DC SUPER HERO GIRLS

™

SUMMER OLYMPUS

an original
graphic novel

WRITTEN BY
Shea Fontana

ART BY
Yancey Labat

COLORS BY
Monica Kubina

LETTERING BY
Janice Chiang

SUPERGIRL BASED ON THE CHARACTERS CREATED BY
JERRY SIEGEL AND JOE SHUSTER. BY SPECIAL ARRANGEMENT WITH THE JERRY SIEGEL FAMILY.

MARIE JAVINS Group Editor
BRITTANY HOLZHERR Associate Editor
STEVE COOK Design Director - Books
AMIE BROCKWAY-METCALF Publication Design

BOB HARRAS Senior VP - Editor-in-Chief, DC Comics
PAT McCALLUM Executive Editor, DC Comics

DIANE NELSON President
DAN DiDIO Publisher
JIM LEE Publisher
GEOFF JOHNS President & Chief Creative Officer
AMIT DESAI Executive VP - Business & Marketing Strategy,
Direct to Consumer & Global Franchise Management
SAM ADES Senior VP & General Manager, Digital Services
BOBBIE CHASE VP & Executive Editor,
Young Reader & Talent Development
MARK CHIARELLO Senior VP - Art, Design & Collected Editions
JOHN CUNNINGHAM Senior VP - Sales & Trade Marketing
ANNE DePIES Senior VP - Business Strategy, Finance & Administration
DON FALLETTI VP - Manufacturing Operations
LAWRENCE GANEM VP - Editorial Administration & Talent Relations
ALISON GILL Senior VP - Manufacturing & Operations
HANK KANALZ Senior VP - Editorial Strategy & Administration
JAY KOGAN VP - Legal Affairs
JACK MAHAN VP - Business Affairs
NICK J. NAPOLITANO VP - Manufacturing Administration
EDDIE SCANNELL VP - Consumer Marketing
COURTNEY SIMMONS Senior VP - Publicity & Communications
JIM (SKI) SOKOLOWSKI VP - Comic Book Specialty Sales
& Trade Marketing
NANCY SPEARS VP - Mass, Book, Digital Sales & Trade Marketing
MICHELE R. WELLS VP - Content Strategy

DC SUPER HERO GIRLS: SUMMER OLYMPUS. Published by DC Comics,
2900 W. Alameda Avenue, Burbank, CA 91505. GST # is R125921072. Copyright © 2017 DC Comics. All Rights Reserved.
All characters featured in this issue, the distinctive likenesses thereof and related elements are trademarks of DC Comics.
The stories, characters and incidents mentioned in this publication are entirely fictional. DC Comics does not read or accept
unsolicited submissions of ideas, stories or artwork. This book is manufactured at a facility holding chain-of-custody
certification. This paper is made with sustainably managed North American fiber. For Advertising and Custom Publishing
contact dccomicsadvertising@dccomics.com. For details on DC Comics Ratings, visit dccomics.com/go/ratings.
Printed by Transcontinental Interglobe, Beauceville, QC, Canada. 12/14/17. Second Printing. ISBN: 978-1-4012-7235-7

TABLE OF CONTENTS

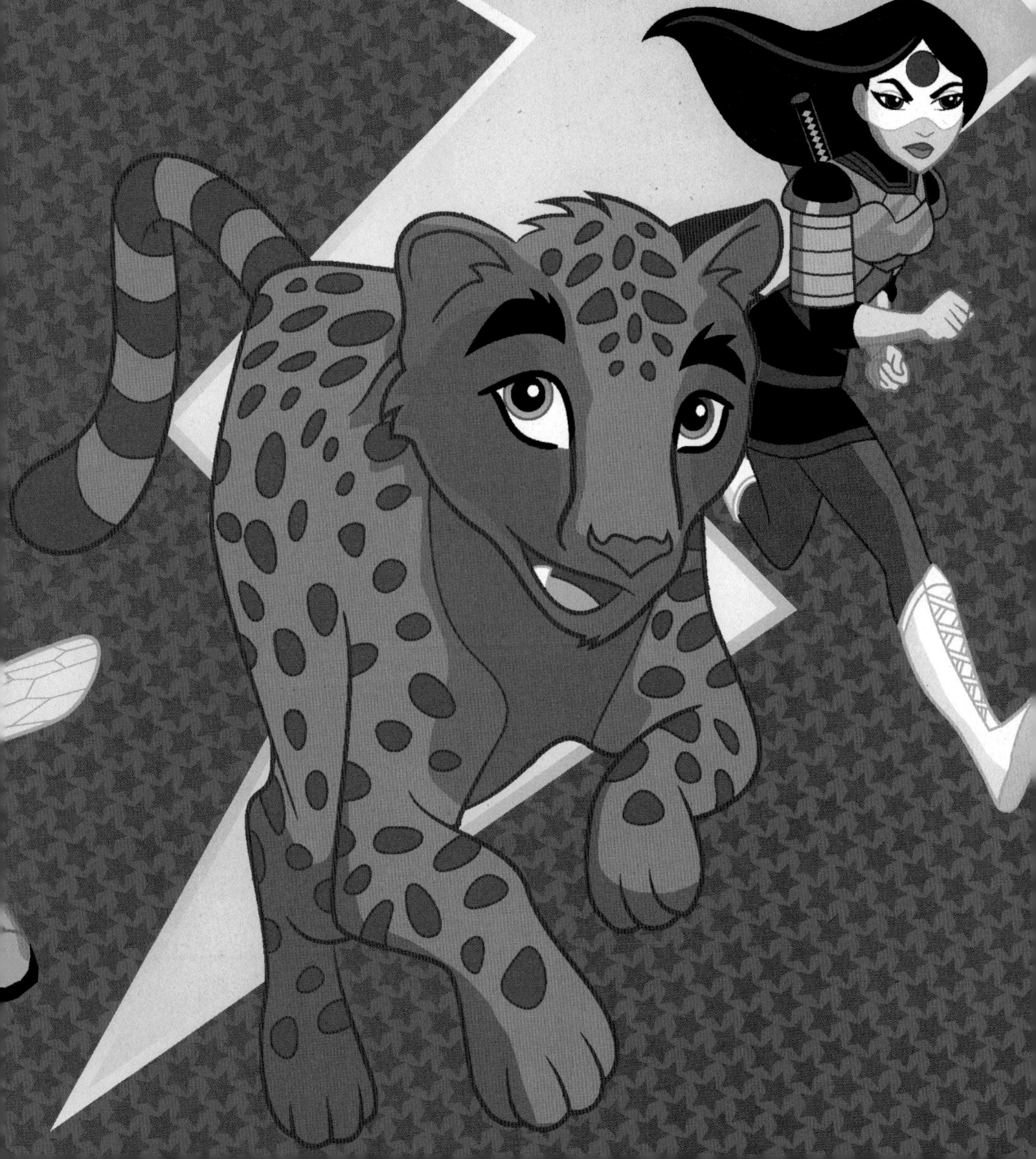

ROLL AT SUPER

SUPER HERO HIGH SCHOOL

WONDER WOMAN

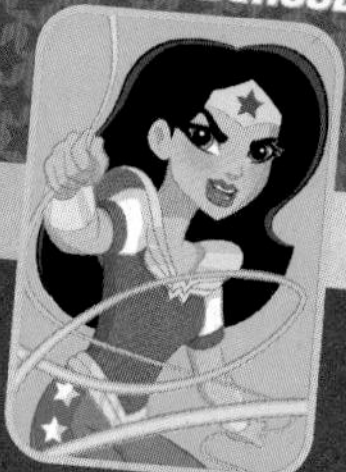

SUPERPOWERS
Super-strength, flight, near-invincibility, super-athleticism

SUPER HERO HIGH SCHOOL

SUPERGIRL

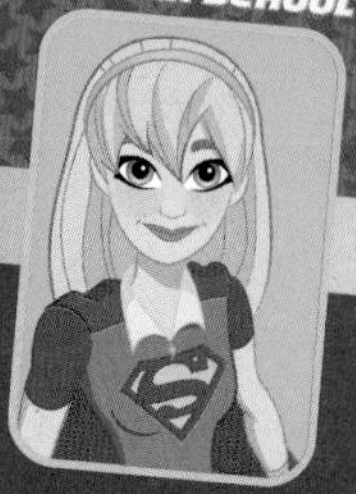

SUPERPOWERS
Super-strength, flight, invincibility, super-hearing, heat vision, x-ray vision

SUPER HERO HIGH SCHOOL

BATGIRL

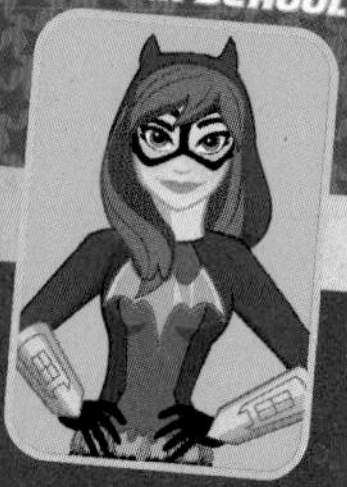

SUPERPOWERS
Computer genius, expert martial artist, photographic memory, legendary detective skills

SUPER HERO HIGH SCHOOL

BUMBLEBEE

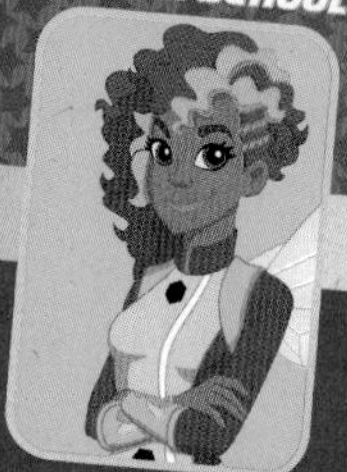

SUPERPOWERS
Enhanced strength, flight, ability to shrink, projects stinger blasts

SUPER HERO HIGH SCHOOL

POISON IVY

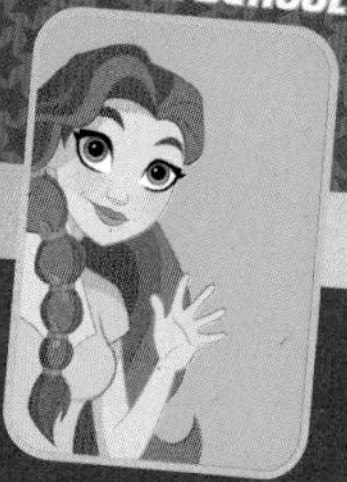

SUPERPOWERS
Genius-level intellect, summons and controls plants

SUPER HERO HIGH SCHOOL

HARLEY QUINN

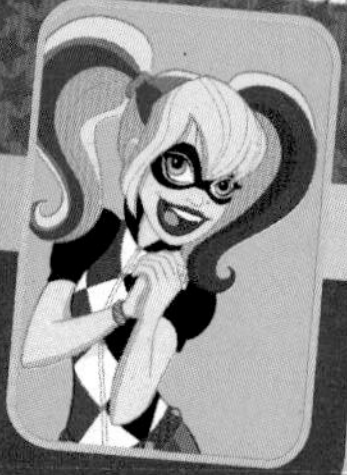

SUPERPOWERS
Expert gymnast, acrobat, quick-witted class clown

SUPER HERO HIGH SCHOOL

KATANA

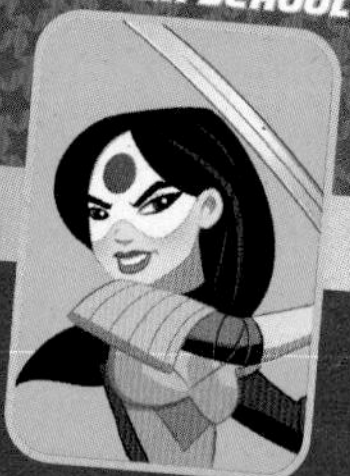

SUPERPOWERS
Superior sword-fighter, expert martial artist, advanced stealth skills

SUPER HERO HIGH SCHOOL

BEAST BOY

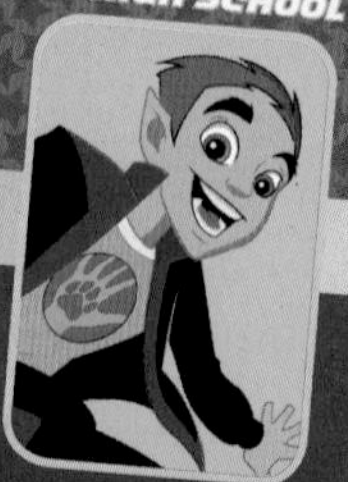

SUPERPOWERS
Shape-shifts into any animal form, world-class slacker

SUPER HERO HIGH SCHOOL

CHEETAH

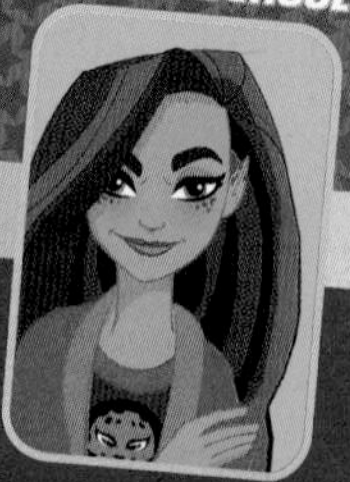

SUPERPOWERS
Agility, speed, sharp reflexes, even sharper claws

CALL HERO HIGH

SUPER HERO HIGH SCHOOL

SHHS

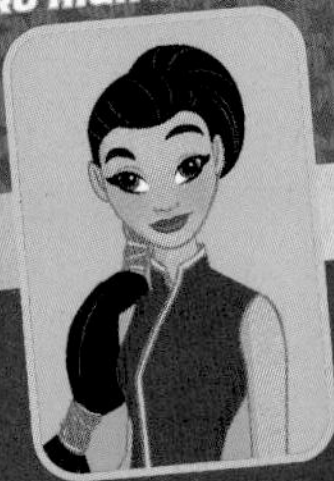

LADY SHIVA

SUPERPOWERS

Expert martial artist, healer, strong-willed, never gives up

SUPER HERO HIGH SCHOOL

SHHS

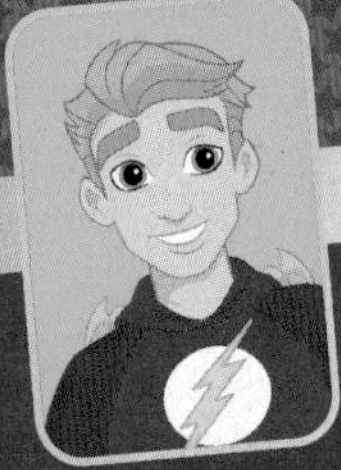

FLASH

SUPERPOWERS

Super-speed, vibrates his molecules through walls, detective skills

SUPER HERO HIGH SCHOOL

SHHS

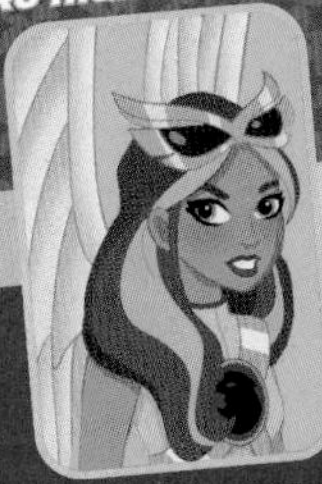

HAWKGIRL

SUPERPOWERS

Flight, super detective skills, weapons expert

SUPER HERO HIGH SCHOOL

SHHS

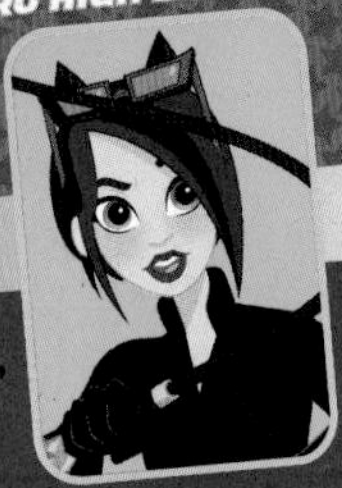

CATWOMAN

SUPERPOWERS

Super-stealth, master gymnast, acrobat, always lands on her feet, loves cats

SUPER HERO HIGH SCHOOL

SHHS

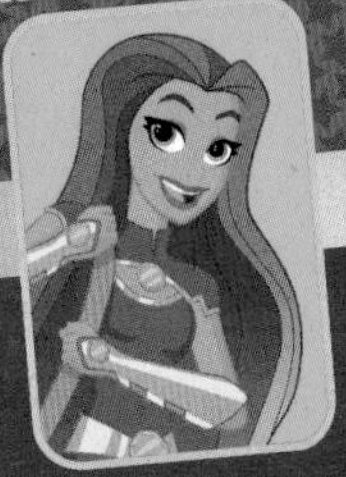

STARFIRE

SUPERPOWERS

Flight, super-strength, can shoot star bolts from her hands

SUPER HERO HIGH SCHOOL

SHHS

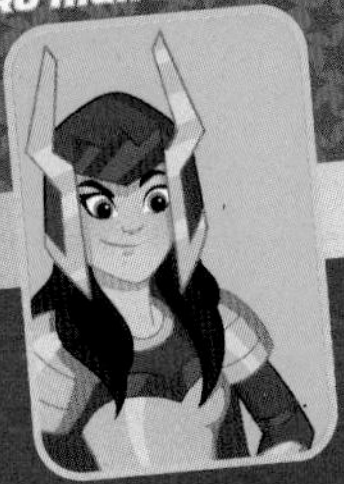

BIG BARDA

SUPERPOWERS

Invincibility, super-reflexes, super-strength, expert at hand-to-hand combat

SUPER HERO HIGH SCHOOL

SHHS

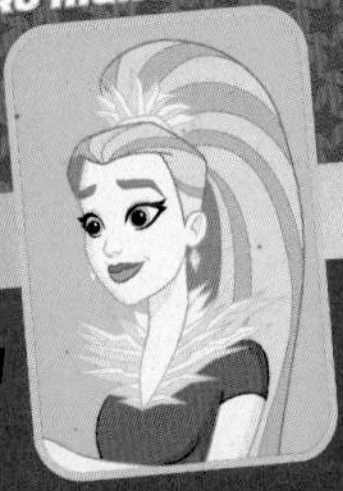

FROST

SUPERPOWERS

Scientific genius, absorbs energy and converts it into sub-zero-temperature ice blasts

SUPER HERO HIGH SCHOOL

SHHS

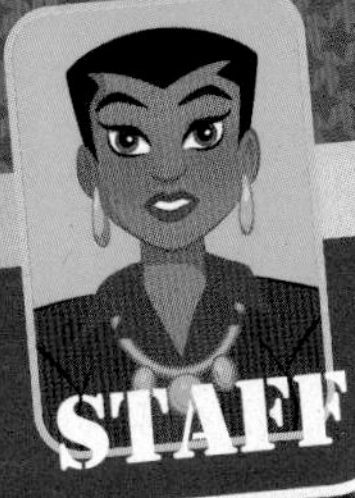
STAFF

AMANDA WALLER

Principal, mentor, stern but fair

SUPER HERO HIGH SCHOOL

SHHS

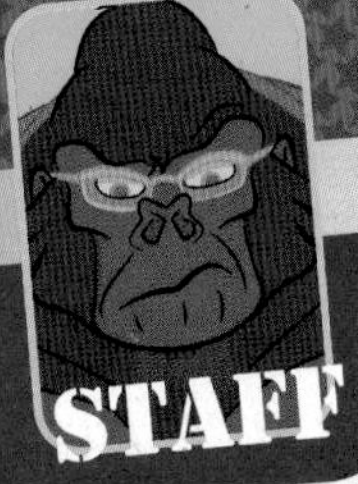
STAFF

GORILLA GRODD

Vice Principal, mind-control powers, in charge of detention

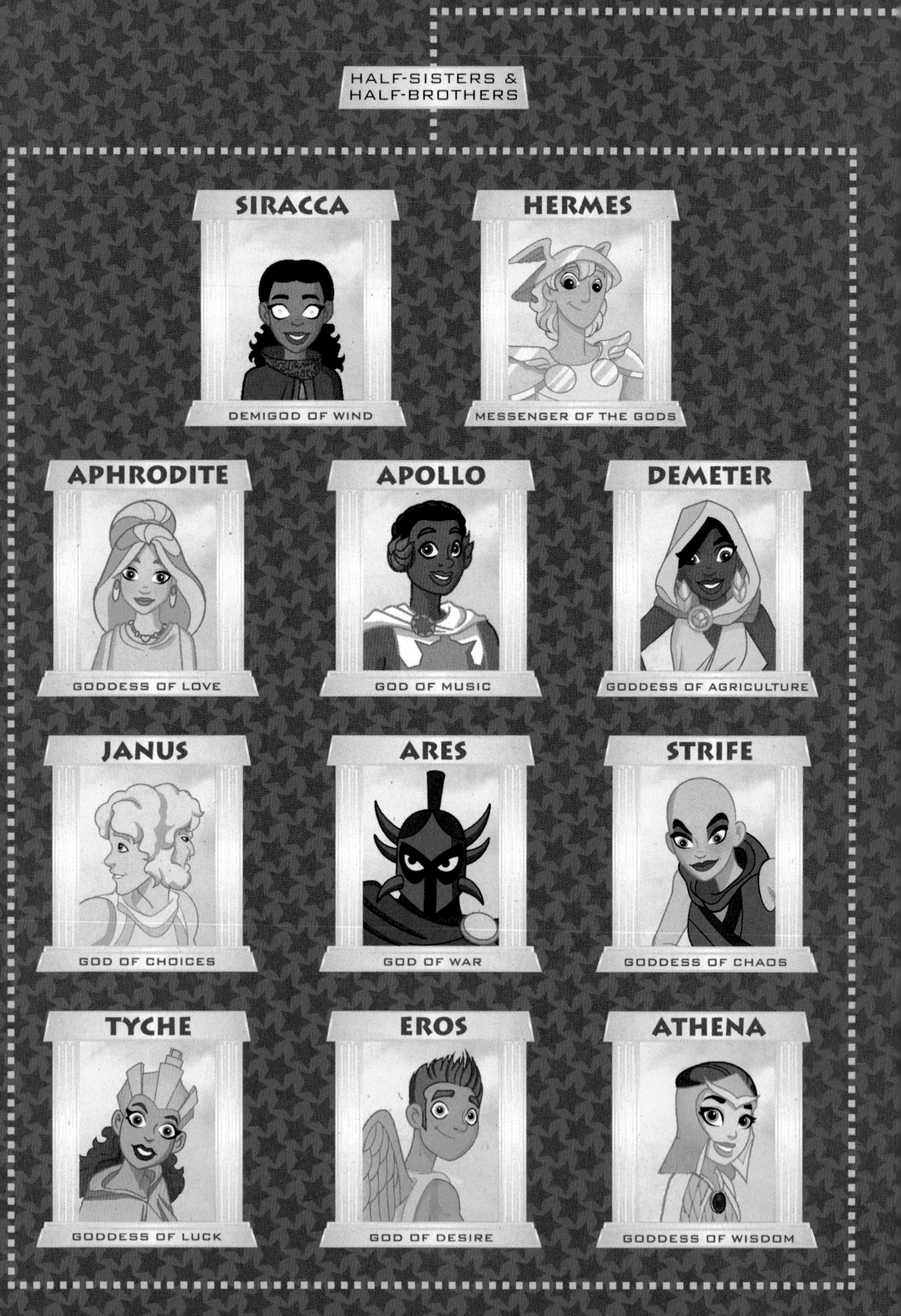
HALF-SISTERS & HALF-BROTHERS
SIRACCA
DEMIGOD OF WIND
HERMES
MESSENGER OF THE GODS
APHRODITE
GODDESS OF LOVE
APOLLO
GOD OF MUSIC
DEMETER
GODDESS OF AGRICULTURE
JANUS
GOD OF CHOICES
ARES
GOD OF WAR
STRIFE
GODDESS OF CHAOS
TYCHE
GODDESS OF LUCK
EROS
GOD OF DESIRE
ATHENA
GODDESS OF WISDOM

WONDER WOMAN'S FAMILY TREE

ZEUS

KING OF THE GODS

FATHER

HIPPOLYTA

QUEEN OF THE AMAZONS

MOTHER

WONDER WOMAN

PRINCESS OF THE AMAZONS
DEMIGOD

CHAPTER ONE
GIMME A SUMMER BREAK

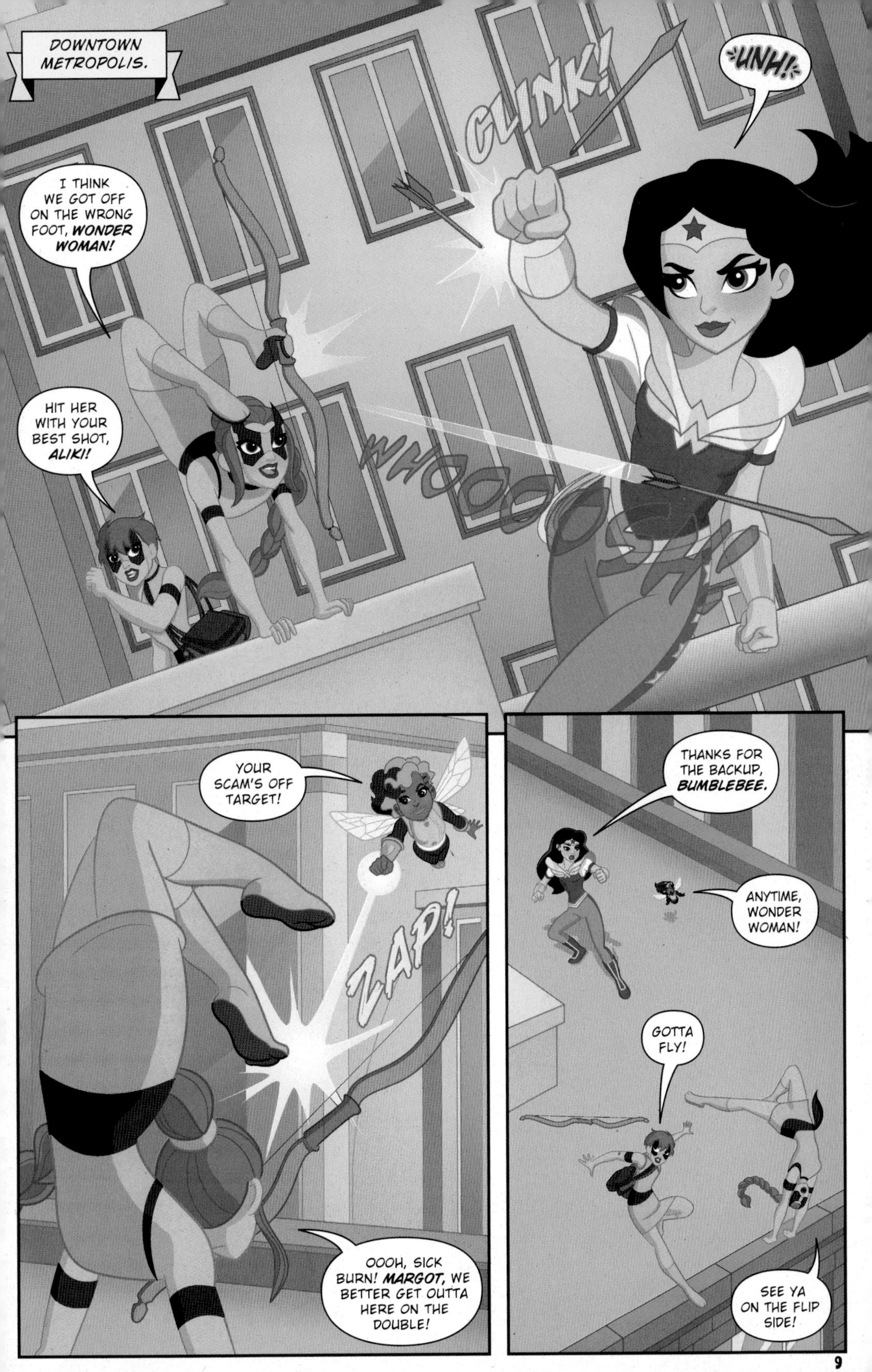

DOWNTOWN METROPOLIS.
CLINK!
UNH!
I THINK WE GOT OFF ON THE WRONG FOOT, WONDER WOMAN!
HIT HER WITH YOUR BEST SHOT, ALIKI!
WHOOOOOSH
YOUR SCAM'S OFF TARGET!
ZAP!
OOOH, SICK BURN! MARGOT, WE BETTER GET OUTTA HERE ON THE DOUBLE!
THANKS FOR THE BACKUP, BUMBLEBEE.
ANYTIME, WONDER WOMAN!
GOTTA FLY!
SEE YA ON THE FLIP SIDE!

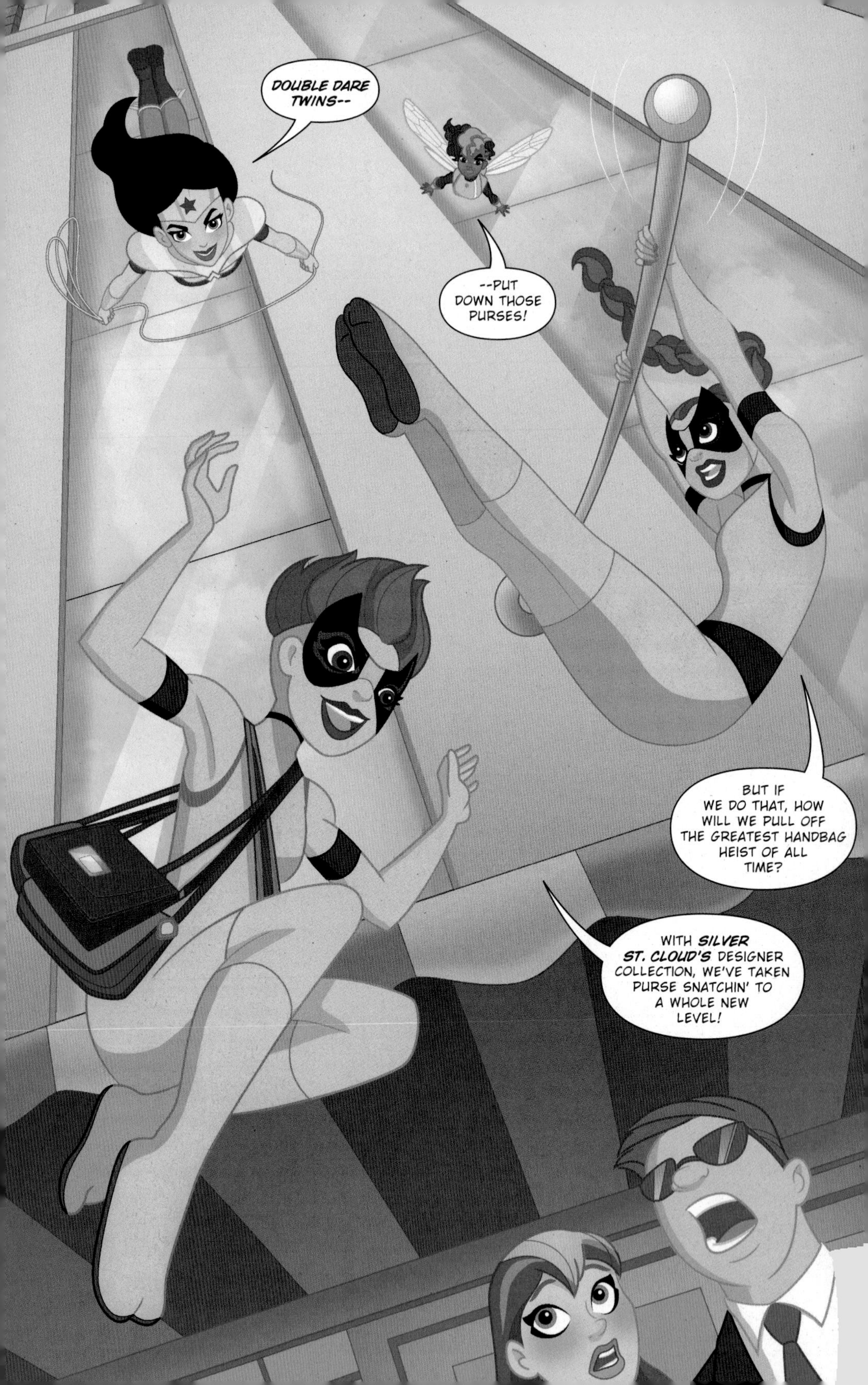
DOUBLE DARE TWINS--
--PUT DOWN THOSE PURSES!
BUT IF WE DO THAT, HOW WILL WE PULL OFF THE GREATEST HANDBAG HEIST OF ALL TIME?
WITH SILVER ST. CLOUD'S DESIGNER COLLECTION, WE'VE TAKEN PURSE SNATCHIN' TO A WHOLE NEW LEVEL!

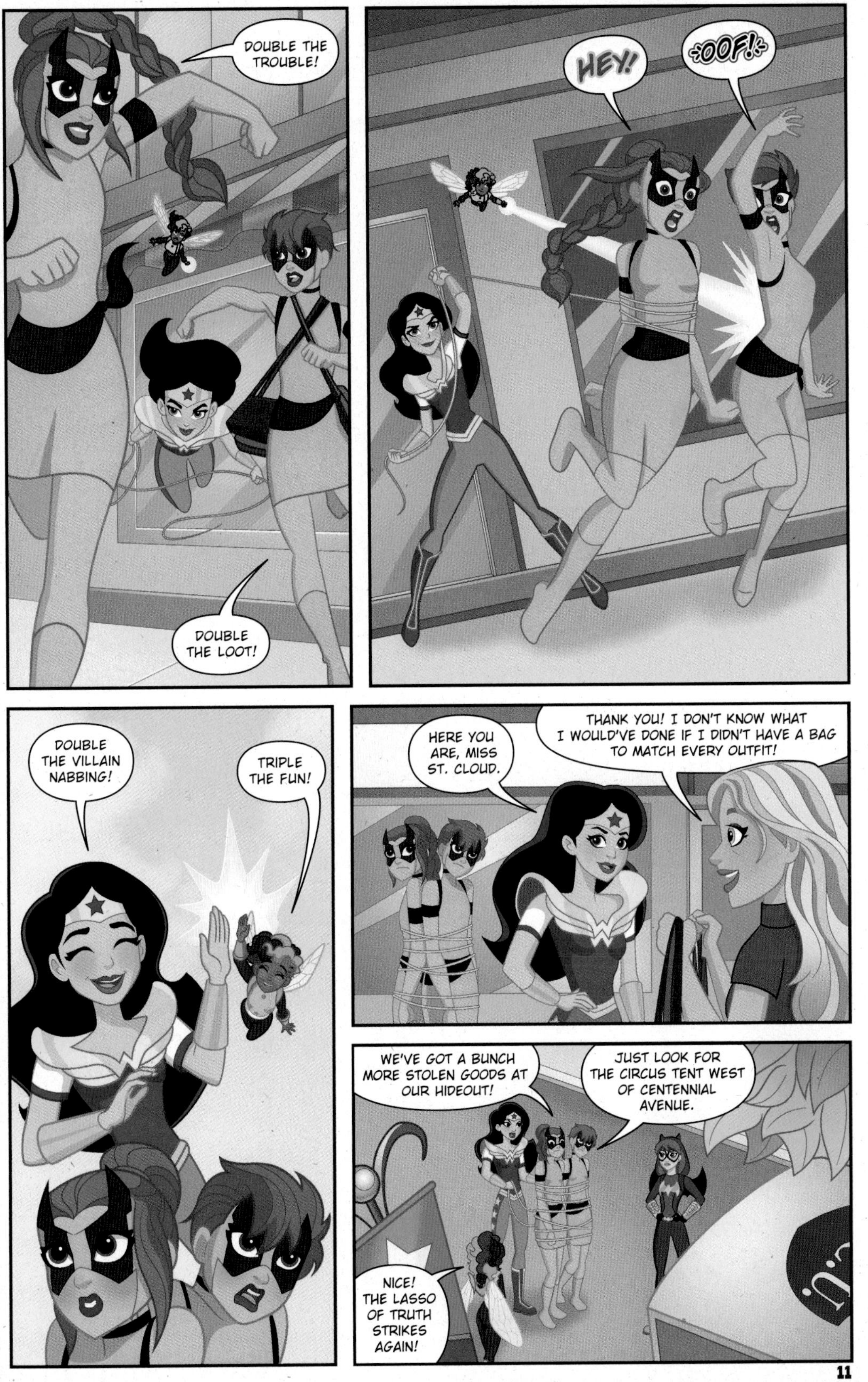
DOUBLE THE TROUBLE!
DOUBLE THE LOOT!
HEY!
OOF!
DOUBLE THE VILLAIN NABBING!
TRIPLE THE FUN!
HERE YOU ARE, MISS ST. CLOUD.
THANK YOU! I DON'T KNOW WHAT I WOULD'VE DONE IF I DIDN'T HAVE A BAG TO MATCH EVERY OUTFIT!
WE'VE GOT A BUNCH MORE STOLEN GOODS AT OUR HIDEOUT!
JUST LOOK FOR THE CIRCUS TENT WEST OF CENTENNIAL AVENUE.
NICE! THE LASSO OF TRUTH STRIKES AGAIN!

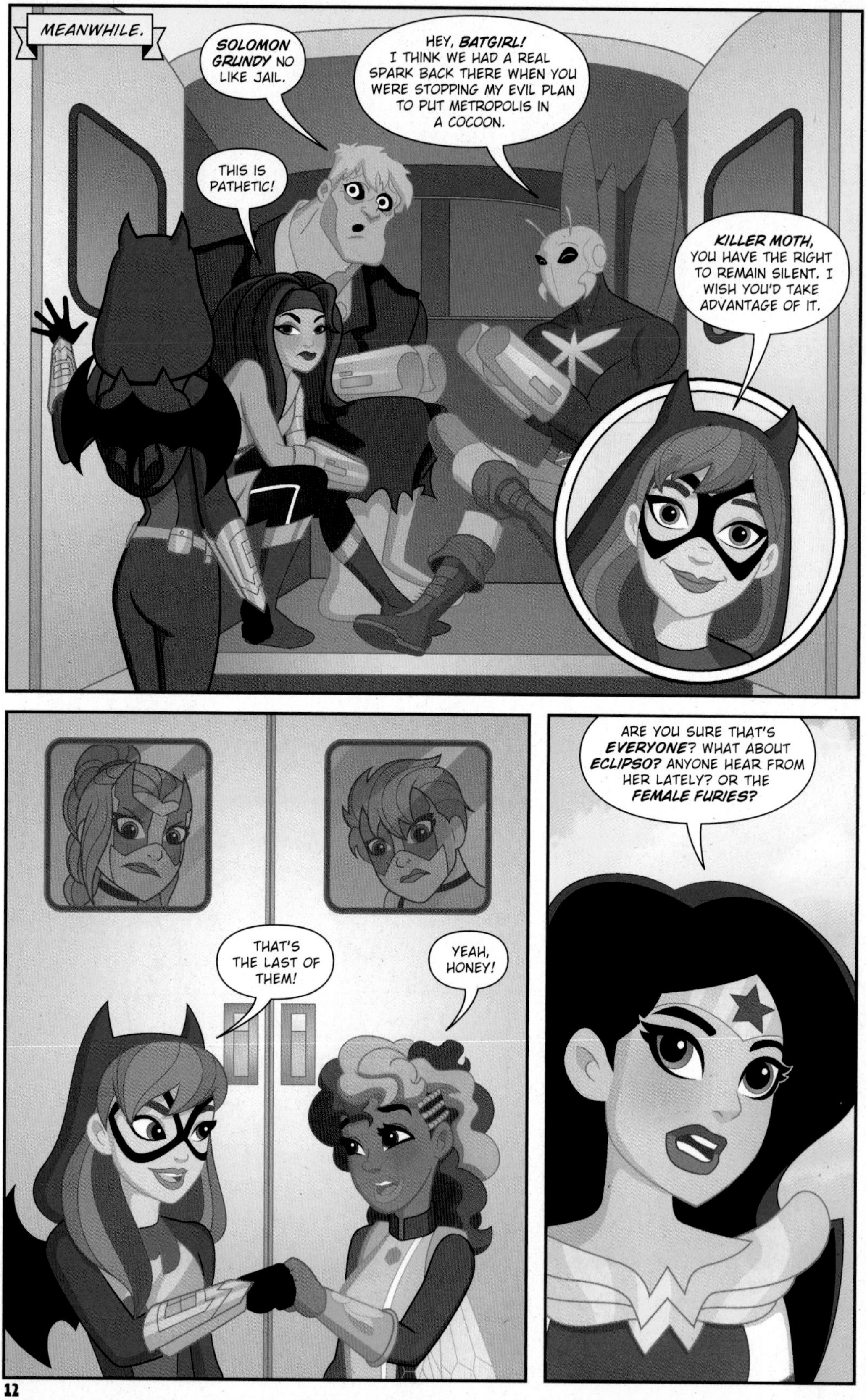
MEANWHILE.
SOLOMON GRUNDY NO LIKE JAIL.
HEY, BATGIRL! I THINK WE HAD A REAL SPARK BACK THERE WHEN YOU WERE STOPPING MY EVIL PLAN TO PUT METROPOLIS IN A COCOON.
THIS IS PATHETIC!
KILLER MOTH, YOU HAVE THE RIGHT TO REMAIN SILENT. I WISH YOU'D TAKE ADVANTAGE OF IT.
THAT'S THE LAST OF THEM!
YEAH, HONEY!
ARE YOU SURE THAT'S EVERYONE? WHAT ABOUT ECLIPSO? ANYONE HEAR FROM HER LATELY? OR THE FEMALE FURIES?

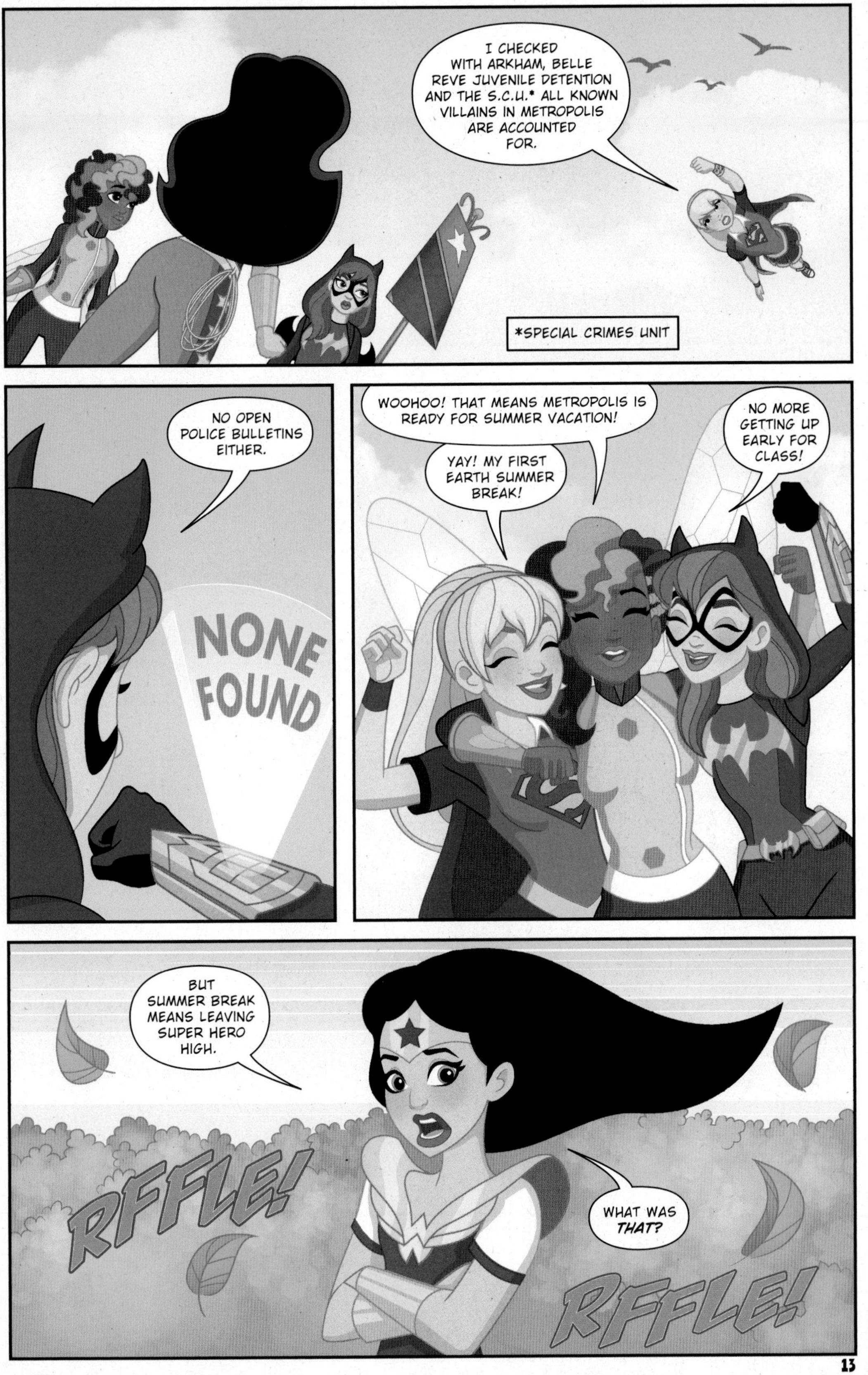

I CHECKED WITH ARKHAM, BELLE REVE JUVENILE DETENTION AND THE S.C.U.* ALL KNOWN VILLAINS IN METROPOLIS ARE ACCOUNTED FOR.
*SPECIAL CRIMES UNIT
NO OPEN POLICE BULLETINS EITHER.
NONE FOUND
WOOHOO! THAT MEANS METROPOLIS IS READY FOR SUMMER VACATION!
YAY! MY FIRST EARTH SUMMER BREAK!
NO MORE GETTING UP EARLY FOR CLASS!
BUT SUMMER BREAK MEANS LEAVING SUPER HERO HIGH.
RFFLE!
WHAT WAS *THAT?*
RFFLE!

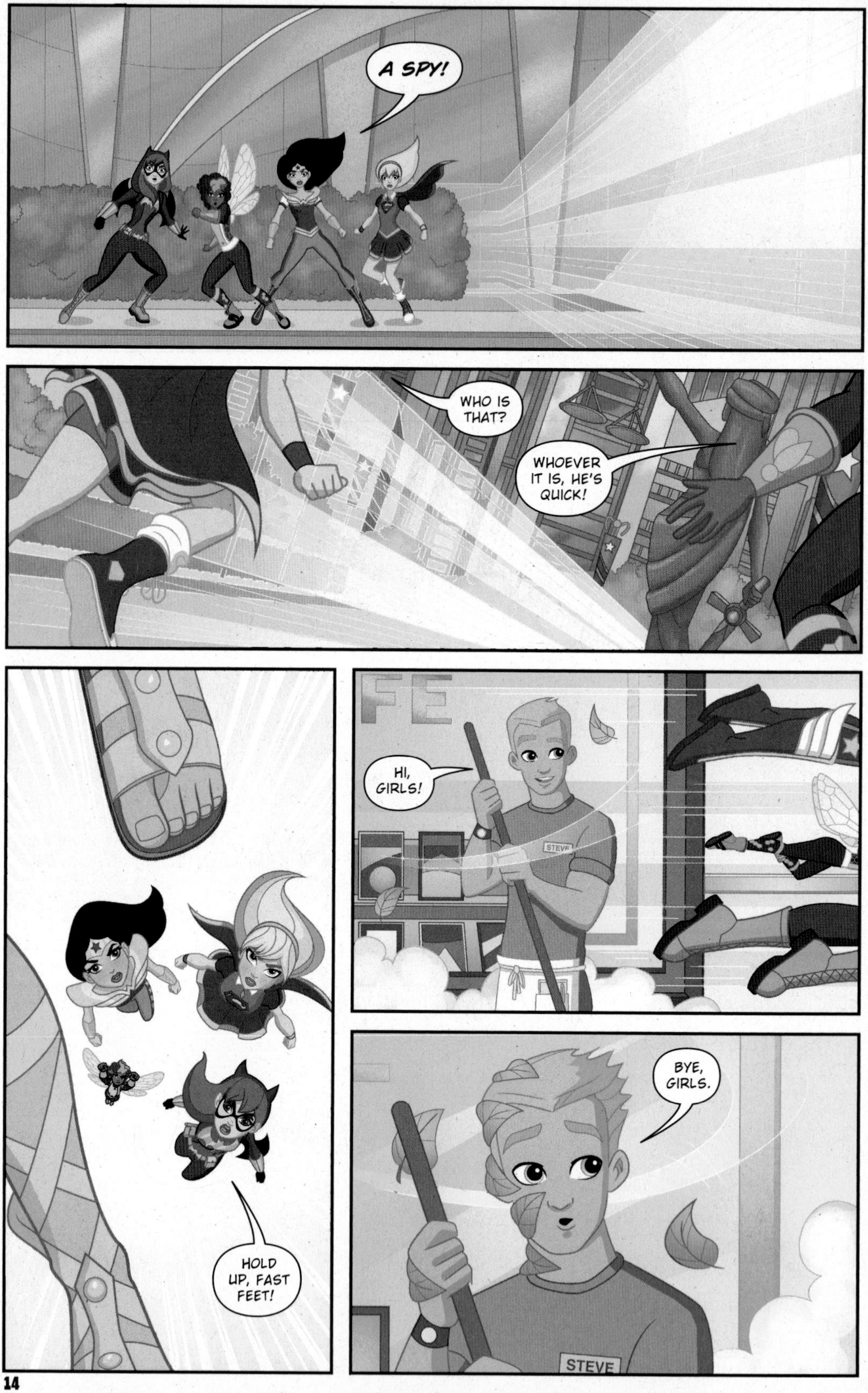
A SPY!
WHO IS THAT?
WHOEVER IT IS, HE'S QUICK!
HOLD UP, FAST FEET!
HI, GIRLS!
STEVE
BYE, GIRLS.
STEVE

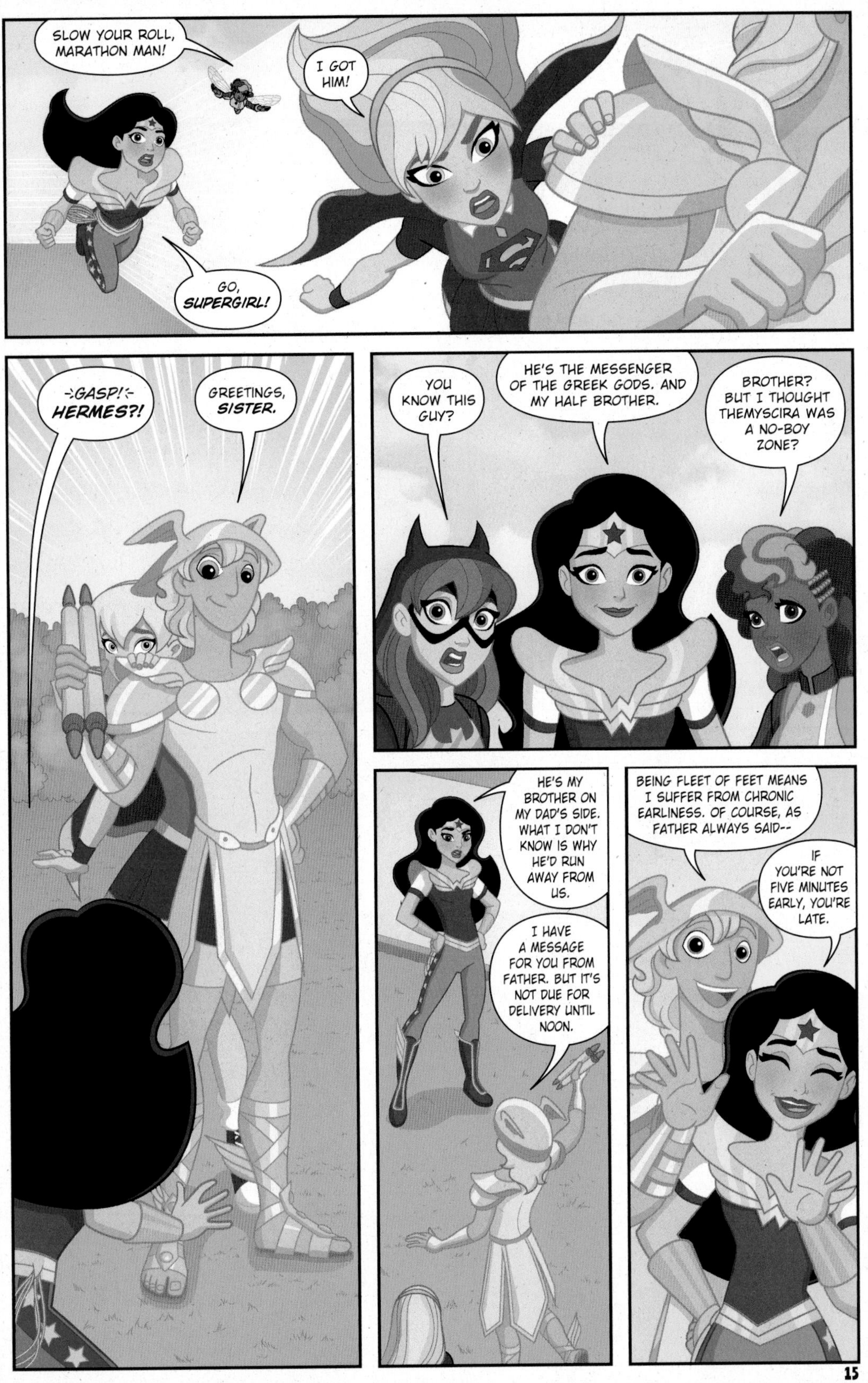
SLOW YOUR ROLL, MARATHON MAN!
I GOT HIM!
GO, SUPERGIRL!
-GASP!- HERMES?!
GREETINGS, SISTER.
YOU KNOW THIS GUY?
HE'S THE MESSENGER OF THE GREEK GODS. AND MY HALF BROTHER.
BROTHER? BUT I THOUGHT THEMYSCIRA WAS A NO-BOY ZONE?
HE'S MY BROTHER ON MY DAD'S SIDE. WHAT I DON'T KNOW IS WHY HE'D RUN AWAY FROM US.
I HAVE A MESSAGE FOR YOU FROM FATHER. BUT IT'S NOT DUE FOR DELIVERY UNTIL NOON.
BEING FLEET OF FEET MEANS I SUFFER FROM CHRONIC EARLINESS. OF COURSE, AS FATHER ALWAYS SAID--
IF YOU'RE NOT FIVE MINUTES EARLY, YOU'RE LATE.

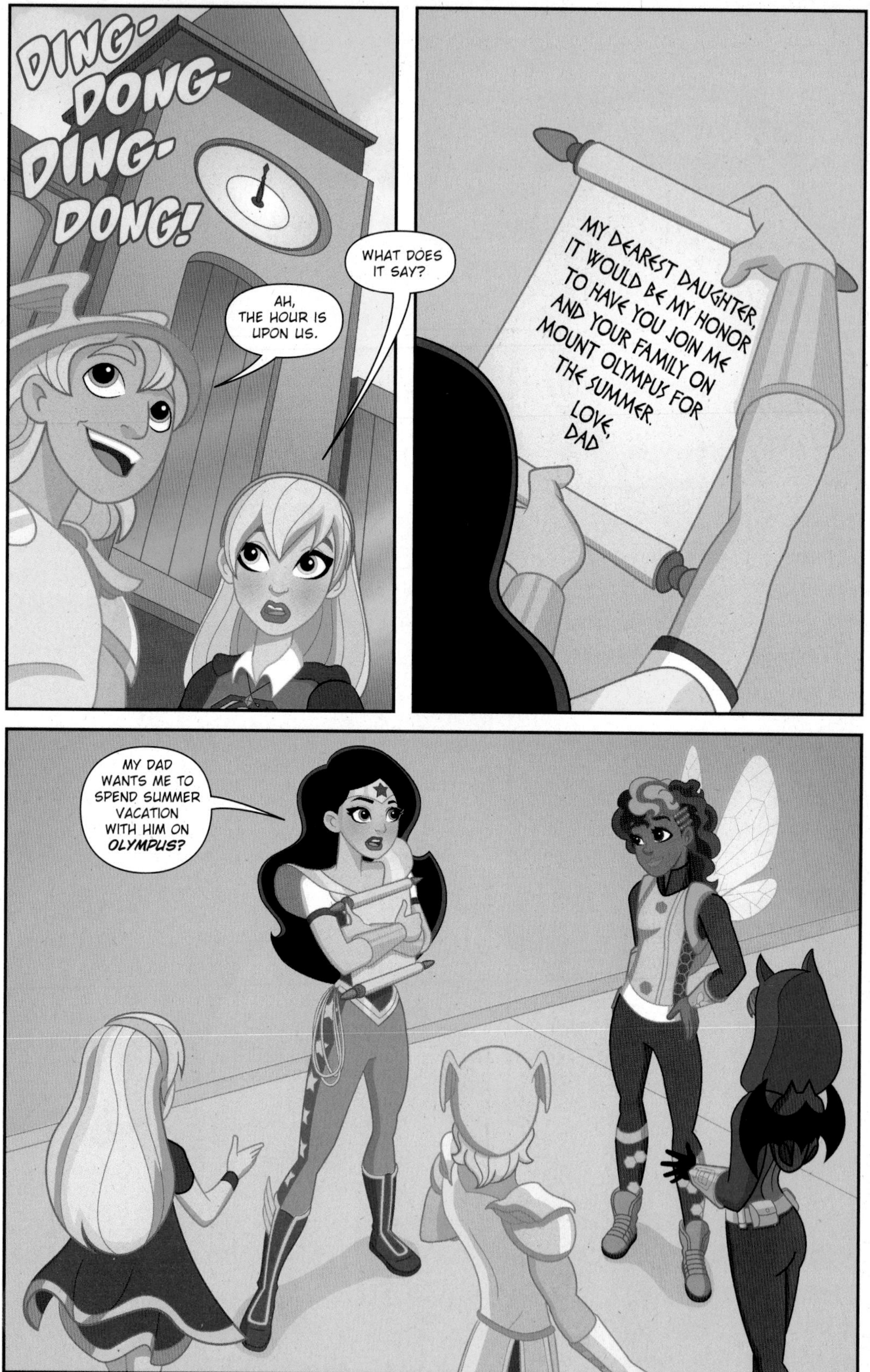
DING-DONG-DING-DONG!
AH, THE HOUR IS UPON US.
WHAT DOES IT SAY?
MY DEAREST DAUGHTER, IT WOULD BE MY HONOR TO HAVE YOU JOIN ME AND YOUR FAMILY ON MOUNT OLYMPUS FOR THE SUMMER. LOVE, DAD
MY DAD WANTS ME TO SPEND SUMMER VACATION WITH HIM ON OLYMPUS?

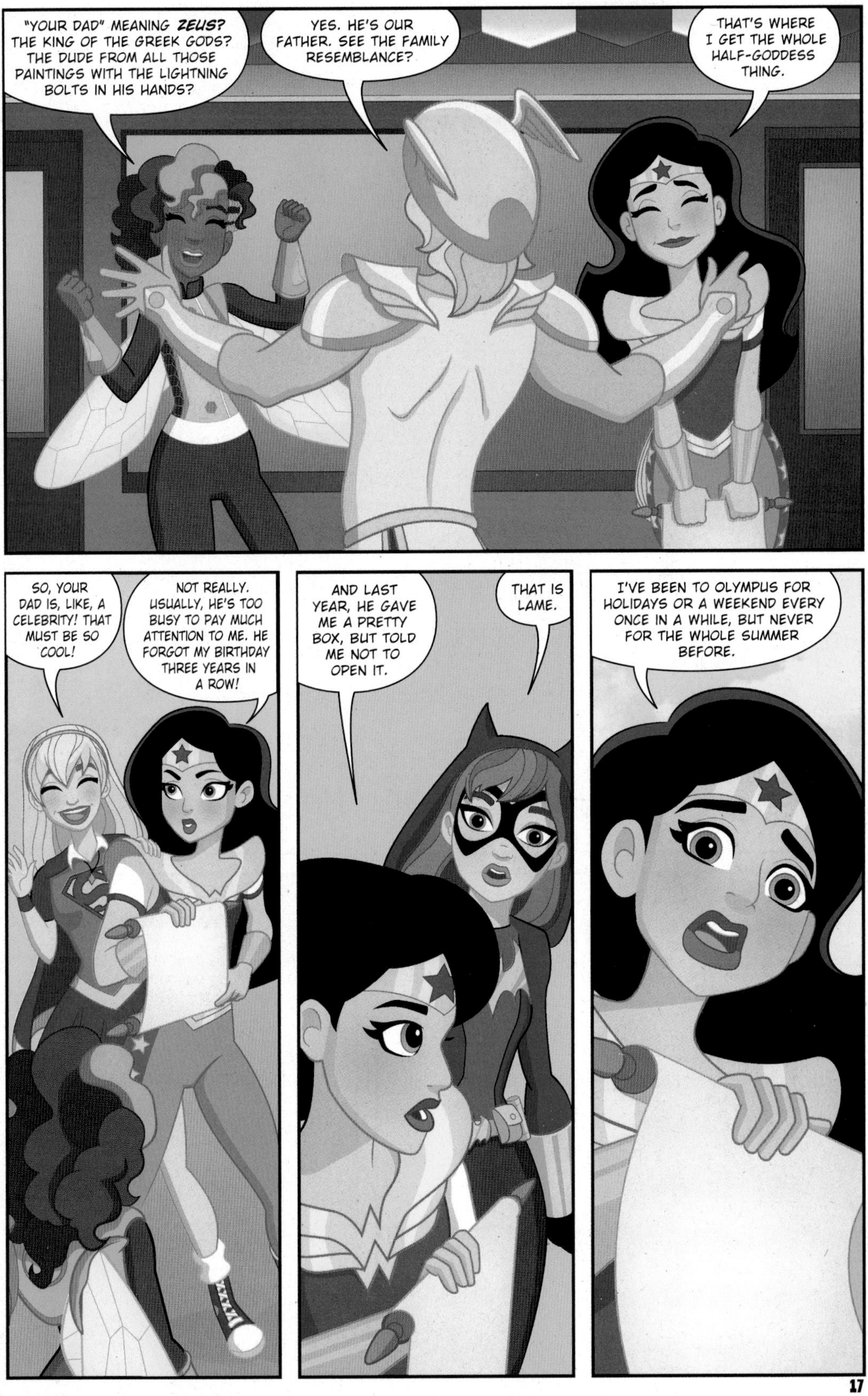
"YOUR DAD" MEANING ZEUS? THE KING OF THE GREEK GODS? THE DUDE FROM ALL THOSE PAINTINGS WITH THE LIGHTNING BOLTS IN HIS HANDS?
YES. HE'S OUR FATHER. SEE THE FAMILY RESEMBLANCE?
THAT'S WHERE I GET THE WHOLE HALF-GODDESS THING.
SO, YOUR DAD IS, LIKE, A CELEBRITY! THAT MUST BE SO COOL!
NOT REALLY. USUALLY, HE'S TOO BUSY TO PAY MUCH ATTENTION TO ME. HE FORGOT MY BIRTHDAY THREE YEARS IN A ROW!
AND LAST YEAR, HE GAVE ME A PRETTY BOX, BUT TOLD ME NOT TO OPEN IT.
THAT IS LAME.
I'VE BEEN TO OLYMPUS FOR HOLIDAYS OR A WEEKEND EVERY ONCE IN A WHILE, BUT NEVER FOR THE WHOLE SUMMER BEFORE.

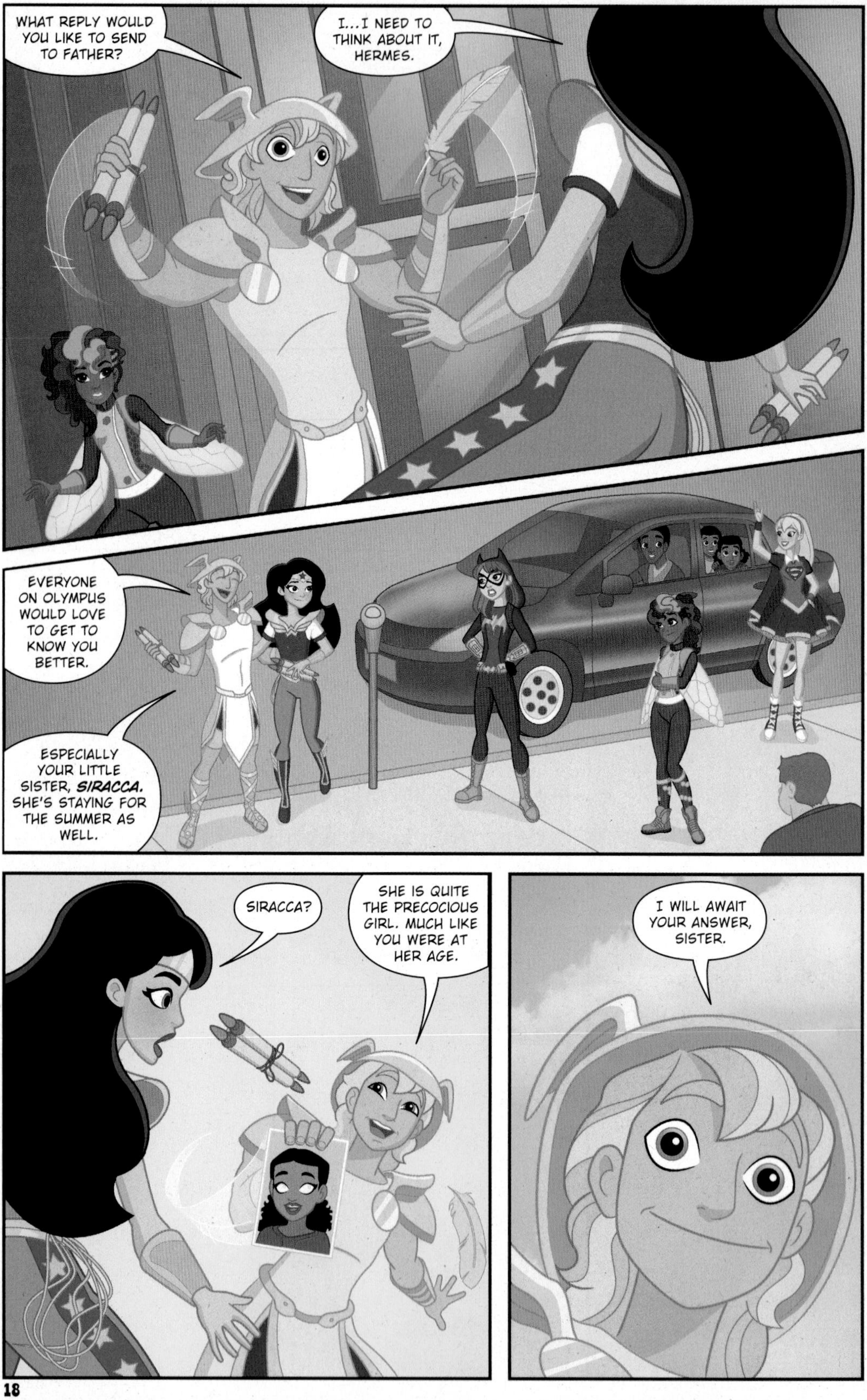

WHAT REPLY WOULD YOU LIKE TO SEND TO FATHER?
I...I NEED TO THINK ABOUT IT, HERMES.
EVERYONE ON OLYMPUS WOULD LOVE TO GET TO KNOW YOU BETTER.
ESPECIALLY YOUR LITTLE SISTER, ***SIRACCA.*** SHE'S STAYING FOR THE SUMMER AS WELL.
SIRACCA?
SHE IS QUITE THE PRECOCIOUS GIRL. MUCH LIKE YOU WERE AT HER AGE.
I WILL AWAIT YOUR ANSWER, SISTER.

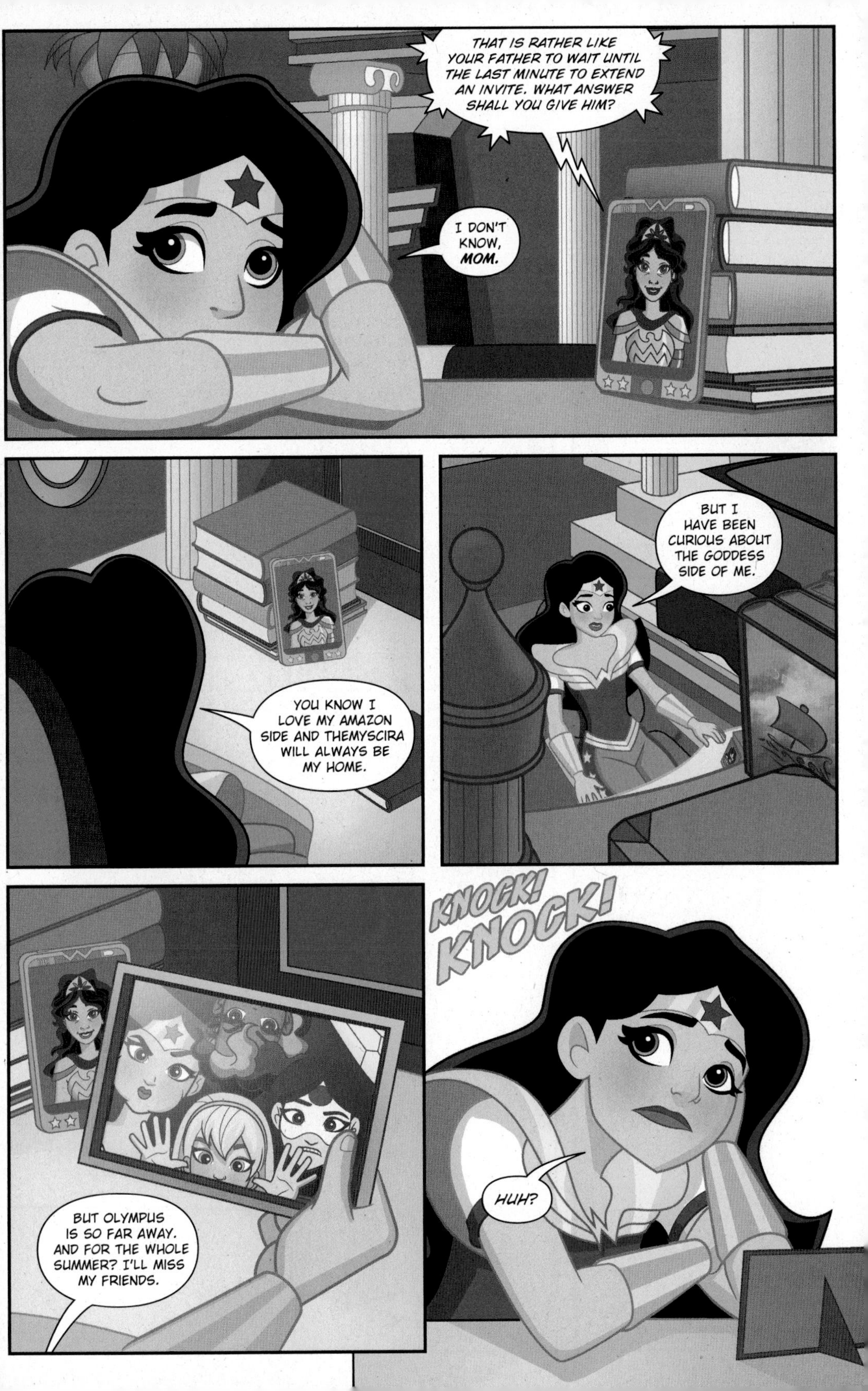
THAT IS RATHER LIKE YOUR FATHER TO WAIT UNTIL THE LAST MINUTE TO EXTEND AN INVITE. WHAT ANSWER SHALL YOU GIVE HIM?
I DON'T KNOW, MOM.
YOU KNOW I LOVE MY AMAZON SIDE AND THEMYSCIRA WILL ALWAYS BE MY HOME.
BUT I HAVE BEEN CURIOUS ABOUT THE GODDESS SIDE OF ME.
BUT OLYMPUS IS SO FAR AWAY. AND FOR THE WHOLE SUMMER? I'LL MISS MY FRIENDS.
KNOCK! KNOCK!
HUH?

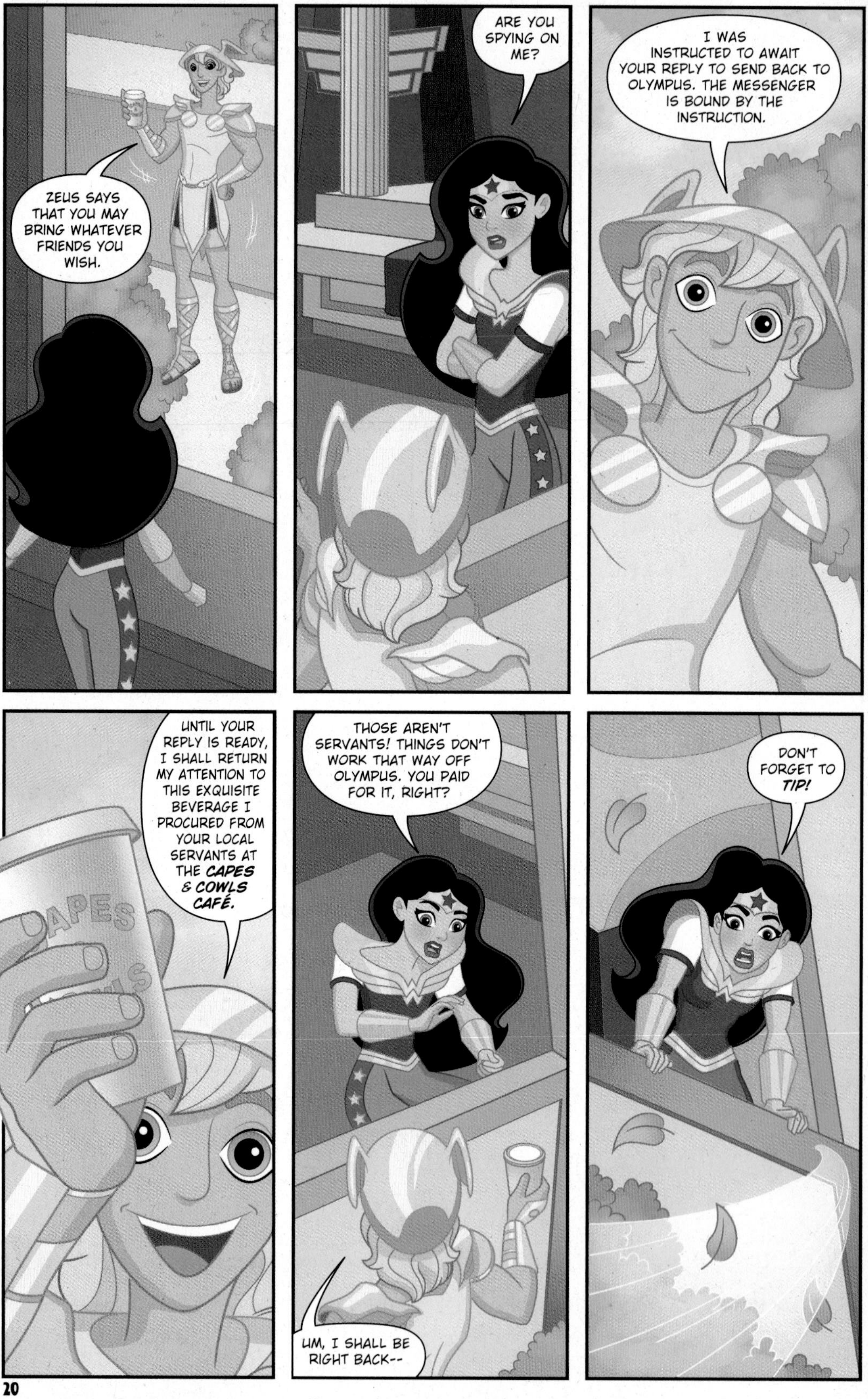
ZEUS SAYS THAT YOU MAY BRING WHATEVER FRIENDS YOU WISH.
ARE YOU SPYING ON ME?
I WAS INSTRUCTED TO AWAIT YOUR REPLY TO SEND BACK TO OLYMPUS. THE MESSENGER IS BOUND BY THE INSTRUCTION.
UNTIL YOUR REPLY IS READY, I SHALL RETURN MY ATTENTION TO THIS EXQUISITE BEVERAGE I PROCURED FROM YOUR LOCAL SERVANTS AT THE CAPES & COWLS CAFÉ.
THOSE AREN'T SERVANTS! THINGS DON'T WORK THAT WAY OFF OLYMPUS. YOU PAID FOR IT, RIGHT?
UM, I SHALL BE RIGHT BACK--
DON'T FORGET TO TIP!

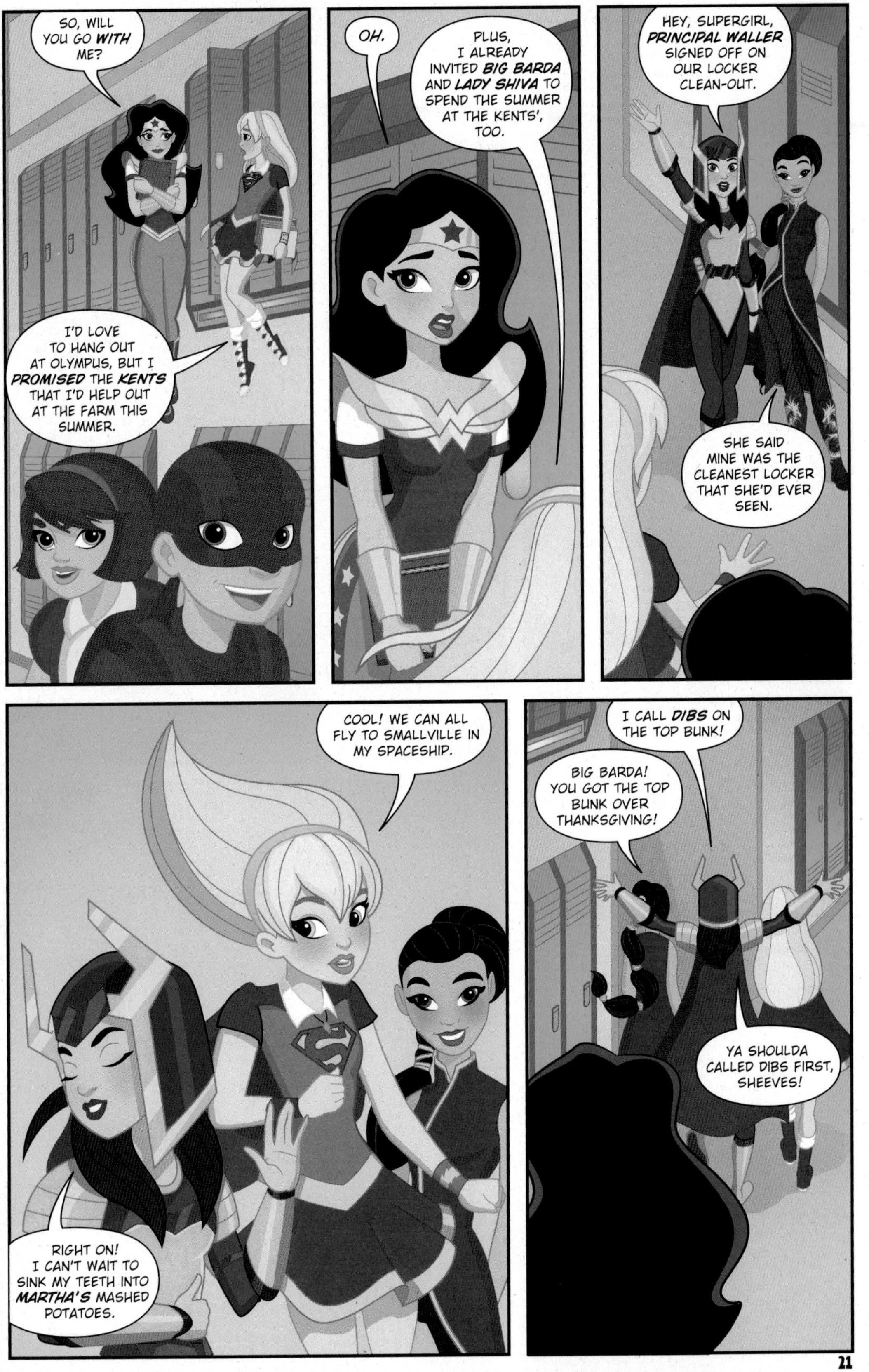

SO, WILL YOU GO WITH ME?
I'D LOVE TO HANG OUT AT OLYMPUS, BUT I PROMISED THE KENTS THAT I'D HELP OUT AT THE FARM THIS SUMMER.
OH.
PLUS, I ALREADY INVITED BIG BARDA AND LADY SHIVA TO SPEND THE SUMMER AT THE KENTS', TOO.
HEY, SUPERGIRL, PRINCIPAL WALLER SIGNED OFF ON OUR LOCKER CLEAN-OUT.
SHE SAID MINE WAS THE CLEANEST LOCKER THAT SHE'D EVER SEEN.
COOL! WE CAN ALL FLY TO SMALLVILLE IN MY SPACESHIP.
RIGHT ON! I CAN'T WAIT TO SINK MY TEETH INTO MARTHA'S MASHED POTATOES.
I CALL DIBS ON THE TOP BUNK!
BIG BARDA! YOU GOT THE TOP BUNK OVER THANKSGIVING!
YA SHOULDA CALLED DIBS FIRST, SHEEVES!

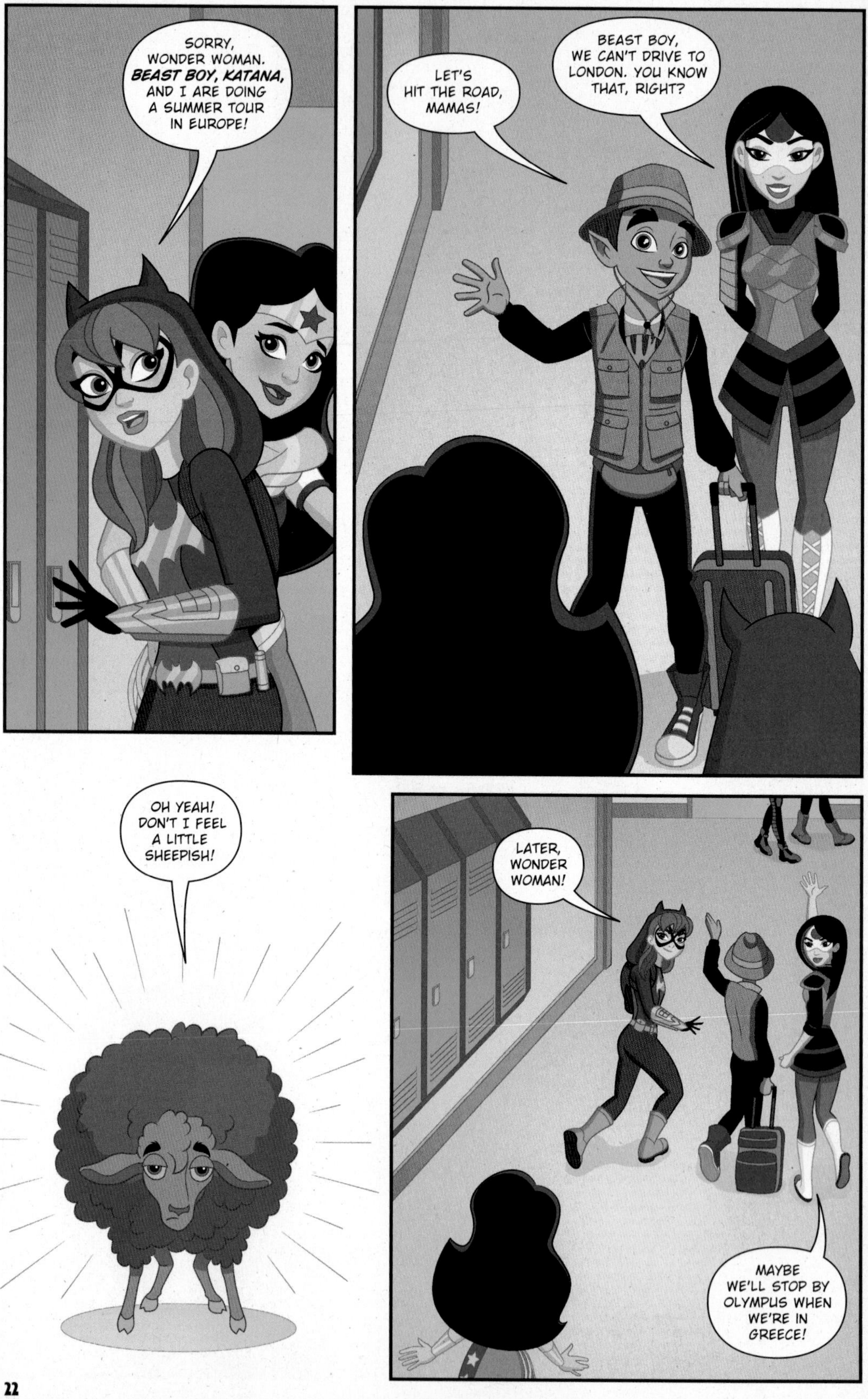
SORRY, WONDER WOMAN. **BEAST BOY, KATANA,** AND I ARE DOING A SUMMER TOUR IN EUROPE!
LET'S HIT THE ROAD, MAMAS!
BEAST BOY, WE CAN'T DRIVE TO LONDON. YOU KNOW THAT, RIGHT?
OH YEAH! DON'T I FEEL A LITTLE SHEEPISH!
LATER, WONDER WOMAN!
MAYBE WE'LL STOP BY OLYMPUS WHEN WE'RE IN GREECE!

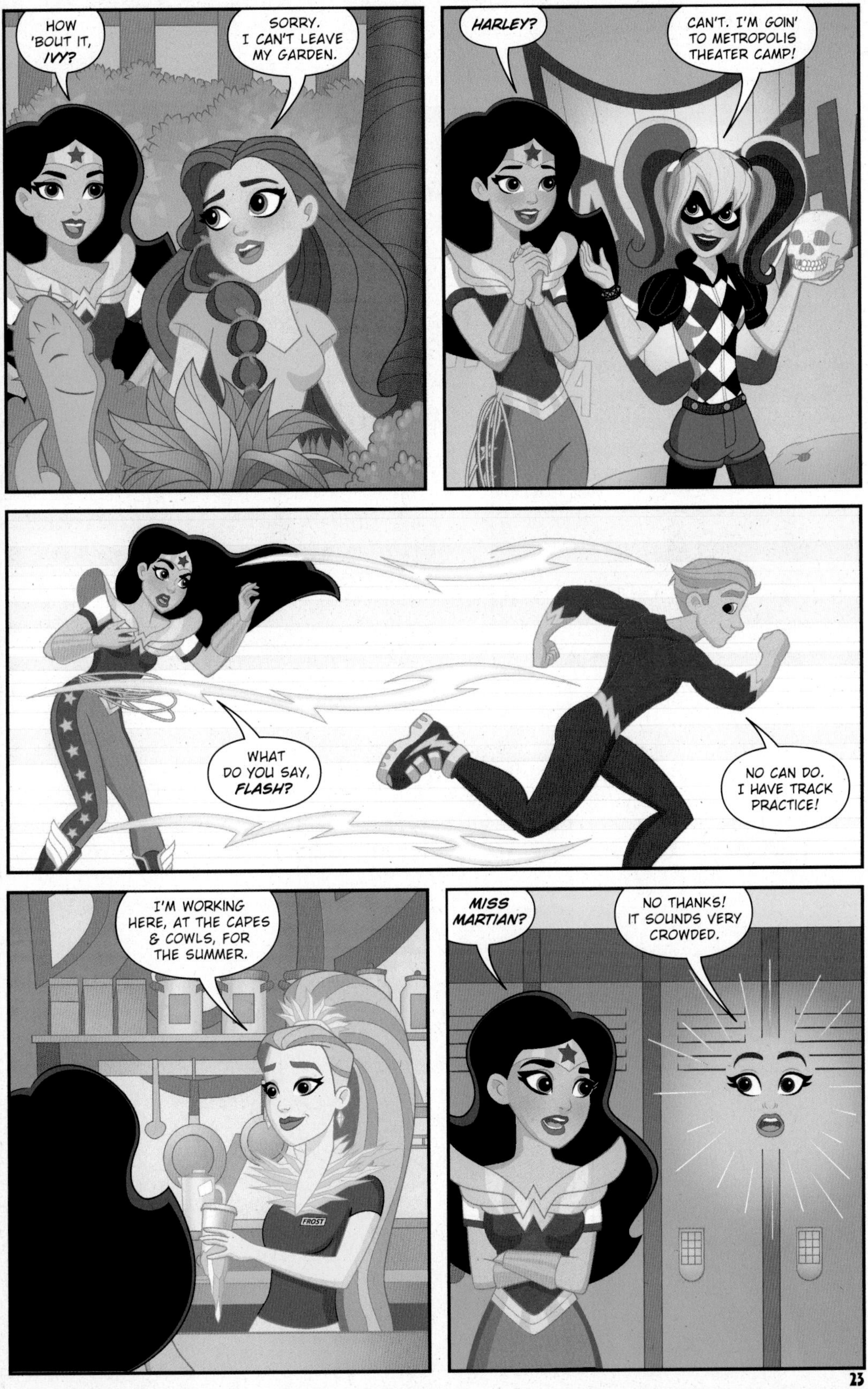
HOW 'BOUT IT, IVY?
SORRY. I CAN'T LEAVE MY GARDEN.
HARLEY?
CAN'T. I'M GOIN' TO METROPOLIS THEATER CAMP!
WHAT DO YOU SAY, FLASH?
NO CAN DO. I HAVE TRACK PRACTICE!
I'M WORKING HERE, AT THE CAPES & COWLS, FOR THE SUMMER.
FROST
MISS MARTIAN?
NO THANKS! IT SOUNDS VERY CROWDED.

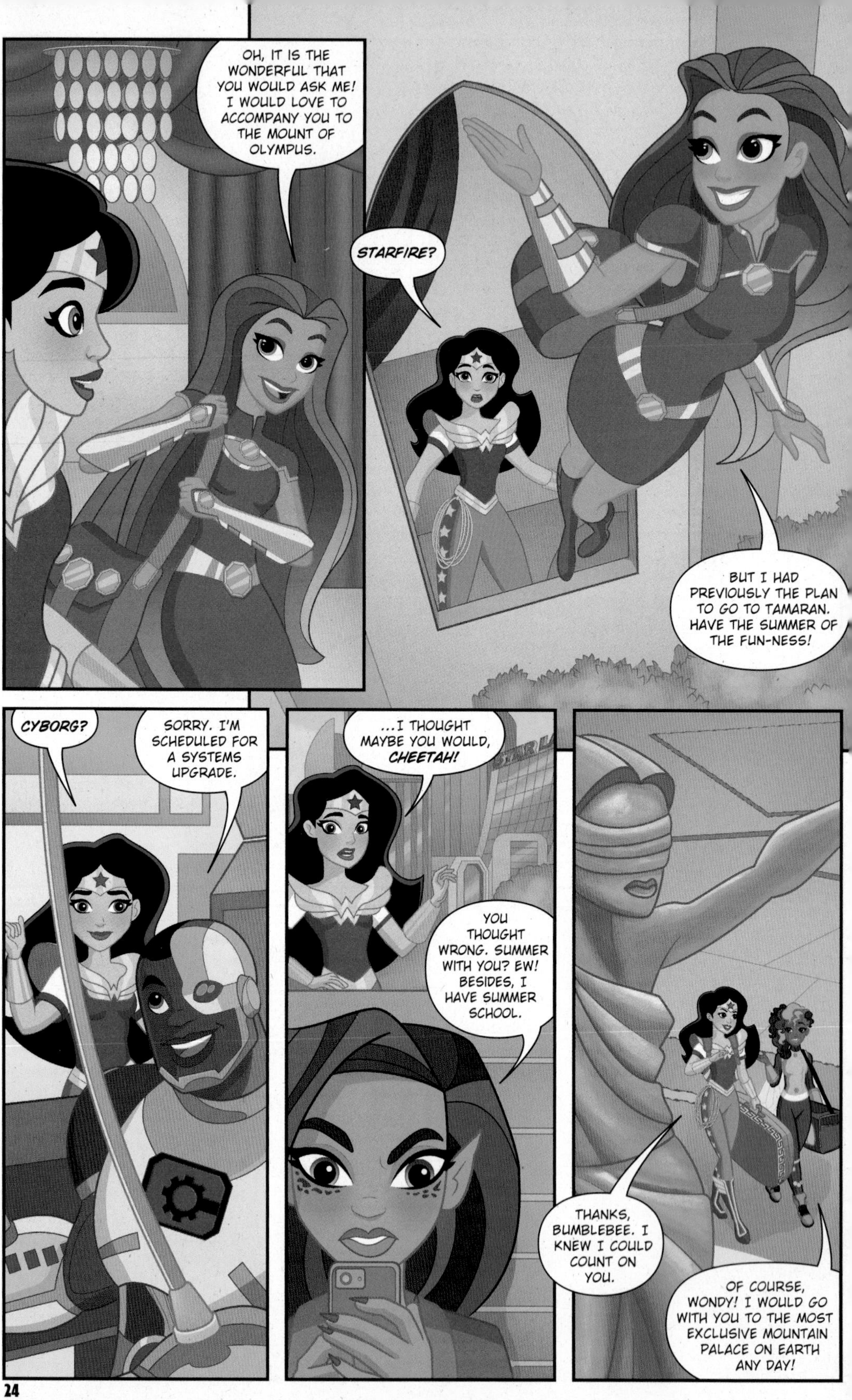
OH, IT IS THE WONDERFUL THAT YOU WOULD ASK ME! I WOULD LOVE TO ACCOMPANY YOU TO THE MOUNT OF OLYMPUS.
STARFIRE?
BUT I HAD PREVIOUSLY THE PLAN TO GO TO TAMARAN. HAVE THE SUMMER OF THE FUN-NESS!
CYBORG?
SORRY. I'M SCHEDULED FOR A SYSTEMS UPGRADE.
...I THOUGHT MAYBE YOU WOULD, CHEETAH!
YOU THOUGHT WRONG. SUMMER WITH YOU? EW! BESIDES, I HAVE SUMMER SCHOOL.
THANKS, BUMBLEBEE. I KNEW I COULD COUNT ON YOU.
OF COURSE, WONDY! I WOULD GO WITH YOU TO THE MOST EXCLUSIVE MOUNTAIN PALACE ON EARTH ANY DAY!

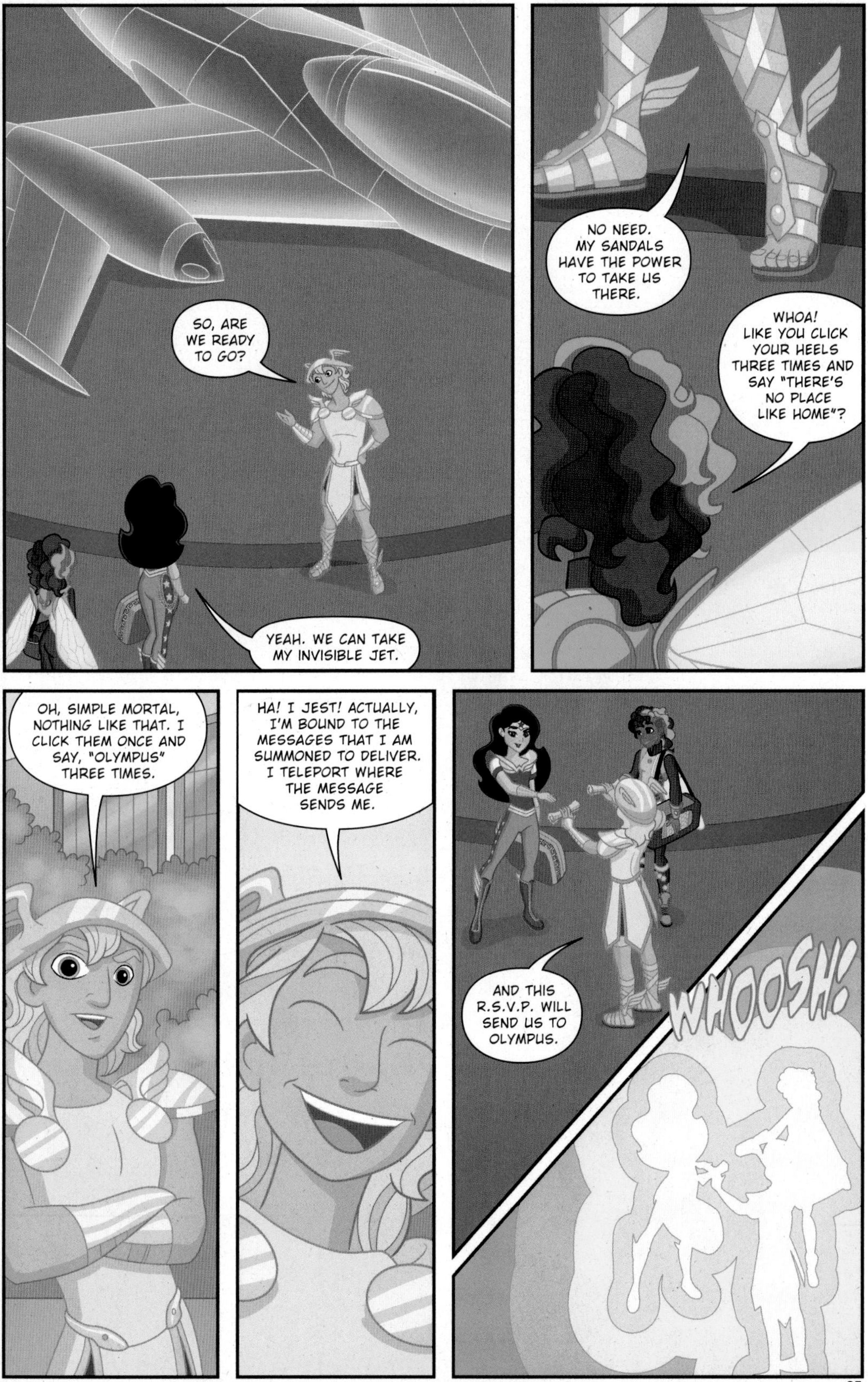
SO, ARE WE READY TO GO?
YEAH. WE CAN TAKE MY INVISIBLE JET.
NO NEED. MY SANDALS HAVE THE POWER TO TAKE US THERE.
WHOA! LIKE YOU CLICK YOUR HEELS THREE TIMES AND SAY "THERE'S NO PLACE LIKE HOME"?
OH, SIMPLE MORTAL, NOTHING LIKE THAT. I CLICK THEM ONCE AND SAY, "OLYMPUS" THREE TIMES.
HA! I JEST! ACTUALLY, I'M BOUND TO THE MESSAGES THAT I AM SUMMONED TO DELIVER. I TELEPORT WHERE THE MESSAGE SENDS ME.
AND THIS R.S.V.P. WILL SEND US TO OLYMPUS.
WHOOSH!

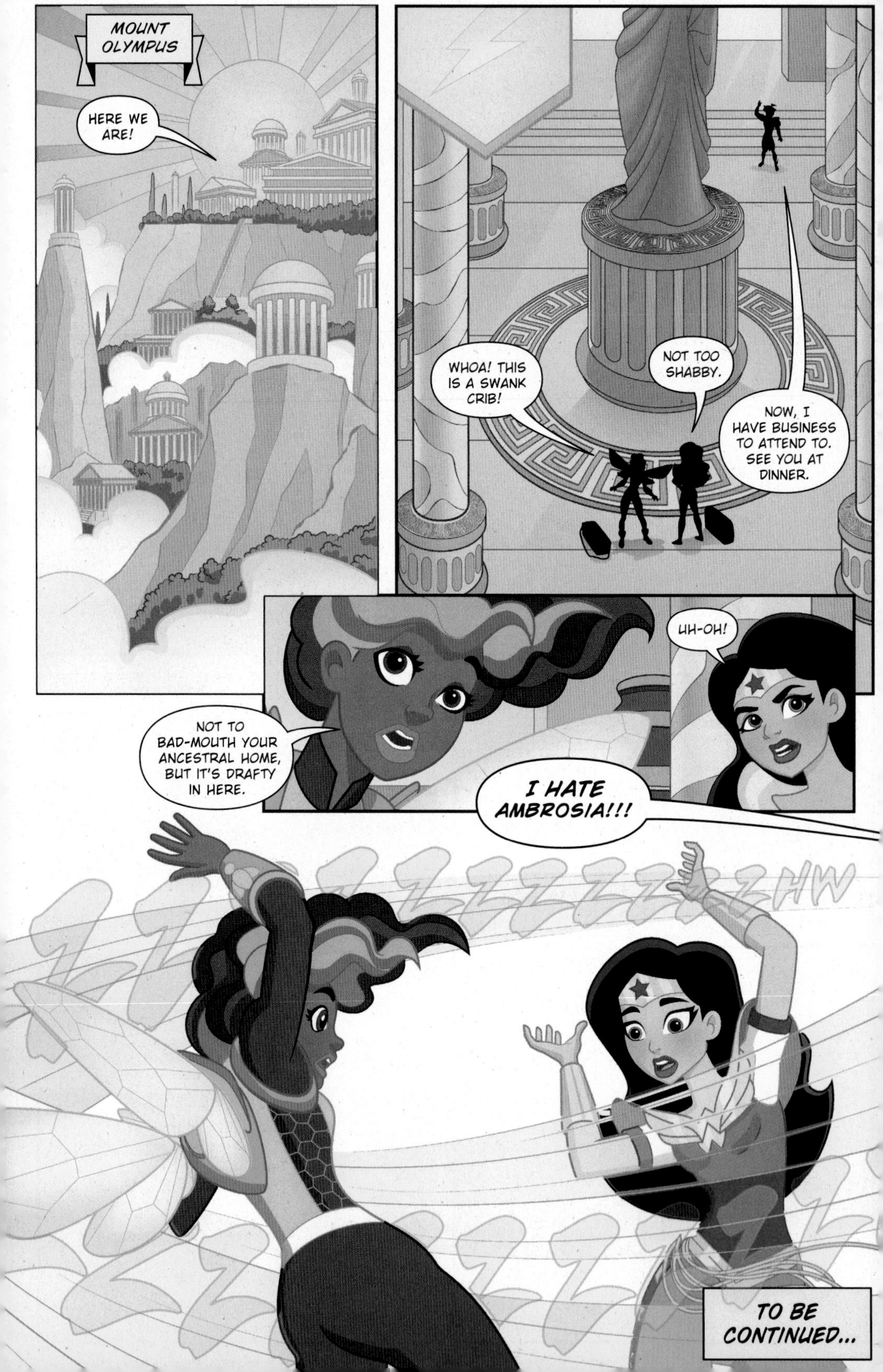
MOUNT OLYMPUS
HERE WE ARE!
WHOA! THIS IS A SWANK CRIB!
NOT TOO SHABBY.
NOW, I HAVE BUSINESS TO ATTEND TO. SEE YOU AT DINNER.
NOT TO BAD-MOUTH YOUR ANCESTRAL HOME, BUT IT'S DRAFTY IN HERE.
UH-OH!
I HATE AMBROSIA!!!
TO BE CONTINUED...

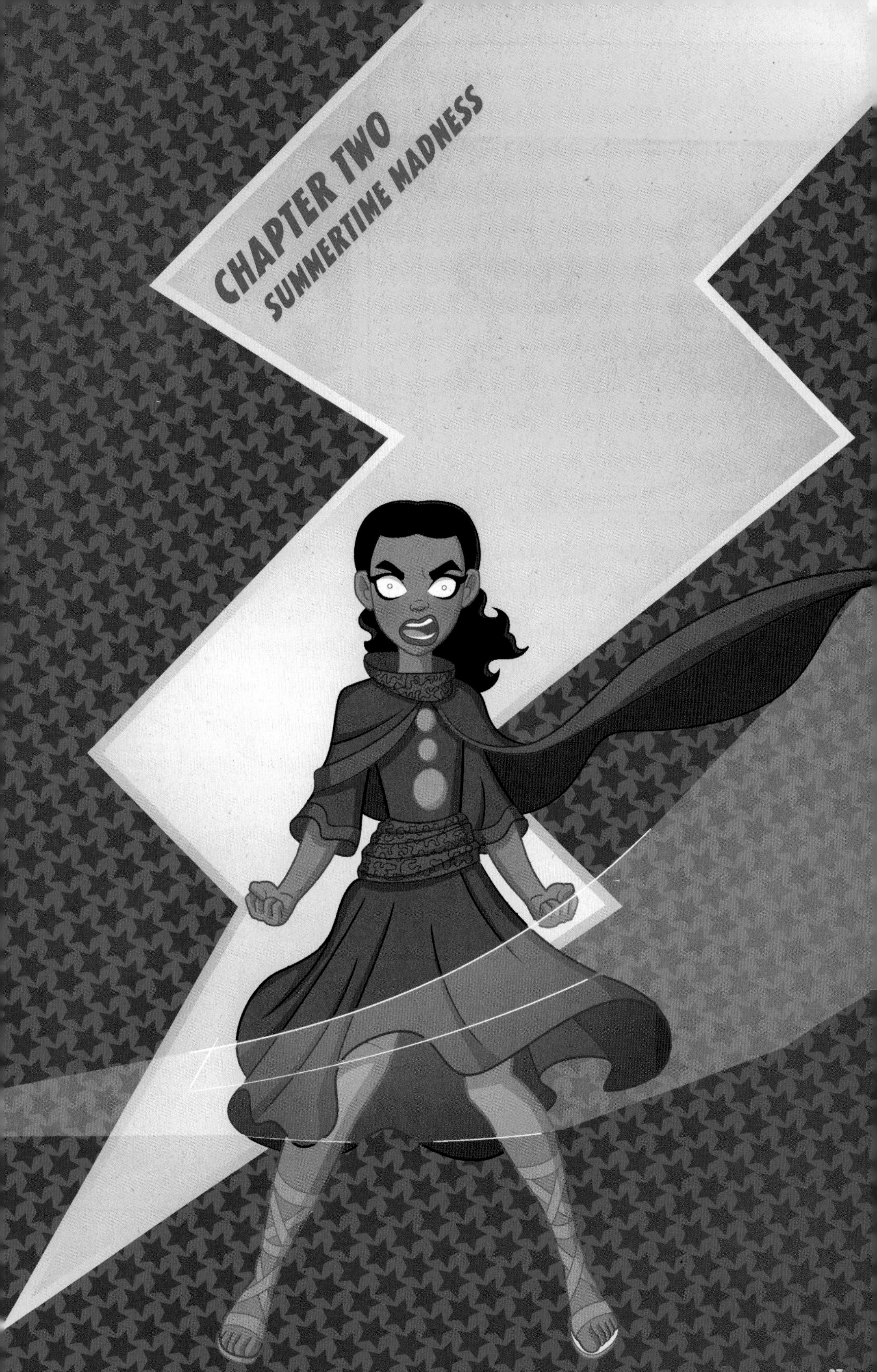
CHAPTER TWO
SUMMERTIME MADNESS

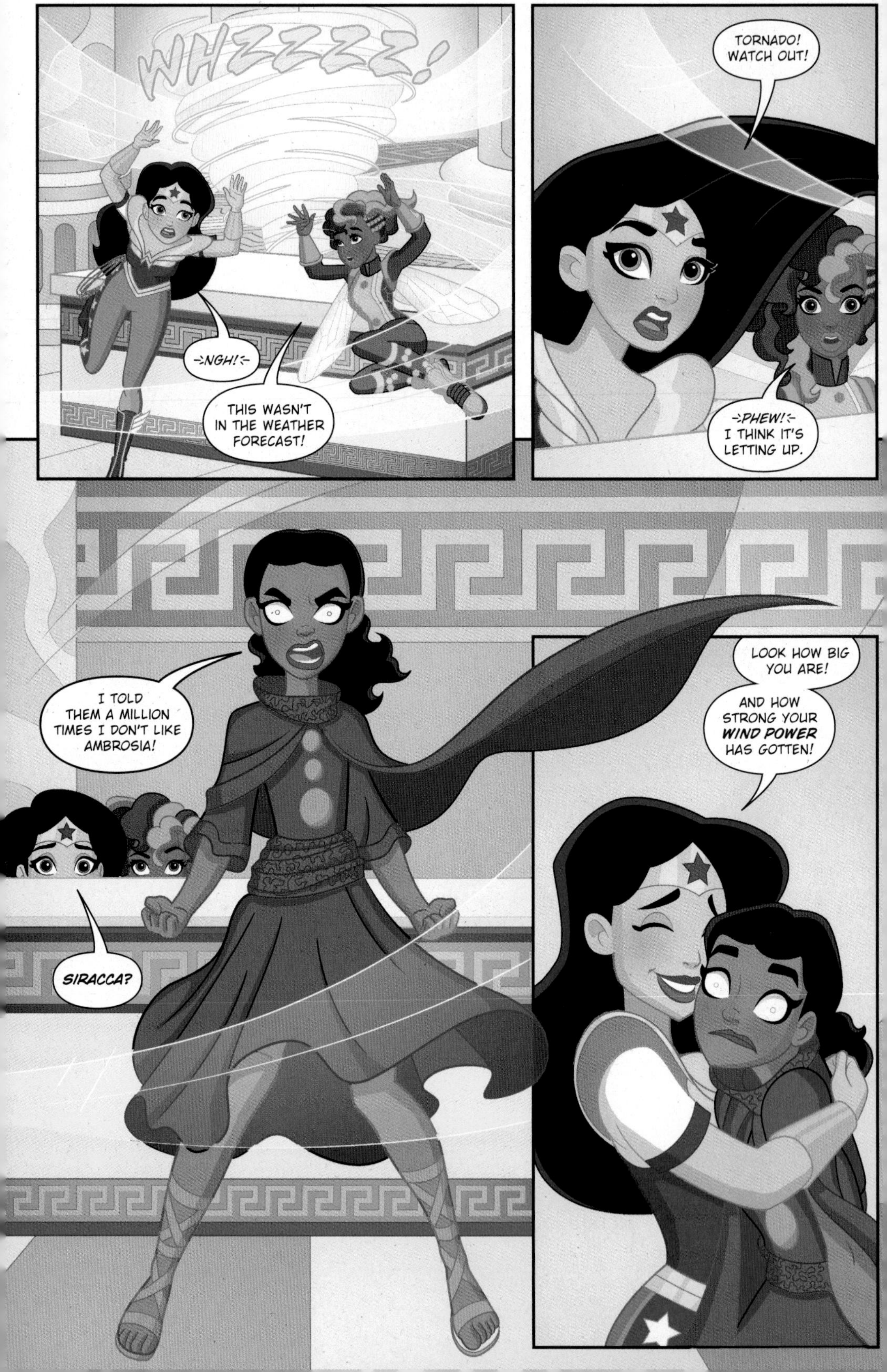
WHZZZZZ!
-NGH!-
THIS WASN'T IN THE WEATHER FORECAST!
TORNADO! WATCH OUT!
-PHEW!- I THINK IT'S LETTING UP.
I TOLD THEM A MILLION TIMES I DON'T LIKE AMBROSIA!
SIRACCA?
LOOK HOW BIG YOU ARE!
AND HOW STRONG YOUR WIND POWER HAS GOTTEN!

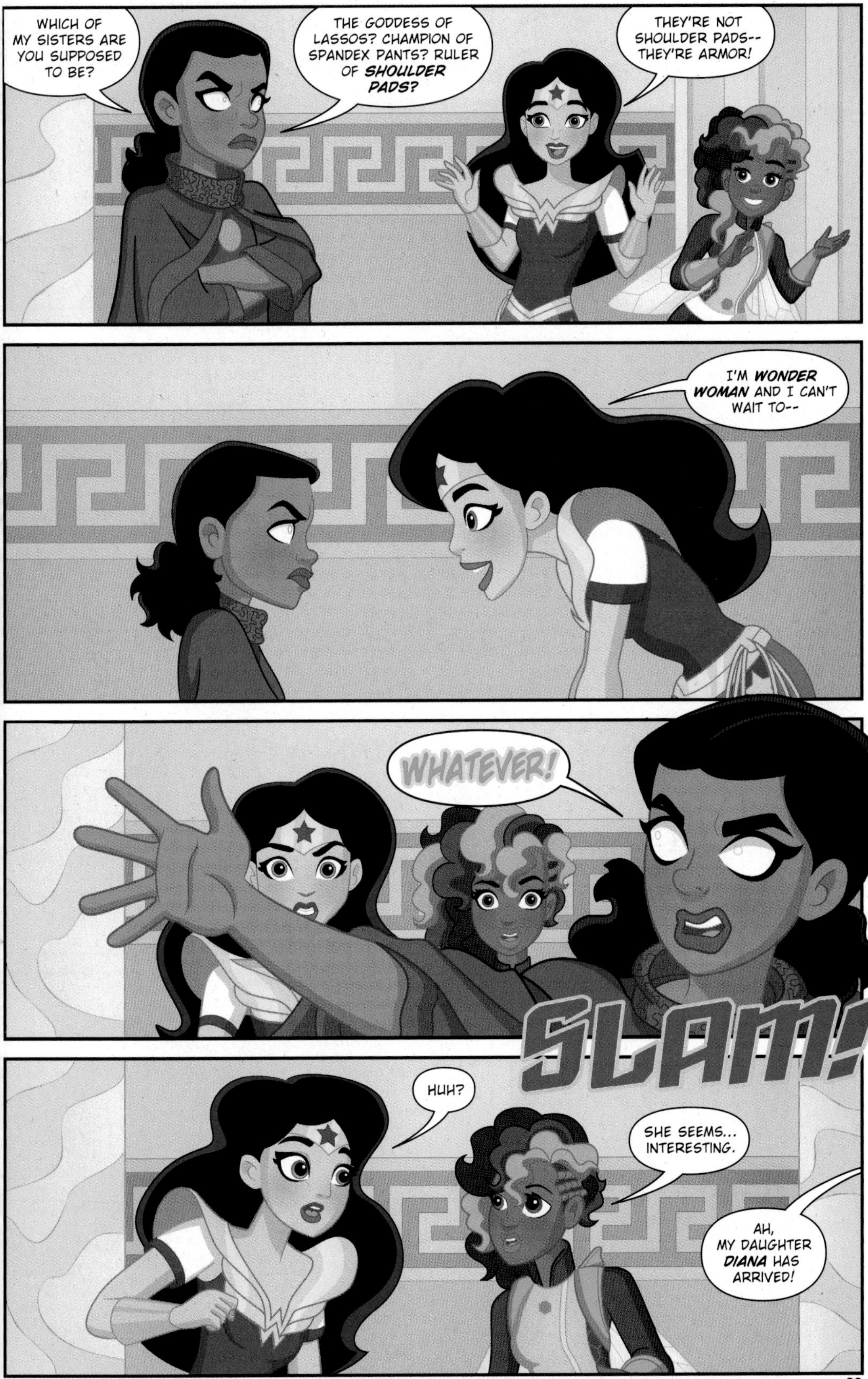

WHICH OF MY SISTERS ARE YOU SUPPOSED TO BE?
THE GODDESS OF LASSOS? CHAMPION OF SPANDEX PANTS? RULER OF SHOULDER PADS?
THEY'RE NOT SHOULDER PADS-- THEY'RE ARMOR!
I'M WONDER WOMAN AND I CAN'T WAIT TO--
WHATEVER!
SLAM!
HUH?
SHE SEEMS... INTERESTING.
AH, MY DAUGHTER DIANA HAS ARRIVED!

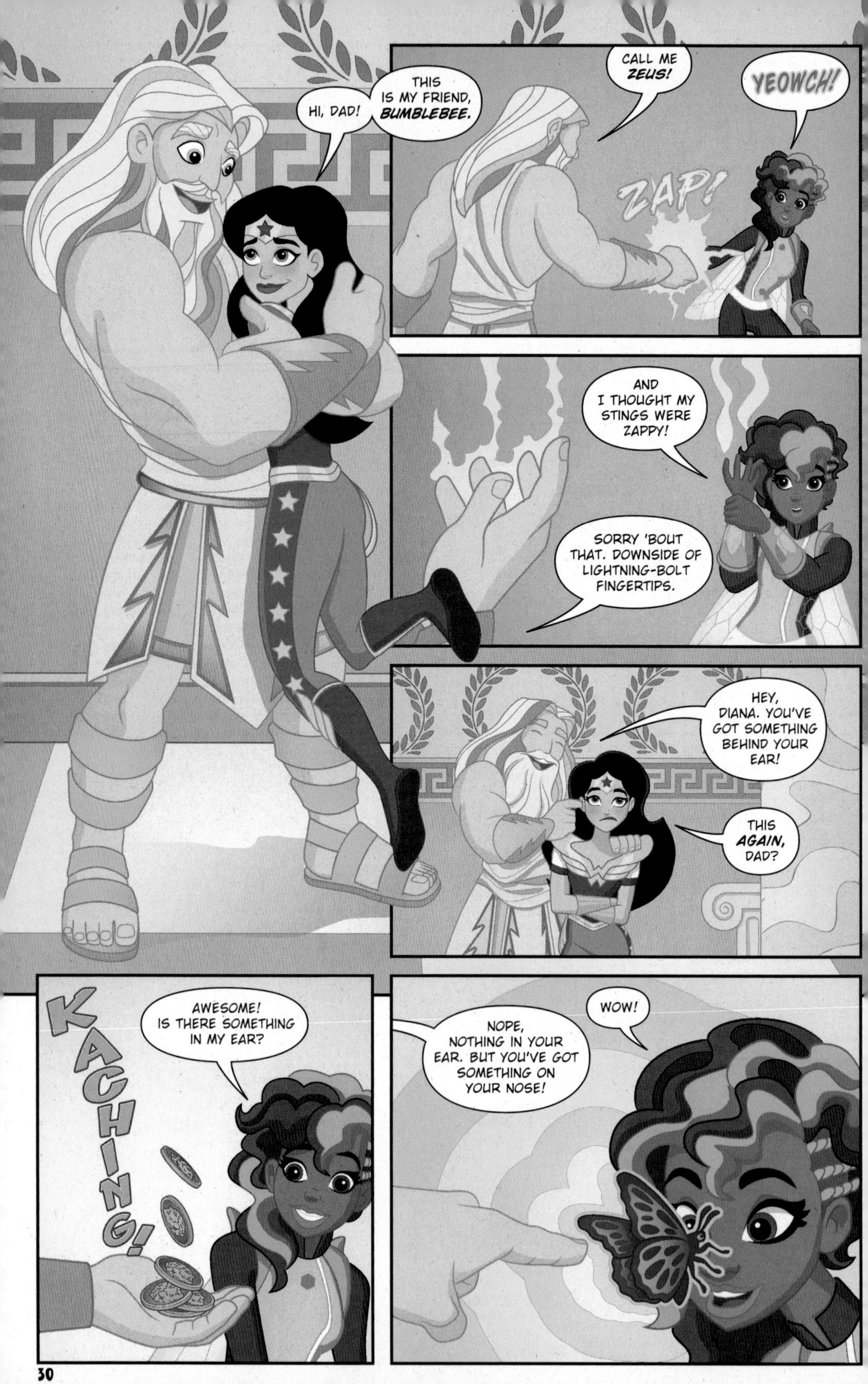
HI, DAD!
THIS IS MY FRIEND, BUMBLEBEE.
CALL ME ZEUS!
ZAP!
YEOWCH!
AND I THOUGHT MY STINGS WERE ZAPPY!
SORRY 'BOUT THAT. DOWNSIDE OF LIGHTNING-BOLT FINGERTIPS.
HEY, DIANA. YOU'VE GOT SOMETHING BEHIND YOUR EAR!
THIS AGAIN, DAD?
KACHING!
AWESOME! IS THERE SOMETHING IN MY EAR?
WOW!
NOPE, NOTHING IN YOUR EAR. BUT YOU'VE GOT SOMETHING ON YOUR NOSE!

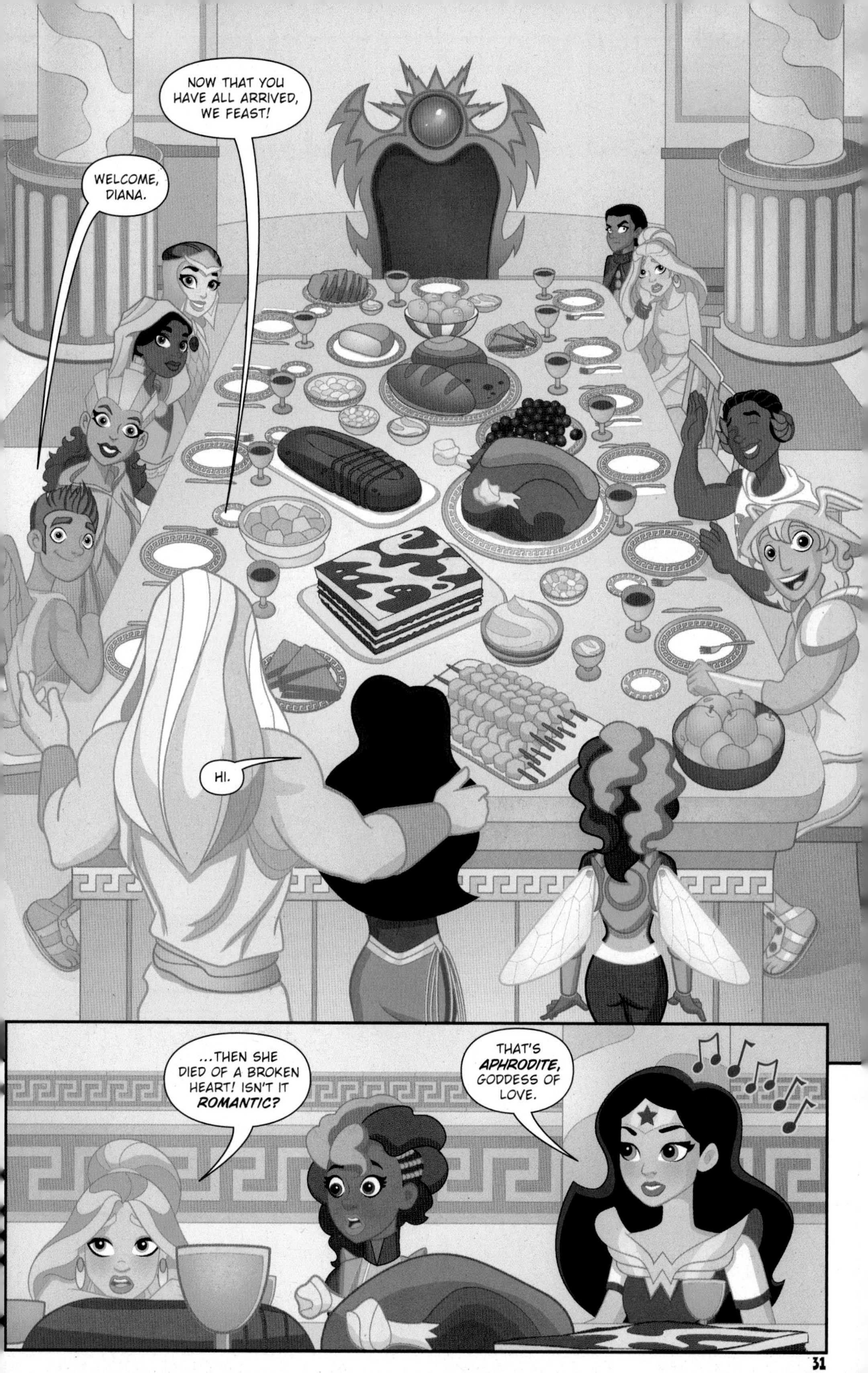
NOW THAT YOU HAVE ALL ARRIVED, WE FEAST!
WELCOME, DIANA.
HI.
...THEN SHE DIED OF A BROKEN HEART! ISN'T IT *ROMANTIC?*
THAT'S *APHRODITE,* GODDESS OF LOVE.

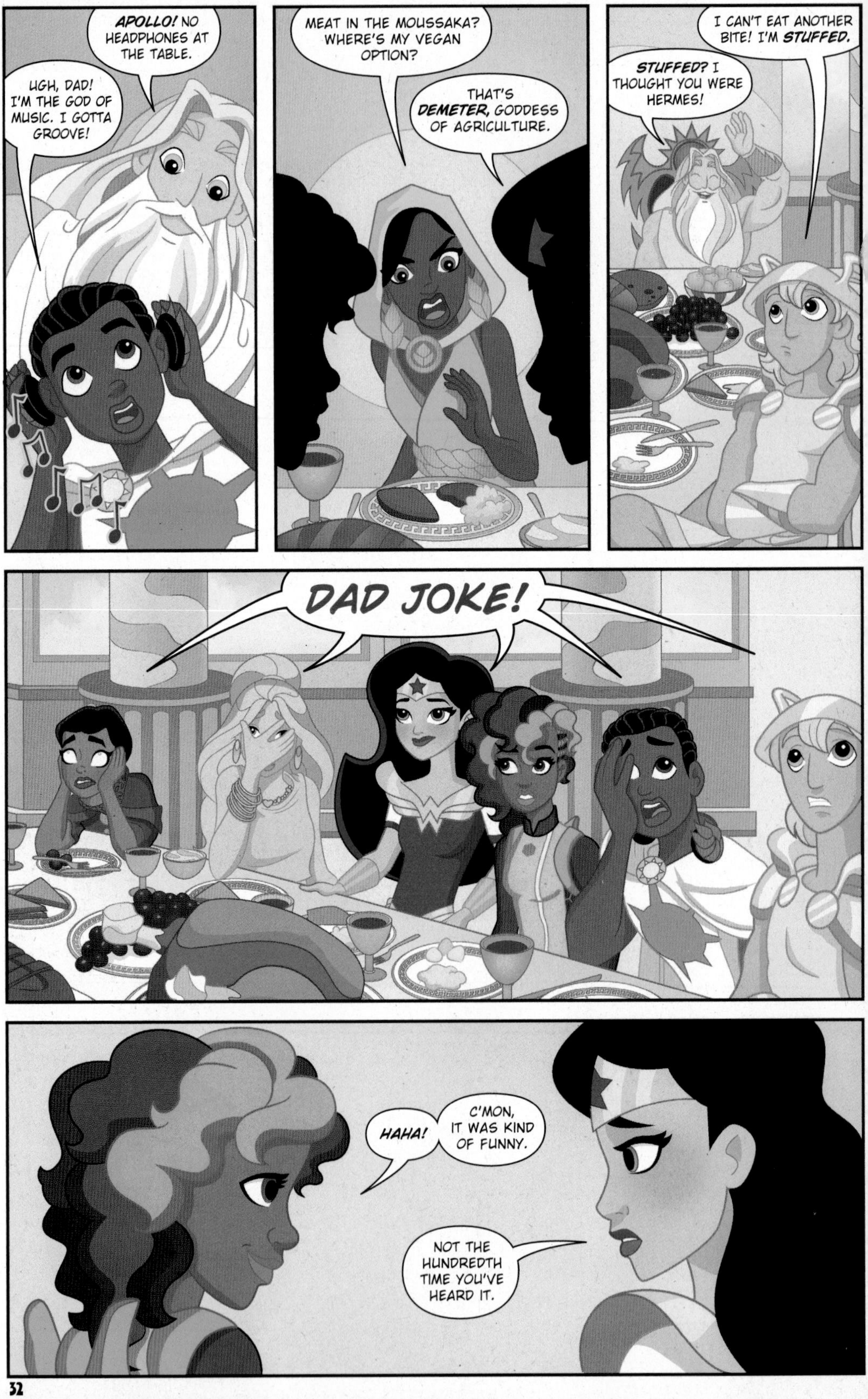
APOLLO! NO HEADPHONES AT THE TABLE.
UGH, DAD! I'M THE GOD OF MUSIC. I GOTTA GROOVE!
MEAT IN THE MOUSSAKA? WHERE'S MY VEGAN OPTION?
THAT'S DEMETER, GODDESS OF AGRICULTURE.
I CAN'T EAT ANOTHER BITE! I'M STUFFED.
STUFFED? I THOUGHT YOU WERE HERMES!
DAD JOKE!
HAHA!
C'MON, IT WAS KIND OF FUNNY.
NOT THE HUNDREDTH TIME YOU'VE HEARD IT.

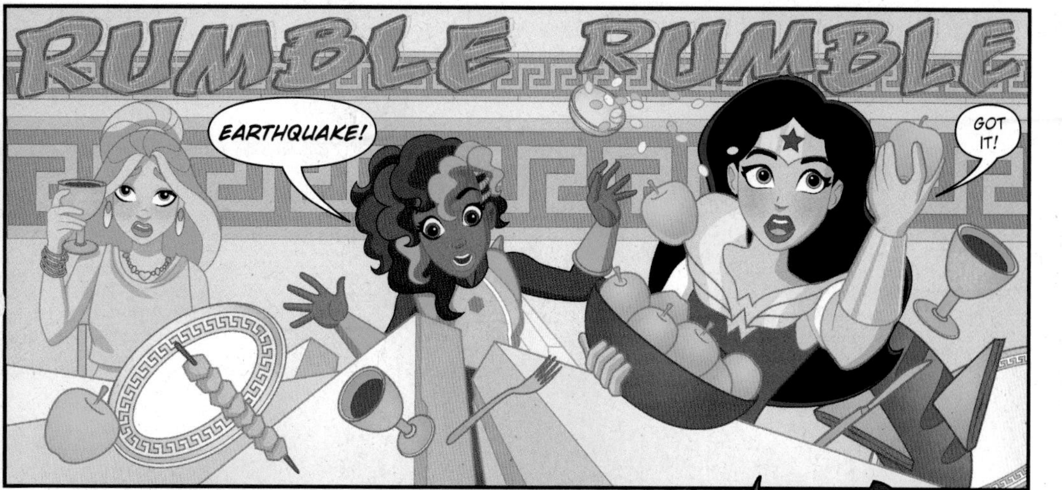
RUMBLE RUMBLE
EARTHQUAKE!
GOT IT!

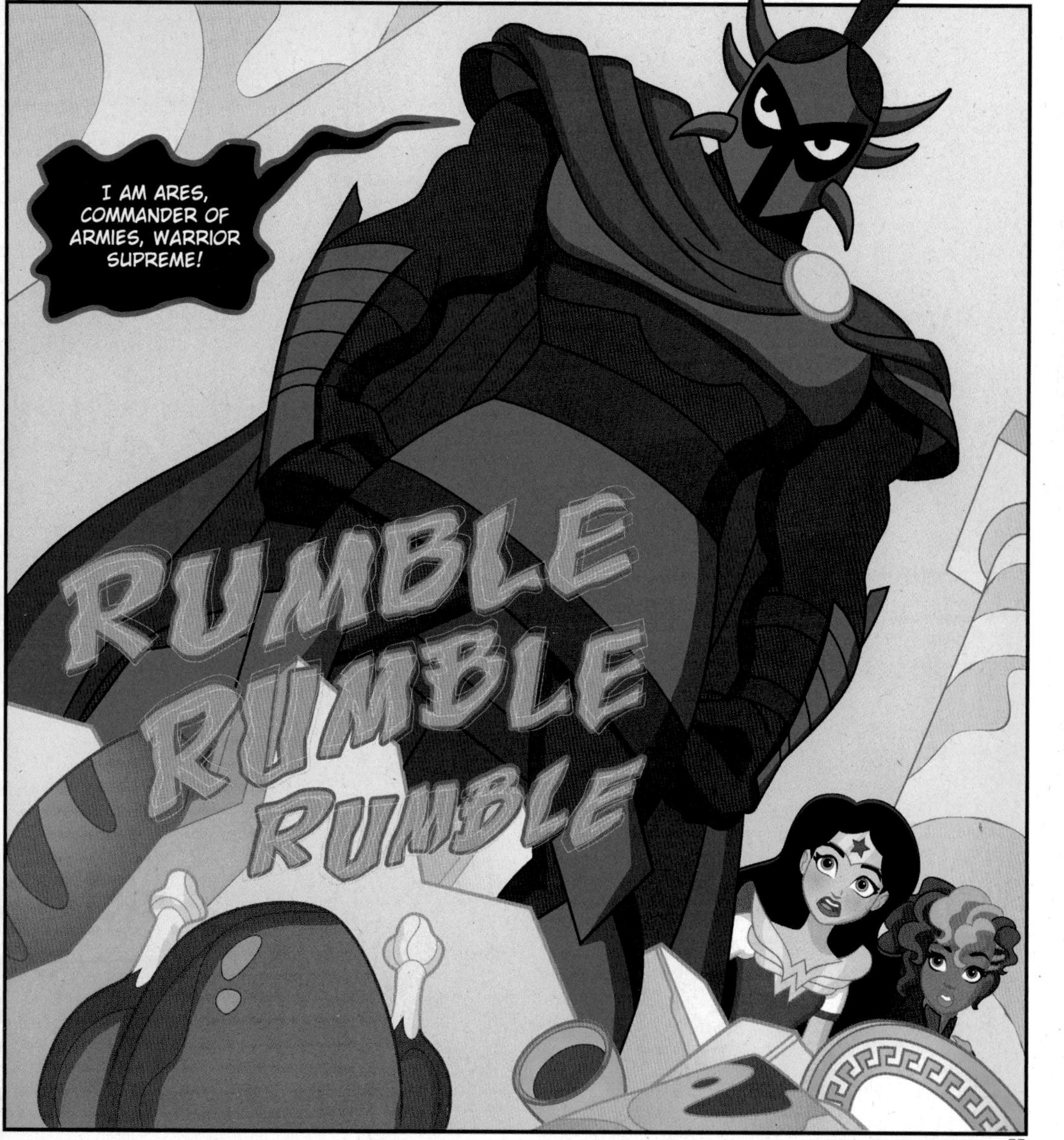
I AM ARES, COMMANDER OF ARMIES, WARRIOR SUPREME!
RUMBLE
RUMBLE
RUMBLE

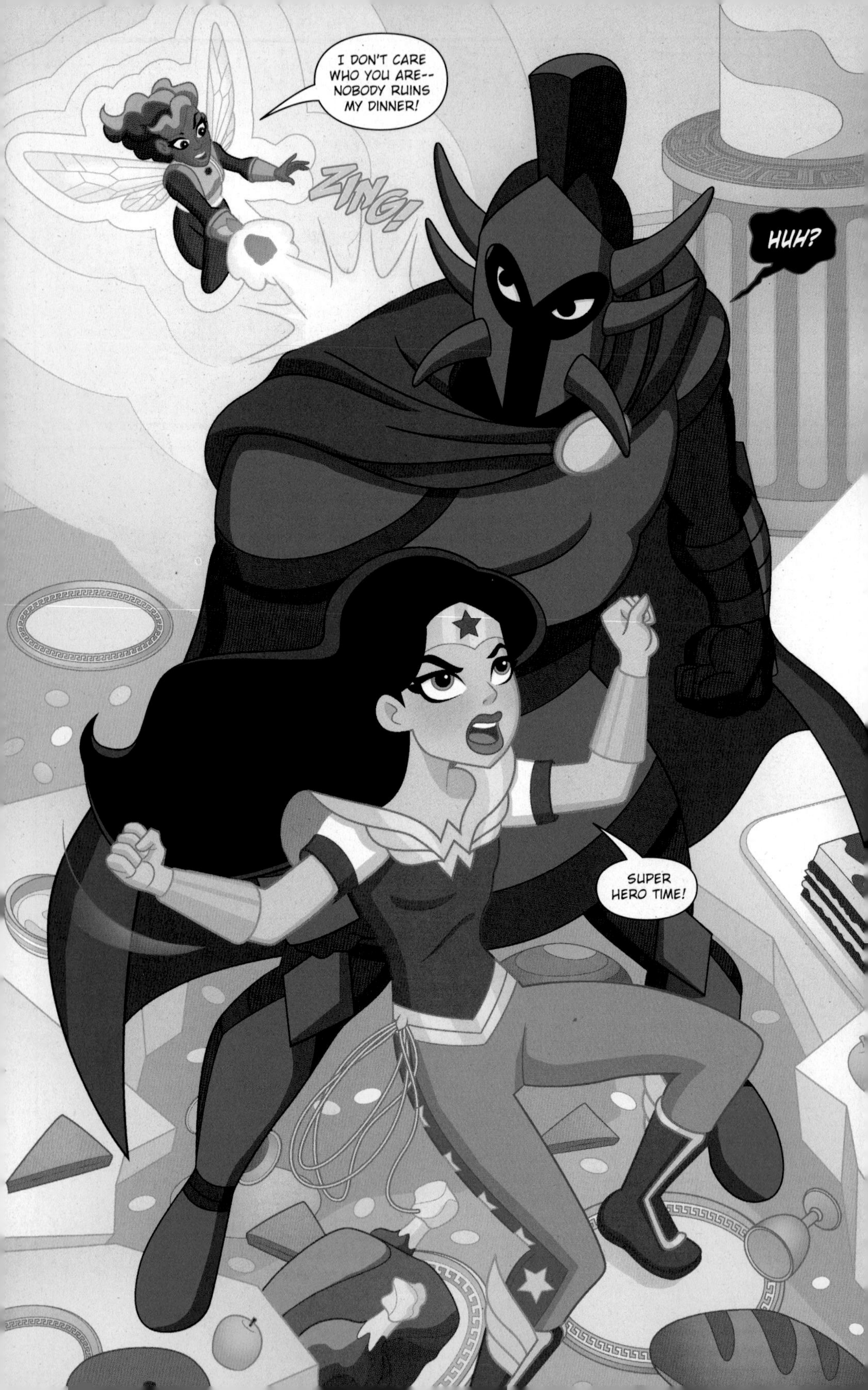
I DON'T CARE WHO YOU ARE-- NOBODY RUINS MY DINNER!
ZING!
HUH?
SUPER HERO TIME!

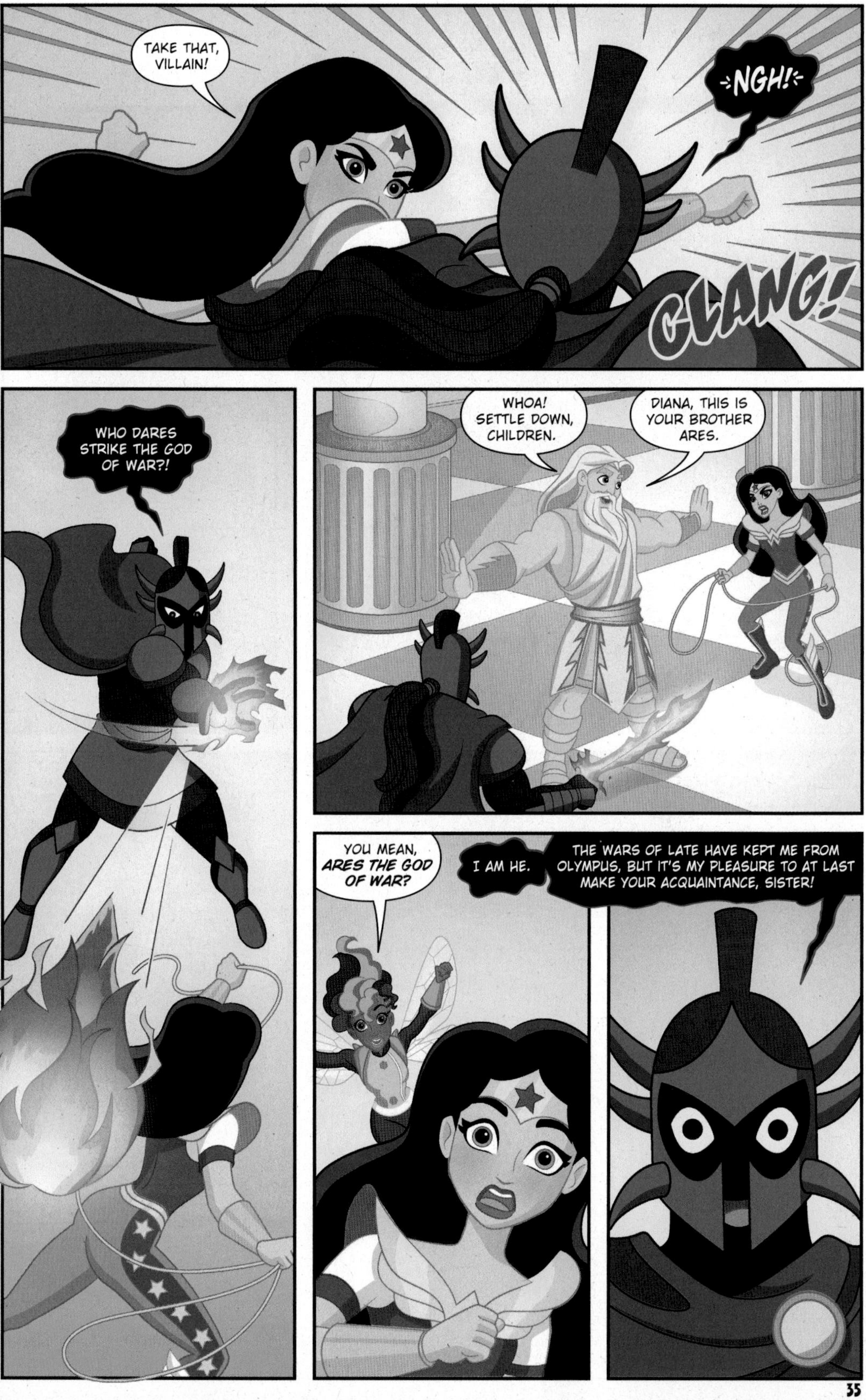
TAKE THAT, VILLAIN!
NGH!
CLANG!
WHO DARES STRIKE THE GOD OF WAR?!
WHOA! SETTLE DOWN, CHILDREN.
DIANA, THIS IS YOUR BROTHER ARES.
YOU MEAN, ARES THE GOD OF WAR?
I AM HE.
THE WARS OF LATE HAVE KEPT ME FROM OLYMPUS, BUT IT'S MY PLEASURE TO AT LAST MAKE YOUR ACQUAINTANCE, SISTER!

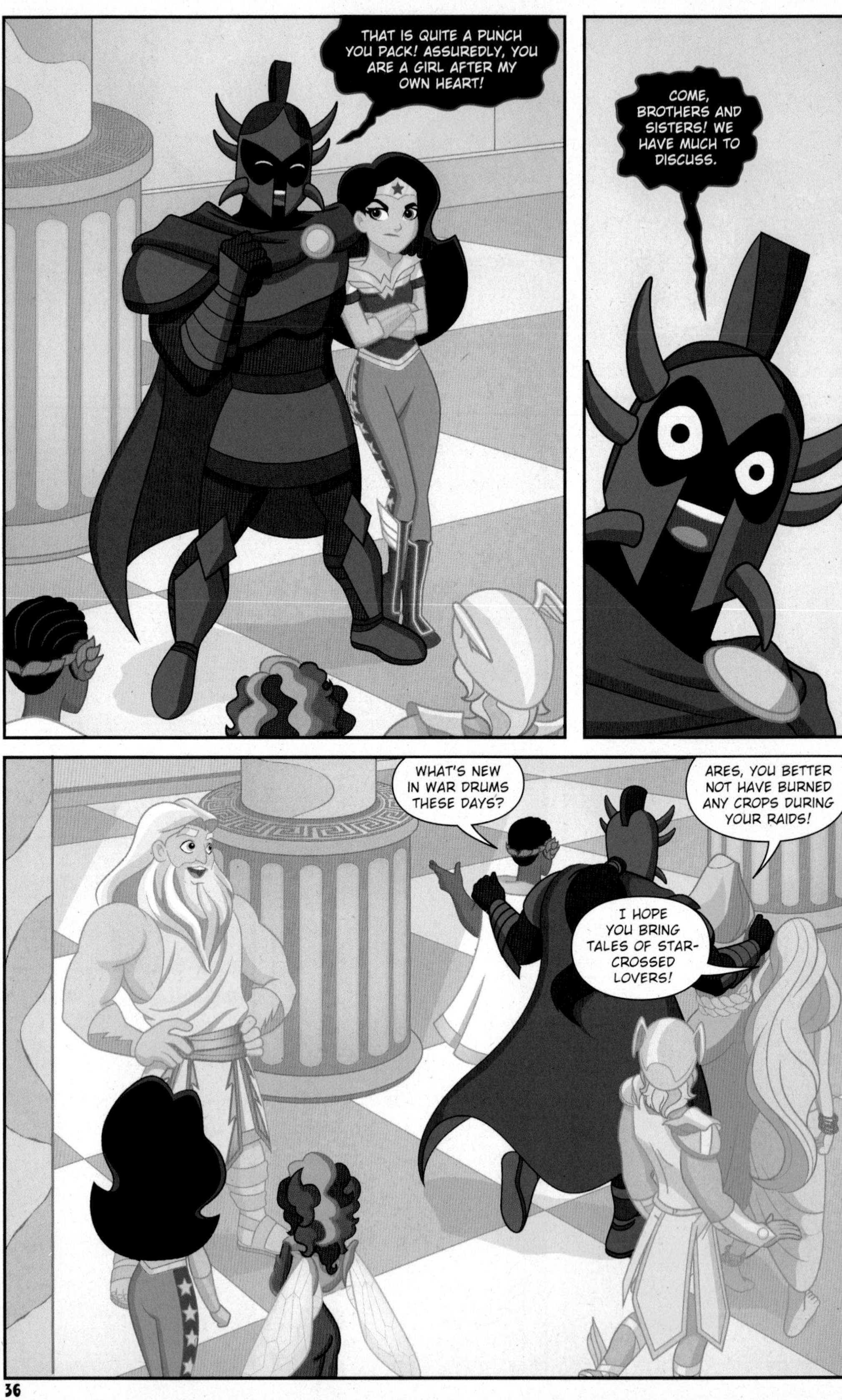
THAT IS QUITE A PUNCH YOU PACK! ASSUREDLY, YOU ARE A GIRL AFTER MY OWN HEART!
COME, BROTHERS AND SISTERS! WE HAVE MUCH TO DISCUSS.
WHAT'S NEW IN WAR DRUMS THESE DAYS?
ARES, YOU BETTER NOT HAVE BURNED ANY CROPS DURING YOUR RAIDS!
I HOPE YOU BRING TALES OF STAR-CROSSED LOVERS!

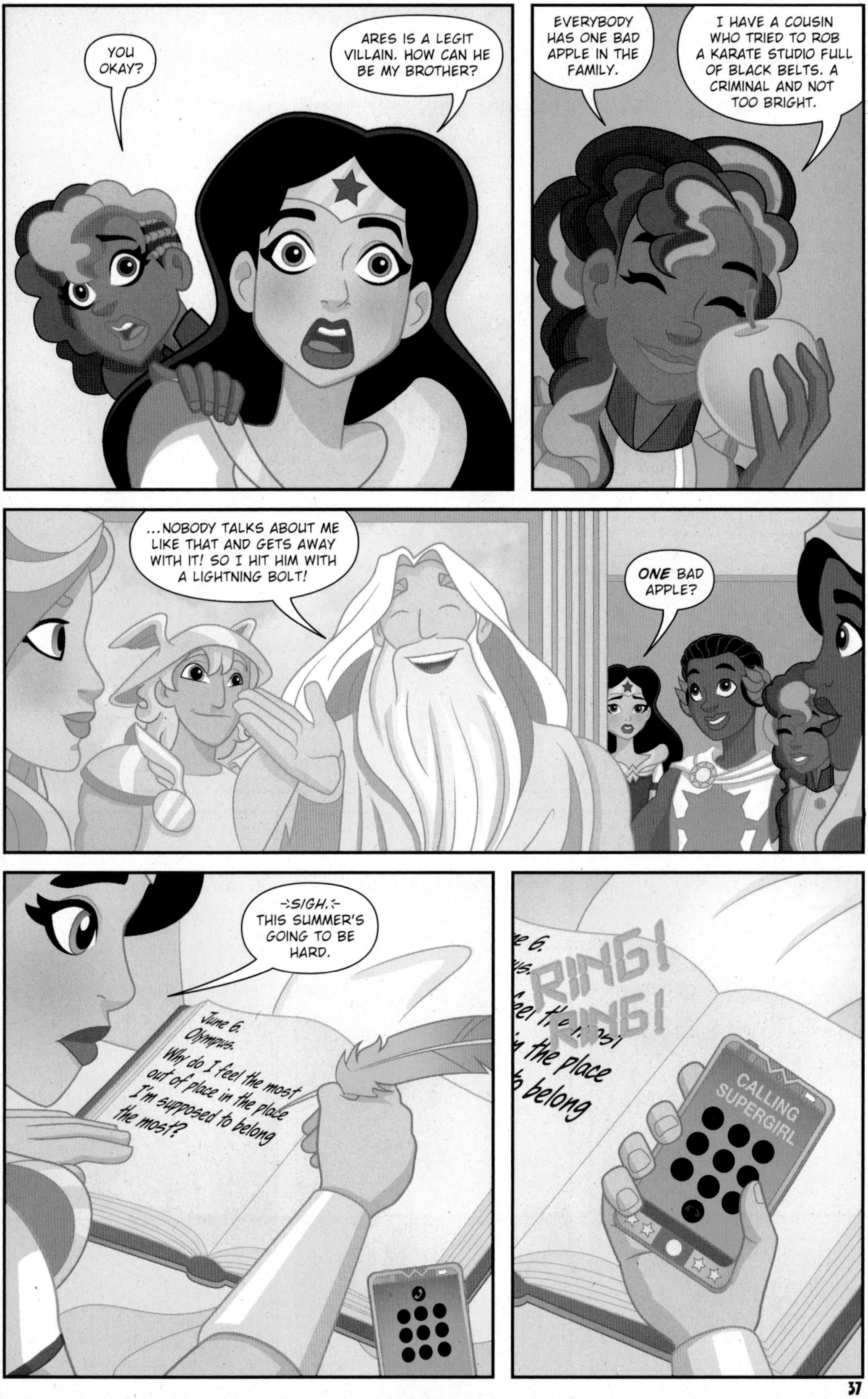
YOU OKAY?
ARES IS A LEGIT VILLAIN. HOW CAN HE BE MY BROTHER?
EVERYBODY HAS ONE BAD APPLE IN THE FAMILY.
I HAVE A COUSIN WHO TRIED TO ROB A KARATE STUDIO FULL OF BLACK BELTS. A CRIMINAL AND NOT TOO BRIGHT.
...NOBODY TALKS ABOUT ME LIKE THAT AND GETS AWAY WITH IT! SO I HIT HIM WITH A LIGHTNING BOLT!
ONE BAD APPLE?
-SIGH.- THIS SUMMER'S GOING TO BE HARD.
June 6. Olympus. Why do I feel the most out of place in the place I'm supposed to belong the most?
RING! RING!
CALLING SUPERGIRL

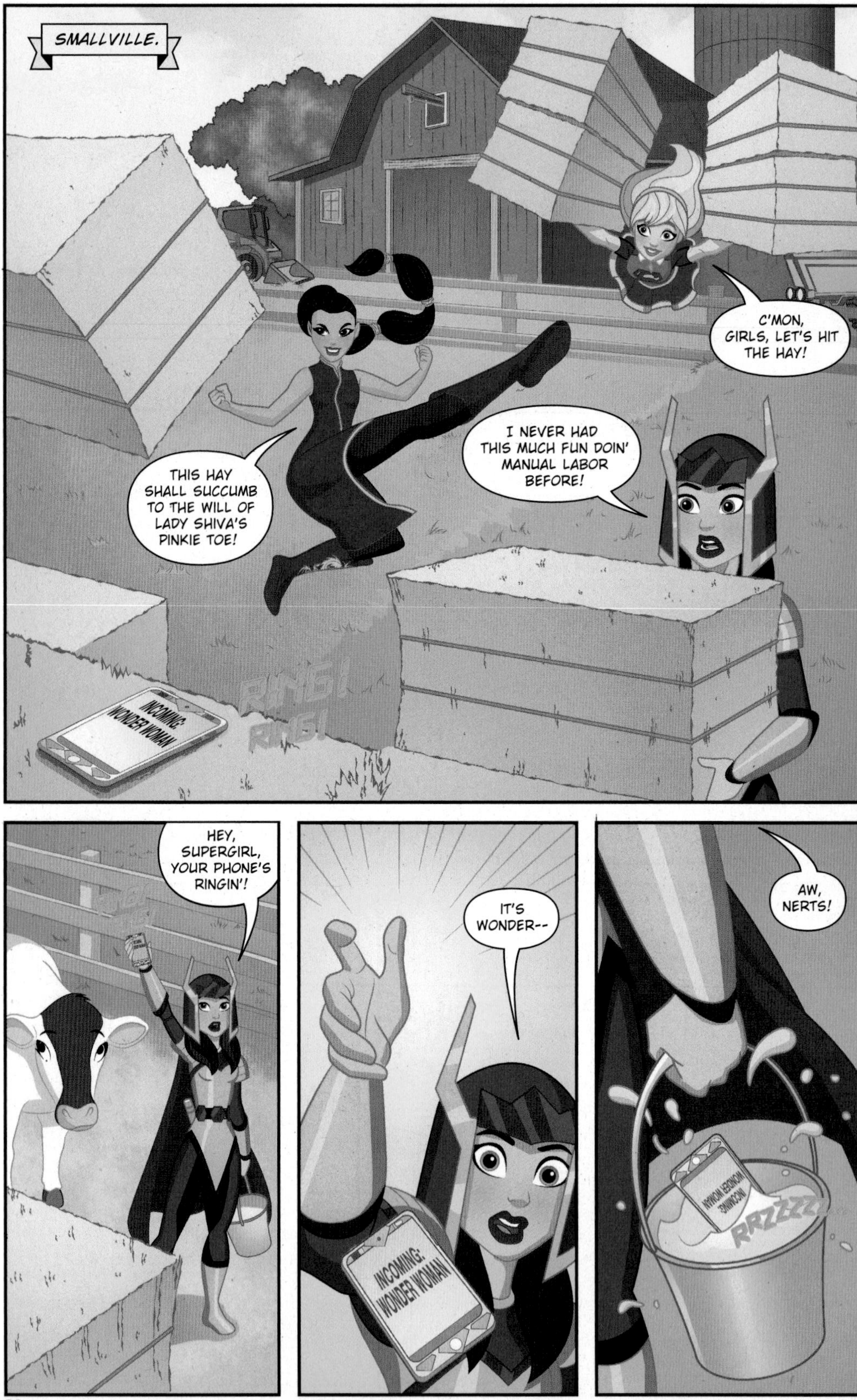

SMALLVILLE.
C'MON, GIRLS, LET'S HIT THE HAY!
THIS HAY SHALL SUCCUMB TO THE WILL OF LADY SHIVA'S PINKIE TOE!
I NEVER HAD THIS MUCH FUN DOIN' MANUAL LABOR BEFORE!
INCOMING: WONDER WOMAN
RING! RING!
HEY, SUPERGIRL, YOUR PHONE'S RINGIN'!
IT'S WONDER--
INCOMING: WONDER WOMAN
AW, NERTS!
INCOMING: WONDER WOMAN
RRZZZZ!

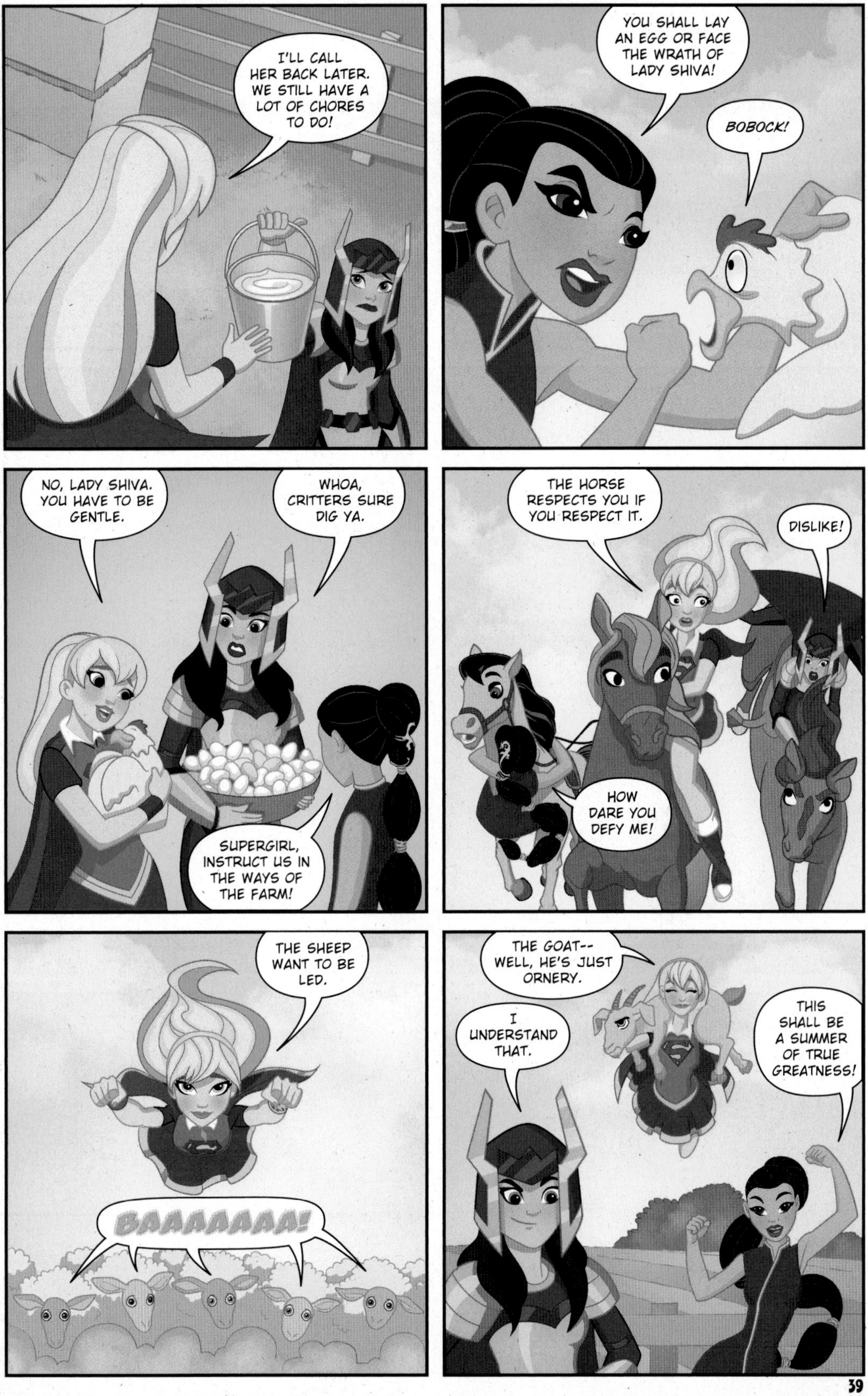
I'LL CALL HER BACK LATER. WE STILL HAVE A LOT OF CHORES TO DO!
YOU SHALL LAY AN EGG OR FACE THE WRATH OF LADY SHIVA!
BOBOCK!
NO, LADY SHIVA. YOU HAVE TO BE GENTLE.
WHOA, CRITTERS SURE DIG YA.
SUPERGIRL, INSTRUCT US IN THE WAYS OF THE FARM!
THE HORSE RESPECTS YOU IF YOU RESPECT IT.
DISLIKE!
HOW DARE YOU DEFY ME!
THE SHEEP WANT TO BE LED.
BAAAAAAA!
THE GOAT-- WELL, HE'S JUST ORNERY.
I UNDERSTAND THAT.
THIS SHALL BE A SUMMER OF TRUE GREATNESS!

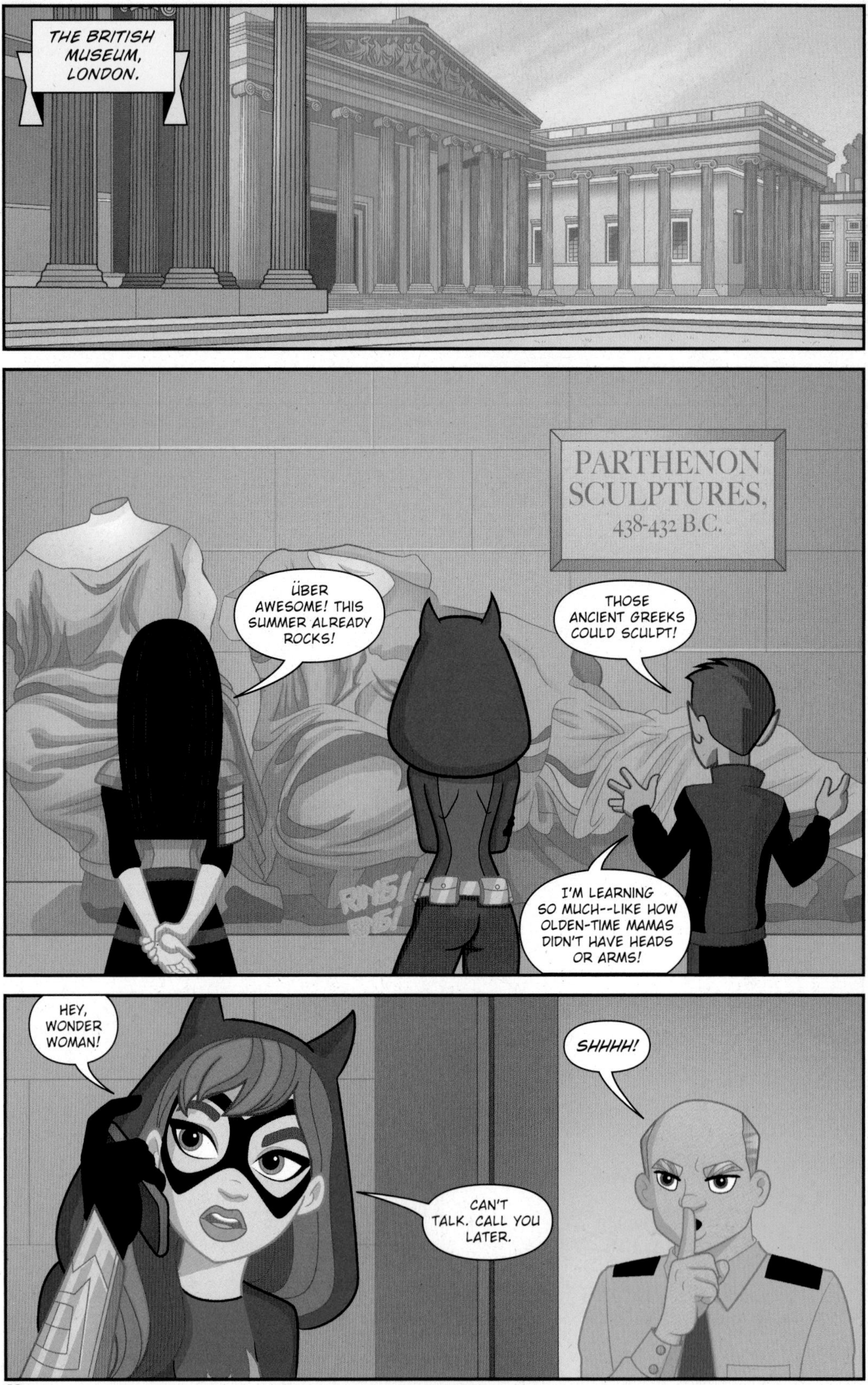
THE BRITISH MUSEUM, LONDON.
PARTHENON SCULPTURES, 438-432 B.C.
ÜBER AWESOME! THIS SUMMER ALREADY ROCKS!
THOSE ANCIENT GREEKS COULD SCULPT!
RING! RING!
I'M LEARNING SO MUCH--LIKE HOW OLDEN-TIME MAMAS DIDN'T HAVE HEADS OR ARMS!
HEY, WONDER WOMAN!
SHHHH!
CAN'T TALK. CALL YOU LATER.

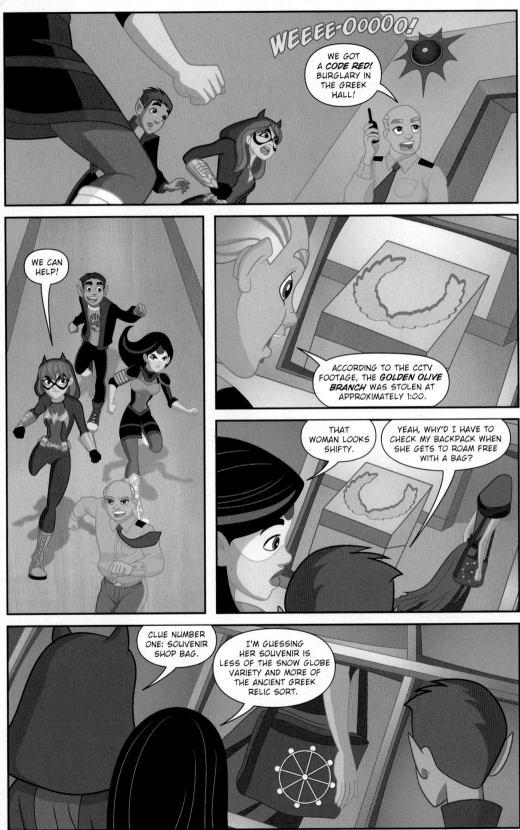

WEEEE-OOOOO!

WE GOT A **CODE RED!** BURGLARY IN THE GREEK HALL!

WE CAN HELP!

ACCORDING TO THE CCTV FOOTAGE, THE **GOLDEN OLIVE BRANCH** WAS STOLEN AT APPROXIMATELY 1:00.

THAT WOMAN LOOKS SHIFTY.

YEAH, WHY'D I HAVE TO CHECK MY BACKPACK WHEN SHE GETS TO ROAM FREE WITH A BAG?

CLUE NUMBER ONE: SOUVENIR SHOP BAG.

I'M GUESSING HER SOUVENIR IS LESS OF THE SNOW GLOBE VARIETY AND MORE OF THE ANCIENT GREEK RELIC SORT.

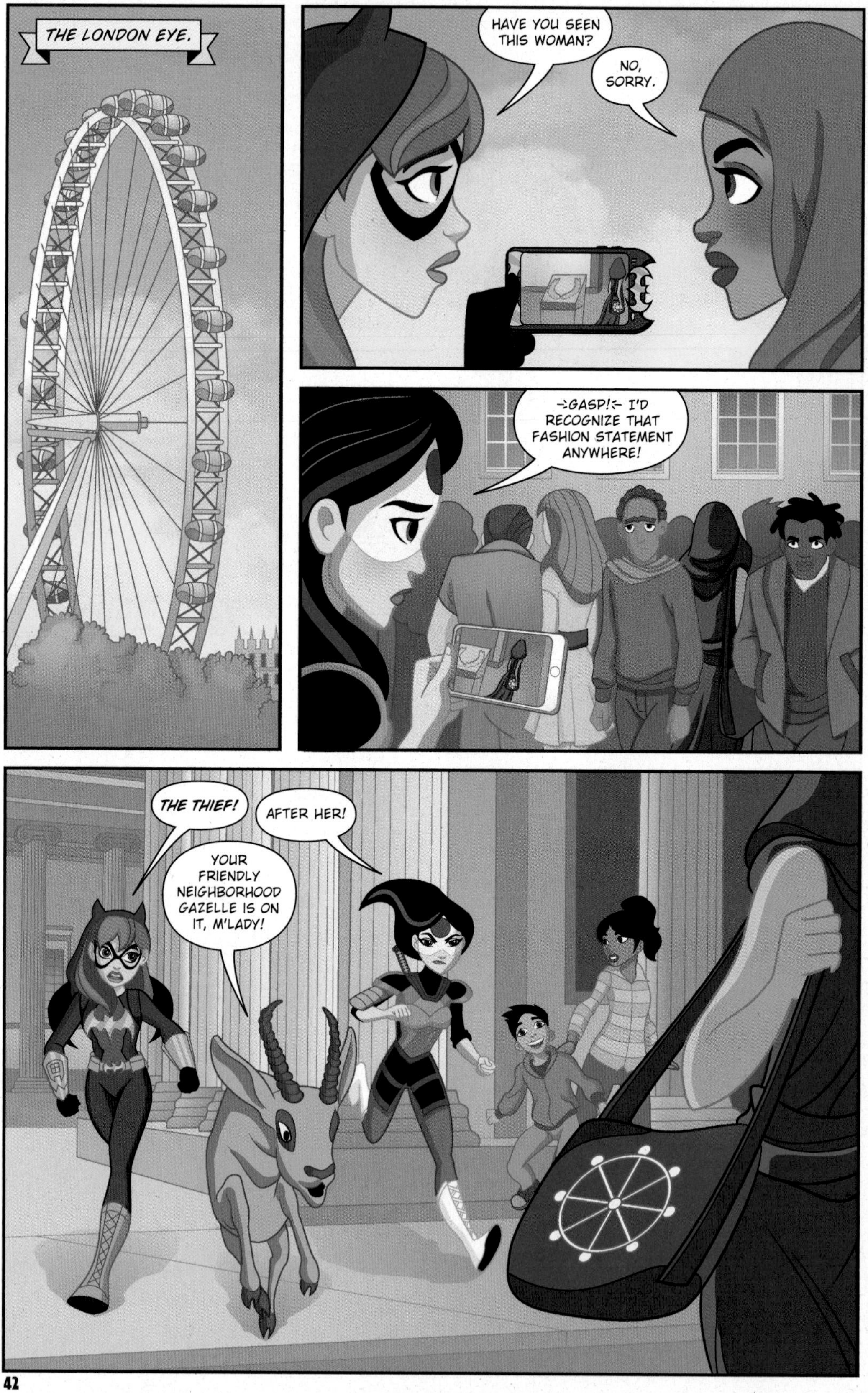
THE LONDON EYE.
HAVE YOU SEEN THIS WOMAN?
NO, SORRY.
→GASP!← I'D RECOGNIZE THAT FASHION STATEMENT ANYWHERE!
THE THIEF!
AFTER HER!
YOUR FRIENDLY NEIGHBORHOOD GAZELLE IS ON IT, M'LADY!

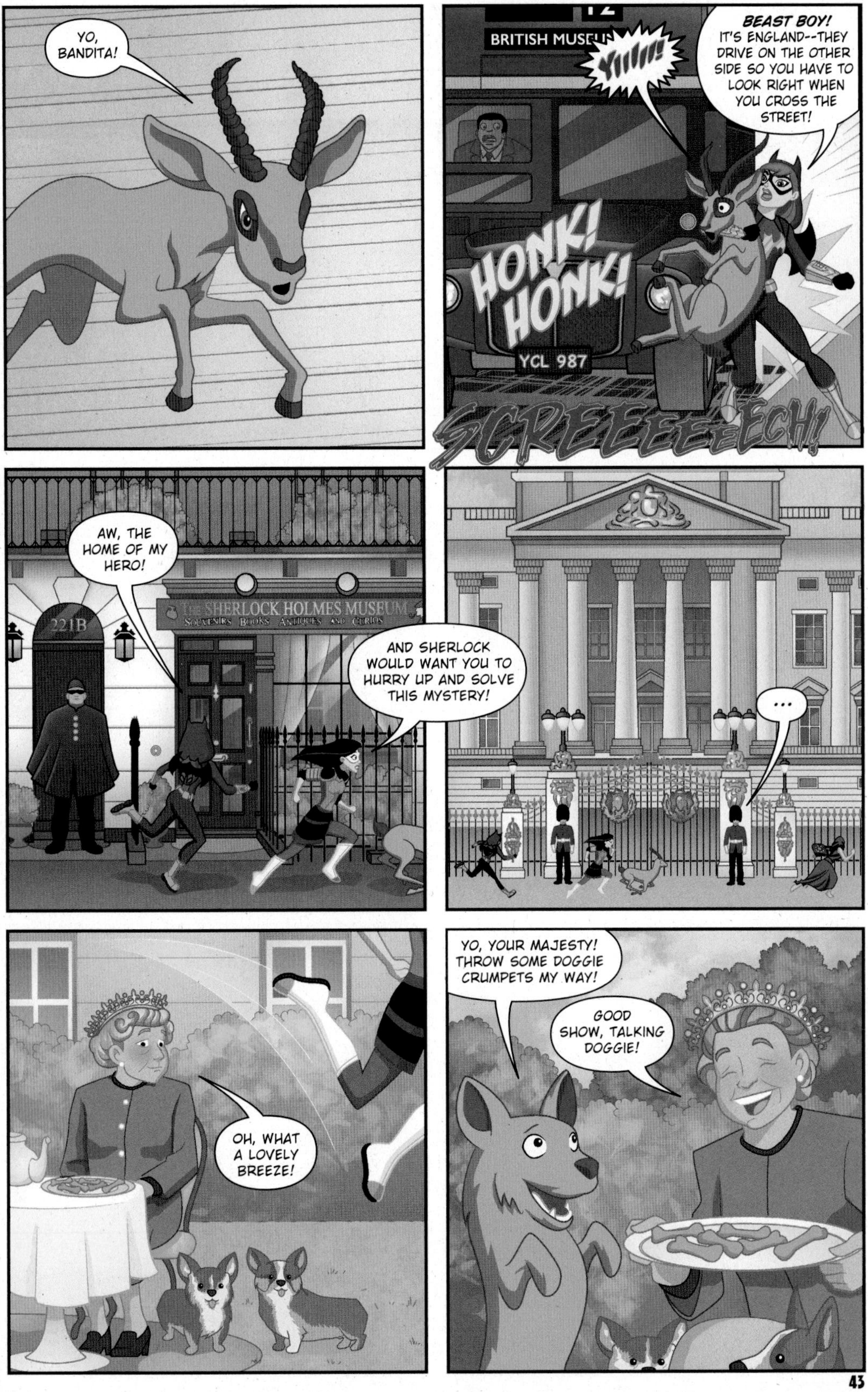
YO, BANDITA!
BRITISH MUSEUM
YIIIII!
BEAST BOY! IT'S ENGLAND--THEY DRIVE ON THE OTHER SIDE SO YOU HAVE TO LOOK RIGHT WHEN YOU CROSS THE STREET!
HONK! HONK!
YCL 987
SCREEEEEEECH!
221B
THE SHERLOCK HOLMES MUSEUM
SOUVENIRS BOOKS ANTIQUES AND CURIOS
AW, THE HOME OF MY HERO!
AND SHERLOCK WOULD WANT YOU TO HURRY UP AND SOLVE THIS MYSTERY!
...
OH, WHAT A LOVELY BREEZE!
YO, YOUR MAJESTY! THROW SOME DOGGIE CRUMPETS MY WAY!
GOOD SHOW, TALKING DOGGIE!

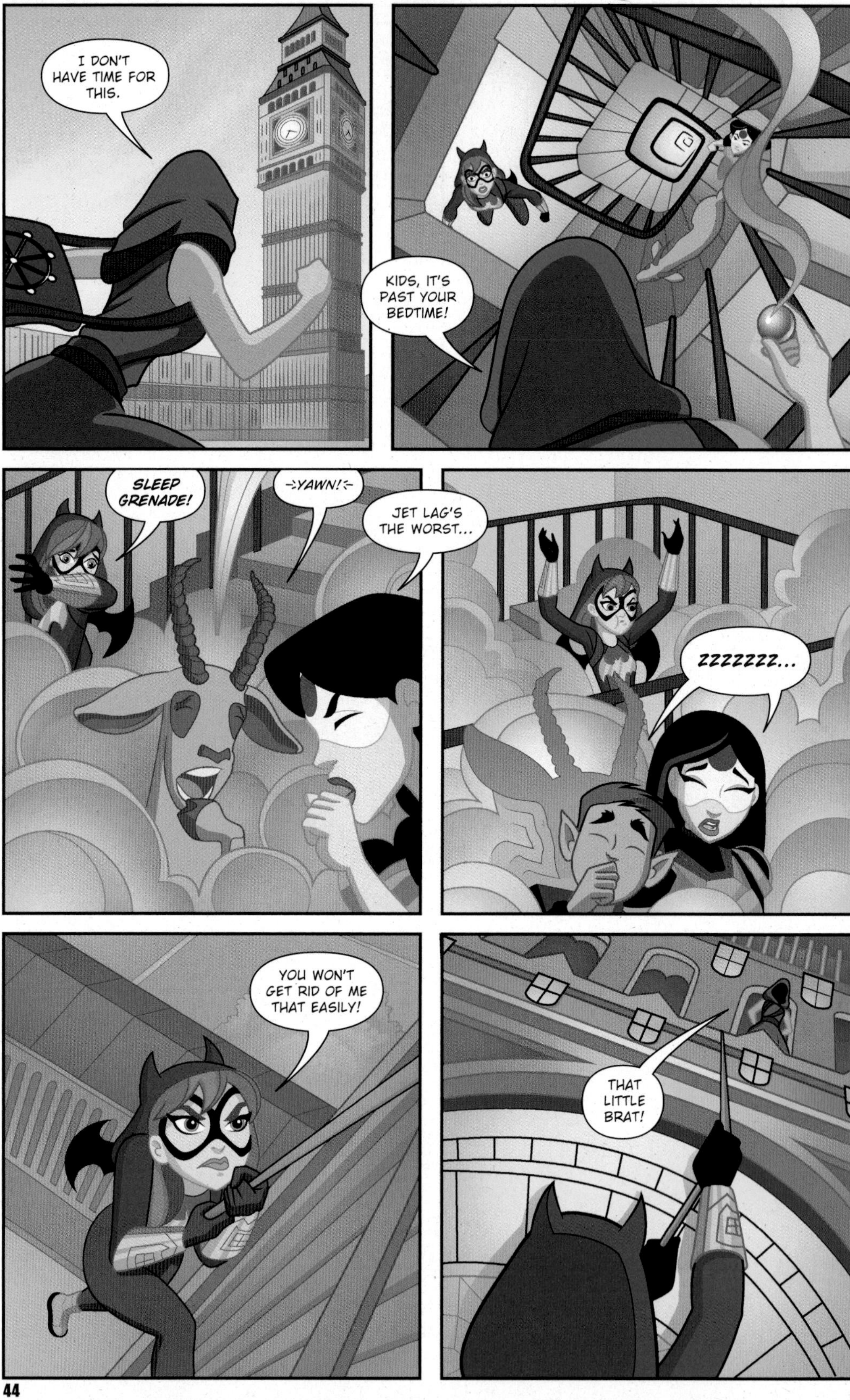
I DON'T HAVE TIME FOR THIS.
KIDS, IT'S PAST YOUR BEDTIME!
SLEEP GRENADE!
-YAWN!-
JET LAG'S THE WORST...
ZZZZZZZ...
YOU WON'T GET RID OF ME THAT EASILY!
THAT LITTLE BRAT!

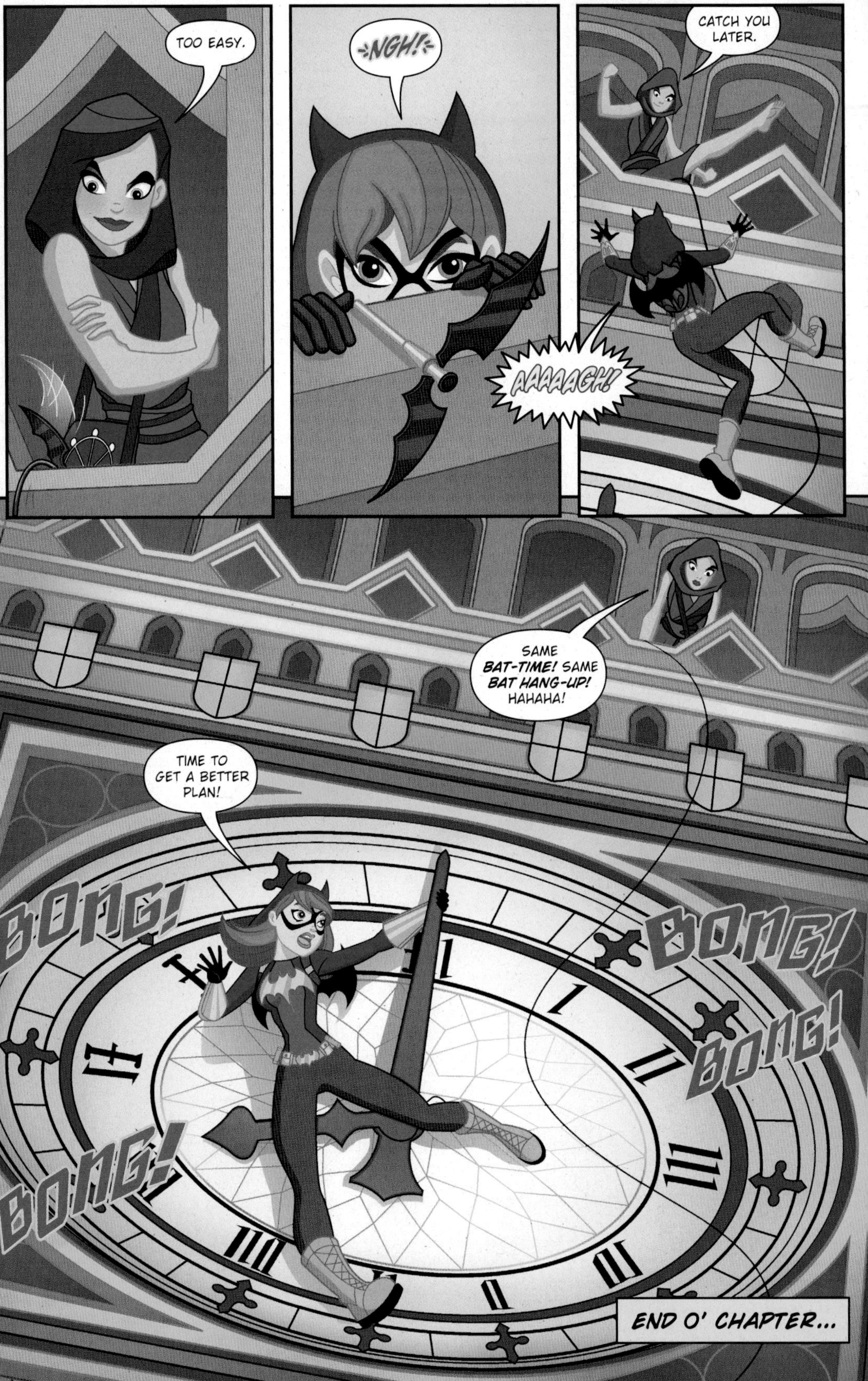

TOO EASY.
-NGH!-
CATCH YOU LATER.
AAAAAGH!
SAME BAT-TIME! SAME BAT HANG-UP! HAHAHA!
TIME TO GET A BETTER PLAN!
BONG!
BONG!
BONG!
BONG!
END O' CHAPTER...

CHAPTER THREE
FUN IN THE SUN

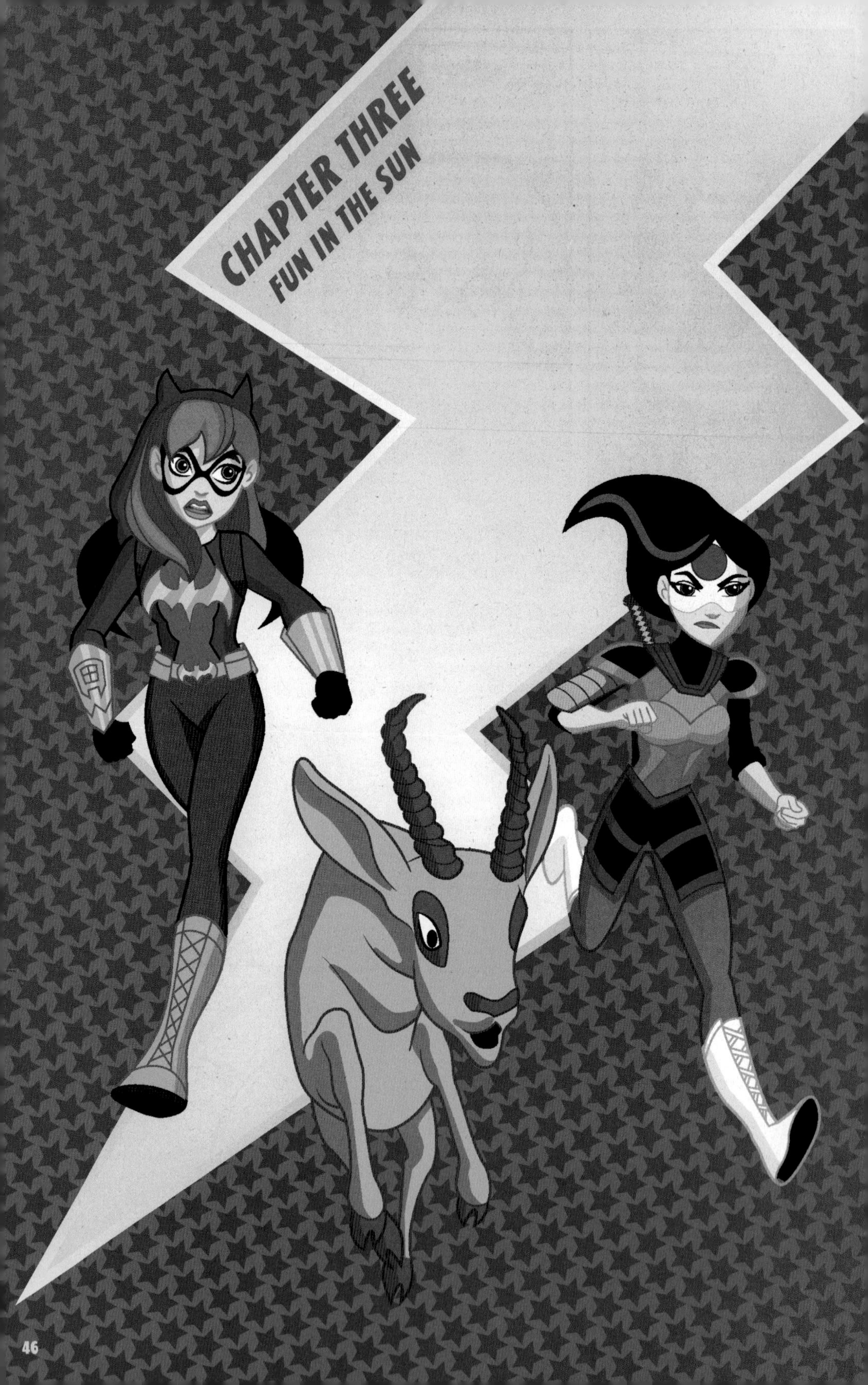

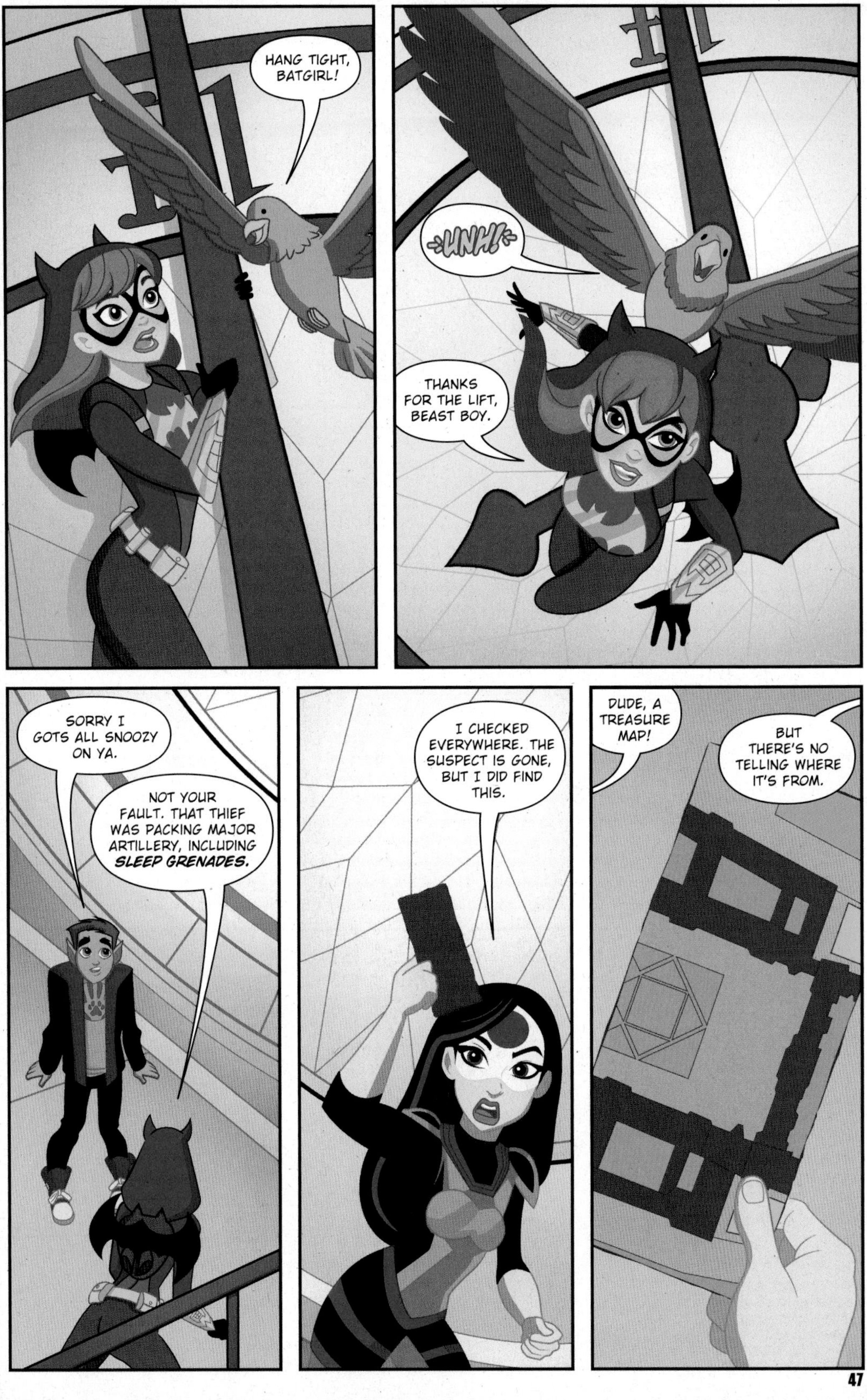
HANG TIGHT, BATGIRL!
UNH!
THANKS FOR THE LIFT, BEAST BOY.
SORRY I GOTS ALL SNOOZY ON YA.
NOT YOUR FAULT. THAT THIEF WAS PACKING MAJOR ARTILLERY, INCLUDING ***SLEEP GRENADES.***
I CHECKED EVERYWHERE. THE SUSPECT IS GONE, BUT I DID FIND THIS.
DUDE, A TREASURE MAP!
BUT THERE'S NO TELLING WHERE IT'S FROM.

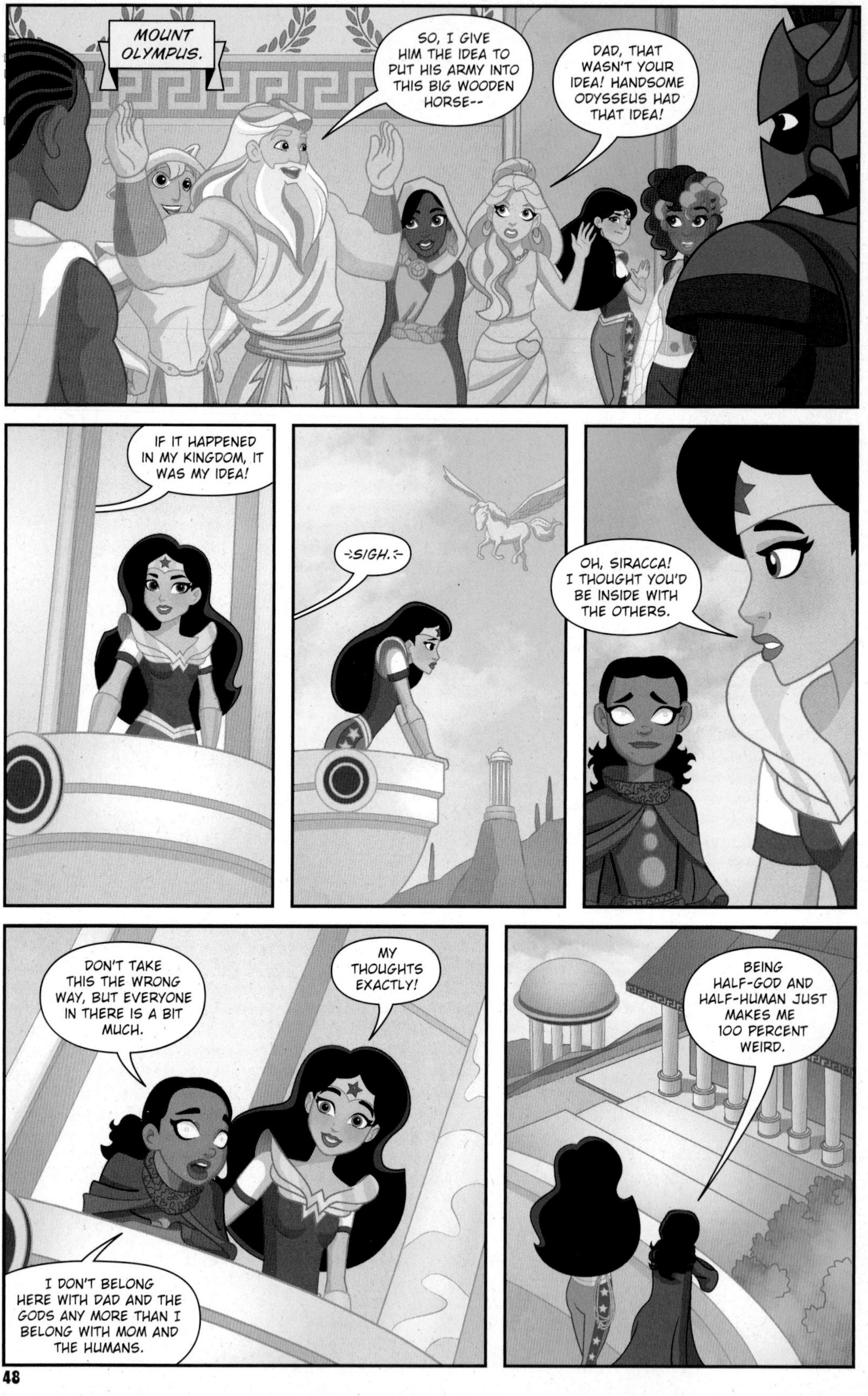
MOUNT OLYMPUS.
SO, I GIVE HIM THE IDEA TO PUT HIS ARMY INTO THIS BIG WOODEN HORSE--
DAD, THAT WASN'T YOUR IDEA! HANDSOME ODYSSEUS HAD THAT IDEA!
IF IT HAPPENED IN MY KINGDOM, IT WAS MY IDEA!
-SIGH.-
OH, SIRACCA! I THOUGHT YOU'D BE INSIDE WITH THE OTHERS.
DON'T TAKE THIS THE WRONG WAY, BUT EVERYONE IN THERE IS A BIT MUCH.
MY THOUGHTS EXACTLY!
I DON'T BELONG HERE WITH DAD AND THE GODS ANY MORE THAN I BELONG WITH MOM AND THE HUMANS.
BEING HALF-GOD AND HALF-HUMAN JUST MAKES ME 100 PERCENT WEIRD.

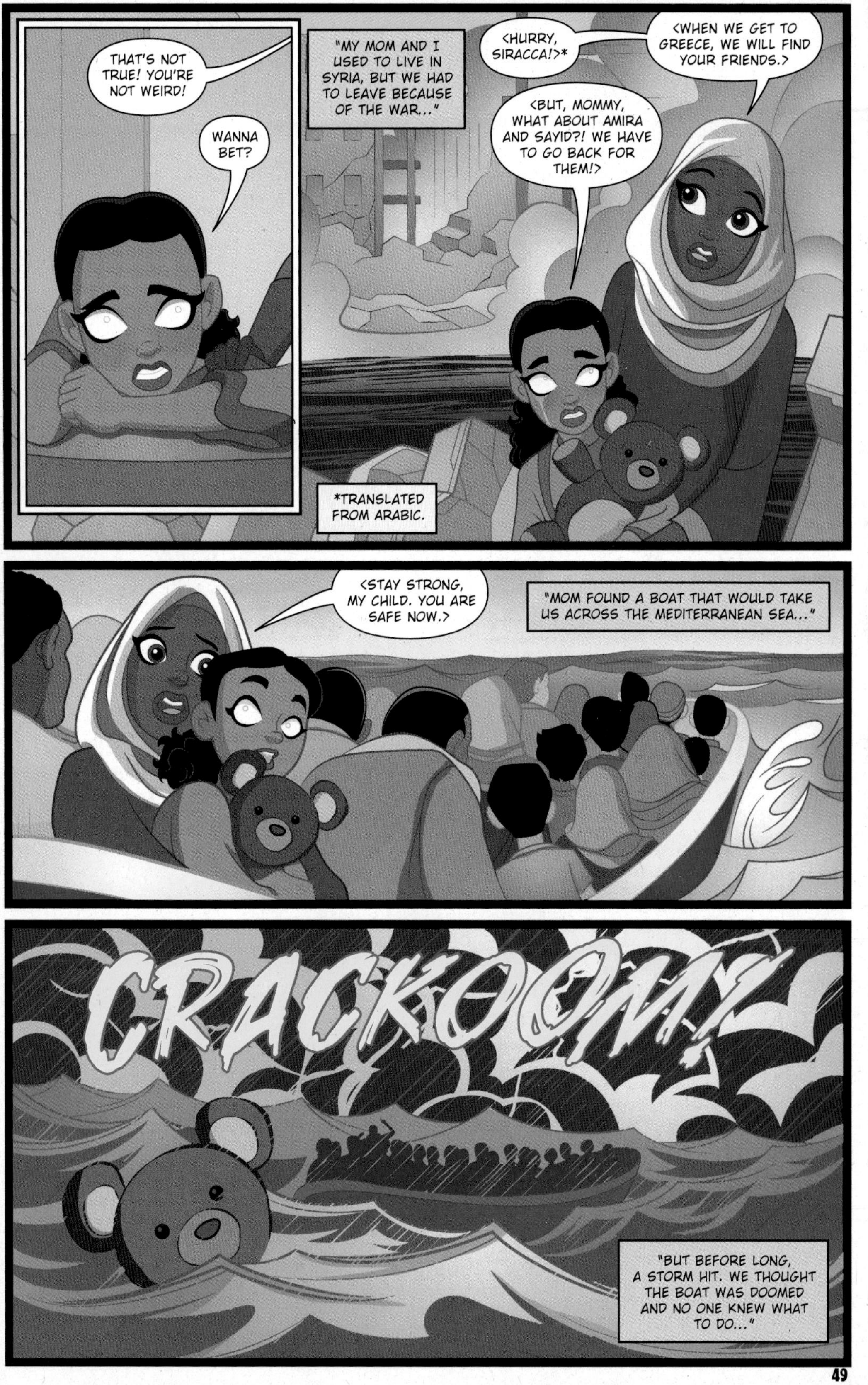
THAT'S NOT TRUE! YOU'RE NOT WEIRD!
WANNA BET?
"MY MOM AND I USED TO LIVE IN SYRIA, BUT WE HAD TO LEAVE BECAUSE OF THE WAR..."
<HURRY, SIRACCA!>*
<WHEN WE GET TO GREECE, WE WILL FIND YOUR FRIENDS.>
<BUT, MOMMY, WHAT ABOUT AMIRA AND SAYID?! WE HAVE TO GO BACK FOR THEM!>
*TRANSLATED FROM ARABIC.
<STAY STRONG, MY CHILD. YOU ARE SAFE NOW.>
"MOM FOUND A BOAT THAT WOULD TAKE US ACROSS THE MEDITERRANEAN SEA..."
CRACKOOM!
"BUT BEFORE LONG, A STORM HIT. WE THOUGHT THE BOAT WAS DOOMED AND NO ONE KNEW WHAT TO DO..."

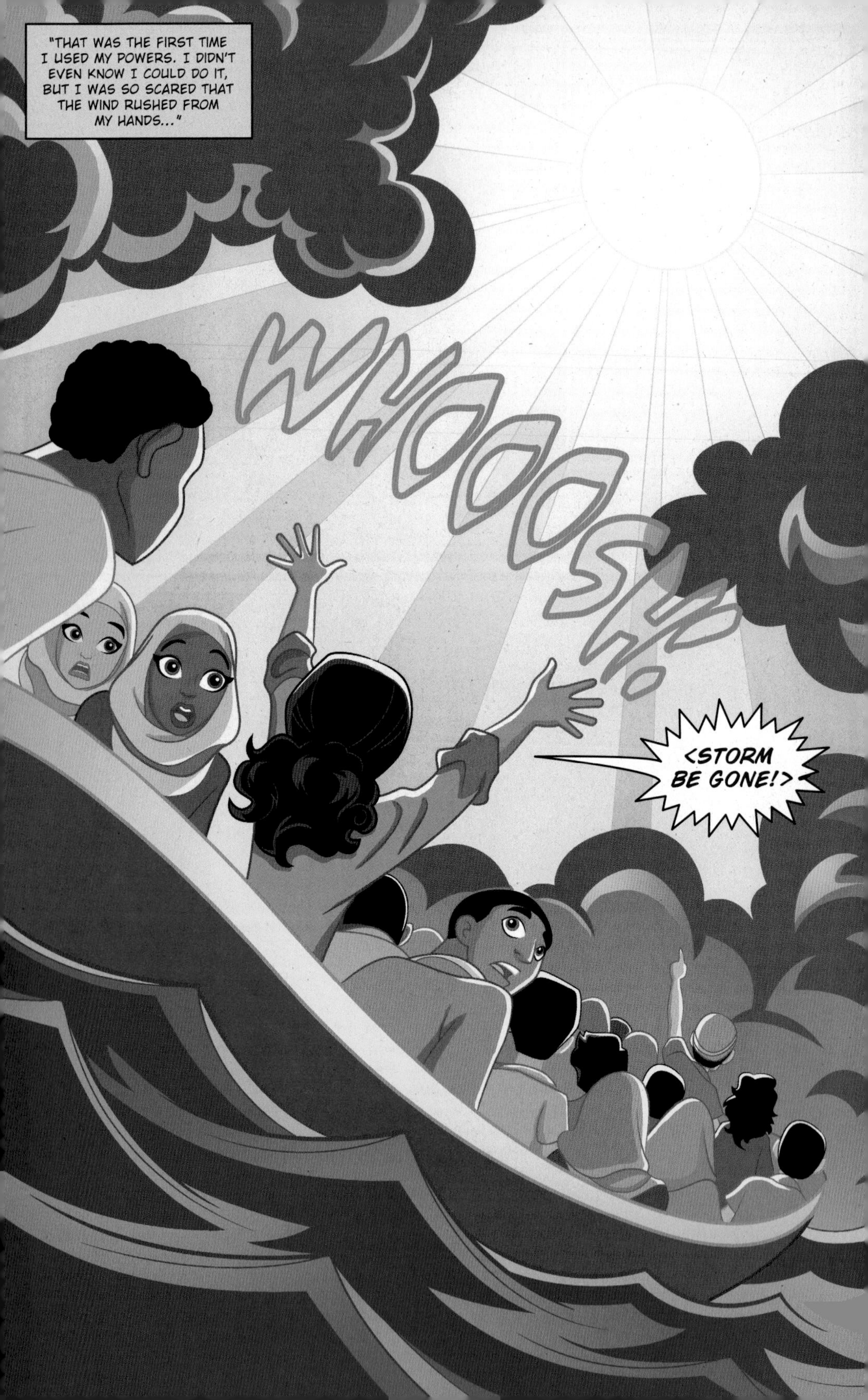
"THAT WAS THE FIRST TIME I USED MY POWERS. I DIDN'T EVEN KNOW I COULD DO IT, BUT I WAS SO SCARED THAT THE WIND RUSHED FROM MY HANDS..."
WHOOOSH!
<STORM BE GONE!>

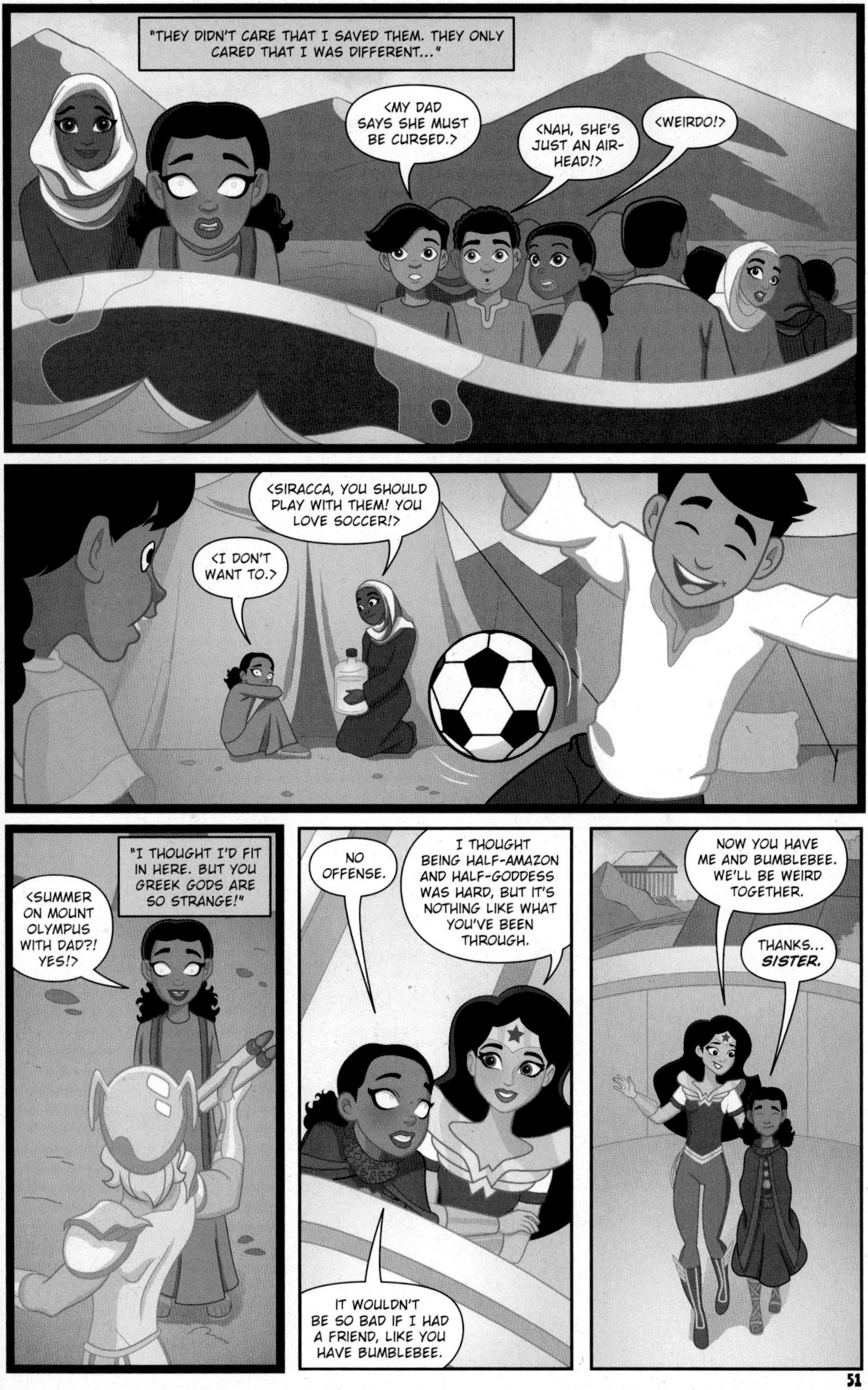
"THEY DIDN'T CARE THAT I SAVED THEM. THEY ONLY CARED THAT I WAS DIFFERENT..."
<MY DAD SAYS SHE MUST BE CURSED.>
<NAH, SHE'S JUST AN AIR-HEAD!>
<WEIRDO!>
<SIRACCA, YOU SHOULD PLAY WITH THEM! YOU LOVE SOCCER!>
<I DON'T WANT TO.>
"I THOUGHT I'D FIT IN HERE. BUT YOU GREEK GODS ARE SO STRANGE!"
<SUMMER ON MOUNT OLYMPUS WITH DAD?! YES!>
NO OFFENSE.
I THOUGHT BEING HALF-AMAZON AND HALF-GODDESS WAS HARD, BUT IT'S NOTHING LIKE WHAT YOU'VE BEEN THROUGH.
IT WOULDN'T BE SO BAD IF I HAD A FRIEND, LIKE YOU HAVE BUMBLEBEE.
NOW YOU HAVE ME AND BUMBLEBEE. WE'LL BE WEIRD TOGETHER.
THANKS... SISTER.

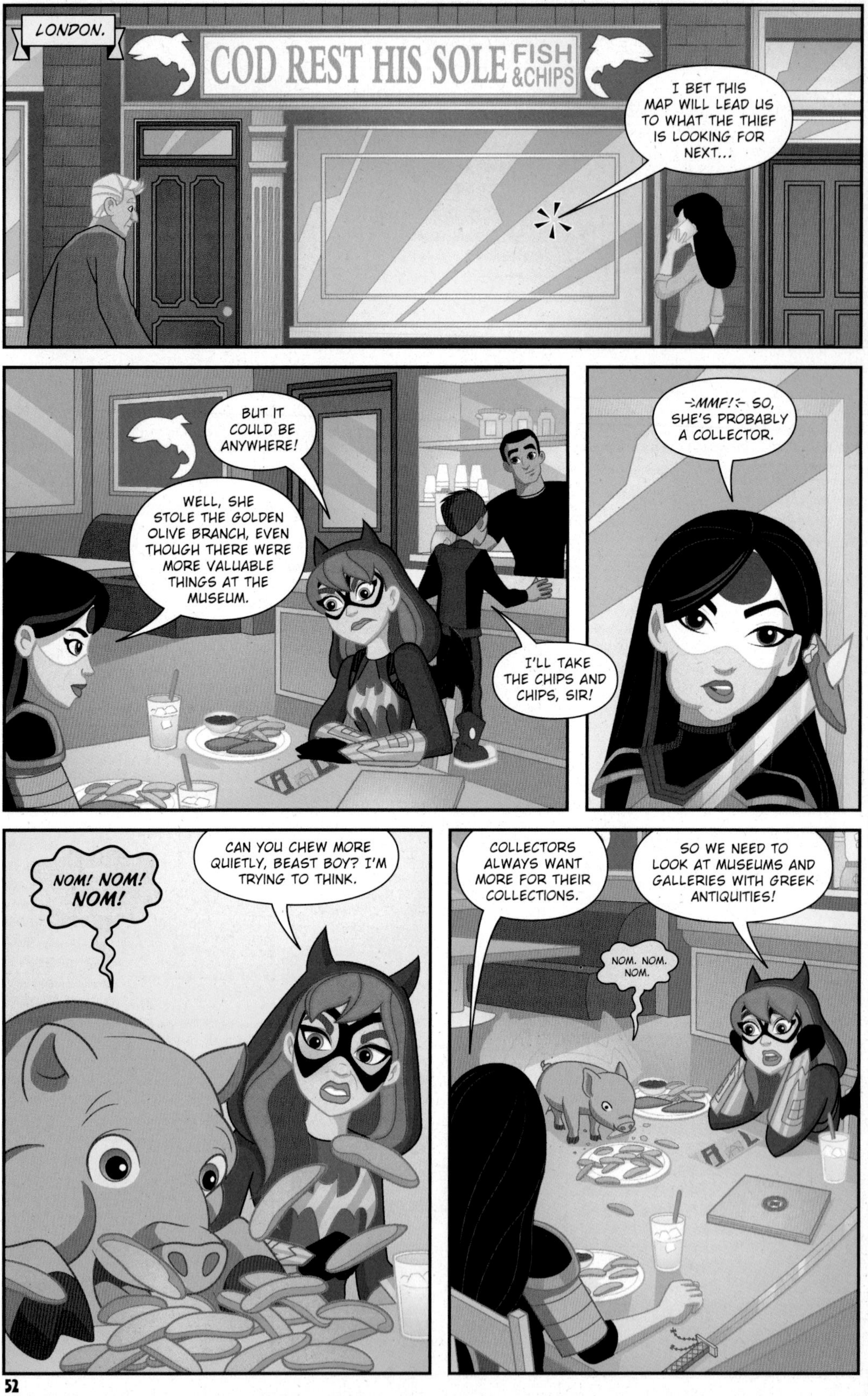
LONDON.
COD REST HIS SOLE FISH &CHIPS
I BET THIS MAP WILL LEAD US TO WHAT THE THIEF IS LOOKING FOR NEXT...
BUT IT COULD BE ANYWHERE!
WELL, SHE STOLE THE GOLDEN OLIVE BRANCH, EVEN THOUGH THERE WERE MORE VALUABLE THINGS AT THE MUSEUM.
I'LL TAKE THE CHIPS AND CHIPS, SIR!
MMF! SO, SHE'S PROBABLY A COLLECTOR.
NOM! NOM! NOM!
CAN YOU CHEW MORE QUIETLY, BEAST BOY? I'M TRYING TO THINK.
COLLECTORS ALWAYS WANT MORE FOR THEIR COLLECTIONS.
NOM. NOM. NOM.
SO WE NEED TO LOOK AT MUSEUMS AND GALLERIES WITH GREEK ANTIQUITIES!

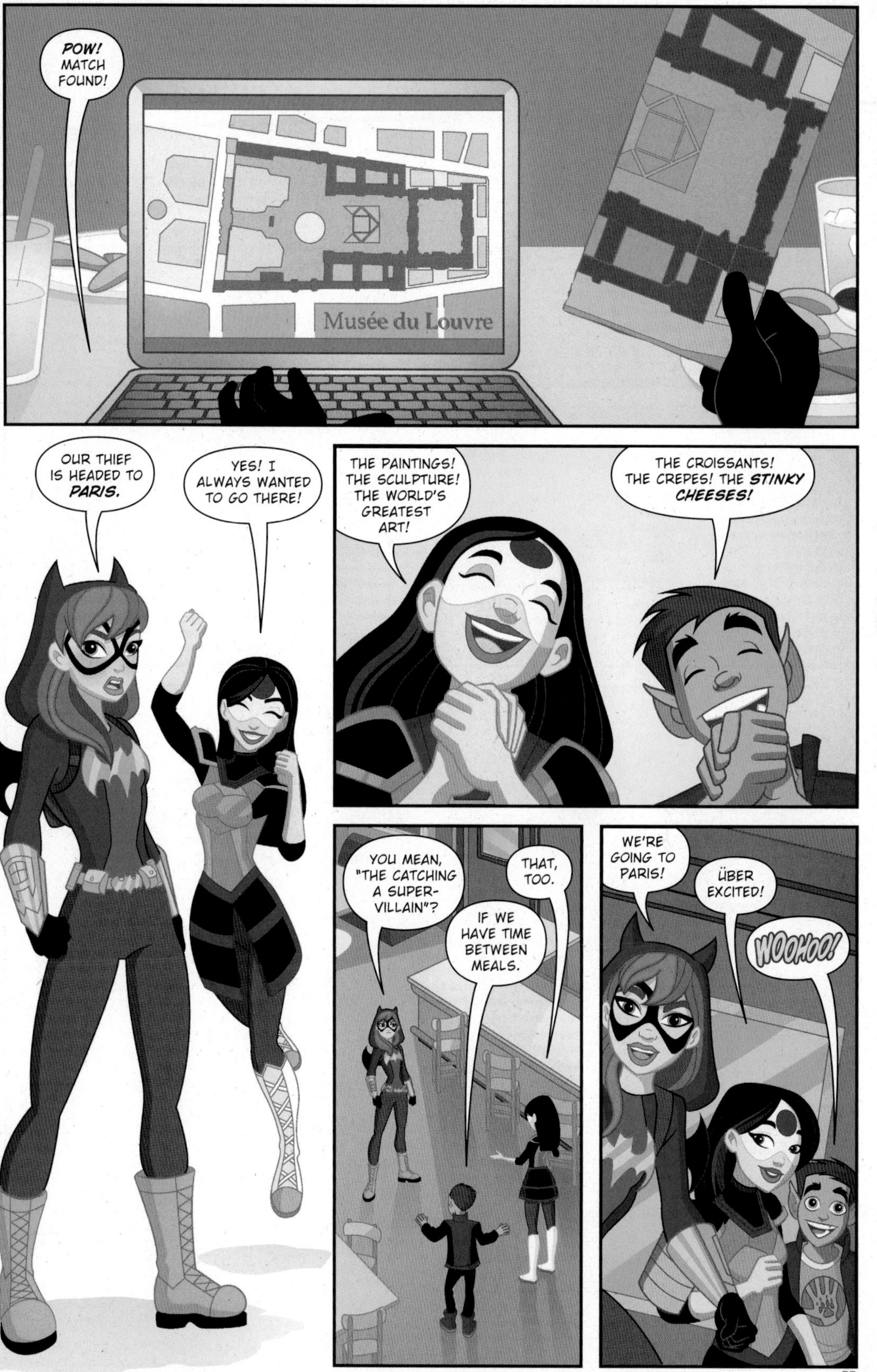
POW! MATCH FOUND!
Musée du Louvre
OUR THIEF IS HEADED TO PARIS.
YES! I ALWAYS WANTED TO GO THERE!
THE PAINTINGS! THE SCULPTURE! THE WORLD'S GREATEST ART!
THE CROISSANTS! THE CREPES! THE STINKY CHEESES!
YOU MEAN, "THE CATCHING A SUPER-VILLAIN"?
THAT, TOO.
IF WE HAVE TIME BETWEEN MEALS.
WE'RE GOING TO PARIS!
ÜBER EXCITED!
WOOHOO!

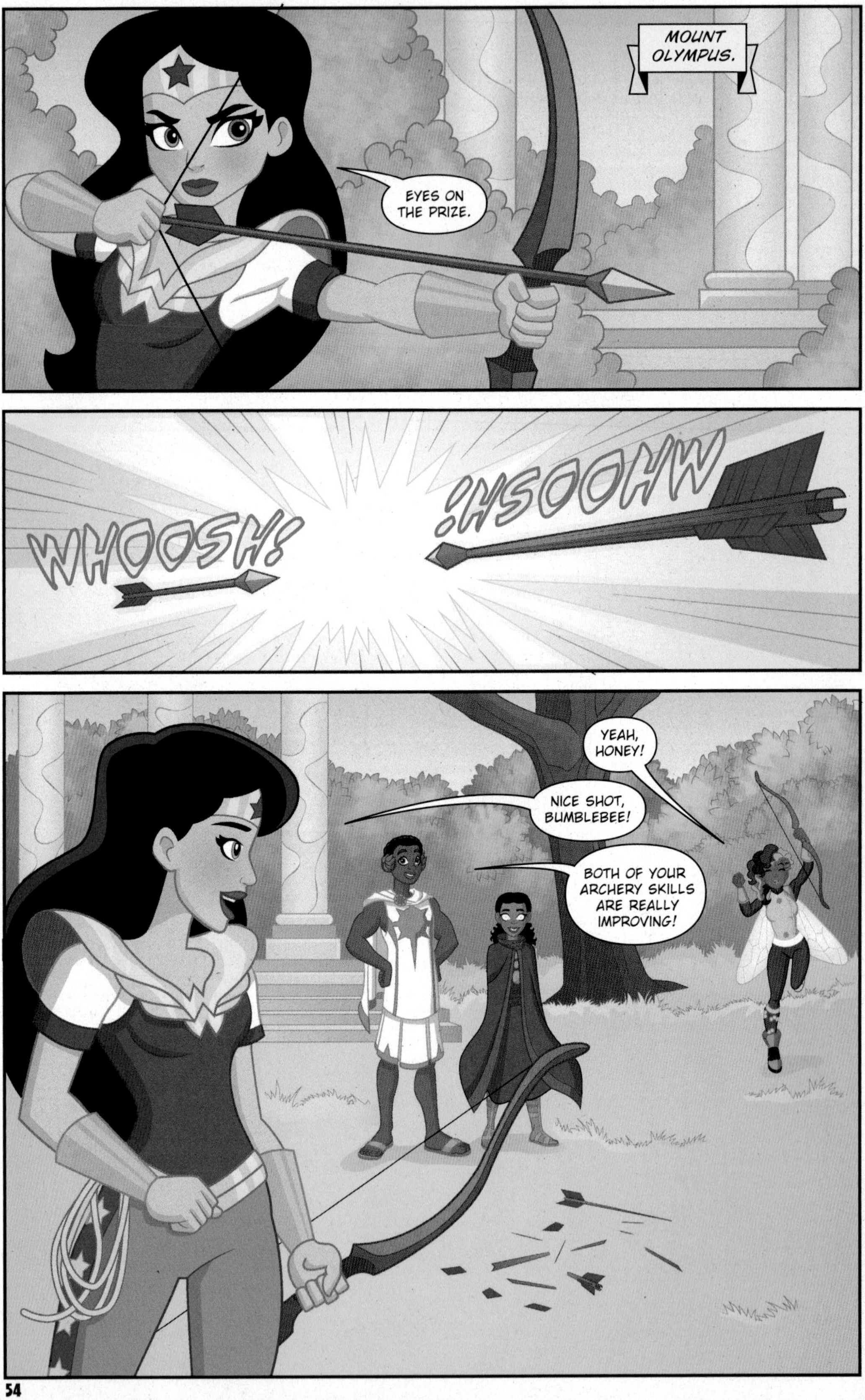
MOUNT OLYMPUS.
EYES ON THE PRIZE.
WHOOSH!
WHOOSH!
YEAH, HONEY!
NICE SHOT, BUMBLEBEE!
BOTH OF YOUR ARCHERY SKILLS ARE REALLY IMPROVING!

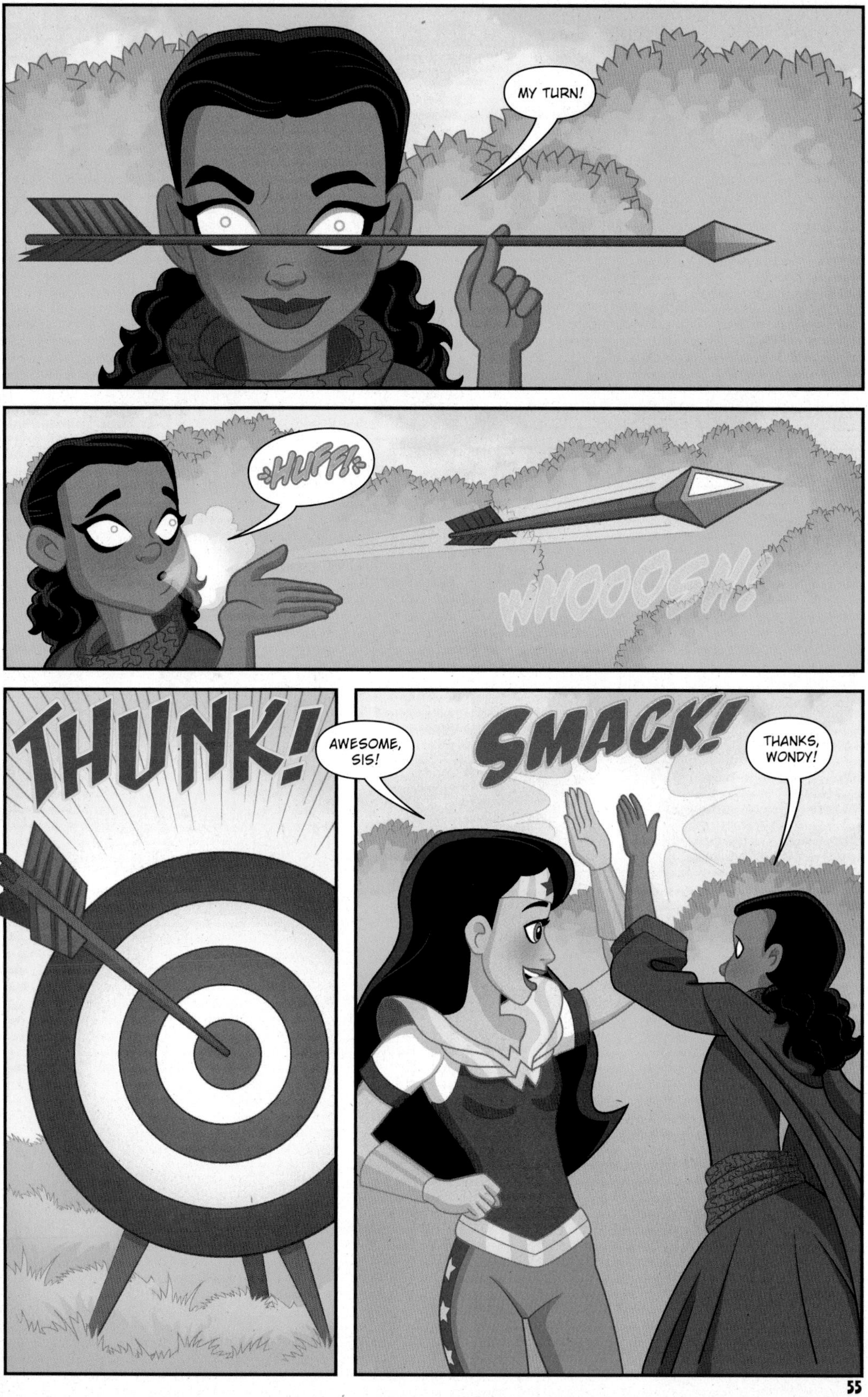
MY TURN!
HUFF!
WHOOOSH!
THUNK!
AWESOME, SIS!
SMACK!
THANKS, WONDY!

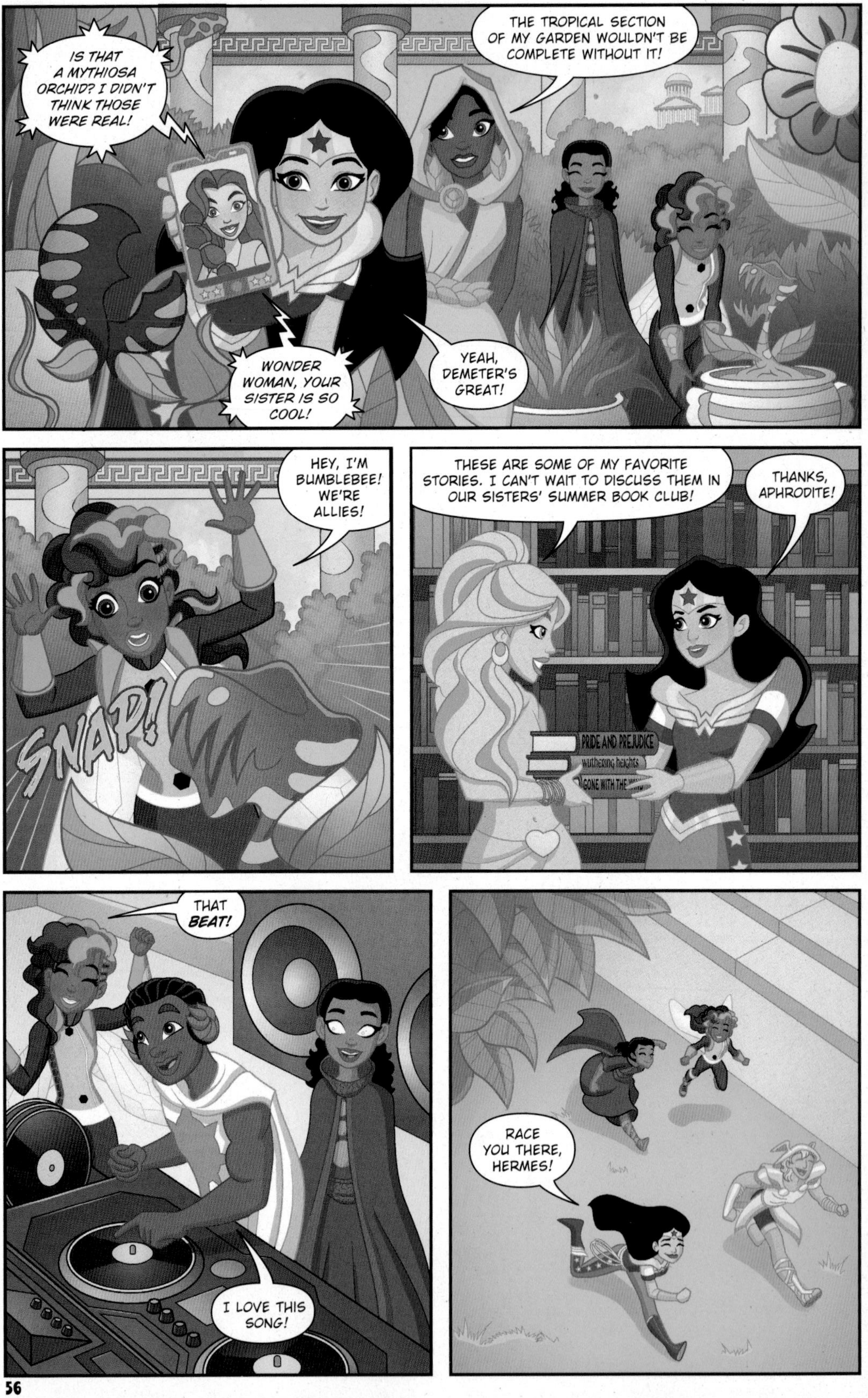
IS THAT A MYTHIOSA ORCHID? I DIDN'T THINK THOSE WERE REAL!
THE TROPICAL SECTION OF MY GARDEN WOULDN'T BE COMPLETE WITHOUT IT!
WONDER WOMAN, YOUR SISTER IS SO COOL!
YEAH, DEMETER'S GREAT!
HEY, I'M BUMBLEBEE! WE'RE ALLIES!
SNAP!
THESE ARE SOME OF MY FAVORITE STORIES. I CAN'T WAIT TO DISCUSS THEM IN OUR SISTERS' SUMMER BOOK CLUB!
PRIDE AND PREJUDICE
wuthering heights
GONE WITH THE
THANKS, APHRODITE!
THAT BEAT!
I LOVE THIS SONG!
RACE YOU THERE, HERMES!

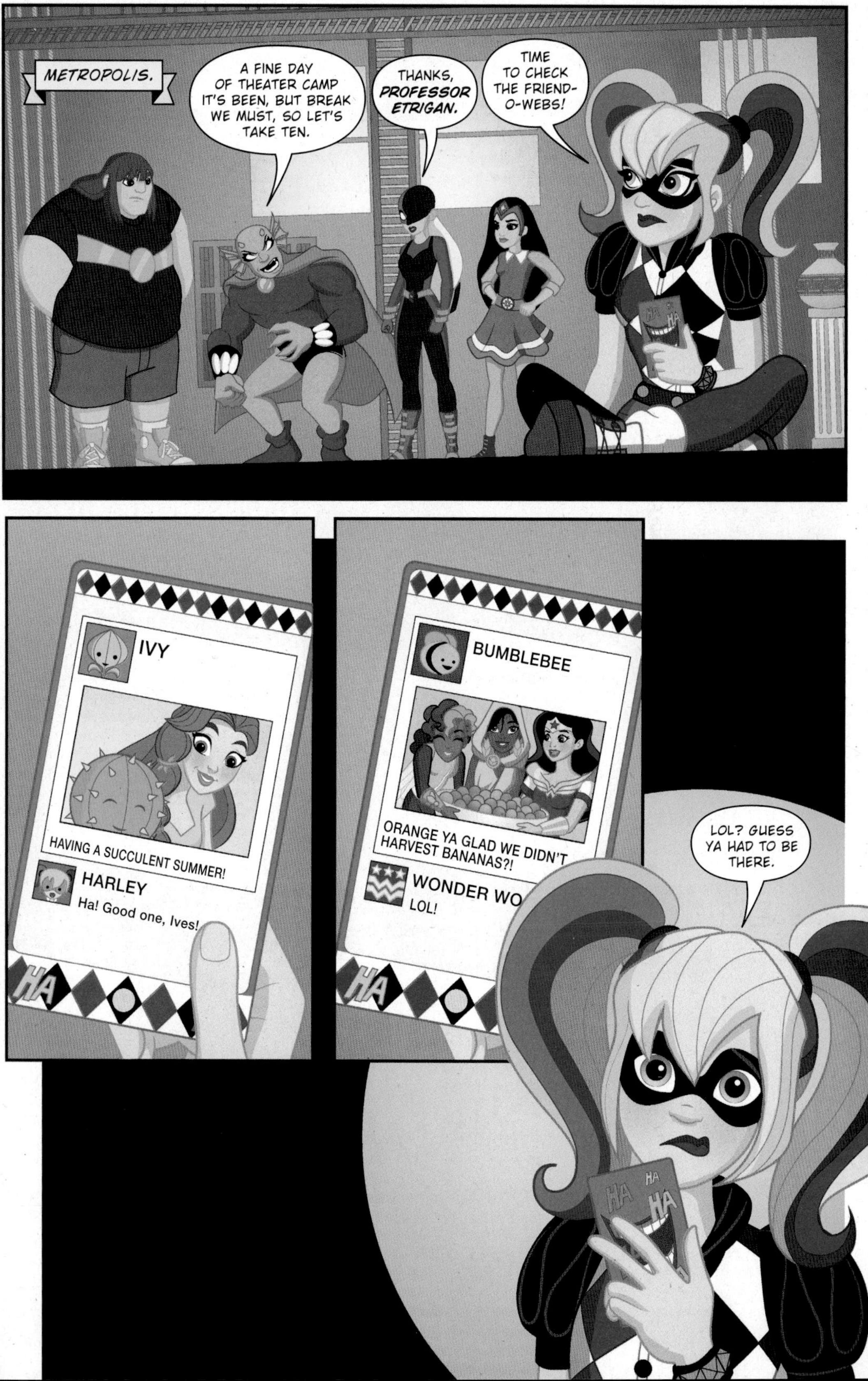
METROPOLIS.
A FINE DAY OF THEATER CAMP IT'S BEEN, BUT BREAK WE MUST, SO LET'S TAKE TEN.
THANKS, PROFESSOR ETRIGAN.
TIME TO CHECK THE FRIEND-O-WEBS!
IVY
HAVING A SUCCULENT SUMMER!
HARLEY
Ha! Good one, Ives!
BUMBLEBEE
ORANGE YA GLAD WE DIDN'T HARVEST BANANAS?!
WONDER WO
LOL!
LOL? GUESS YA HAD TO BE THERE.

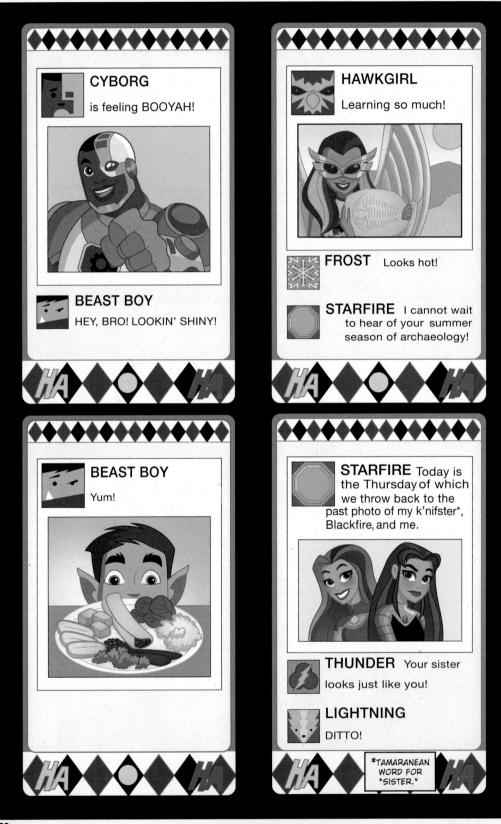

CYBORG
is feeling BOOYAH!

BEAST BOY
HEY, BRO! LOOKIN' SHINY!

HAWKGIRL
Learning so much!

FROST Looks hot!

STARFIRE I cannot wait to hear of your summer season of archaeology!

BEAST BOY
Yum!

STARFIRE Today is the Thursday of which we throw back to the past photo of my k'nifster*, Blackfire, and me.

THUNDER Your sister looks just like you!

LIGHTNING
DITTO!

*TAMARANEAN WORD FOR "SISTER."

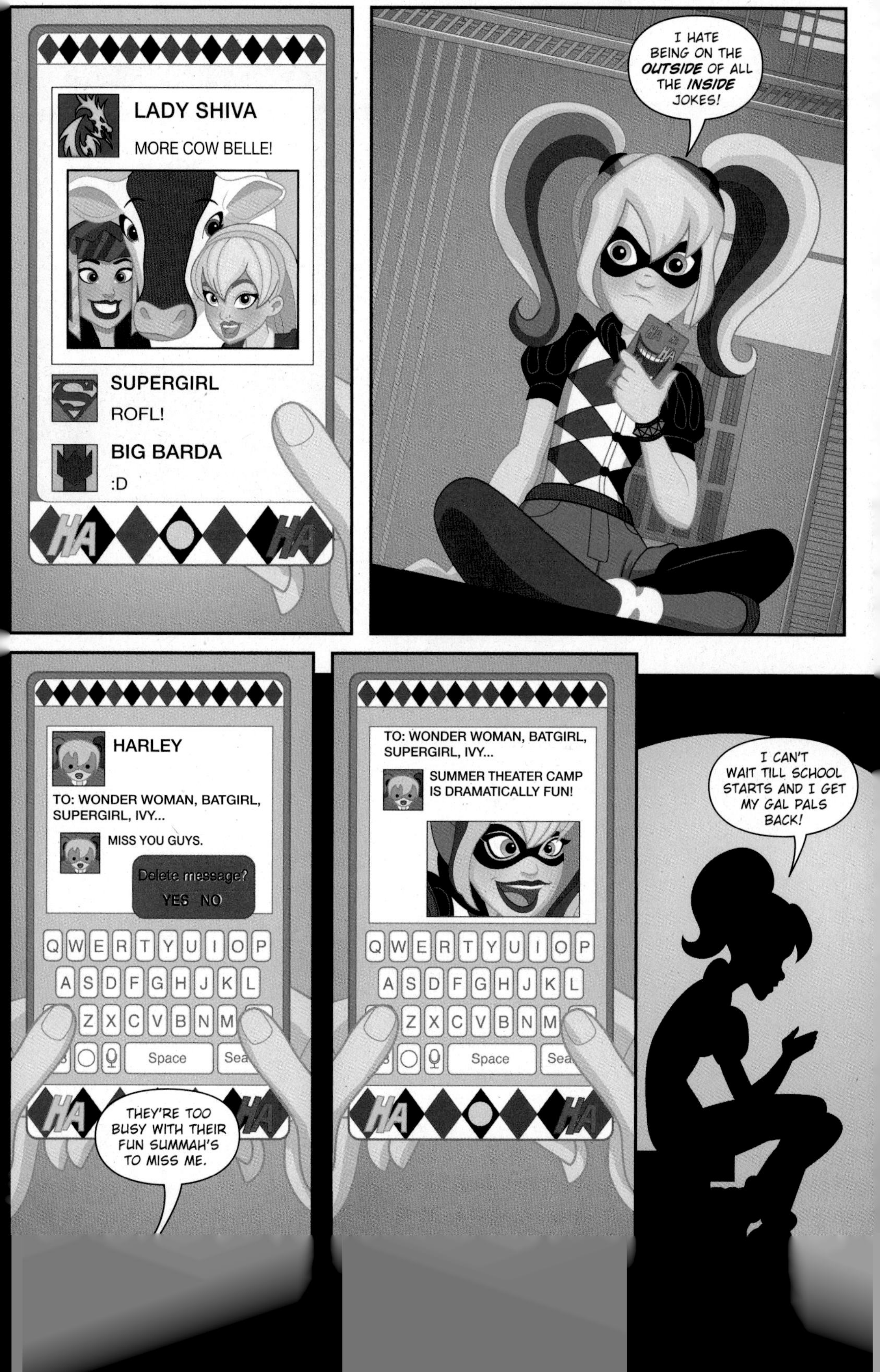
LADY SHIVA
MORE COW BELLE!
SUPERGIRL
ROFL!
BIG BARDA
:D
HA
HA
I HATE BEING ON THE *OUTSIDE* OF ALL THE *INSIDE* JOKES!
HARLEY
TO: WONDER WOMAN, BATGIRL, SUPERGIRL, IVY...
MISS YOU GUYS.
Delete message?
YES NO
THEY'RE TOO BUSY WITH THEIR FUN SUMMAH'S TO MISS ME.
TO: WONDER WOMAN, BATGIRL, SUPERGIRL, IVY...
SUMMER THEATER CAMP IS DRAMATICALLY FUN!
I CAN'T WAIT TILL SCHOOL STARTS AND I GET MY GAL PALS BACK!

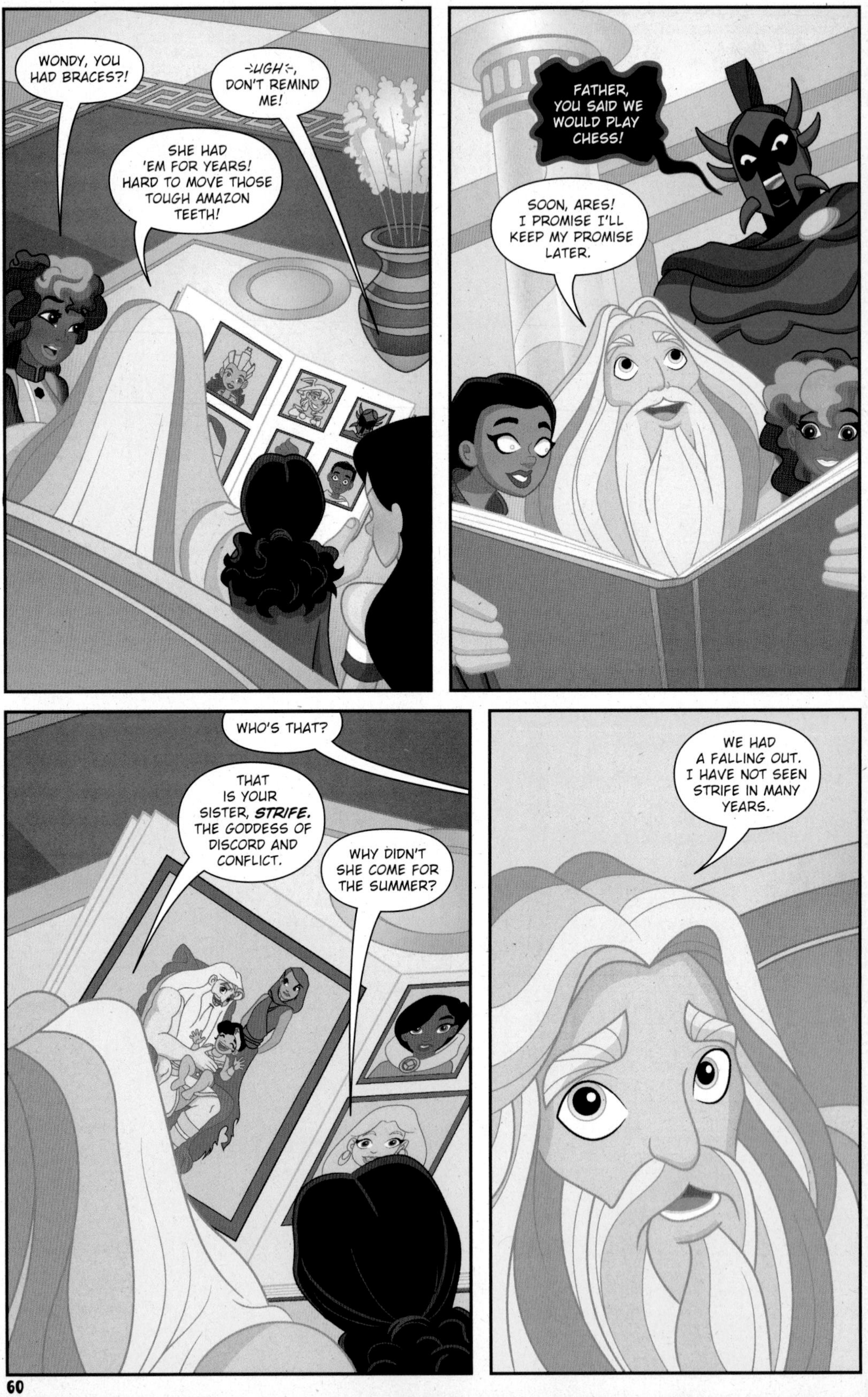
WONDY, YOU HAD BRACES?!
-UGH-, DON'T REMIND ME!
SHE HAD 'EM FOR YEARS! HARD TO MOVE THOSE TOUGH AMAZON TEETH!
FATHER, YOU SAID WE WOULD PLAY CHESS!
SOON, ARES! I PROMISE I'LL KEEP MY PROMISE LATER.
WHO'S THAT?
THAT IS YOUR SISTER, STRIFE. THE GODDESS OF DISCORD AND CONFLICT.
WHY DIDN'T SHE COME FOR THE SUMMER?
WE HAD A FALLING OUT. I HAVE NOT SEEN STRIFE IN MANY YEARS.

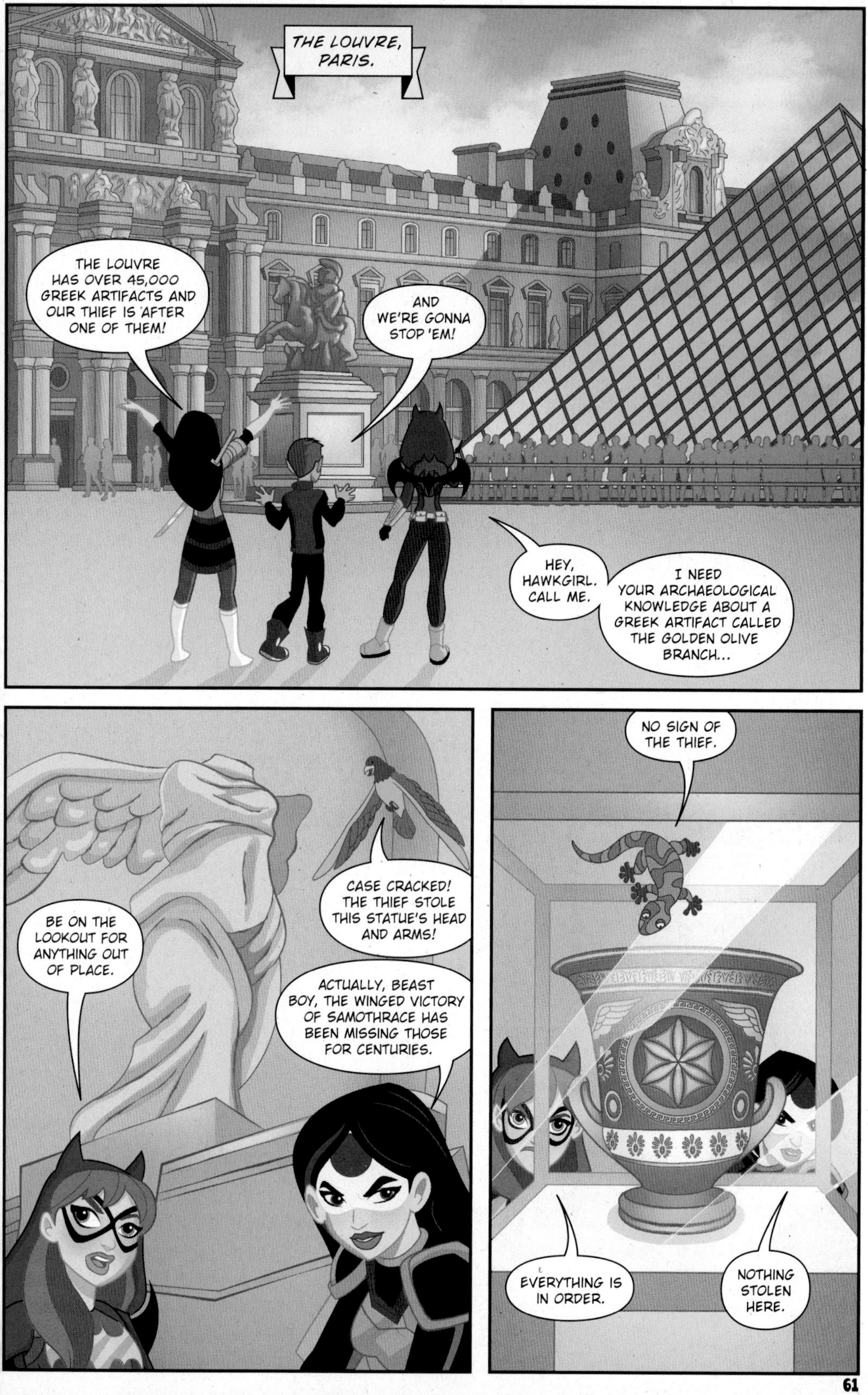
THE LOUVRE, PARIS.
THE LOUVRE HAS OVER 45,000 GREEK ARTIFACTS AND OUR THIEF IS AFTER ONE OF THEM!
AND WE'RE GONNA STOP 'EM!
HEY, HAWKGIRL. CALL ME.
I NEED YOUR ARCHAEOLOGICAL KNOWLEDGE ABOUT A GREEK ARTIFACT CALLED THE GOLDEN OLIVE BRANCH...
BE ON THE LOOKOUT FOR ANYTHING OUT OF PLACE.
CASE CRACKED! THE THIEF STOLE THIS STATUE'S HEAD AND ARMS!
ACTUALLY, BEAST BOY, THE WINGED VICTORY OF SAMOTHRACE HAS BEEN MISSING THOSE FOR CENTURIES.
NO SIGN OF THE THIEF.
EVERYTHING IS IN ORDER.
NOTHING STOLEN HERE.

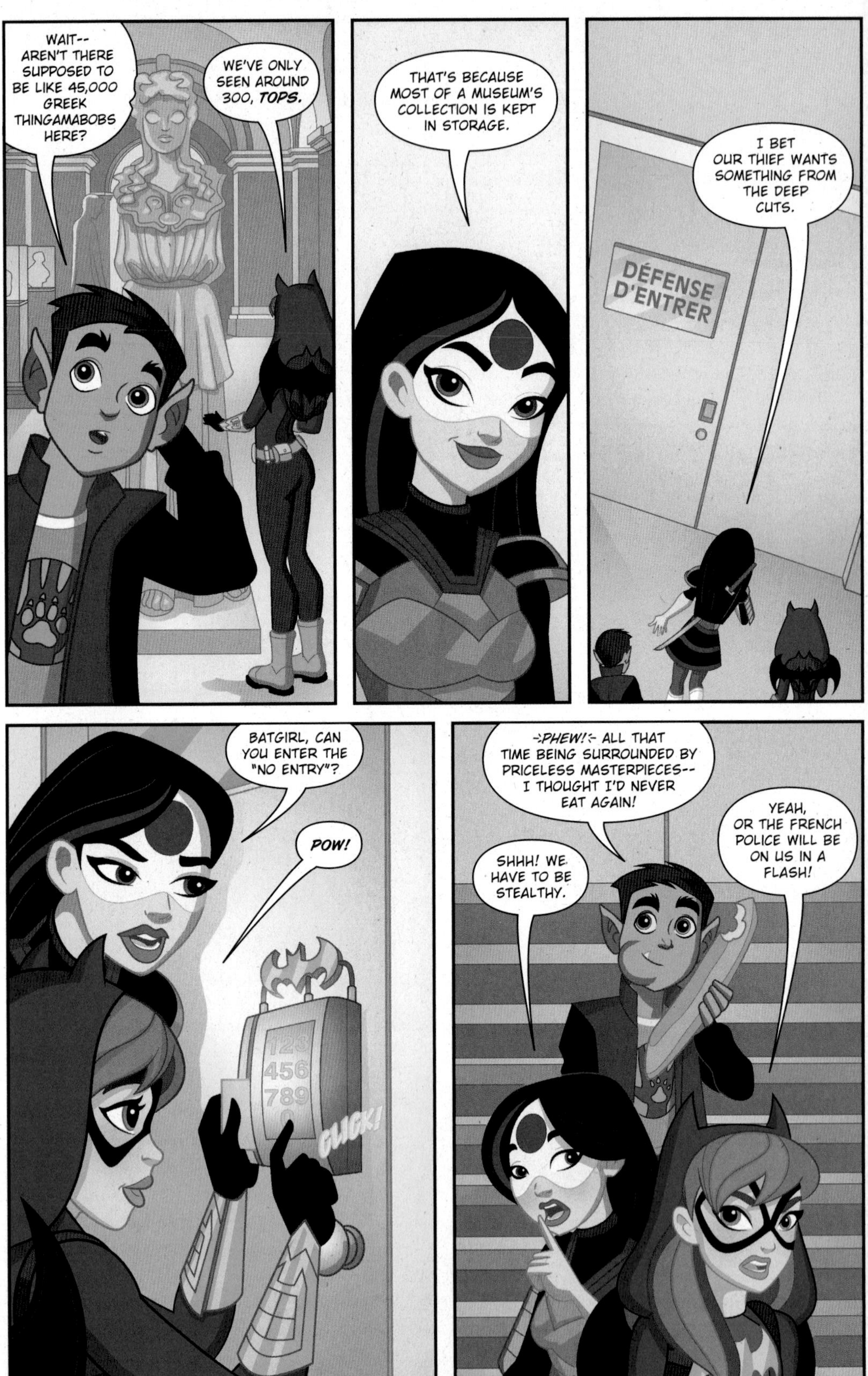

WAIT-- AREN'T THERE SUPPOSED TO BE LIKE 45,000 GREEK THINGAMABOBS HERE?
WE'VE ONLY SEEN AROUND 300, TOPS.
THAT'S BECAUSE MOST OF A MUSEUM'S COLLECTION IS KEPT IN STORAGE.
I BET OUR THIEF WANTS SOMETHING FROM THE DEEP CUTS.
DÉFENSE D'ENTRER
BATGIRL, CAN YOU ENTER THE "NO ENTRY"?
POW!
CLICK!
-PHEW!- ALL THAT TIME BEING SURROUNDED BY PRICELESS MASTERPIECES-- I THOUGHT I'D NEVER EAT AGAIN!
SHHH! WE HAVE TO BE STEALTHY.
YEAH, OR THE FRENCH POLICE WILL BE ON US IN A FLASH!

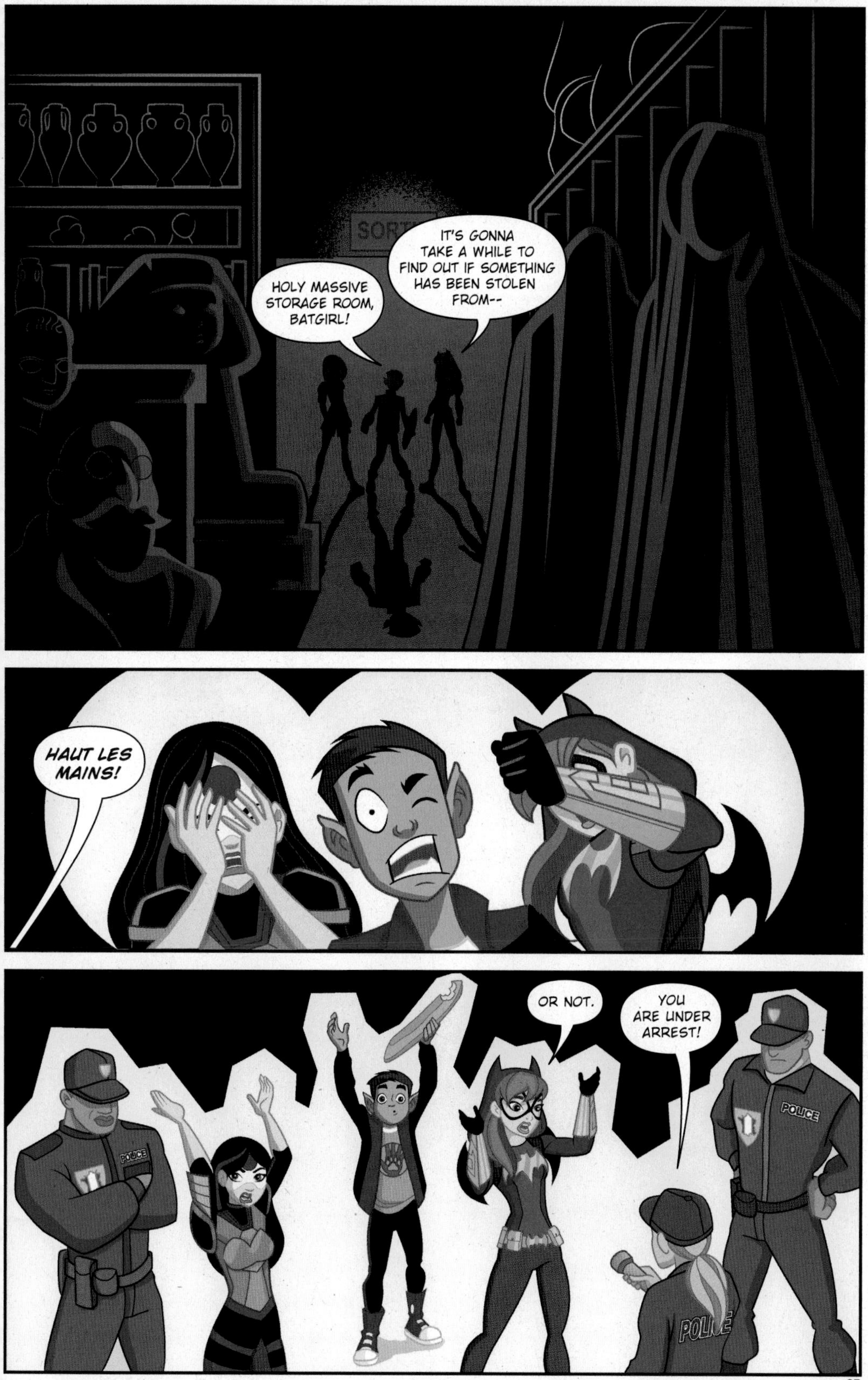
HOLY MASSIVE STORAGE ROOM, BATGIRL!
IT'S GONNA TAKE A WHILE TO FIND OUT IF SOMETHING HAS BEEN STOLEN FROM--
HAUT LES MAINS!
OR NOT.
YOU ARE UNDER ARREST!
POLICE
POLICE
POLICE

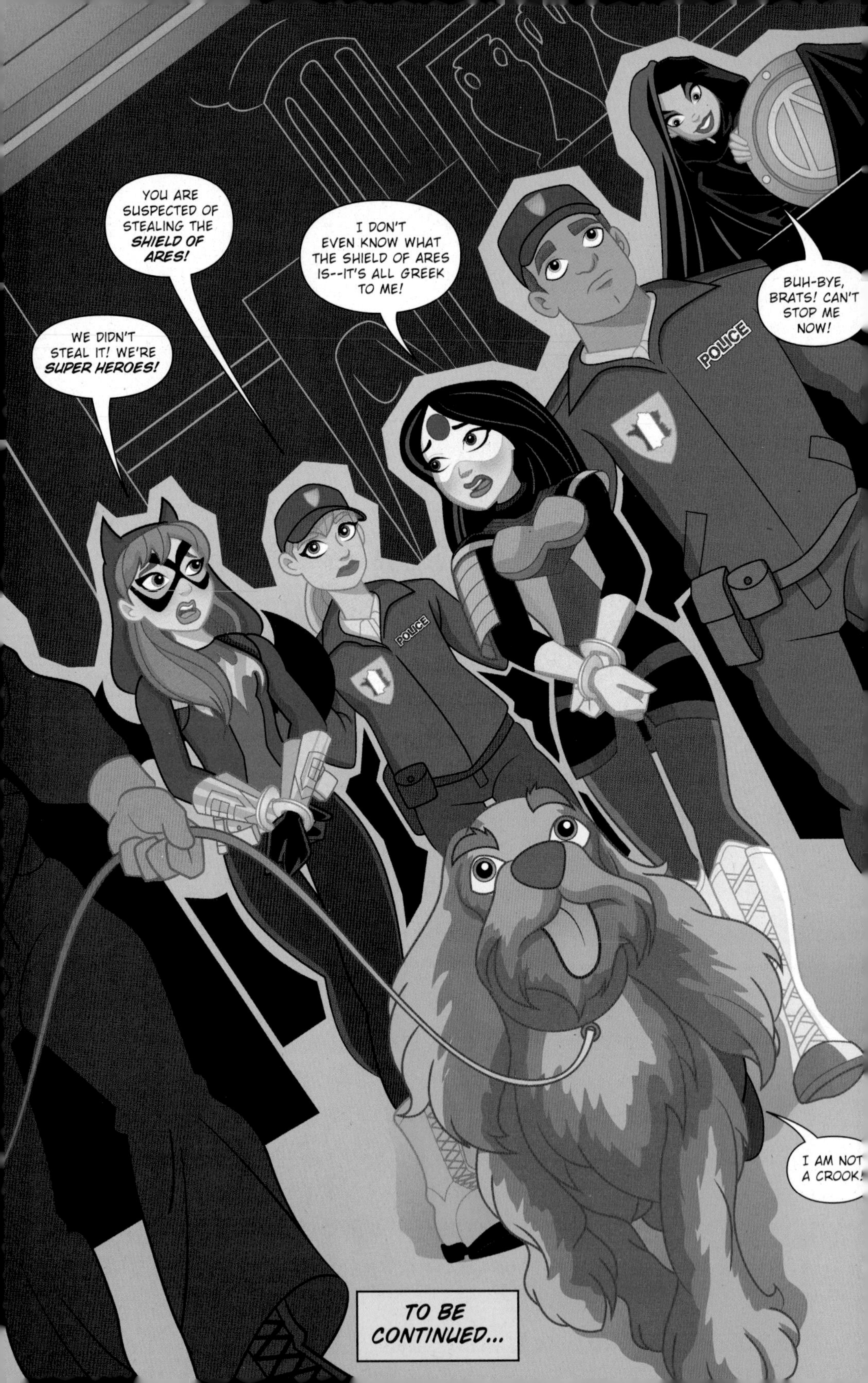
YOU ARE SUSPECTED OF STEALING THE SHIELD OF ARES!
I DON'T EVEN KNOW WHAT THE SHIELD OF ARES IS--IT'S ALL GREEK TO ME!
BUH-BYE, BRATS! CAN'T STOP ME NOW!
WE DIDN'T STEAL IT! WE'RE SUPER HEROES!
POLICE
POLICE
I AM NOT A CROOK!
TO BE CONTINUED...

CHAPTER FOUR
THE HUNT

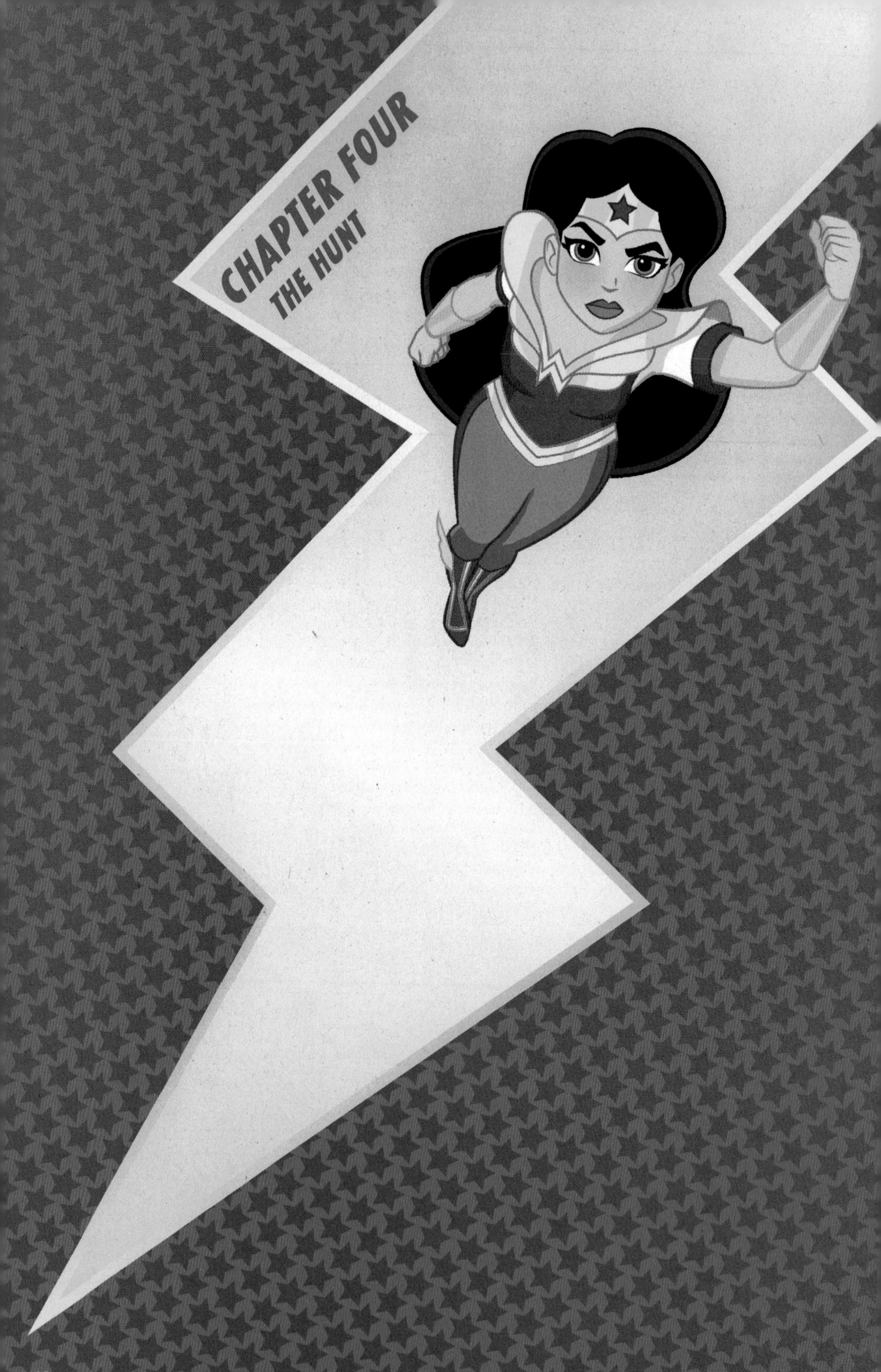

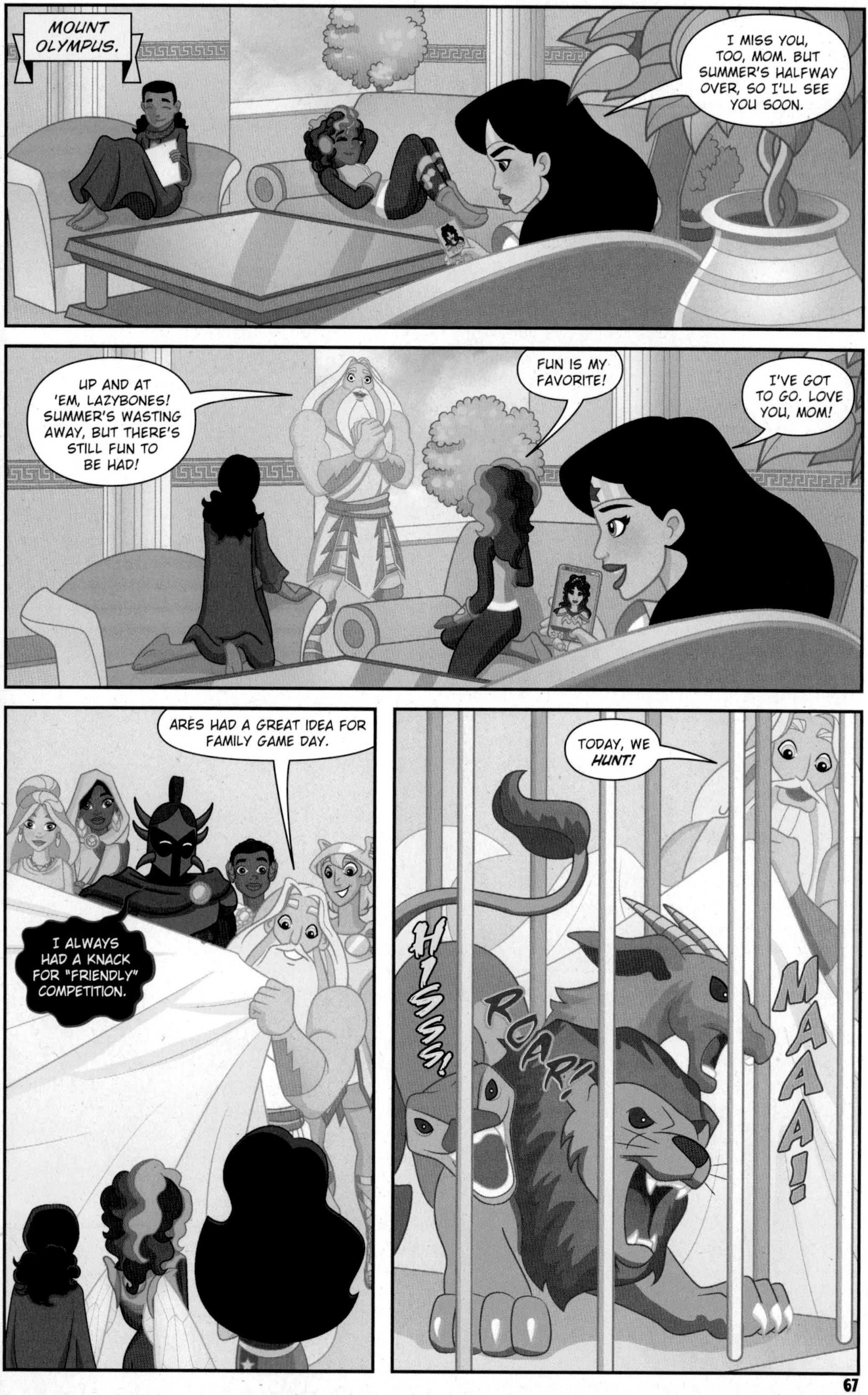
MOUNT OLYMPUS.
I MISS YOU, TOO, MOM. BUT SUMMER'S HALFWAY OVER, SO I'LL SEE YOU SOON.
UP AND AT 'EM, LAZYBONES! SUMMER'S WASTING AWAY, BUT THERE'S STILL FUN TO BE HAD!
FUN IS MY FAVORITE!
I'VE GOT TO GO. LOVE YOU, MOM!
ARES HAD A GREAT IDEA FOR FAMILY GAME DAY.
I ALWAYS HAD A KNACK FOR "FRIENDLY" COMPETITION.
TODAY, WE HUNT!
HISSS!
ROAR!
MAAAA!

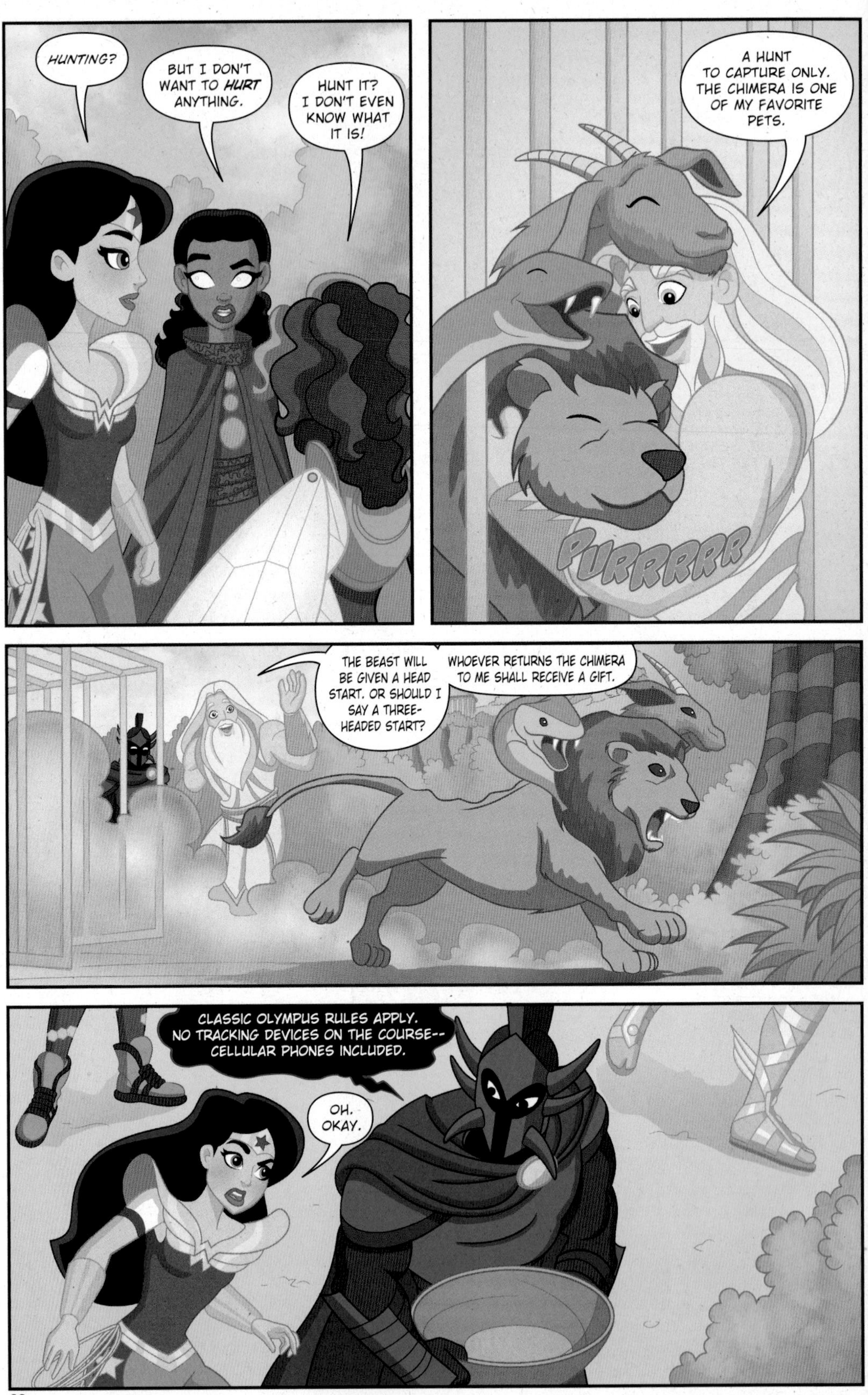
HUNTING?
BUT I DON'T WANT TO HURT ANYTHING.
HUNT IT? I DON'T EVEN KNOW WHAT IT IS!
A HUNT TO CAPTURE ONLY. THE CHIMERA IS ONE OF MY FAVORITE PETS.
PURRRRR
THE BEAST WILL BE GIVEN A HEAD START. OR SHOULD I SAY A THREE-HEADED START?
WHOEVER RETURNS THE CHIMERA TO ME SHALL RECEIVE A GIFT.
CLASSIC OLYMPUS RULES APPLY. NO TRACKING DEVICES ON THE COURSE--CELLULAR PHONES INCLUDED.
OH. OKAY.

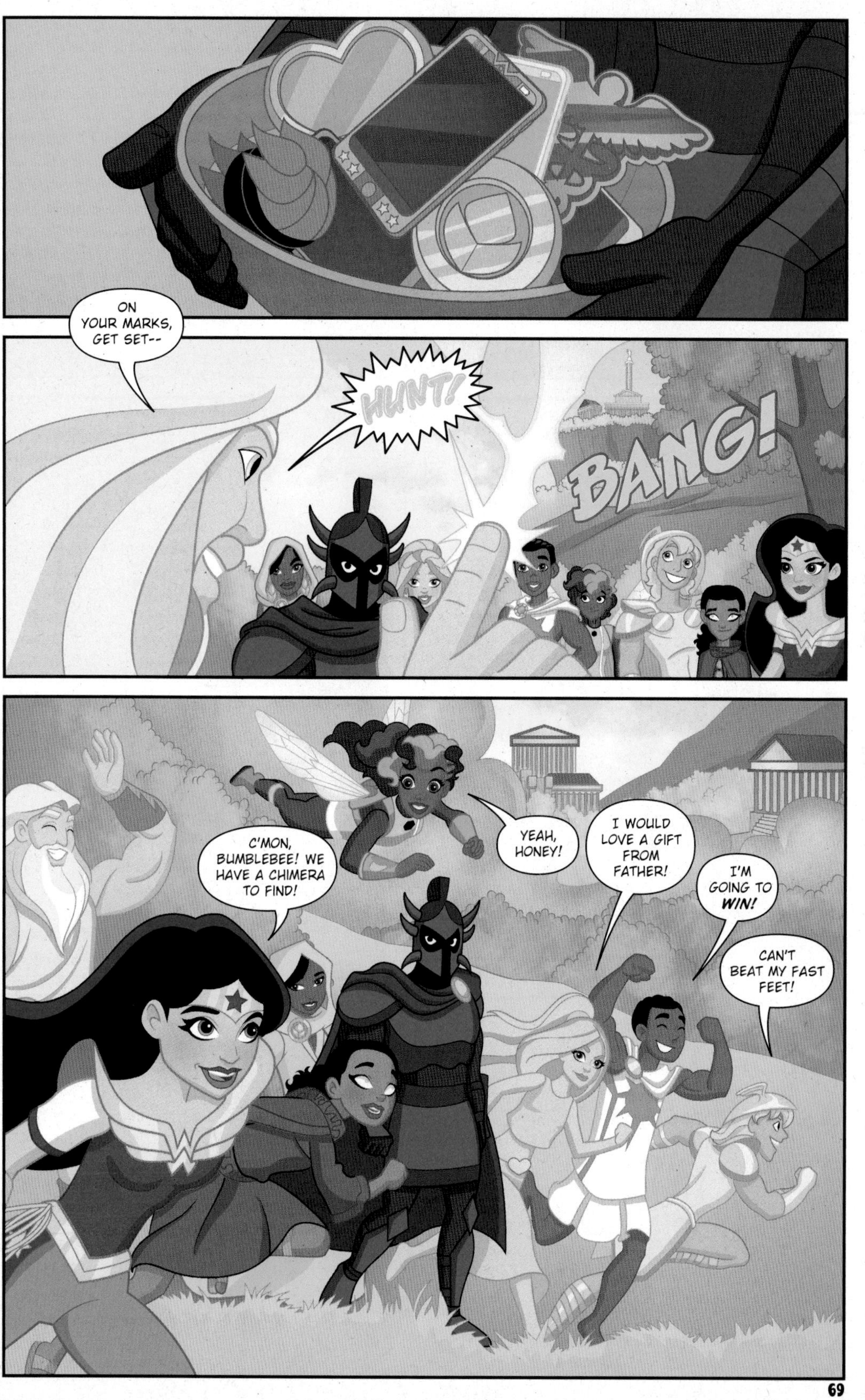
ON YOUR MARKS, GET SET--
HUNT!
BANG!
C'MON, BUMBLEBEE! WE HAVE A CHIMERA TO FIND!
YEAH, HONEY!
I WOULD LOVE A GIFT FROM FATHER!
I'M GOING TO **WIN!**
CAN'T BEAT MY FAST FEET!

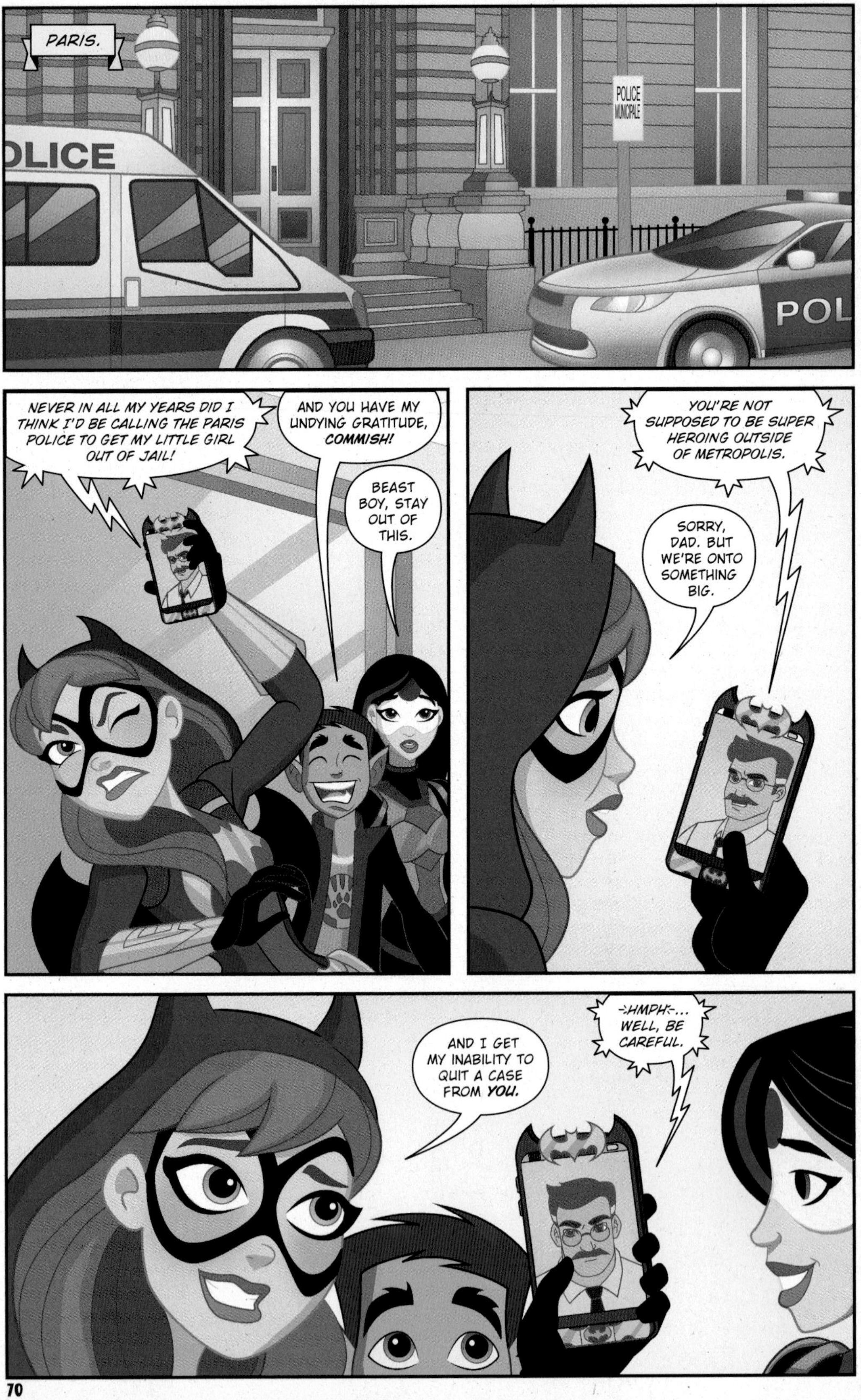
PARIS.
POLICE MUNICIPALE
POLICE
POLICE
NEVER IN ALL MY YEARS DID I THINK I'D BE CALLING THE PARIS POLICE TO GET MY LITTLE GIRL OUT OF JAIL!
AND YOU HAVE MY UNDYING GRATITUDE, COMMISH!
BEAST BOY, STAY OUT OF THIS.
YOU'RE NOT SUPPOSED TO BE SUPER HEROING OUTSIDE OF METROPOLIS.
SORRY, DAD. BUT WE'RE ONTO SOMETHING BIG.
AND I GET MY INABILITY TO QUIT A CASE FROM YOU.
HMPH... WELL, BE CAREFUL.

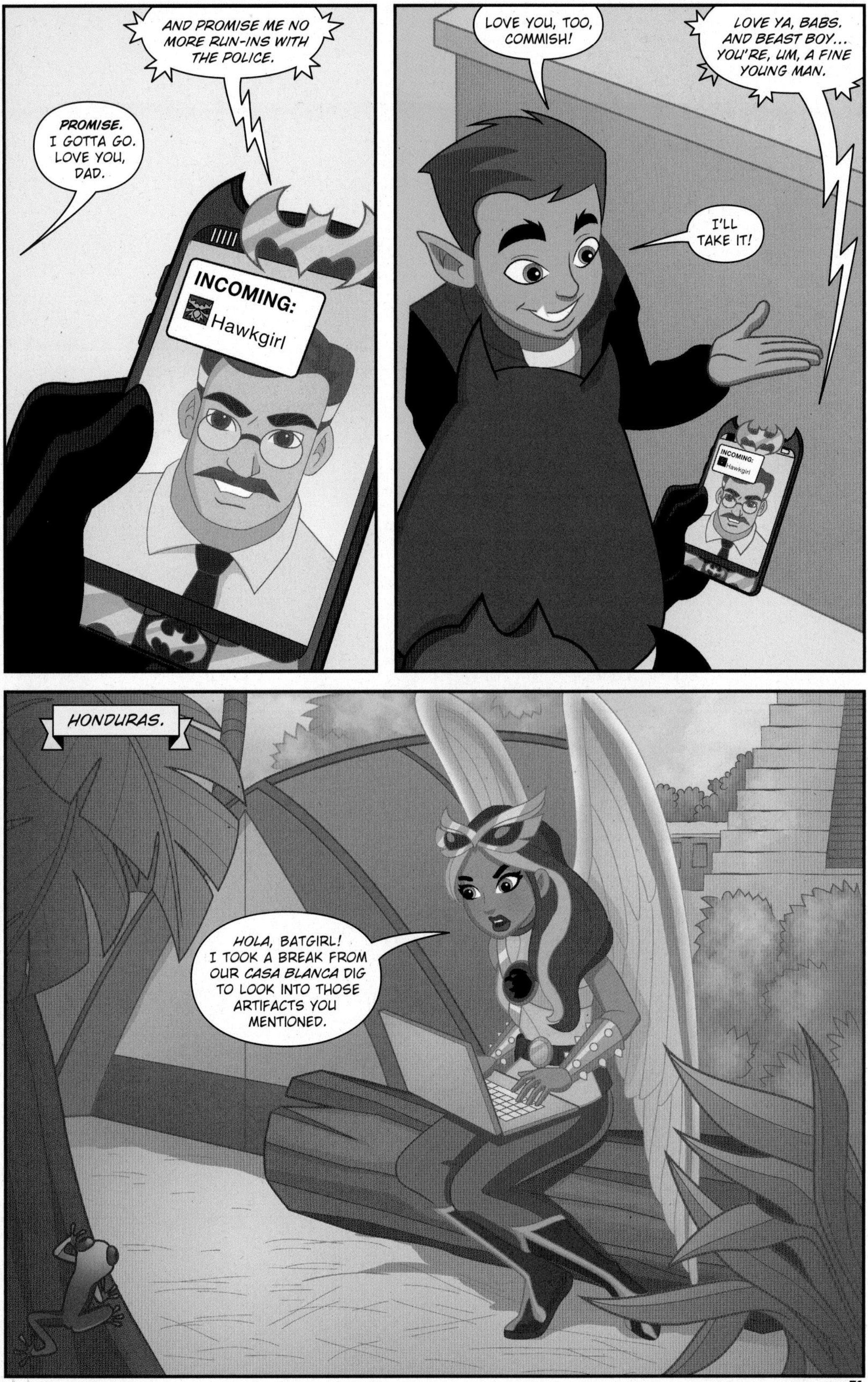
AND PROMISE ME NO MORE RUN-INS WITH THE POLICE.
PROMISE. I GOTTA GO. LOVE YOU, DAD.
INCOMING:
Hawkgirl
LOVE YOU, TOO, COMMISH!
LOVE YA, BABS. AND BEAST BOY... YOU'RE, UM, A FINE YOUNG MAN.
I'LL TAKE IT!
INCOMING:
Hawkgirl
HONDURAS.
HOLA, BATGIRL! I TOOK A BREAK FROM OUR CASA BLANCA DIG TO LOOK INTO THOSE ARTIFACTS YOU MENTIONED.

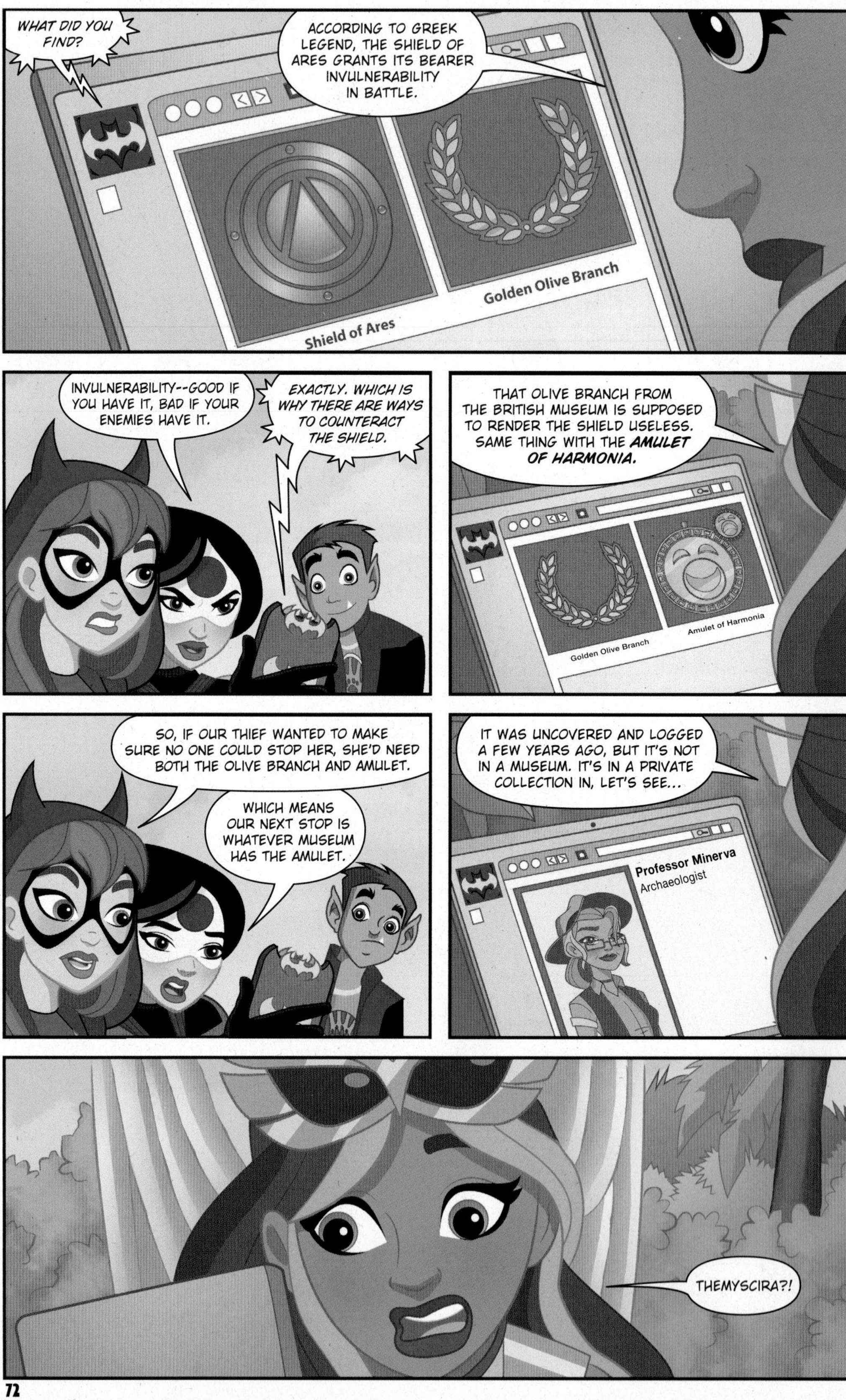
WHAT DID YOU FIND?
ACCORDING TO GREEK LEGEND, THE SHIELD OF ARES GRANTS ITS BEARER INVULNERABILITY IN BATTLE.
Shield of Ares
Golden Olive Branch
INVULNERABILITY--GOOD IF YOU HAVE IT, BAD IF YOUR ENEMIES HAVE IT.
EXACTLY. WHICH IS WHY THERE ARE WAYS TO COUNTERACT THE SHIELD.
THAT OLIVE BRANCH FROM THE BRITISH MUSEUM IS SUPPOSED TO RENDER THE SHIELD USELESS. SAME THING WITH THE **AMULET OF HARMONIA.**
Golden Olive Branch
Amulet of Harmonia
SO, IF OUR THIEF WANTED TO MAKE SURE NO ONE COULD STOP HER, SHE'D NEED BOTH THE OLIVE BRANCH AND AMULET.
WHICH MEANS OUR NEXT STOP IS WHATEVER MUSEUM HAS THE AMULET.
IT WAS UNCOVERED AND LOGGED A FEW YEARS AGO, BUT IT'S NOT IN A MUSEUM. IT'S IN A PRIVATE COLLECTION IN, LET'S SEE...
Professor Minerva
Archaeologist
THEMYSCIRA?!

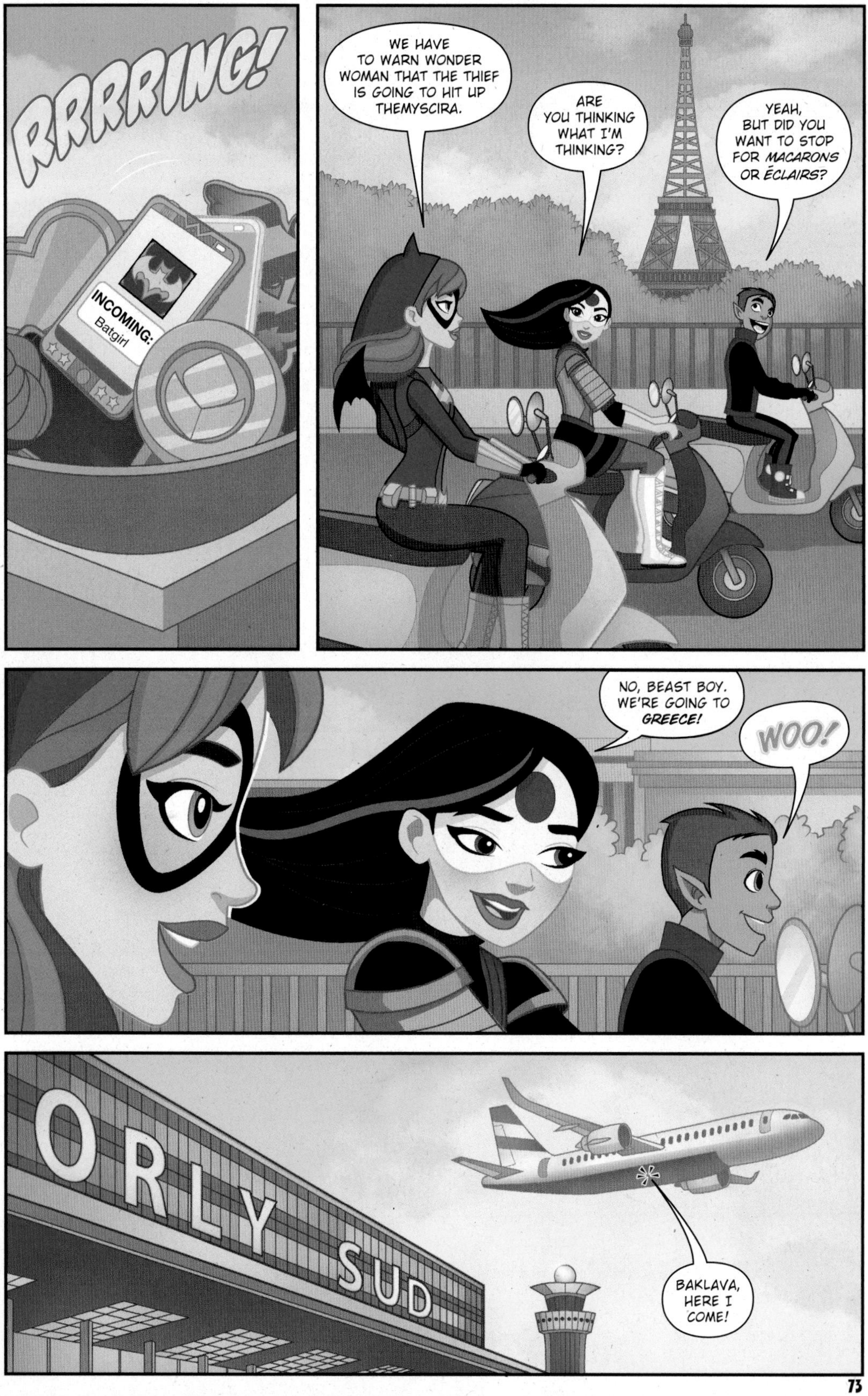
RRRRING!
INCOMING:
Batgirl
WE HAVE TO WARN WONDER WOMAN THAT THE THIEF IS GOING TO HIT UP THEMYSCIRA.
ARE YOU THINKING WHAT I'M THINKING?
YEAH, BUT DID YOU WANT TO STOP FOR *MACARONS* OR *ÉCLAIRS?*
NO, BEAST BOY. WE'RE GOING TO ***GREECE!***
WOO!
ORLY SUD
BAKLAVA, HERE I COME!

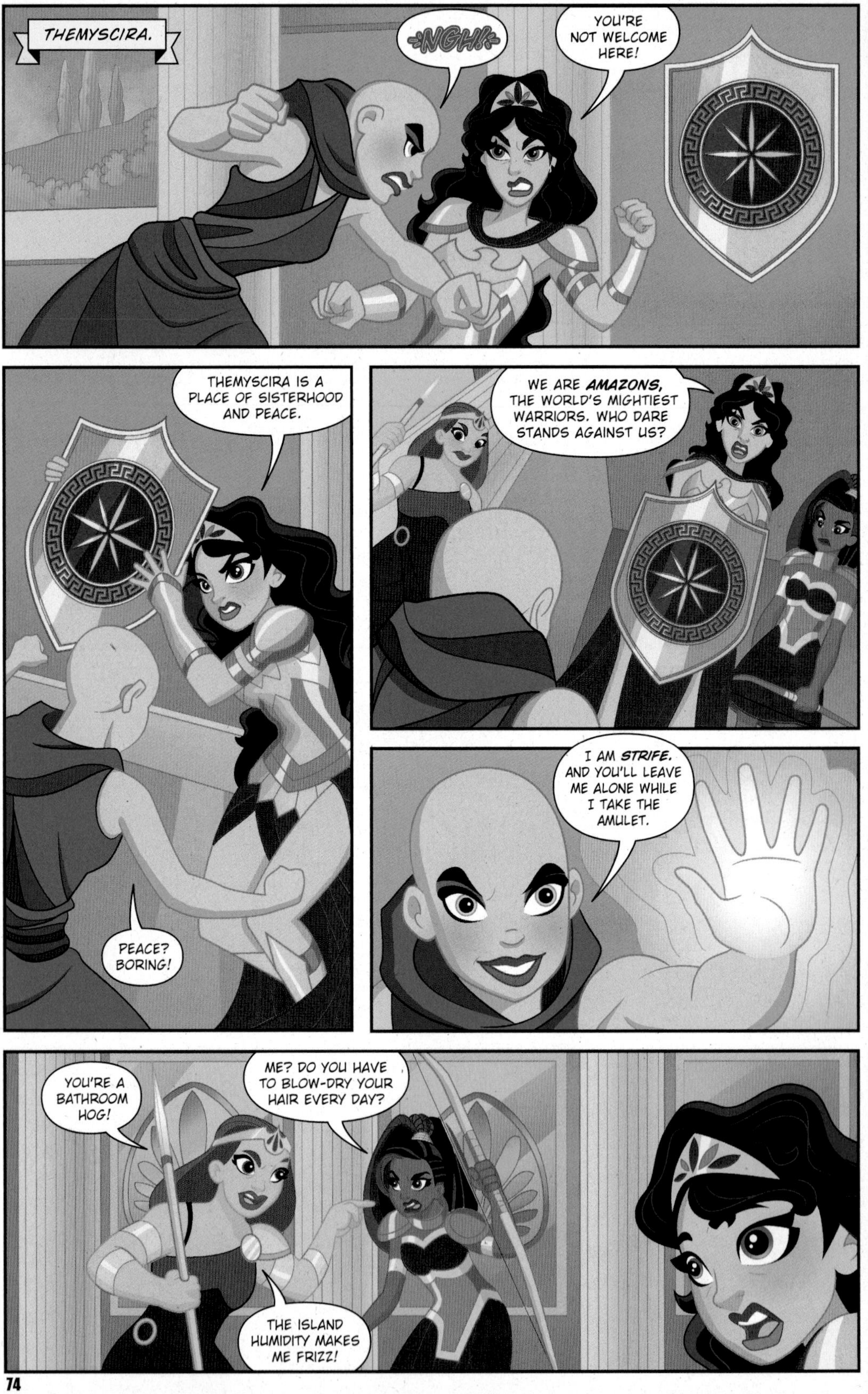
THEMYSCIRA.
NGH!
YOU'RE NOT WELCOME HERE!
THEMYSCIRA IS A PLACE OF SISTERHOOD AND PEACE.
PEACE? BORING!
WE ARE AMAZONS, THE WORLD'S MIGHTIEST WARRIORS. WHO DARE STANDS AGAINST US?
I AM STRIFE. AND YOU'LL LEAVE ME ALONE WHILE I TAKE THE AMULET.
YOU'RE A BATHROOM HOG!
ME? DO YOU HAVE TO BLOW-DRY YOUR HAIR EVERY DAY?
THE ISLAND HUMIDITY MAKES ME FRIZZ!

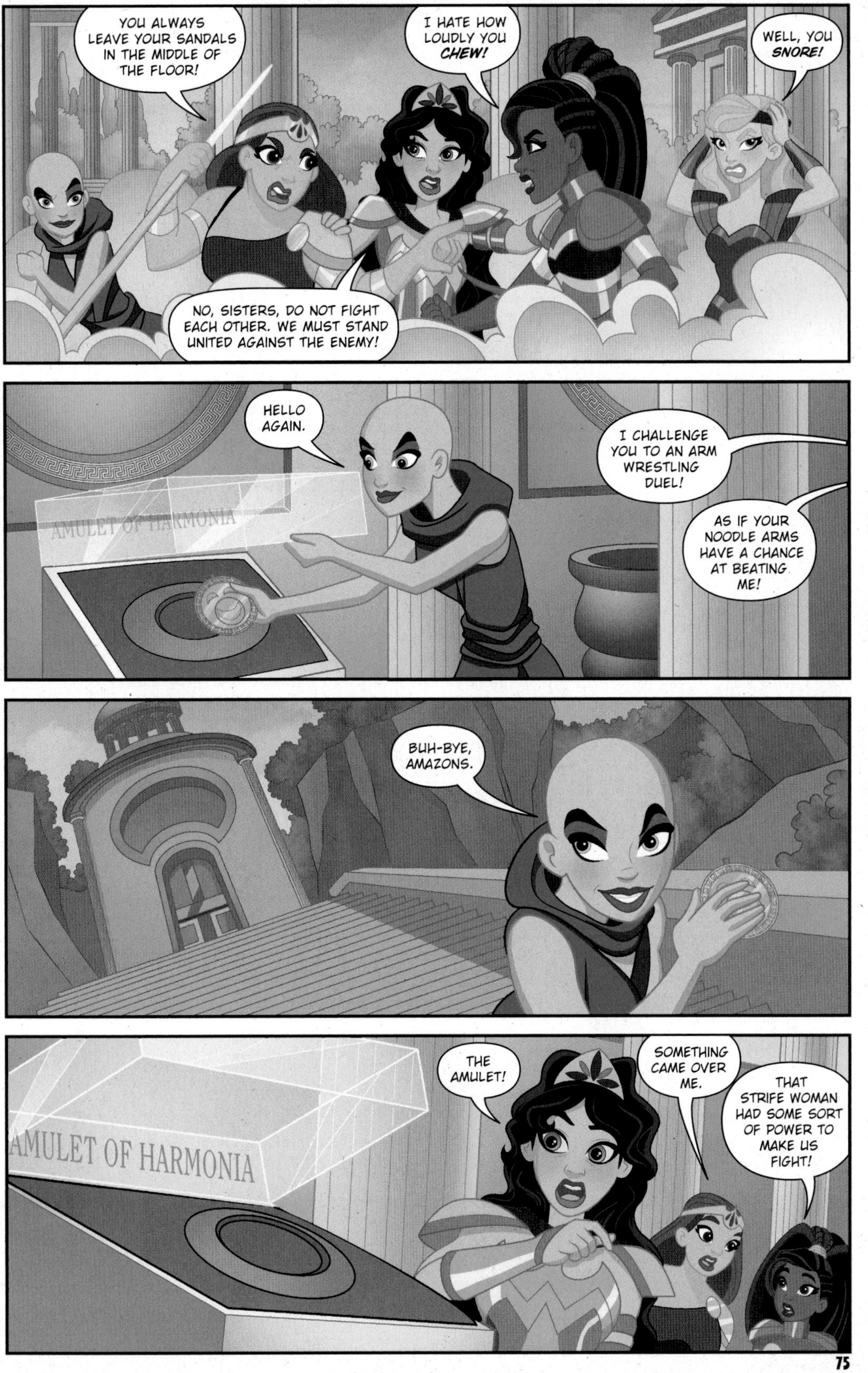
YOU ALWAYS LEAVE YOUR SANDALS IN THE MIDDLE OF THE FLOOR!
I HATE HOW LOUDLY YOU **CHEW!**
WELL, YOU **SNORE!**
NO, SISTERS, DO NOT FIGHT EACH OTHER. WE MUST STAND UNITED AGAINST THE ENEMY!
HELLO AGAIN.
AMULET OF HARMONIA
I CHALLENGE YOU TO AN ARM WRESTLING DUEL!
AS IF YOUR NOODLE ARMS HAVE A CHANCE AT BEATING ME!
BUH-BYE, AMAZONS.
AMULET OF HARMONIA
THE AMULET!
SOMETHING CAME OVER ME.
THAT STRIFE WOMAN HAD SOME SORT OF POWER TO MAKE US FIGHT!

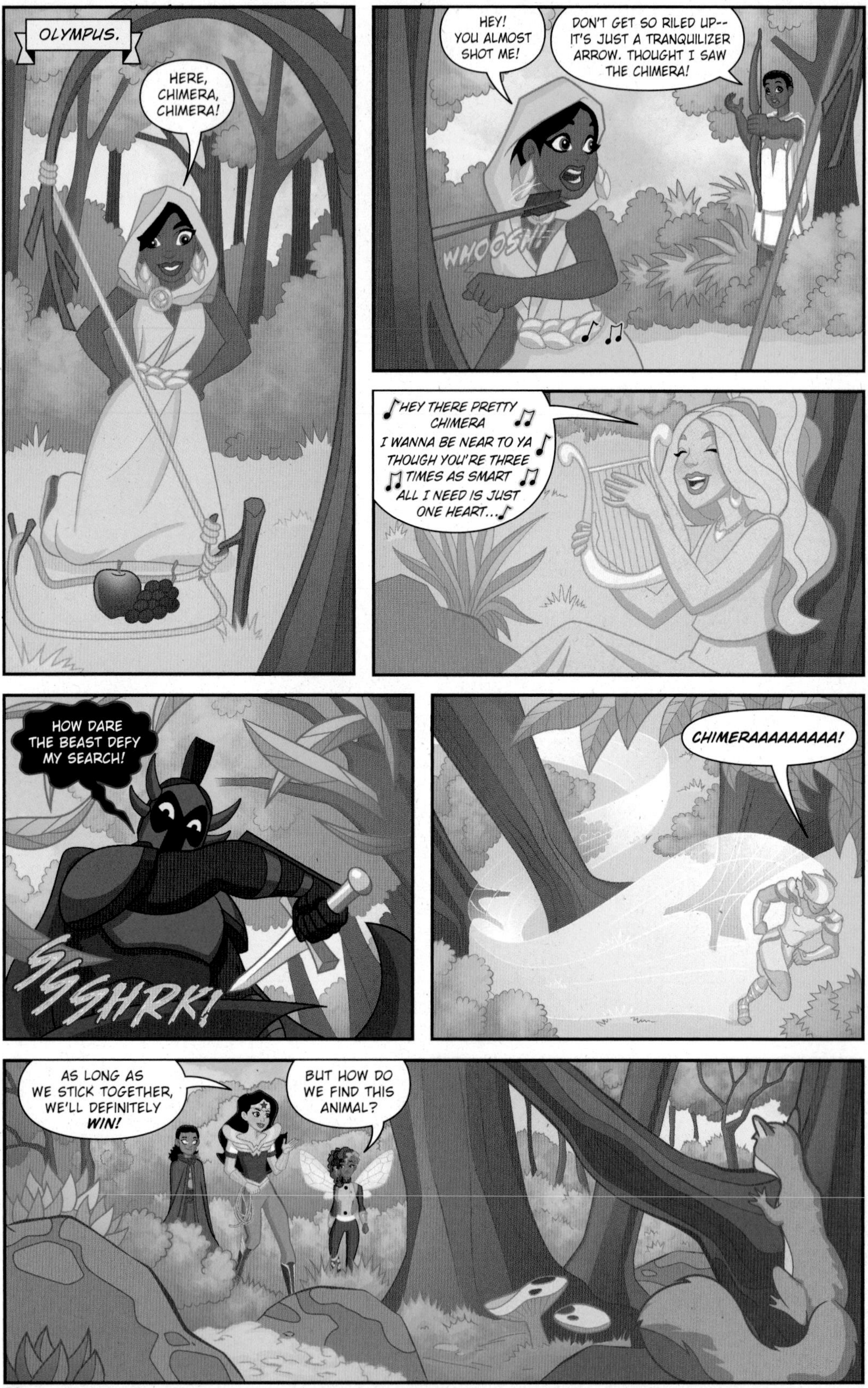
OLYMPUS.
HERE, CHIMERA, CHIMERA!
HEY! YOU ALMOST SHOT ME!
DON'T GET SO RILED UP-- IT'S JUST A TRANQUILIZER ARROW. THOUGHT I SAW THE CHIMERA!
WHOOSH!
HEY THERE PRETTY CHIMERA I WANNA BE NEAR TO YA THOUGH YOU'RE THREE TIMES AS SMART ALL I NEED IS JUST ONE HEART...
HOW DARE THE BEAST DEFY MY SEARCH!
SSSHRK!
CHIMERAAAAAAAAA!
AS LONG AS WE STICK TOGETHER, WE'LL DEFINITELY WIN!
BUT HOW DO WE FIND THIS ANIMAL?

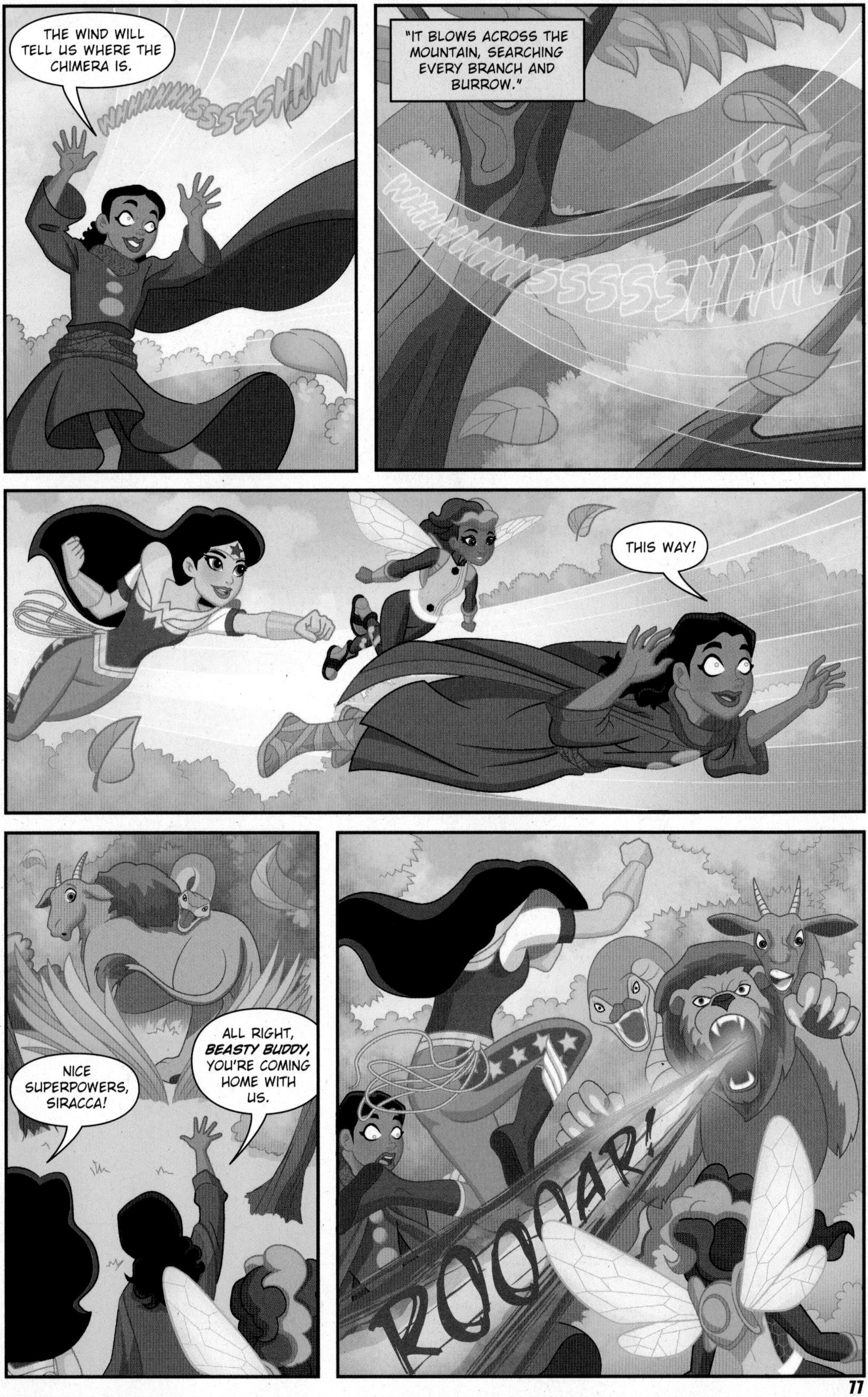
THE WIND WILL TELL US WHERE THE CHIMERA IS.
WHHHHHHHSSSSSHHHH
"IT BLOWS ACROSS THE MOUNTAIN, SEARCHING EVERY BRANCH AND BURROW."
WHHHHHHHSSSSSSHHHH
THIS WAY!
NICE SUPERPOWERS, SIRACCA!
ALL RIGHT, **BEASTY BUDDY**, YOU'RE COMING HOME WITH US.
ROOOAR!

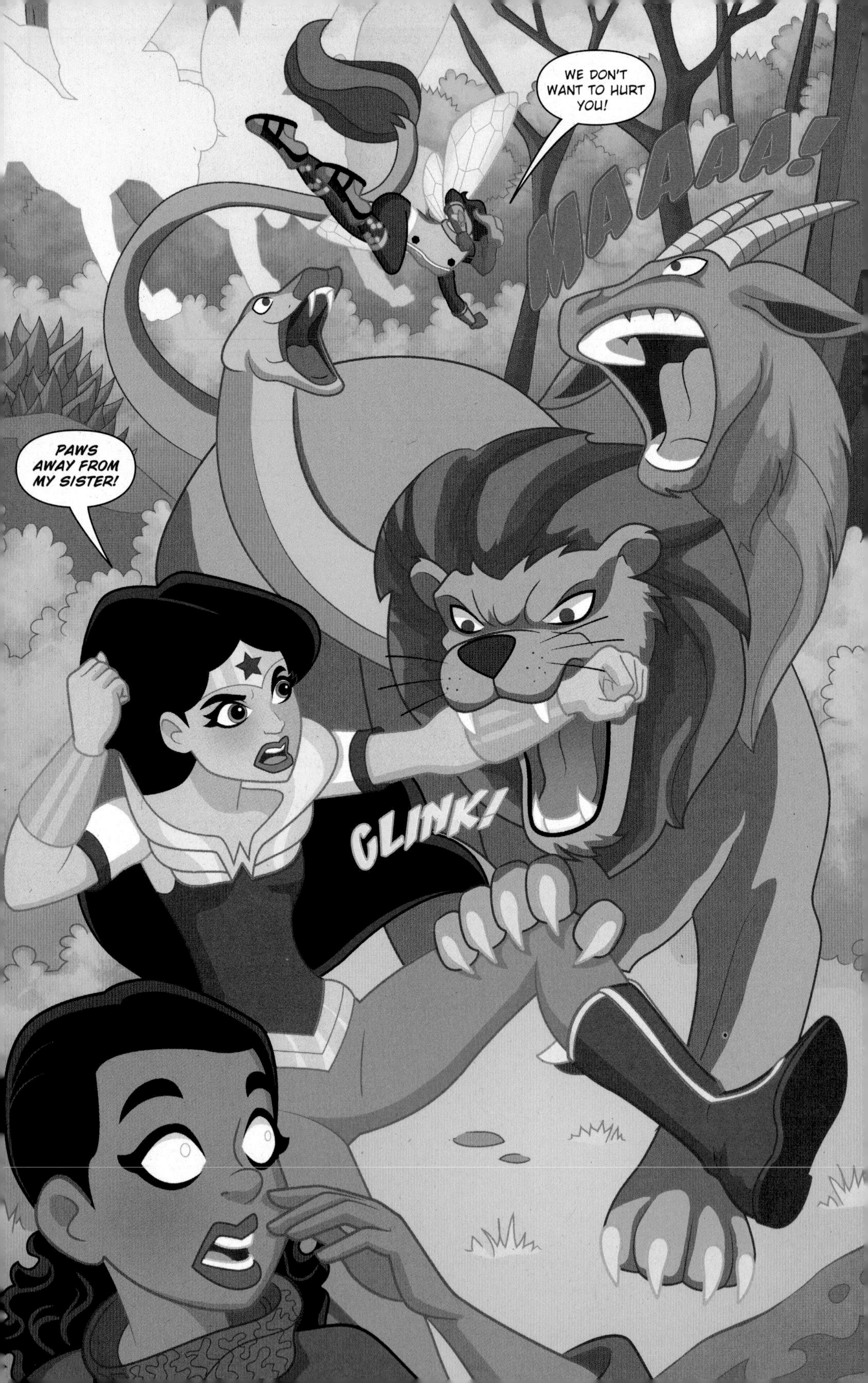
WE DON'T WANT TO HURT YOU!
MAAAA!
PAWS AWAY FROM MY SISTER!
CLINK!

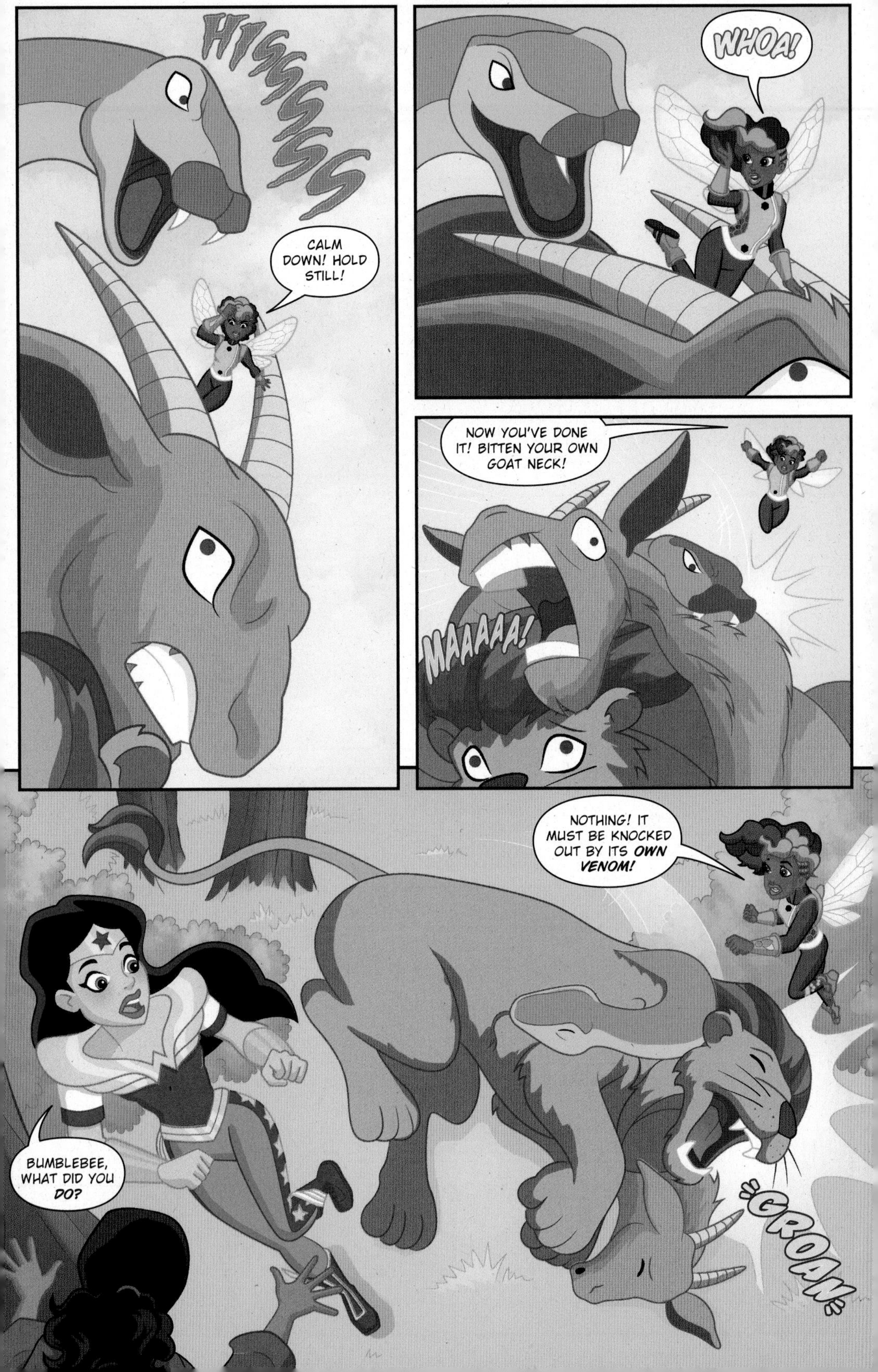
HISSSSSS
CALM DOWN! HOLD STILL!
WHOA!
NOW YOU'VE DONE IT! BITTEN YOUR OWN GOAT NECK!
MAAAAA!
BUMBLEBEE, WHAT DID YOU *DO?*
NOTHING! IT MUST BE KNOCKED OUT BY ITS ***OWN VENOM!***
GROAN

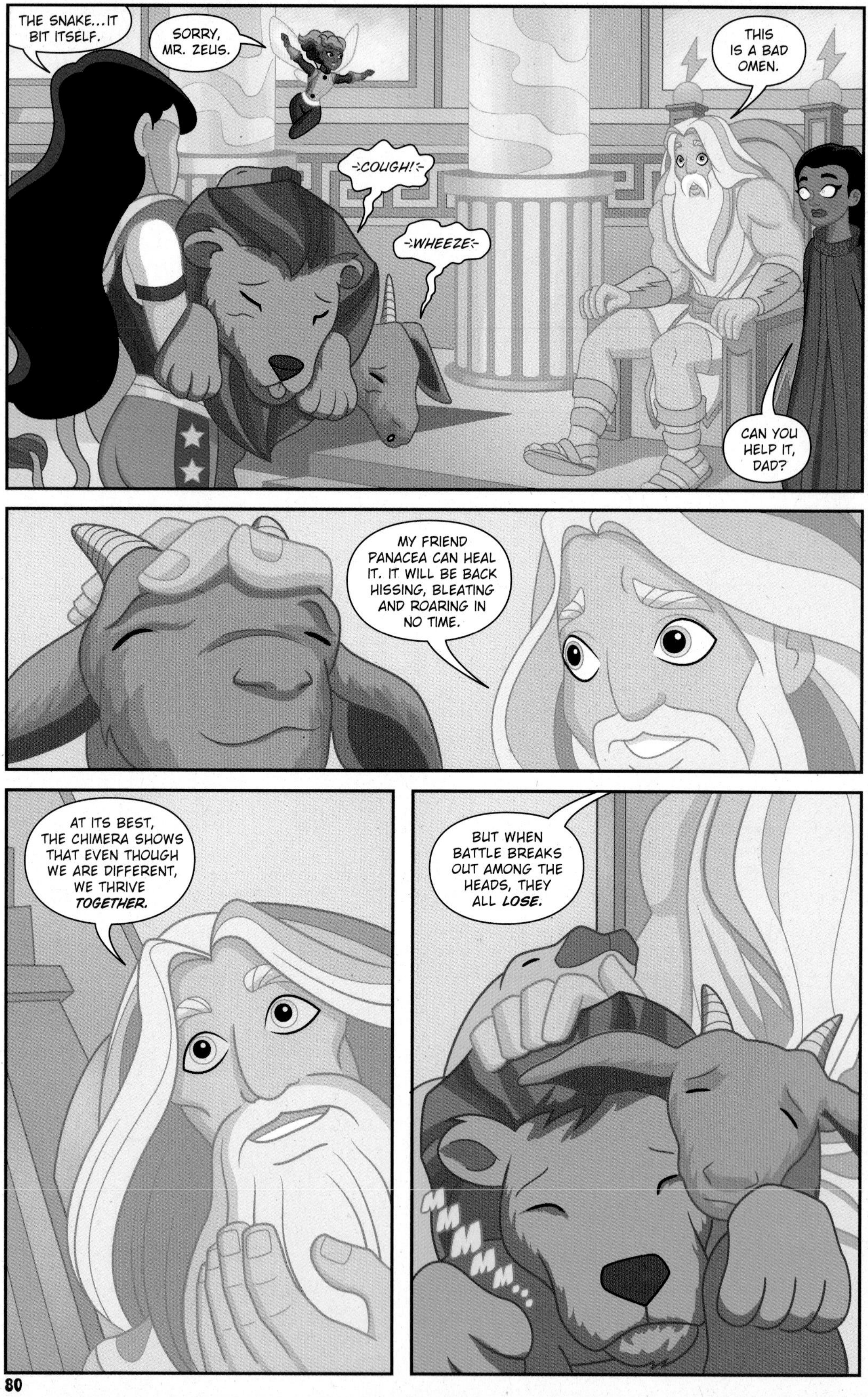
THE SNAKE...IT BIT ITSELF.
SORRY, MR. ZEUS.
THIS IS A BAD OMEN.
COUGH!
WHEEZE
CAN YOU HELP IT, DAD?
MY FRIEND PANACEA CAN HEAL IT. IT WILL BE BACK HISSING, BLEATING AND ROARING IN NO TIME.
AT ITS BEST, THE CHIMERA SHOWS THAT EVEN THOUGH WE ARE DIFFERENT, WE THRIVE *TOGETHER.*
BUT WHEN BATTLE BREAKS OUT AMONG THE HEADS, THEY ALL *LOSE.*
MMMMMM...

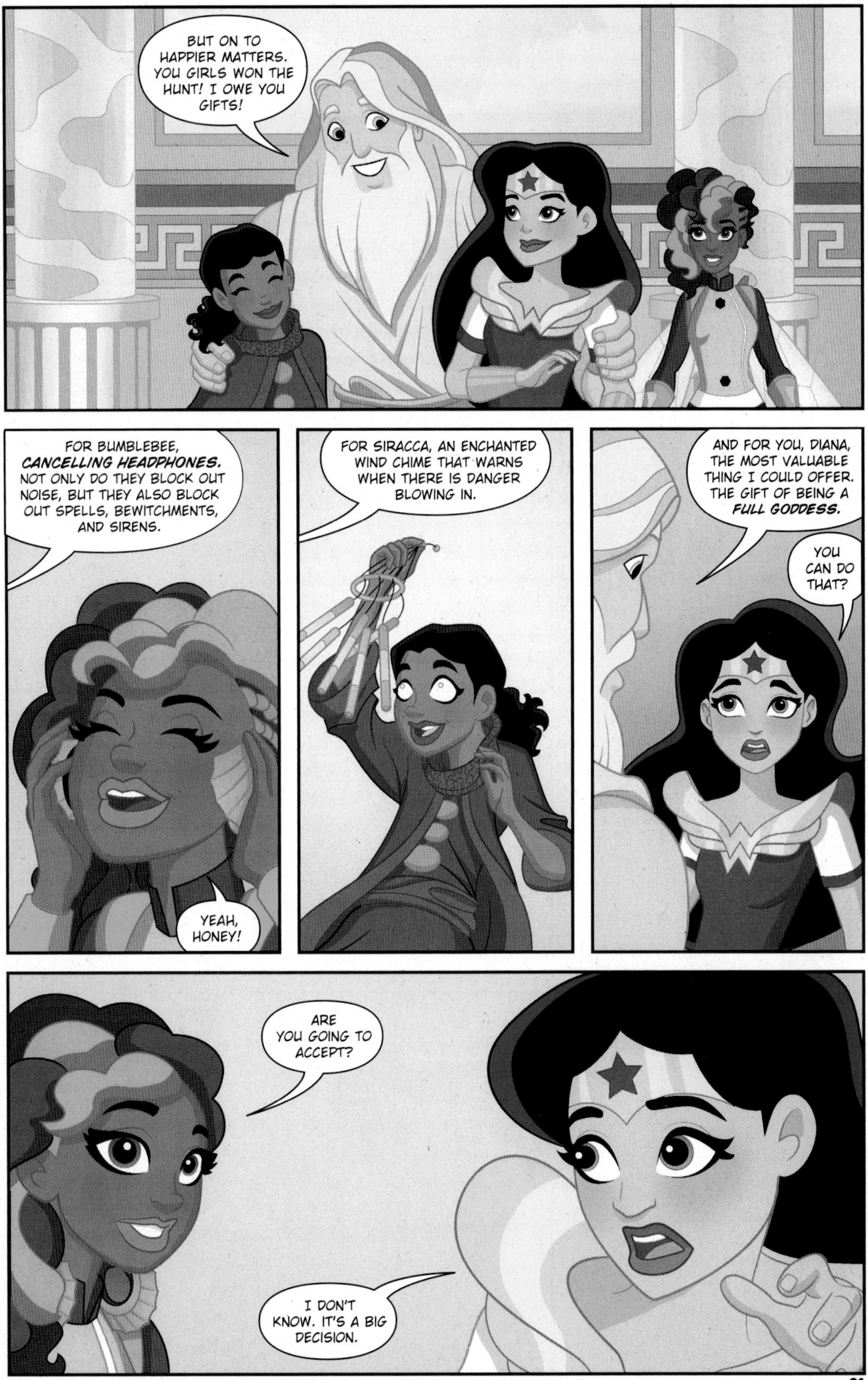
BUT ON TO HAPPIER MATTERS. YOU GIRLS WON THE HUNT! I OWE YOU GIFTS!
FOR BUMBLEBEE, **CANCELLING HEADPHONES.** NOT ONLY DO THEY BLOCK OUT NOISE, BUT THEY ALSO BLOCK OUT SPELLS, BEWITCHMENTS, AND SIRENS.
YEAH, HONEY!
FOR SIRACCA, AN ENCHANTED WIND CHIME THAT WARNS WHEN THERE IS DANGER BLOWING IN.
AND FOR YOU, DIANA, THE MOST VALUABLE THING I COULD OFFER. THE GIFT OF BEING A ***FULL GODDESS.***
YOU CAN DO THAT?
ARE YOU GOING TO ACCEPT?
I DON'T KNOW. IT'S A BIG DECISION.

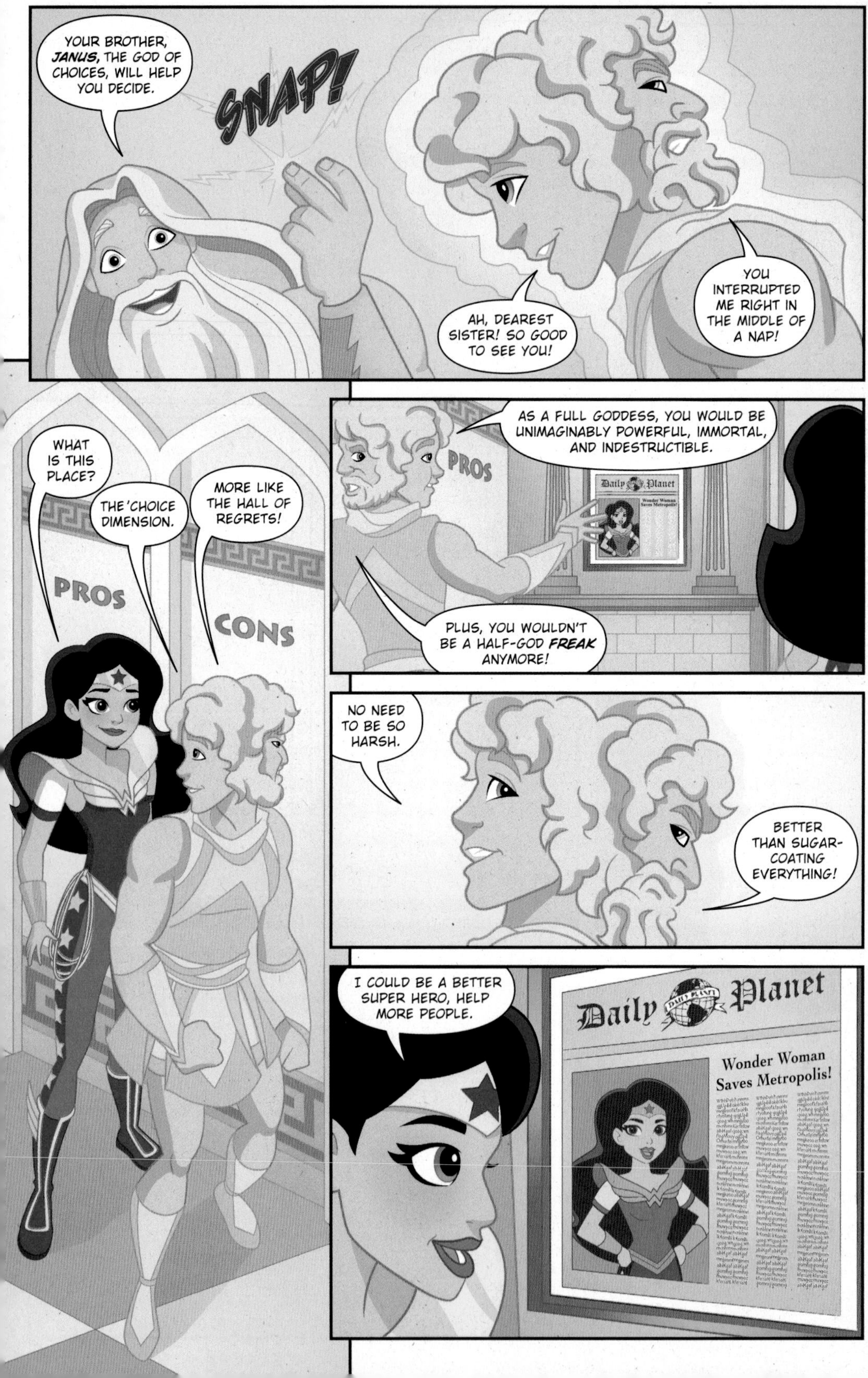
YOUR BROTHER, JANUS, THE GOD OF CHOICES, WILL HELP YOU DECIDE.
SNAP!
AH, DEAREST SISTER! SO GOOD TO SEE YOU!
YOU INTERRUPTED ME RIGHT IN THE MIDDLE OF A NAP!
WHAT IS THIS PLACE?
THE 'CHOICE DIMENSION.
MORE LIKE THE HALL OF REGRETS!
PROS
CONS
AS A FULL GODDESS, YOU WOULD BE UNIMAGINABLY POWERFUL, IMMORTAL, AND INDESTRUCTIBLE.
PROS
PLUS, YOU WOULDN'T BE A HALF-GOD FREAK ANYMORE!
NO NEED TO BE SO HARSH.
BETTER THAN SUGAR-COATING EVERYTHING!
I COULD BE A BETTER SUPER HERO, HELP MORE PEOPLE.
Daily Planet
Wonder Woman Saves Metropolis!

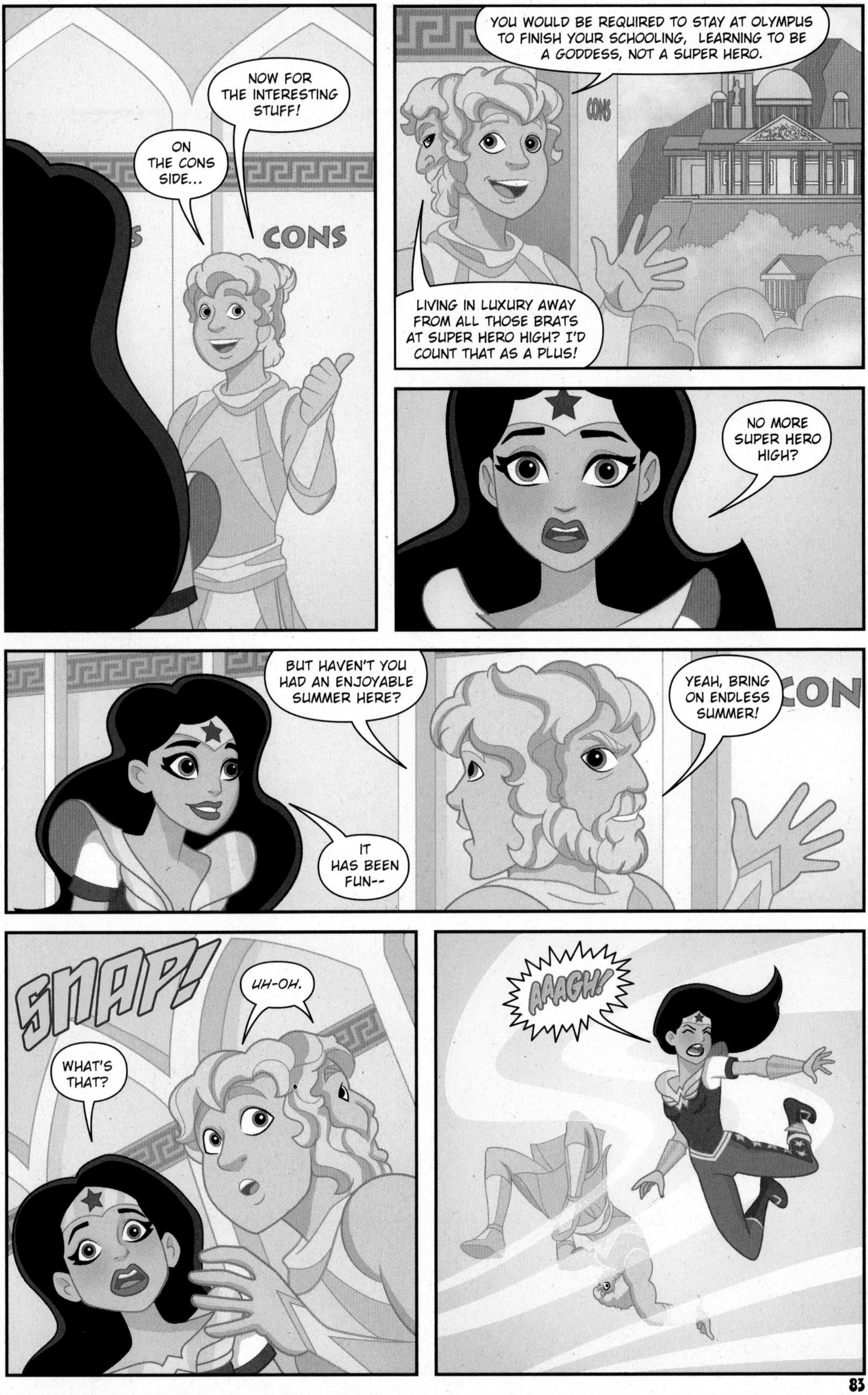
NOW FOR THE INTERESTING STUFF!
ON THE CONS SIDE...
CONS
YOU WOULD BE REQUIRED TO STAY AT OLYMPUS TO FINISH YOUR SCHOOLING, LEARNING TO BE A GODDESS, NOT A SUPER HERO.
CONS
LIVING IN LUXURY AWAY FROM ALL THOSE BRATS AT SUPER HERO HIGH? I'D COUNT THAT AS A PLUS!
NO MORE SUPER HERO HIGH?
BUT HAVEN'T YOU HAD AN ENJOYABLE SUMMER HERE?
IT HAS BEEN FUN--
YEAH, BRING ON ENDLESS SUMMER!
CON
SNAP!
UH-OH.
WHAT'S THAT?
AAAGH!

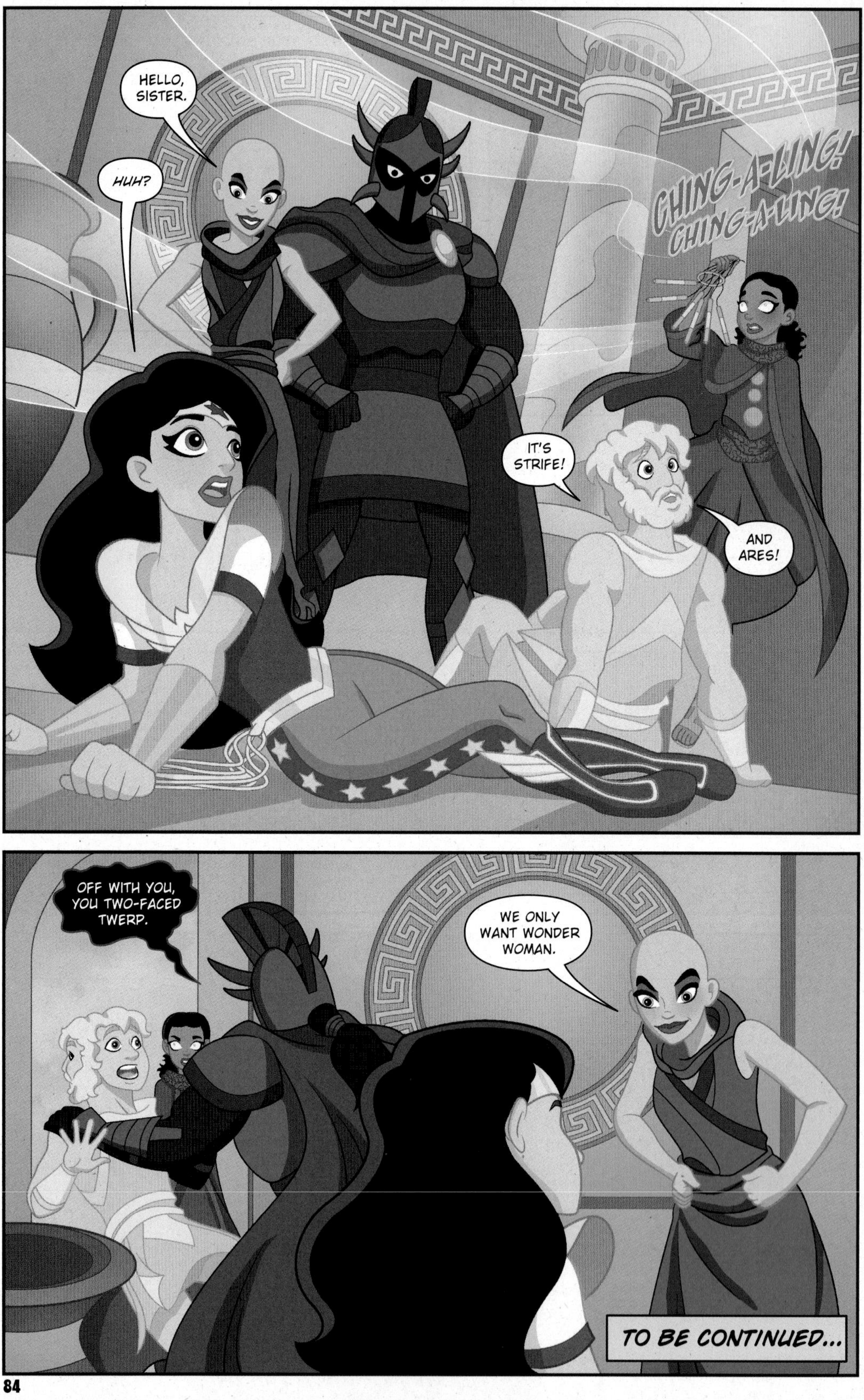
HELLO, SISTER.
HUH?
CHING-A-LING!
CHING-A-LING!
IT'S STRIFE!
AND ARES!
OFF WITH YOU, YOU TWO-FACED TWERP.
WE ONLY WANT WONDER WOMAN.
TO BE CONTINUED...

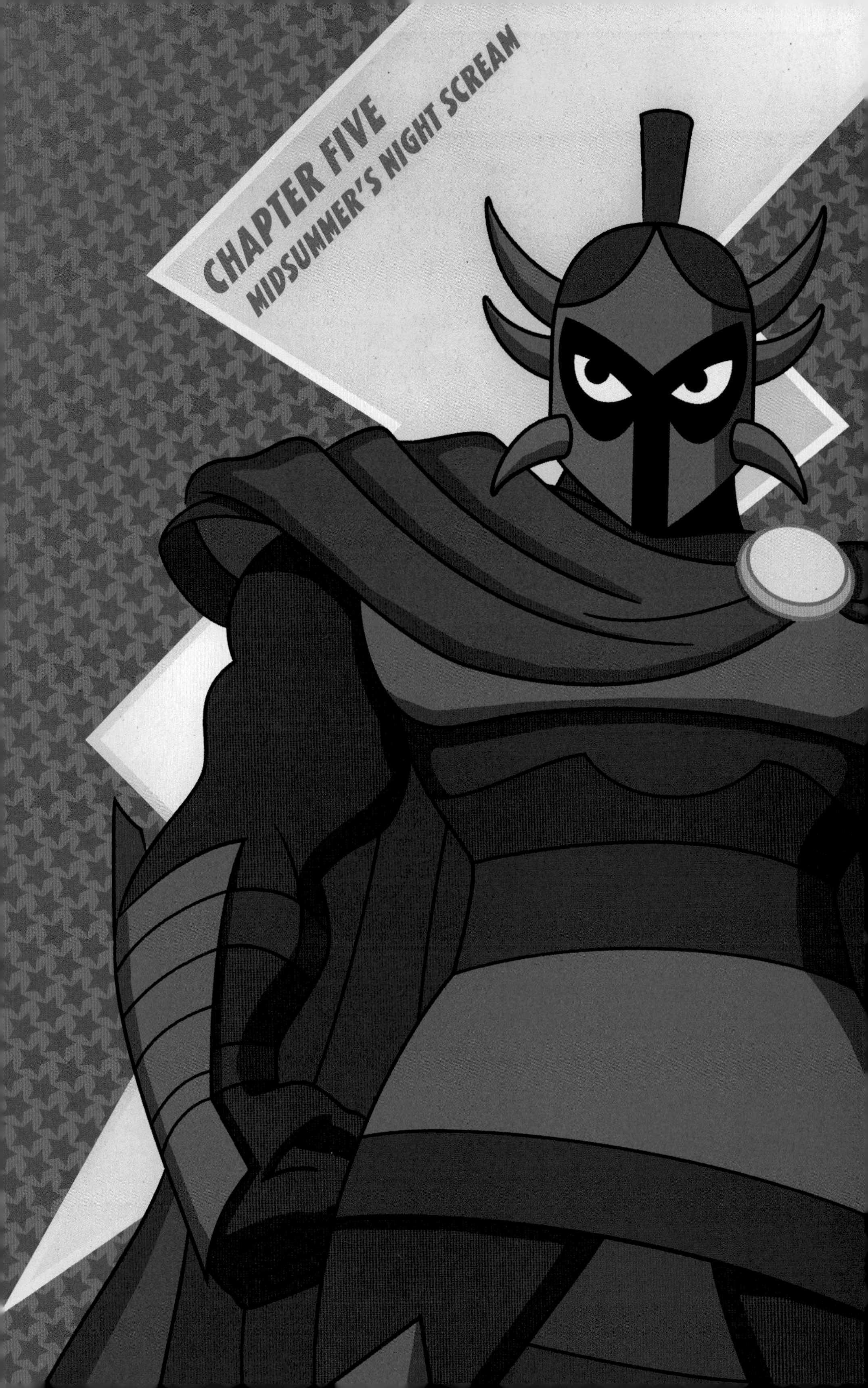
CHAPTER FIVE
MIDSUMMER'S NIGHT SCREAM

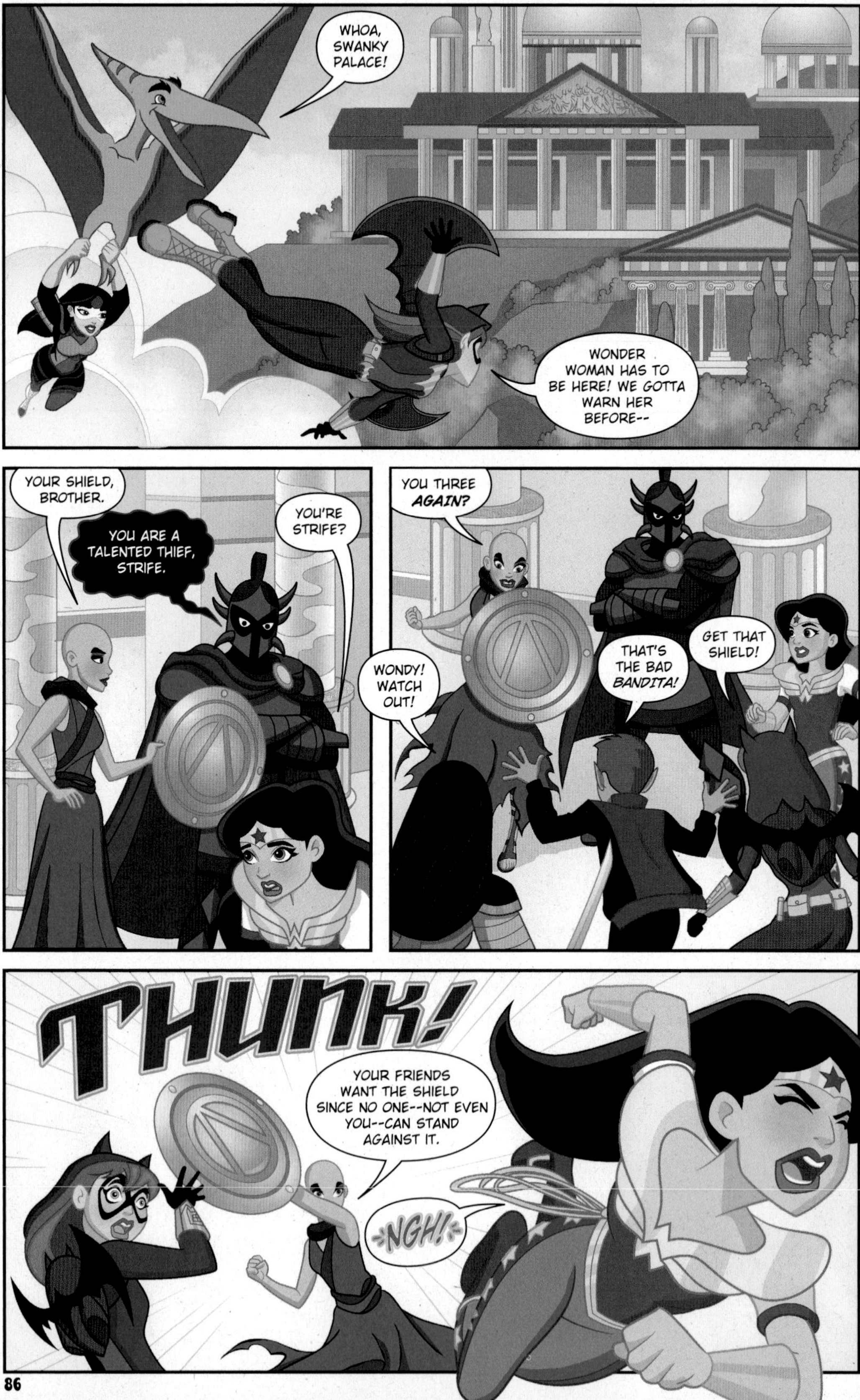
WHOA, SWANKY PALACE!
WONDER WOMAN HAS TO BE HERE! WE GOTTA WARN HER BEFORE--
YOUR SHIELD, BROTHER.
YOU ARE A TALENTED THIEF, STRIFE.
YOU'RE STRIFE?
YOU THREE AGAIN?
WONDY! WATCH OUT!
THAT'S THE BAD BANDITA!
GET THAT SHIELD!
THUNK!
YOUR FRIENDS WANT THE SHIELD SINCE NO ONE--NOT EVEN YOU--CAN STAND AGAINST IT.
NGH!

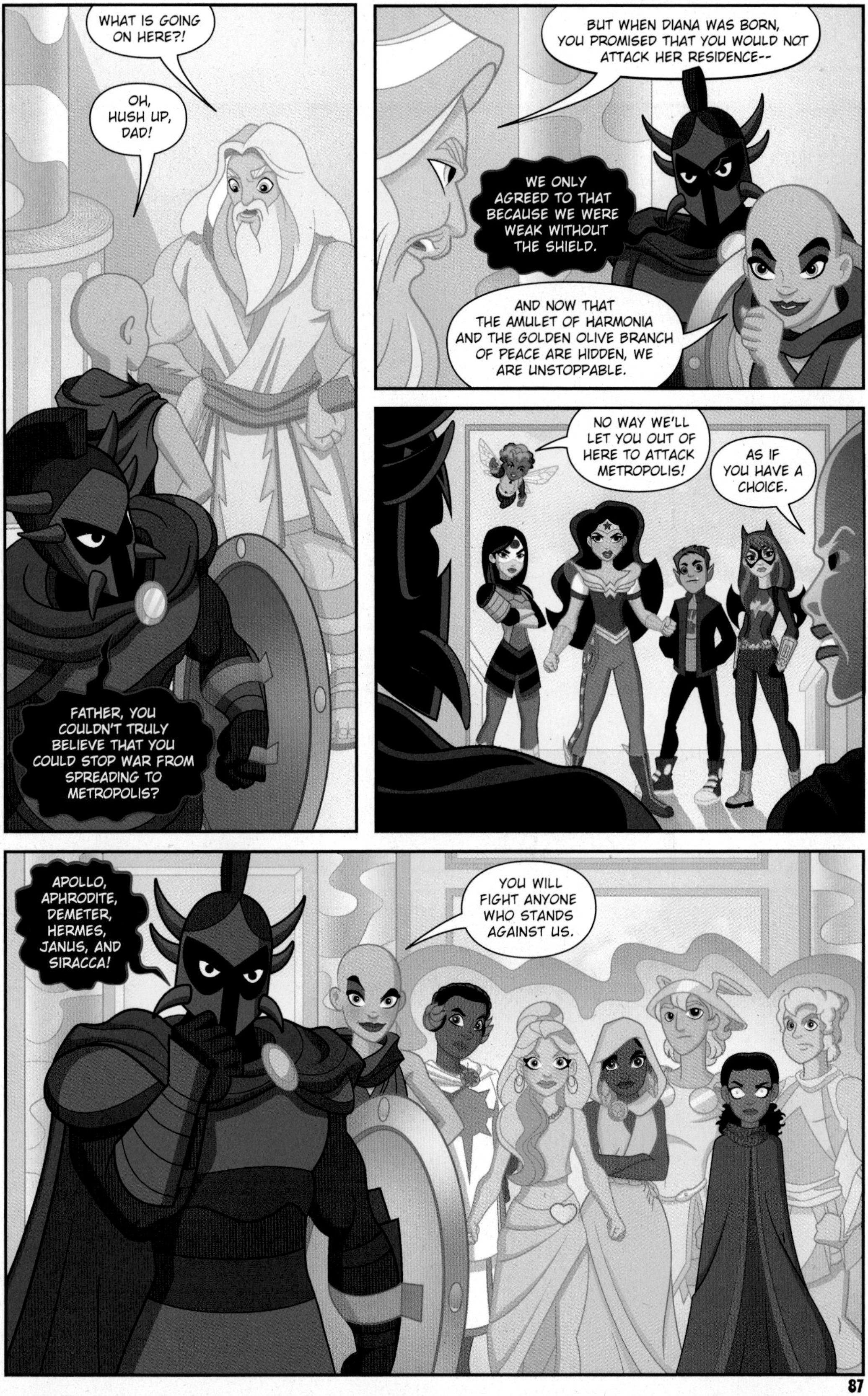
WHAT IS GOING ON HERE?!
OH, HUSH UP, DAD!
FATHER, YOU COULDN'T TRULY BELIEVE THAT YOU COULD STOP WAR FROM SPREADING TO METROPOLIS?
BUT WHEN DIANA WAS BORN, YOU PROMISED THAT YOU WOULD NOT ATTACK HER RESIDENCE--
WE ONLY AGREED TO THAT BECAUSE WE WERE WEAK WITHOUT THE SHIELD.
AND NOW THAT THE AMULET OF HARMONIA AND THE GOLDEN OLIVE BRANCH OF PEACE ARE HIDDEN, WE ARE UNSTOPPABLE.
NO WAY WE'LL LET YOU OUT OF HERE TO ATTACK METROPOLIS!
AS IF YOU HAVE A CHOICE.
APOLLO, APHRODITE, DEMETER, HERMES, JANUS, AND SIRACCA!
YOU WILL FIGHT ANYONE WHO STANDS AGAINST US.

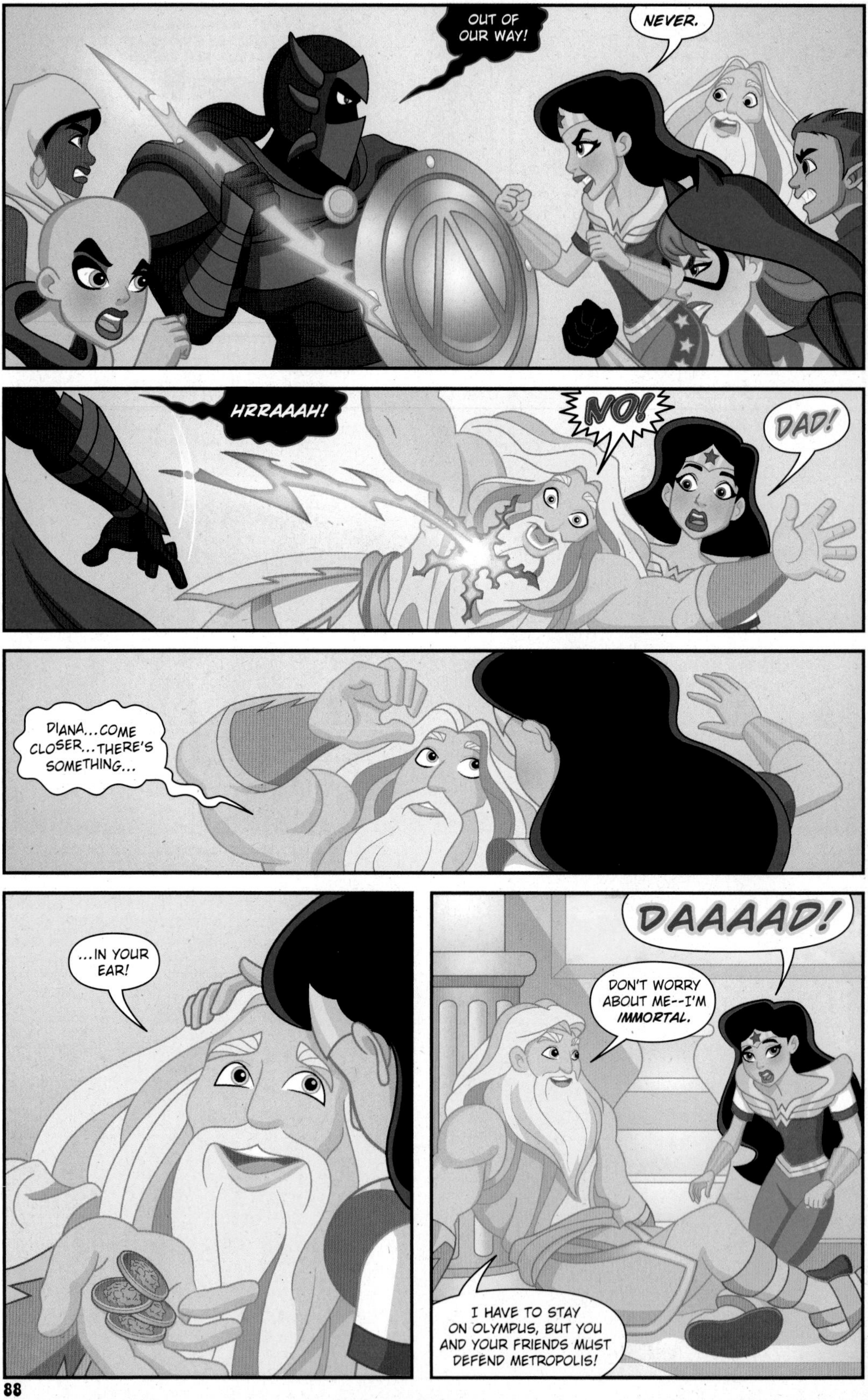

OUT OF OUR WAY!
NEVER.
HRRAAAH!
NO!
DAD!
DIANA...COME CLOSER...THERE'S SOMETHING...
...IN YOUR EAR!
DAAAAD!
DON'T WORRY ABOUT ME--I'M *IMMORTAL.*
I HAVE TO STAY ON OLYMPUS, BUT YOU AND YOUR FRIENDS MUST DEFEND METROPOLIS!

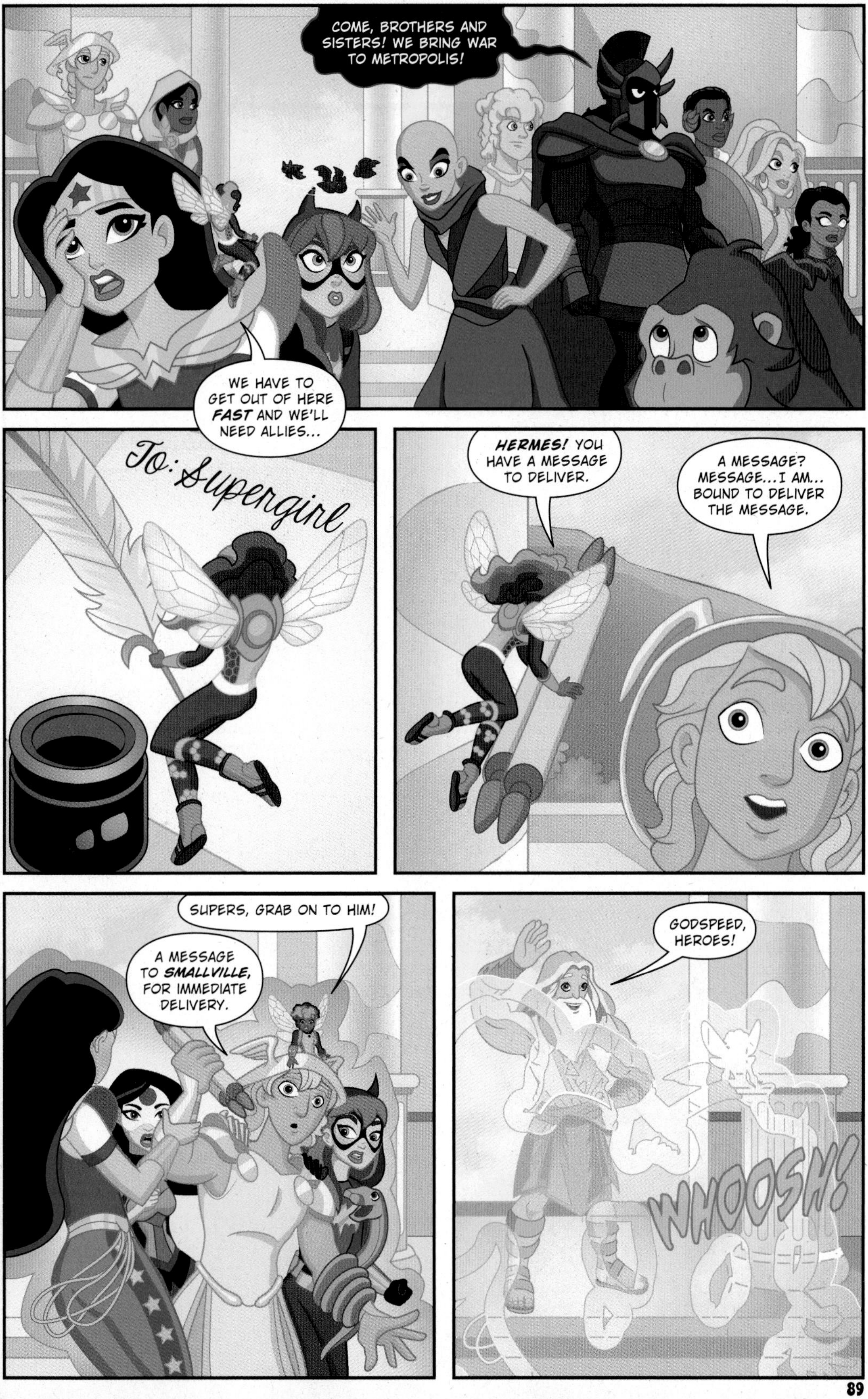
COME, BROTHERS AND SISTERS! WE BRING WAR TO METROPOLIS!
WE HAVE TO GET OUT OF HERE FAST AND WE'LL NEED ALLIES...
To: Supergirl
HERMES! YOU HAVE A MESSAGE TO DELIVER.
A MESSAGE? MESSAGE...I AM... BOUND TO DELIVER THE MESSAGE.
SUPERS, GRAB ON TO HIM!
A MESSAGE TO SMALLVILLE, FOR IMMEDIATE DELIVERY.
GODSPEED, HEROES!
WHOOSH!

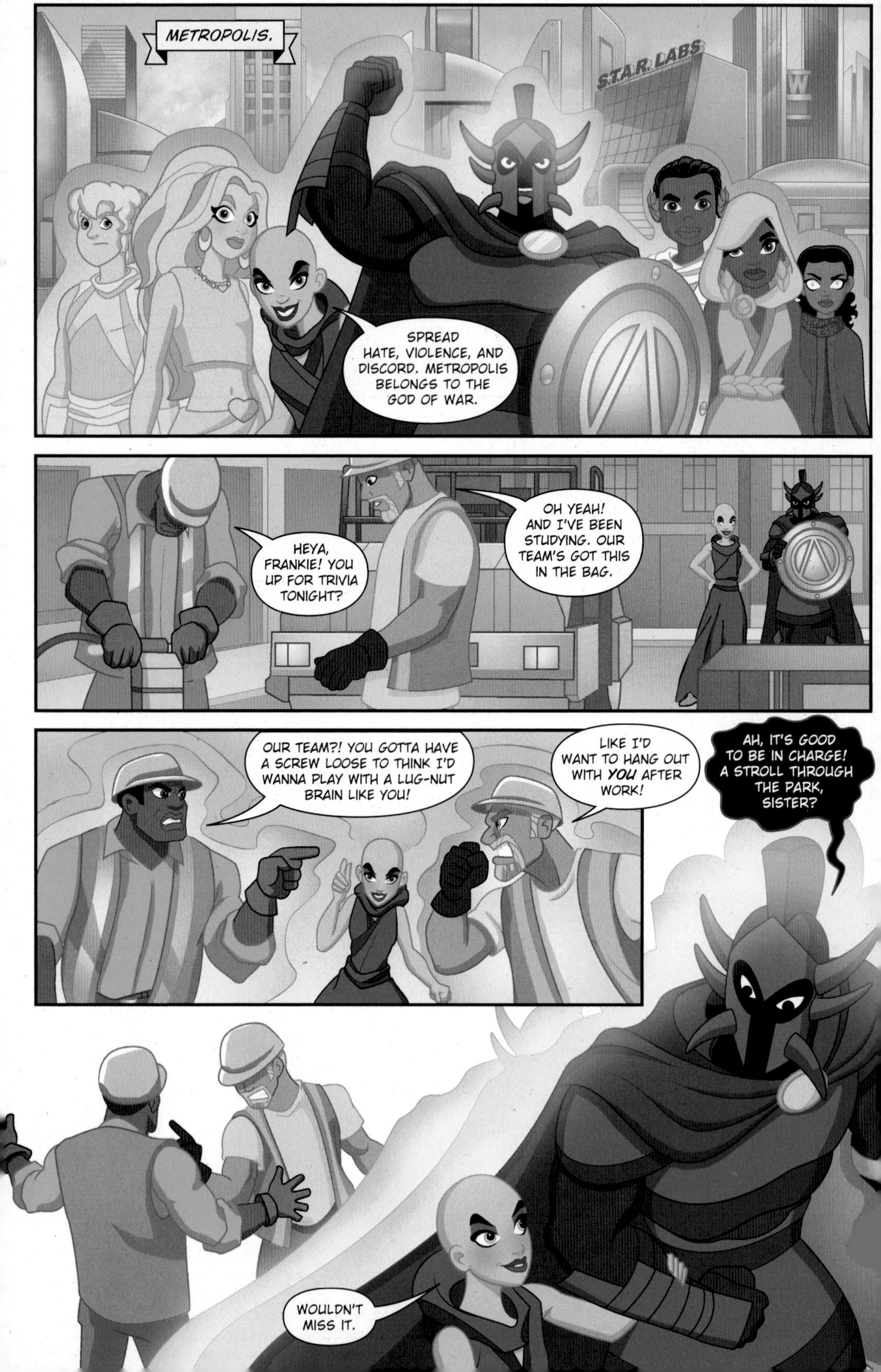

METROPOLIS.
S.T.A.R. LABS
SPREAD HATE, VIOLENCE, AND DISCORD. METROPOLIS BELONGS TO THE GOD OF WAR.
HEYA, FRANKIE! YOU UP FOR TRIVIA TONIGHT?
OH YEAH! AND I'VE BEEN STUDYING. OUR TEAM'S GOT THIS IN THE BAG.
OUR TEAM?! YOU GOTTA HAVE A SCREW LOOSE TO THINK I'D WANNA PLAY WITH A LUG-NUT BRAIN LIKE YOU!
LIKE I'D WANT TO HANG OUT WITH YOU AFTER WORK!
AH, IT'S GOOD TO BE IN CHARGE! A STROLL THROUGH THE PARK, SISTER?
WOULDN'T MISS IT.

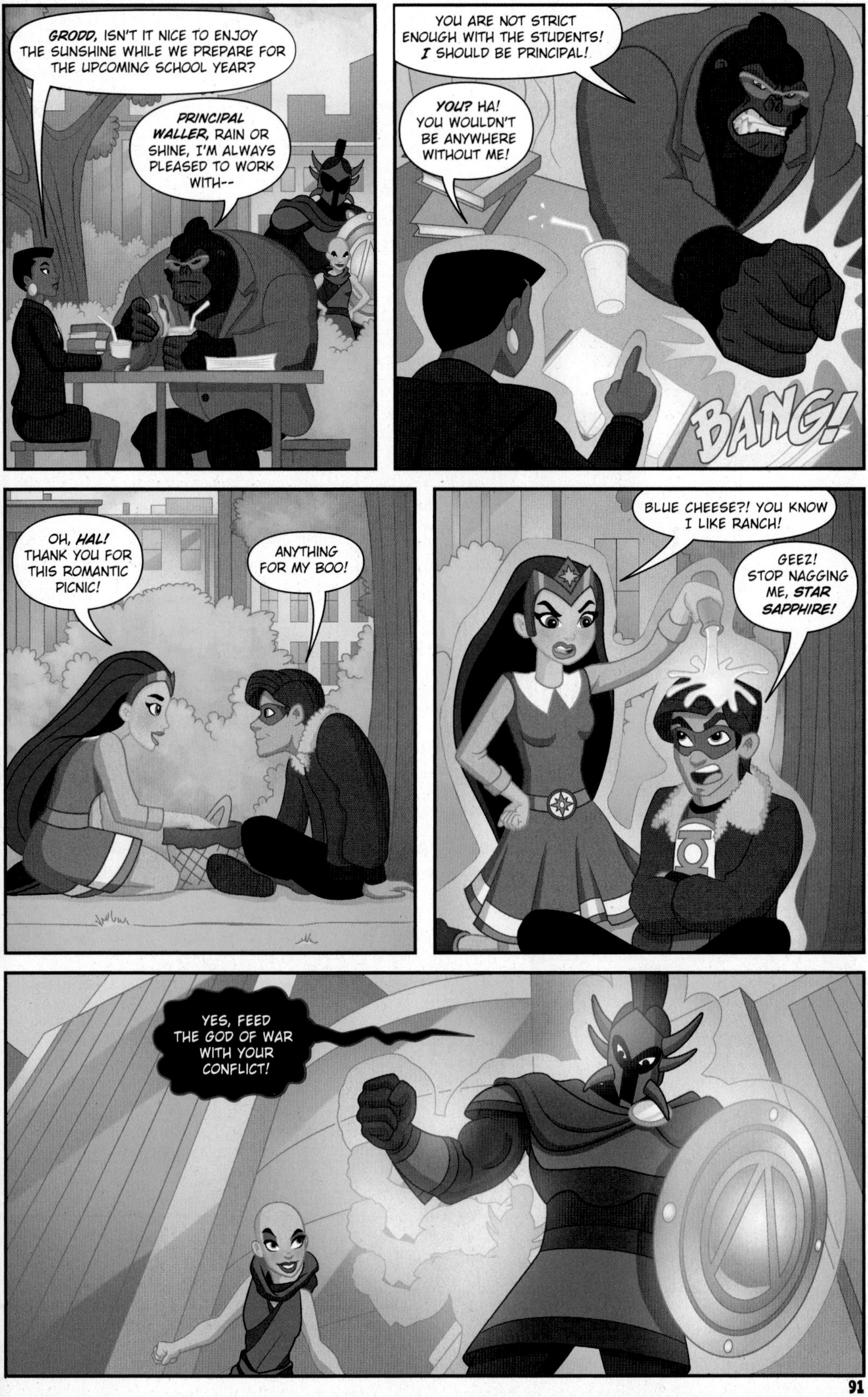
GRODD, ISN'T IT NICE TO ENJOY THE SUNSHINE WHILE WE PREPARE FOR THE UPCOMING SCHOOL YEAR?
PRINCIPAL WALLER, RAIN OR SHINE, I'M ALWAYS PLEASED TO WORK WITH--
YOU ARE NOT STRICT ENOUGH WITH THE STUDENTS! I SHOULD BE PRINCIPAL!
YOU? HA! YOU WOULDN'T BE ANYWHERE WITHOUT ME!
BANG!
OH, HAL! THANK YOU FOR THIS ROMANTIC PICNIC!
ANYTHING FOR MY BOO!
BLUE CHEESE?! YOU KNOW I LIKE RANCH!
GEEZ! STOP NAGGING ME, STAR SAPPHIRE!
YES, FEED THE GOD OF WAR WITH YOUR CONFLICT!

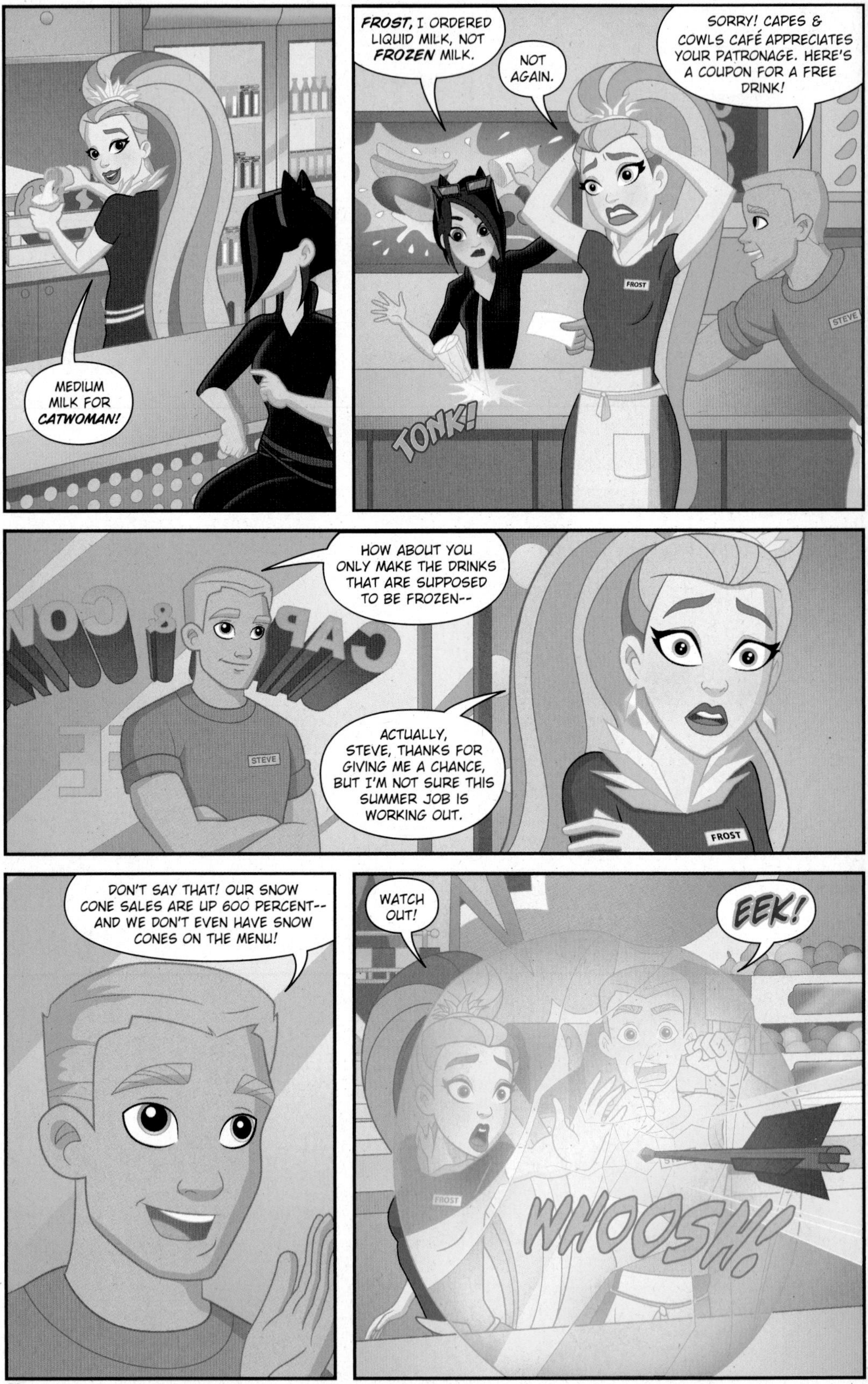
MEDIUM MILK FOR CATWOMAN!
FROST, I ORDERED LIQUID MILK, NOT FROZEN MILK.
NOT AGAIN.
SORRY! CAPES & COWLS CAFÉ APPRECIATES YOUR PATRONAGE. HERE'S A COUPON FOR A FREE DRINK!
TONK!
FROST
STEVE
HOW ABOUT YOU ONLY MAKE THE DRINKS THAT ARE SUPPOSED TO BE FROZEN--
ACTUALLY, STEVE, THANKS FOR GIVING ME A CHANCE, BUT I'M NOT SURE THIS SUMMER JOB IS WORKING OUT.
STEVE
FROST
DON'T SAY THAT! OUR SNOW CONE SALES ARE UP 600 PERCENT--AND WE DON'T EVEN HAVE SNOW CONES ON THE MENU!
WATCH OUT!
EEK!
FROST
WHOOSH!

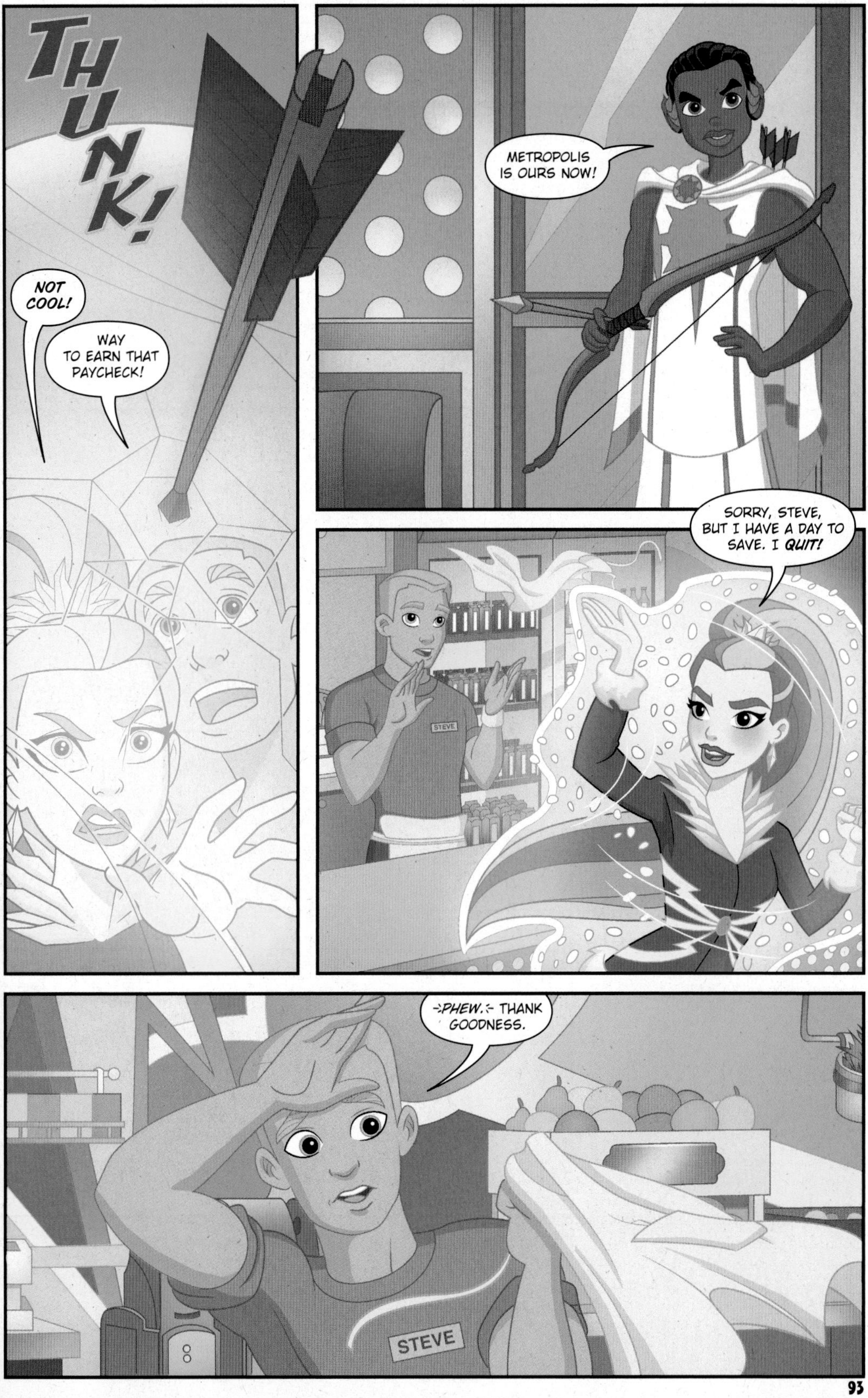
THUNK!
NOT COOL!
WAY TO EARN THAT PAYCHECK!
METROPOLIS IS OURS NOW!
SORRY, STEVE, BUT I HAVE A DAY TO SAVE. I QUIT!
STEVE
-PHEW.- THANK GOODNESS.
STEVE

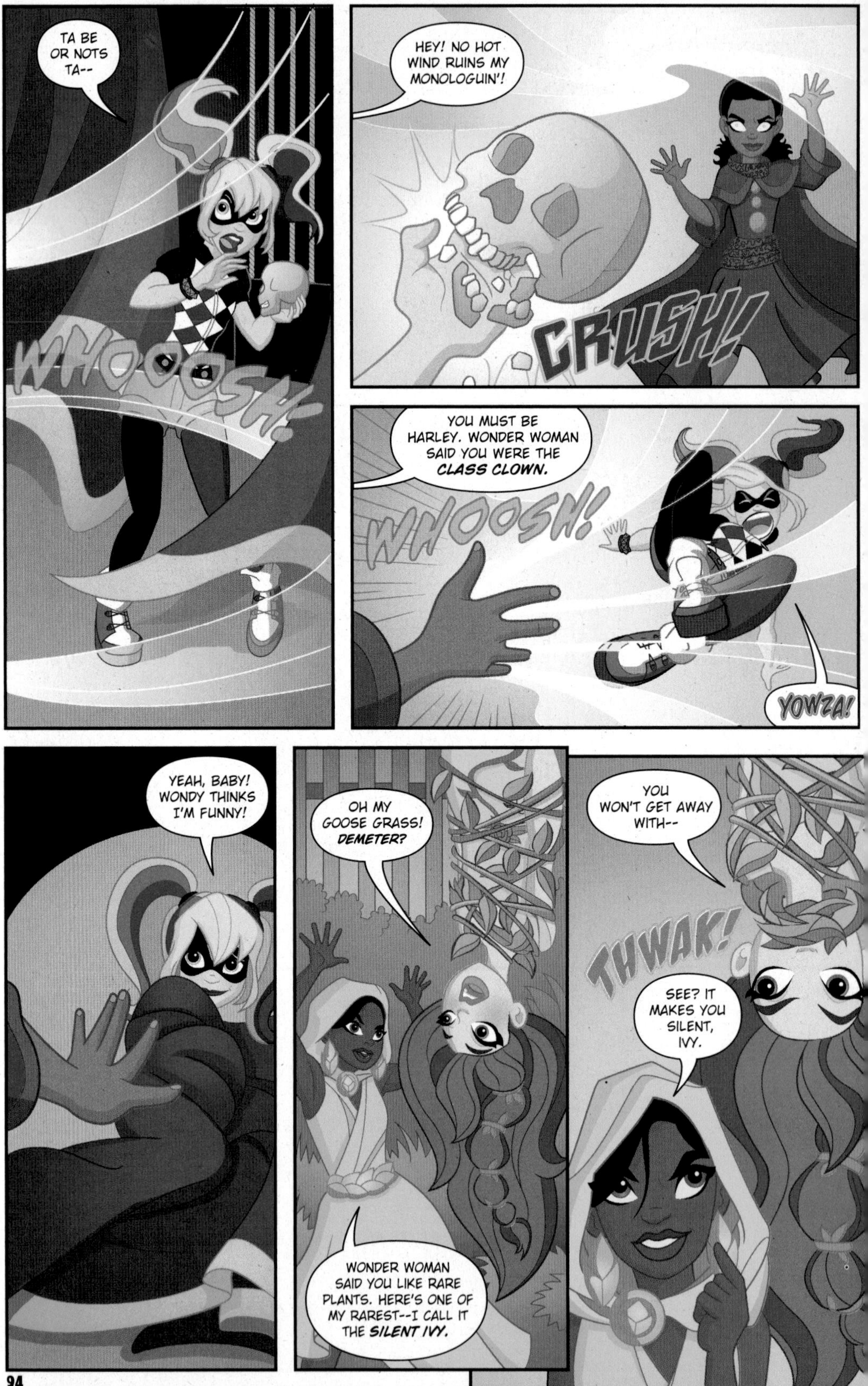

TA BE OR NOTS TA--
WHOOOSH!
HEY! NO HOT WIND RUINS MY MONOLOGUIN'!
CRUSH!
YOU MUST BE HARLEY. WONDER WOMAN SAID YOU WERE THE CLASS CLOWN.
WHOOSH!
YOWZA!
YEAH, BABY! WONDY THINKS I'M FUNNY!
OH MY GOOSE GRASS! DEMETER?
WONDER WOMAN SAID YOU LIKE RARE PLANTS. HERE'S ONE OF MY RAREST--I CALL IT THE SILENT IVY.
YOU WON'T GET AWAY WITH--
THWAK!
SEE? IT MAKES YOU SILENT, IVY.

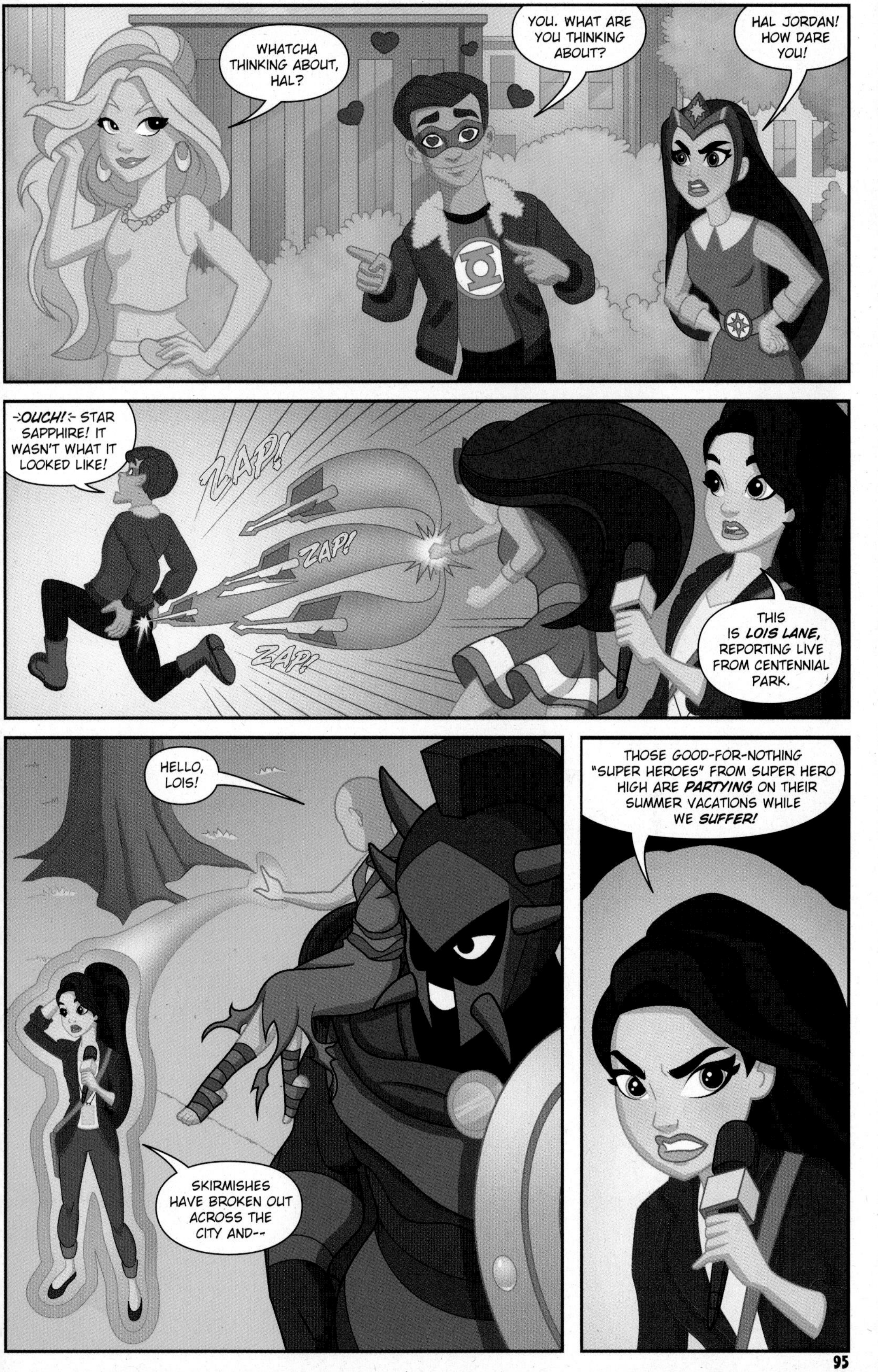

WHATCHA THINKING ABOUT, HAL?
YOU. WHAT ARE YOU THINKING ABOUT?
HAL JORDAN! HOW DARE YOU!
-OUCH!- STAR SAPPHIRE! IT WASN'T WHAT IT LOOKED LIKE!
ZAP!
ZAP!
ZAP!
THIS IS LOIS LANE, REPORTING LIVE FROM CENTENNIAL PARK.
HELLO, LOIS!
SKIRMISHES HAVE BROKEN OUT ACROSS THE CITY AND--
THOSE GOOD-FOR-NOTHING "SUPER HEROES" FROM SUPER HERO HIGH ARE PARTYING ON THEIR SUMMER VACATIONS WHILE WE SUFFER!

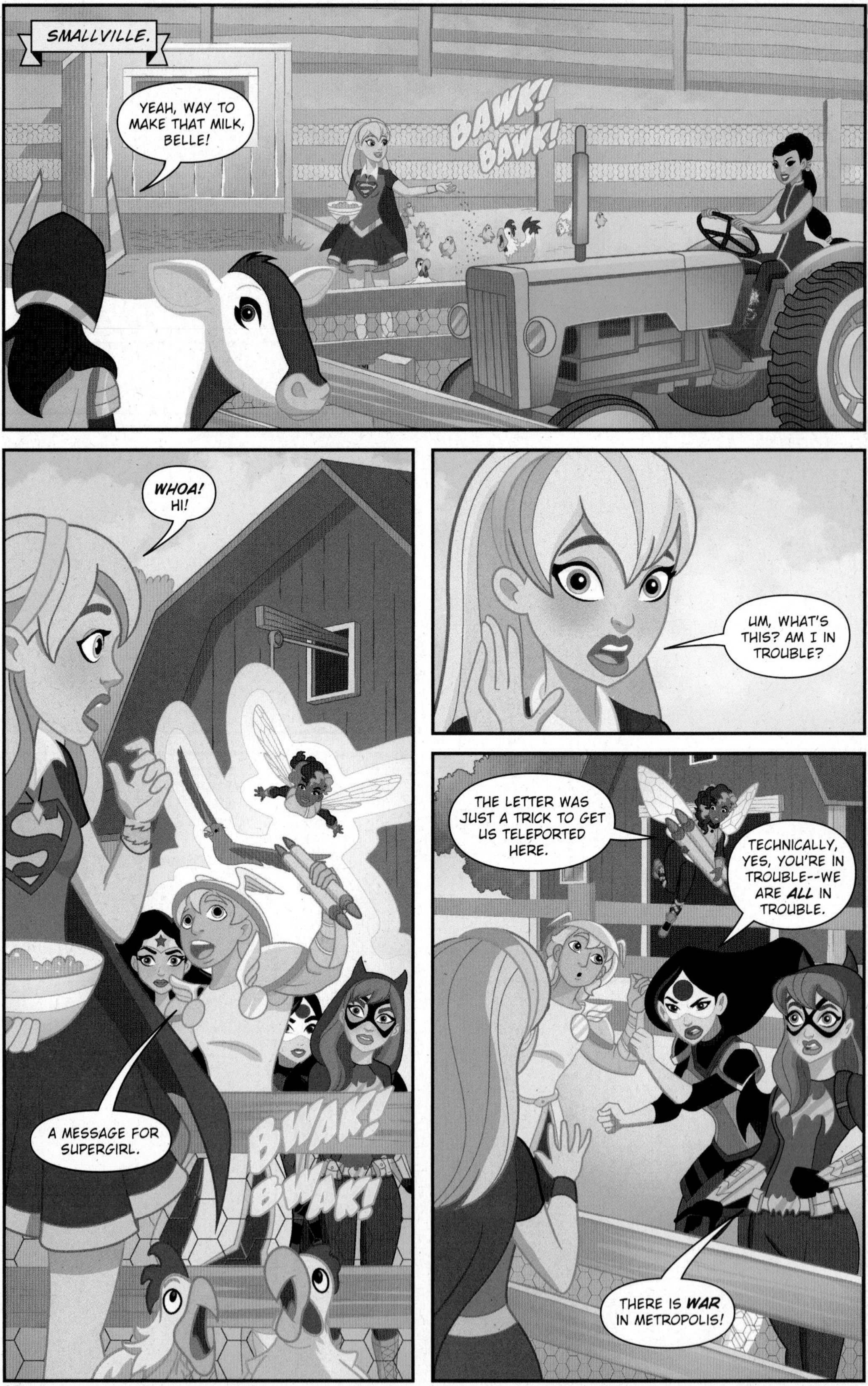

SMALLVILLE.
YEAH, WAY TO MAKE THAT MILK, BELLE!
BAWK! BAWK!
WHOA! HI!
A MESSAGE FOR SUPERGIRL.
BWAK! BWAK!
UM, WHAT'S THIS? AM I IN TROUBLE?
THE LETTER WAS JUST A TRICK TO GET US TELEPORTED HERE.
TECHNICALLY, YES, YOU'RE IN TROUBLE--WE ARE ALL IN TROUBLE.
THERE IS WAR IN METROPOLIS!

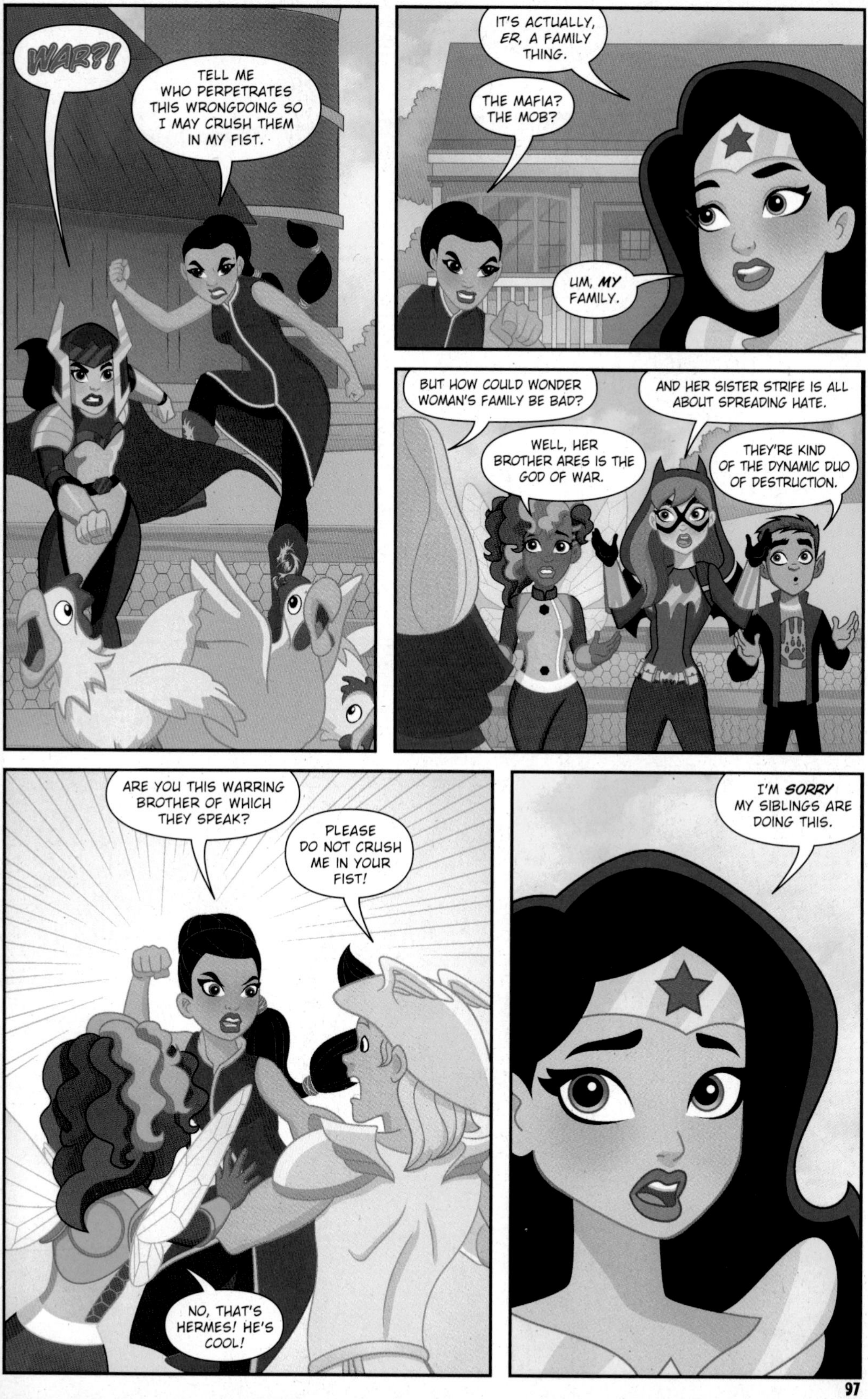
WAR?!
TELL ME WHO PERPETRATES THIS WRONGDOING SO I MAY CRUSH THEM IN MY FIST.
IT'S ACTUALLY, ER, A FAMILY THING.
THE MAFIA? THE MOB?
UM, MY FAMILY.
BUT HOW COULD WONDER WOMAN'S FAMILY BE BAD?
WELL, HER BROTHER ARES IS THE GOD OF WAR.
AND HER SISTER STRIFE IS ALL ABOUT SPREADING HATE.
THEY'RE KIND OF THE DYNAMIC DUO OF DESTRUCTION.
ARE YOU THIS WARRING BROTHER OF WHICH THEY SPEAK?
PLEASE DO NOT CRUSH ME IN YOUR FIST!
NO, THAT'S HERMES! HE'S COOL!
I'M SORRY MY SIBLINGS ARE DOING THIS.

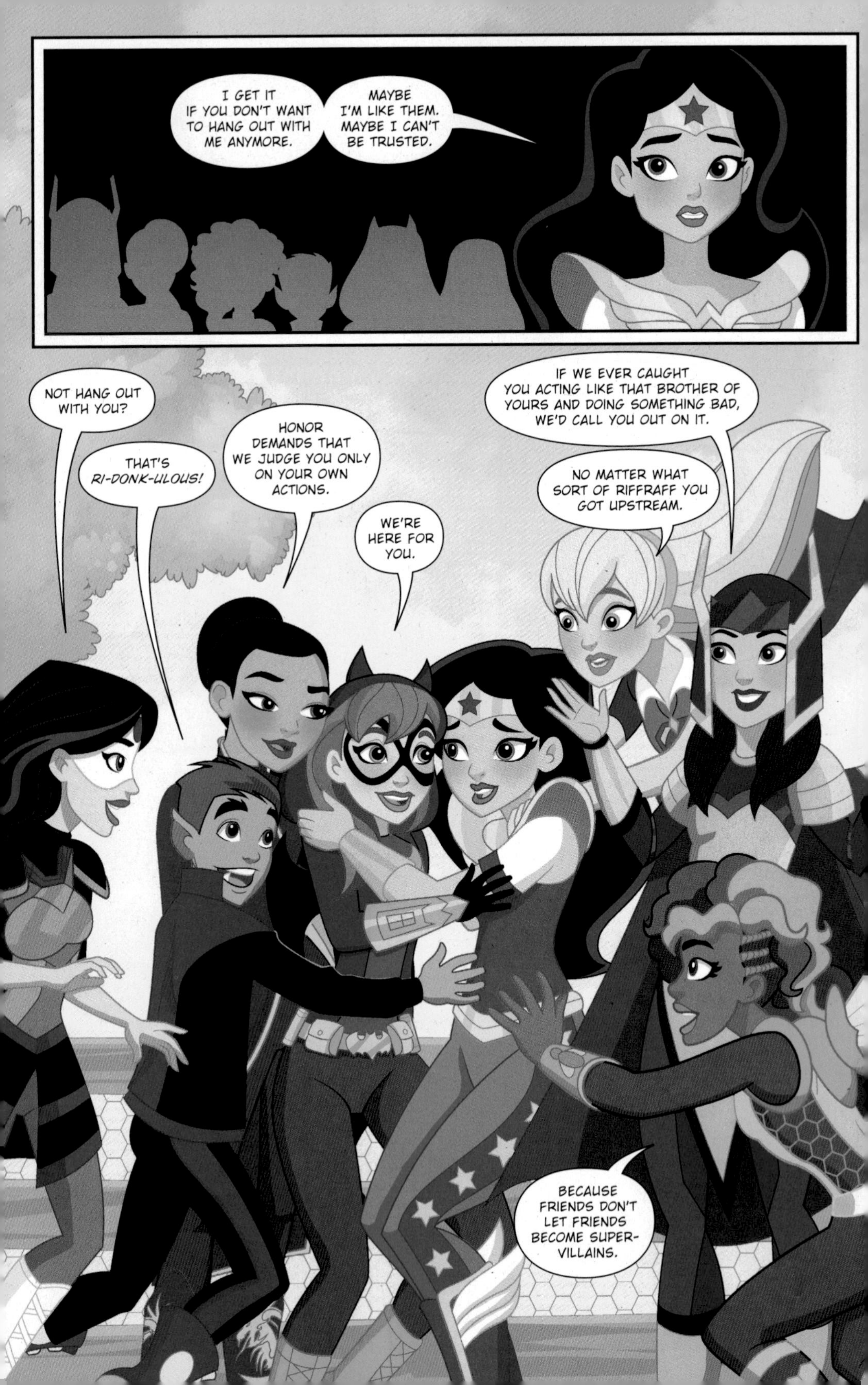
I GET IT IF YOU DON'T WANT TO HANG OUT WITH ME ANYMORE.
MAYBE I'M LIKE THEM. MAYBE I CAN'T BE TRUSTED.
NOT HANG OUT WITH YOU?
THAT'S *RI-DONK-ULOUS!*
HONOR DEMANDS THAT WE JUDGE YOU ONLY ON YOUR OWN ACTIONS.
WE'RE HERE FOR YOU.
IF WE EVER CAUGHT YOU ACTING LIKE THAT BROTHER OF YOURS AND DOING SOMETHING BAD, WE'D CALL YOU OUT ON IT.
NO MATTER WHAT SORT OF RIFFRAFF YOU GOT UPSTREAM.
BECAUSE FRIENDS DON'T LET FRIENDS BECOME SUPER-VILLAINS.

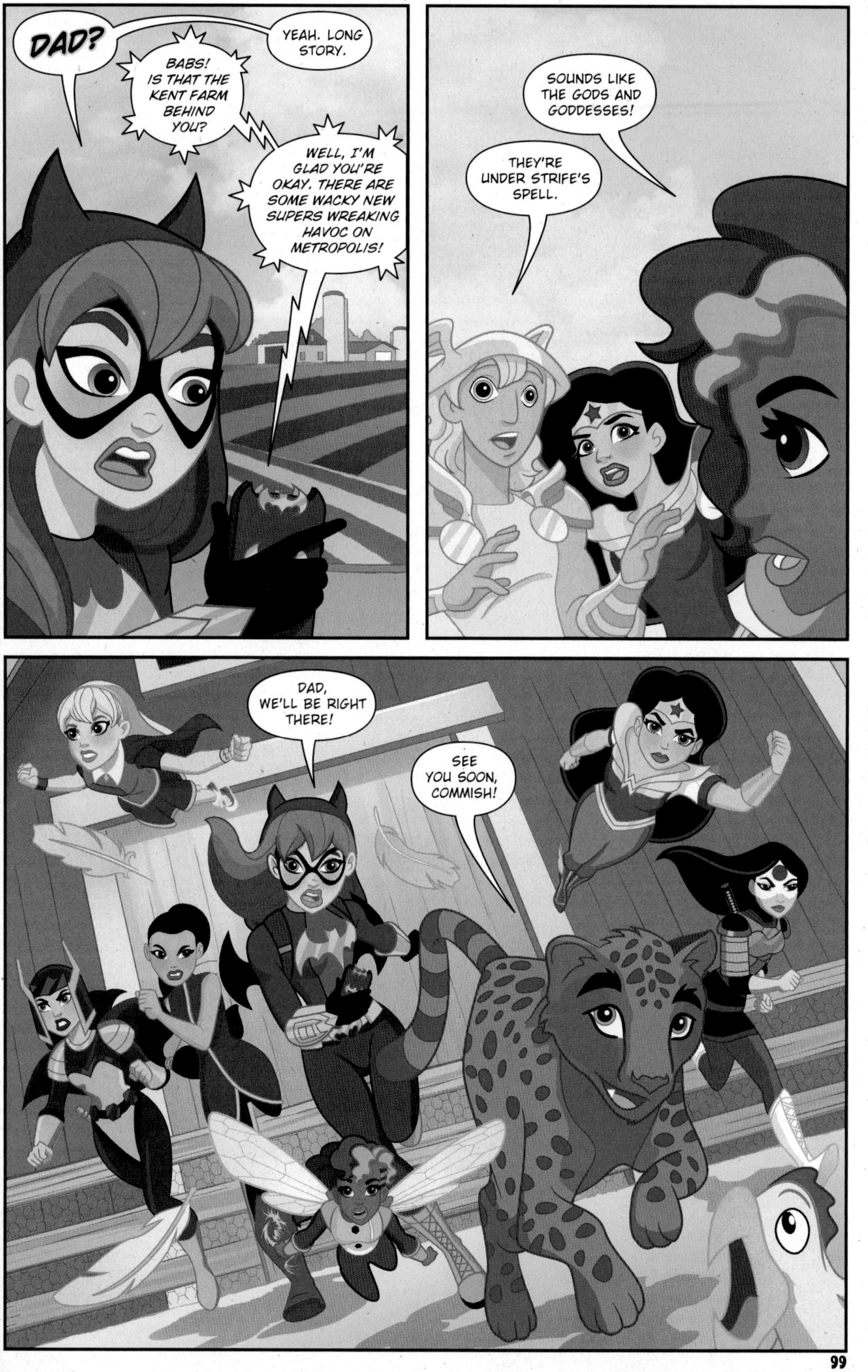
DAD?
YEAH. LONG STORY.
BABS! IS THAT THE KENT FARM BEHIND YOU?
WELL, I'M GLAD YOU'RE OKAY. THERE ARE SOME WACKY NEW SUPERS WREAKING HAVOC ON METROPOLIS!
SOUNDS LIKE THE GODS AND GODDESSES!
THEY'RE UNDER STRIFE'S SPELL.
DAD, WE'LL BE RIGHT THERE!
SEE YOU SOON, COMMISH!

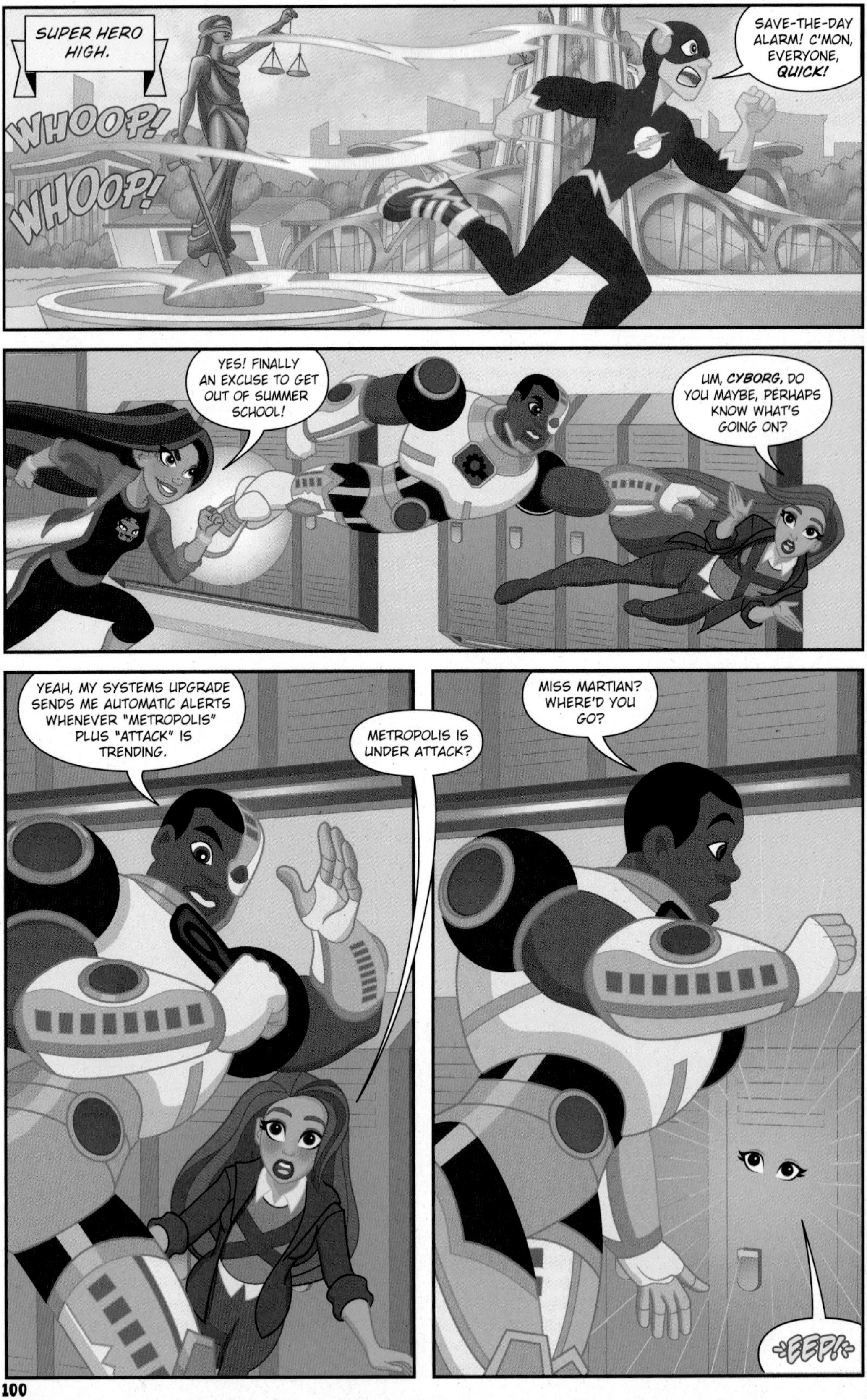
SUPER HERO HIGH.
WHOOP!
WHOOP!
SAVE-THE-DAY ALARM! C'MON, EVERYONE, QUICK!
YES! FINALLY AN EXCUSE TO GET OUT OF SUMMER SCHOOL!
UM, CYBORG, DO YOU MAYBE, PERHAPS KNOW WHAT'S GOING ON?
YEAH, MY SYSTEMS UPGRADE SENDS ME AUTOMATIC ALERTS WHENEVER "METROPOLIS" PLUS "ATTACK" IS TRENDING.
METROPOLIS IS UNDER ATTACK?
MISS MARTIAN? WHERE'D YOU GO?
EEP!

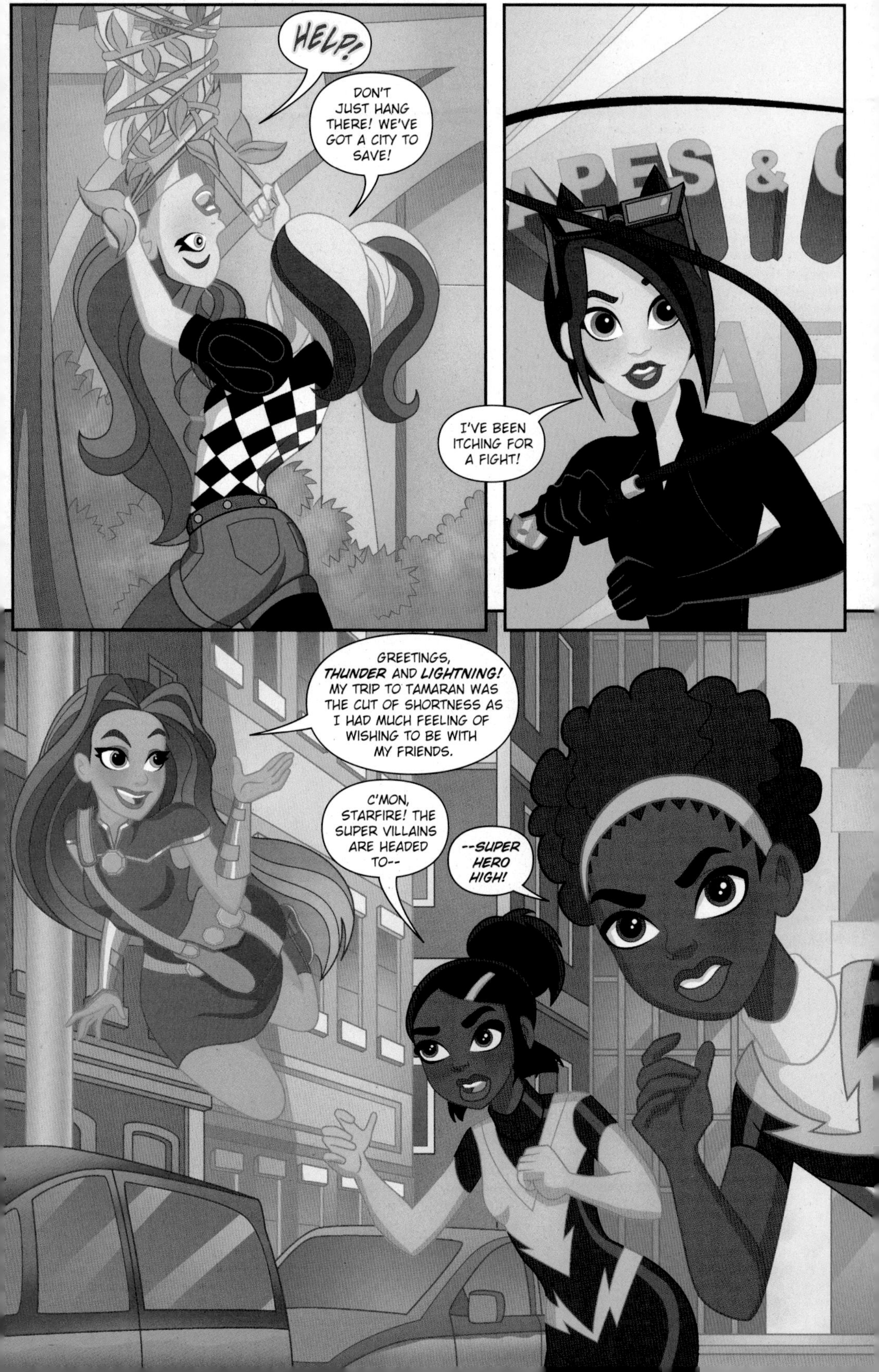
HELP?!
DON'T JUST HANG THERE! WE'VE GOT A CITY TO SAVE!
I'VE BEEN ITCHING FOR A FIGHT!
GREETINGS, THUNDER AND LIGHTNING! MY TRIP TO TAMARAN WAS THE CUT OF SHORTNESS AS I HAD MUCH FEELING OF WISHING TO BE WITH MY FRIENDS.
C'MON, STARFIRE! THE SUPER VILLAINS ARE HEADED TO--
--SUPER HERO HIGH!

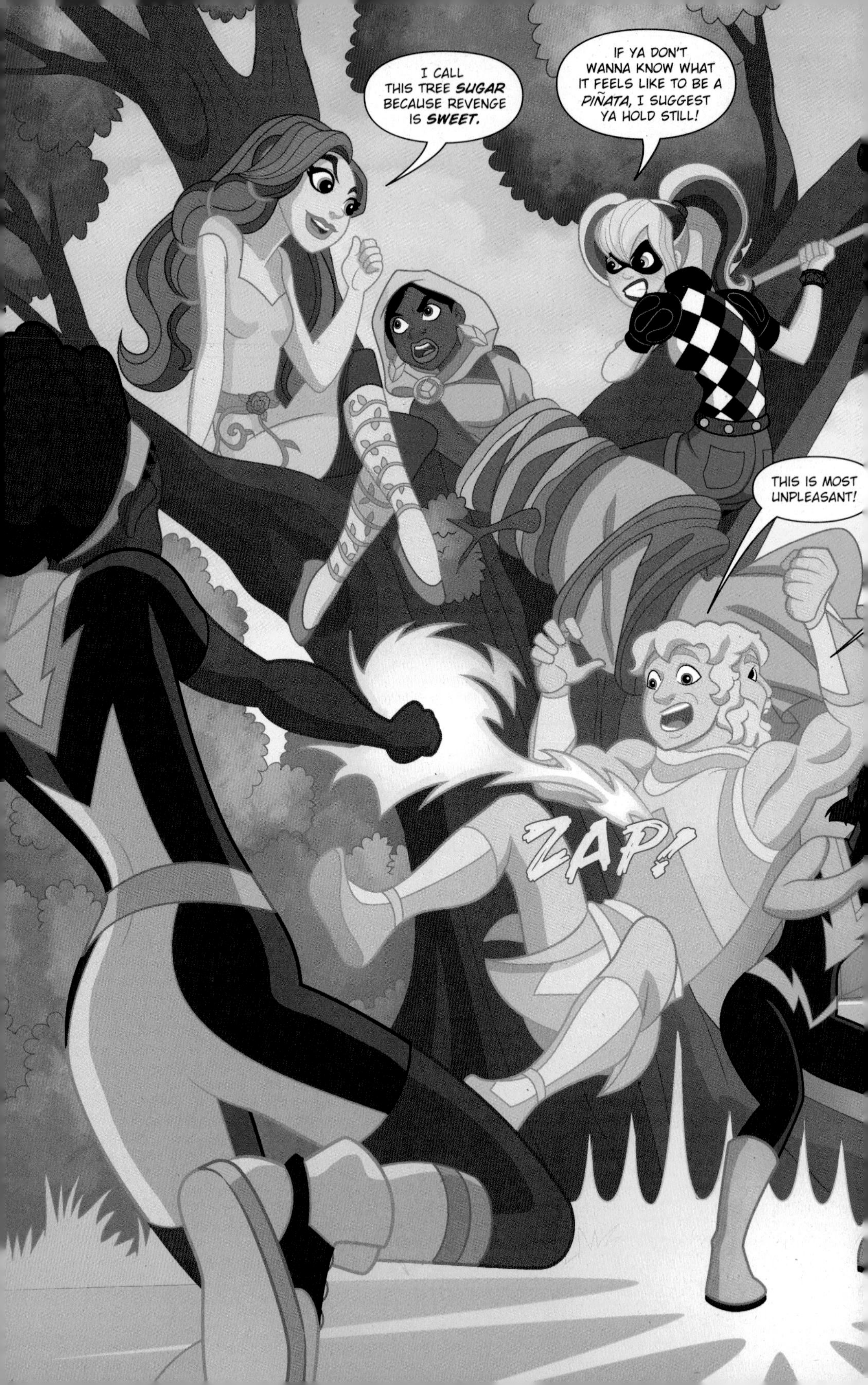
I CALL THIS TREE **SUGAR** BECAUSE REVENGE IS **SWEET.**
IF YA DON'T WANNA KNOW WHAT IT FEELS LIKE TO BE A *PIÑATA*, I SUGGEST YA HOLD STILL!
THIS IS MOST UNPLEASANT!
ZAP!

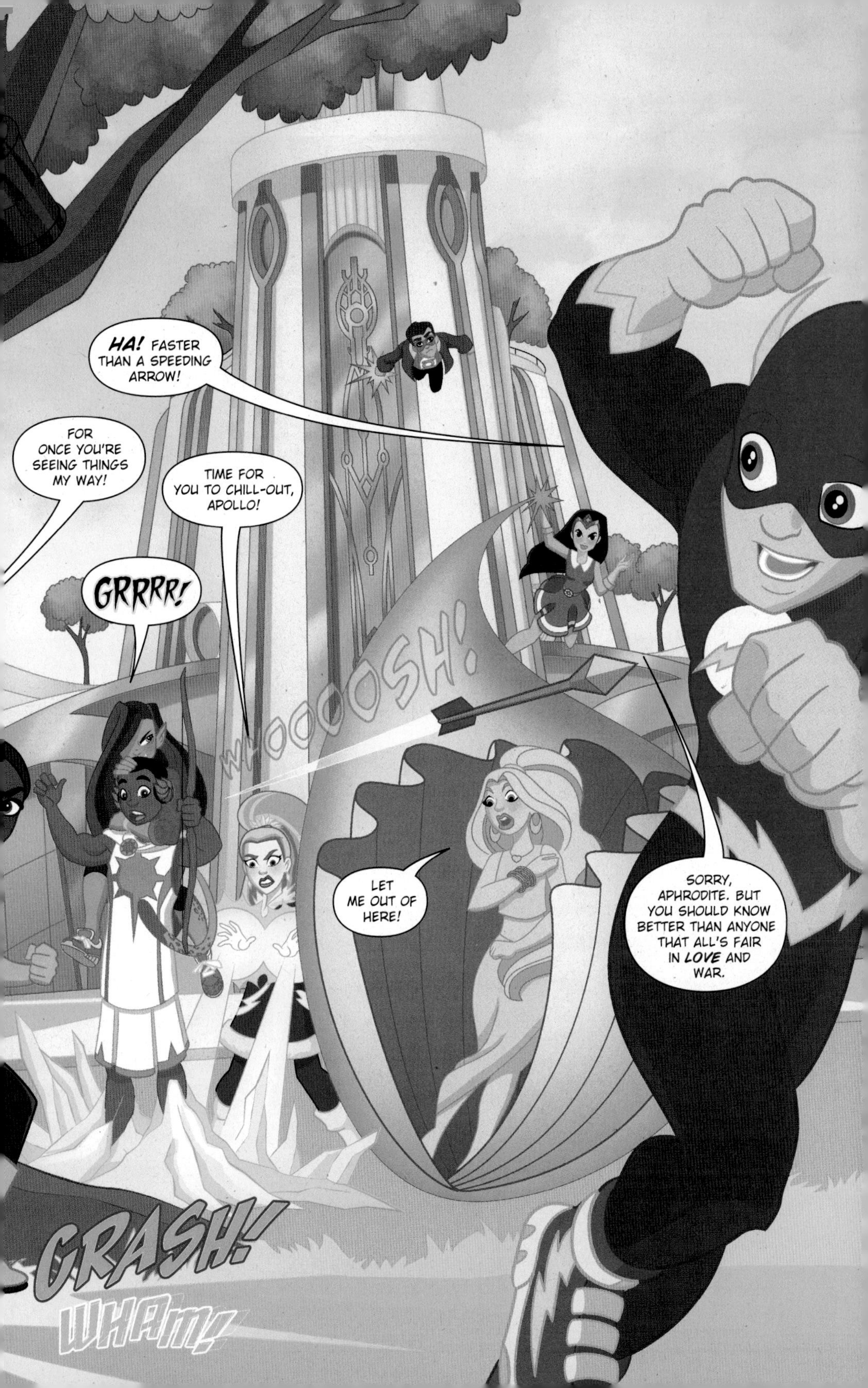

HA! FASTER THAN A SPEEDING ARROW!
FOR ONCE YOU'RE SEEING THINGS MY WAY!
TIME FOR YOU TO CHILL-OUT, APOLLO!
GRRRR!
WHOOOOOSH!
LET ME OUT OF HERE!
SORRY, APHRODITE. BUT YOU SHOULD KNOW BETTER THAN ANYONE THAT ALL'S FAIR IN LOVE AND WAR.
CRASH!
WHAM!

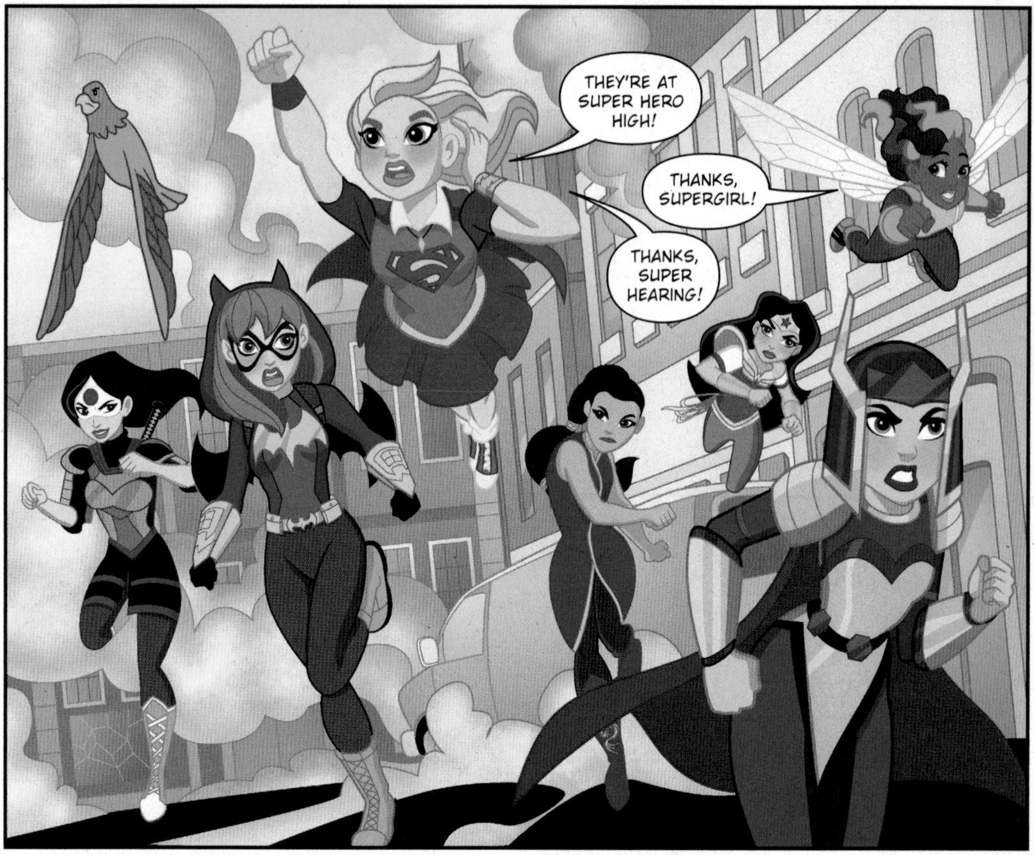
THEY'RE AT SUPER HERO HIGH!
THANKS, SUPERGIRL!
THANKS, SUPER HEARING!

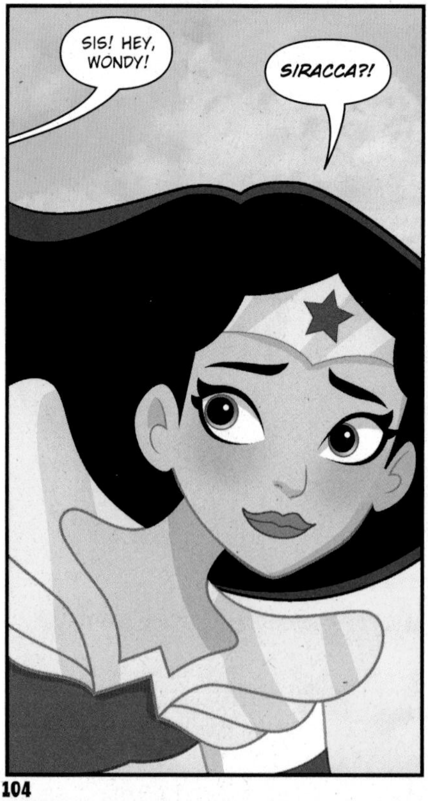
SIS! HEY, WONDY!
SIRACCA?!

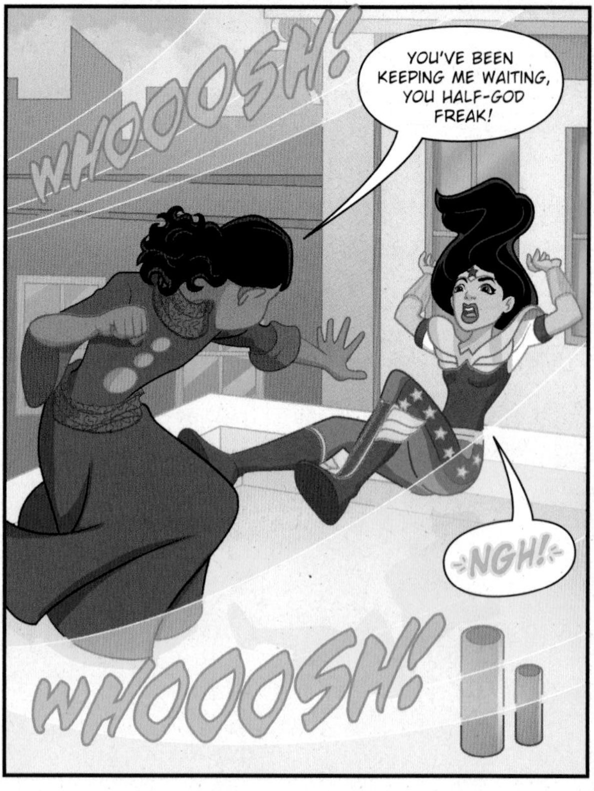
WHOOOSH!
YOU'VE BEEN KEEPING ME WAITING, YOU HALF-GOD FREAK!
NGH!
WHOOOSH!

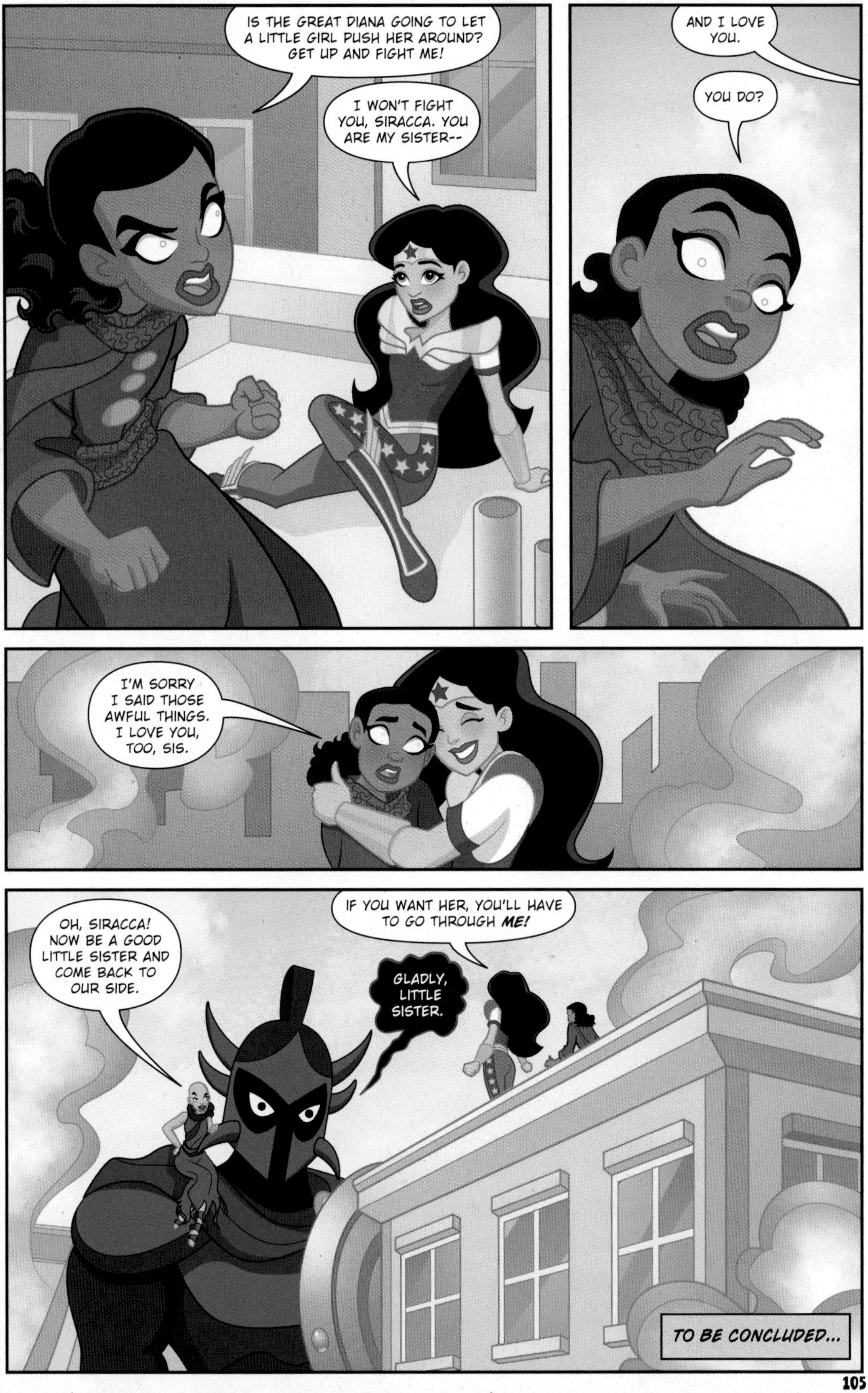
IS THE GREAT DIANA GOING TO LET A LITTLE GIRL PUSH HER AROUND? GET UP AND FIGHT ME!
I WON'T FIGHT YOU, SIRACCA. YOU ARE MY SISTER--
AND I LOVE YOU.
YOU DO?
I'M SORRY I SAID THOSE AWFUL THINGS. I LOVE YOU, TOO, SIS.
OH, SIRACCA! NOW BE A GOOD LITTLE SISTER AND COME BACK TO OUR SIDE.
GLADLY, LITTLE SISTER.
IF YOU WANT HER, YOU'LL HAVE TO GO THROUGH ME!
TO BE CONCLUDED...

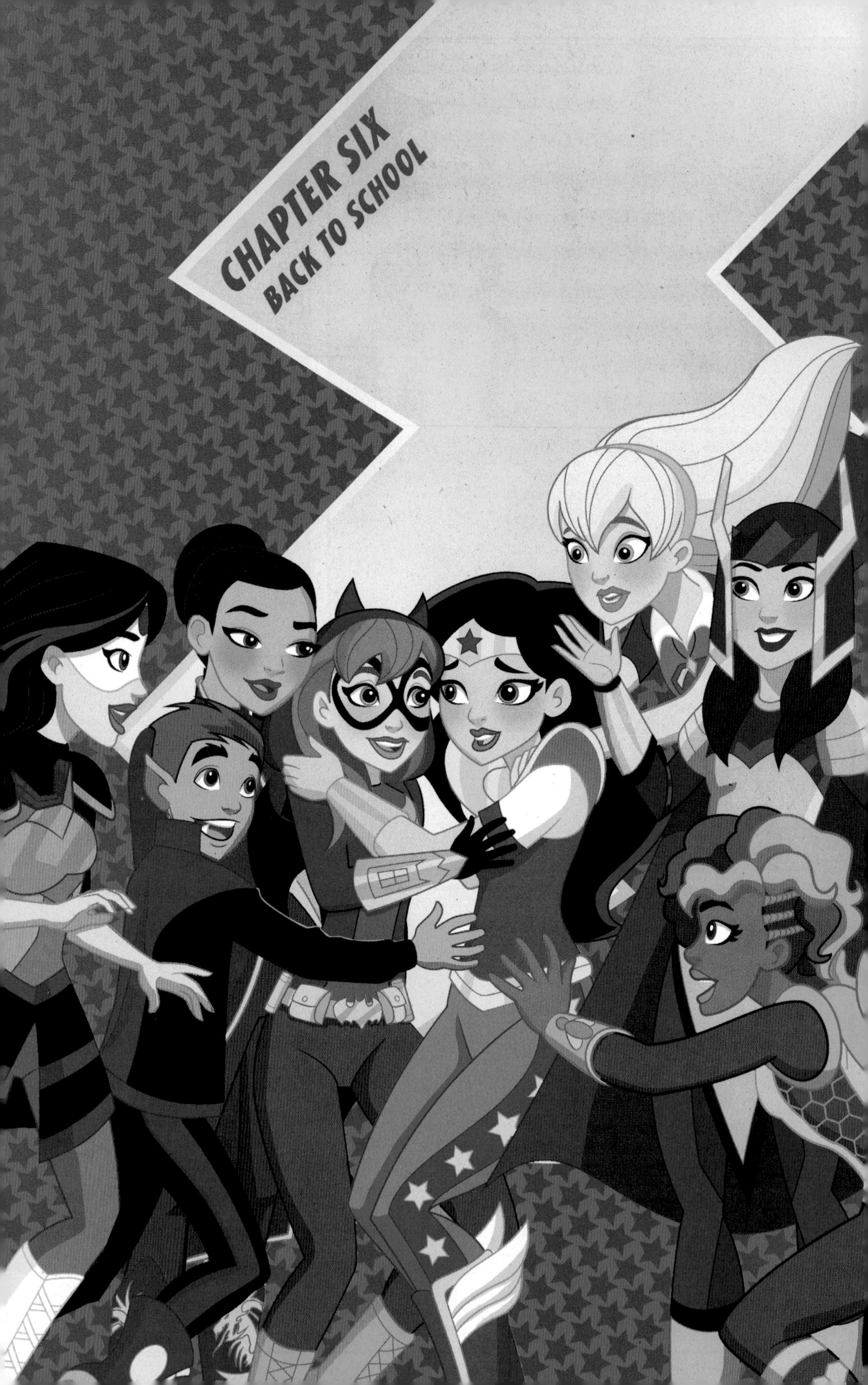
CHAPTER SIX
BACK TO SCHOOL

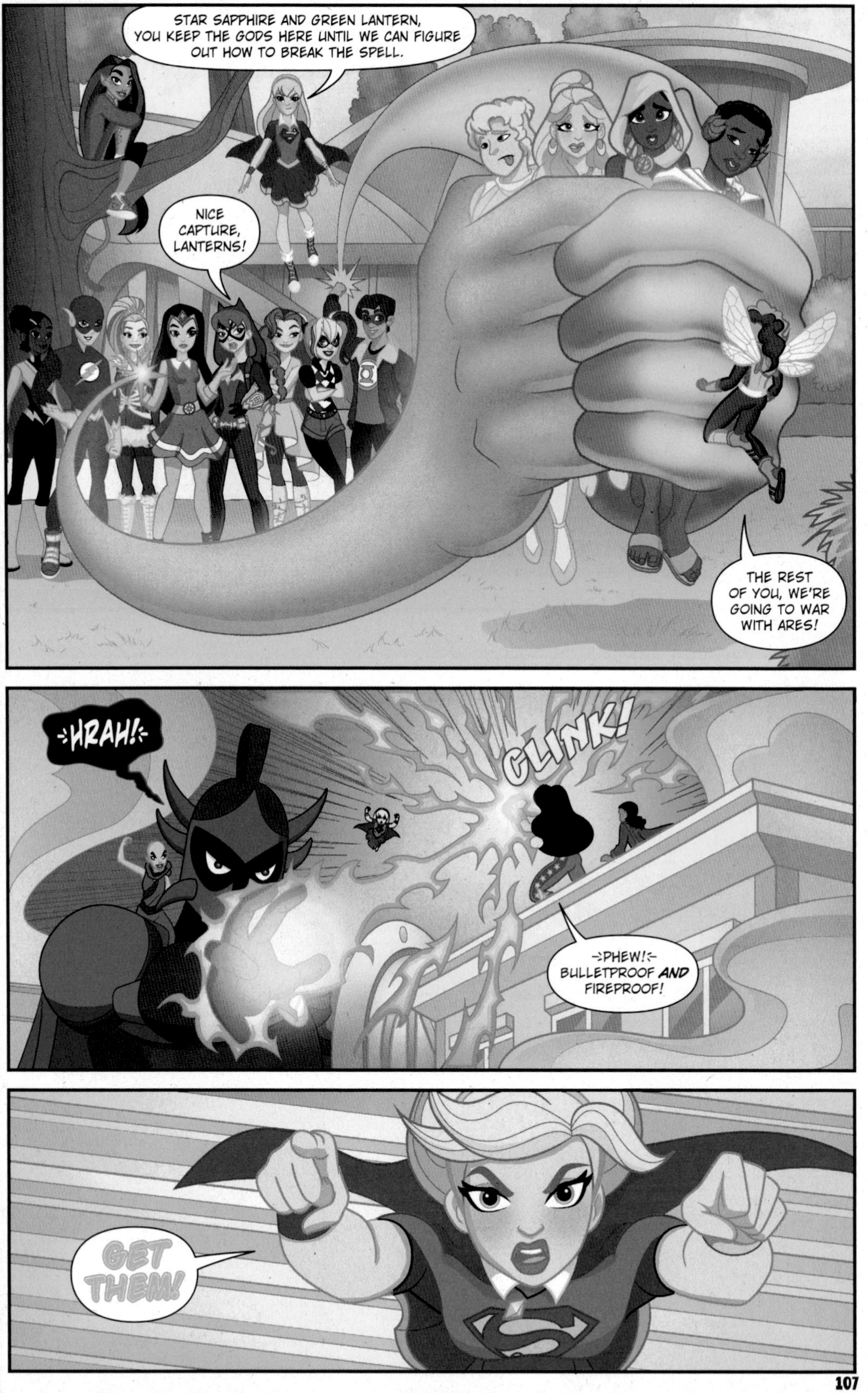
STAR SAPPHIRE AND GREEN LANTERN, YOU KEEP THE GODS HERE UNTIL WE CAN FIGURE OUT HOW TO BREAK THE SPELL.
NICE CAPTURE, LANTERNS!
THE REST OF YOU, WE'RE GOING TO WAR WITH ARES!
HRAH!
CLINK!
PHEW! BULLETPROOF AND FIREPROOF!
GET THEM!

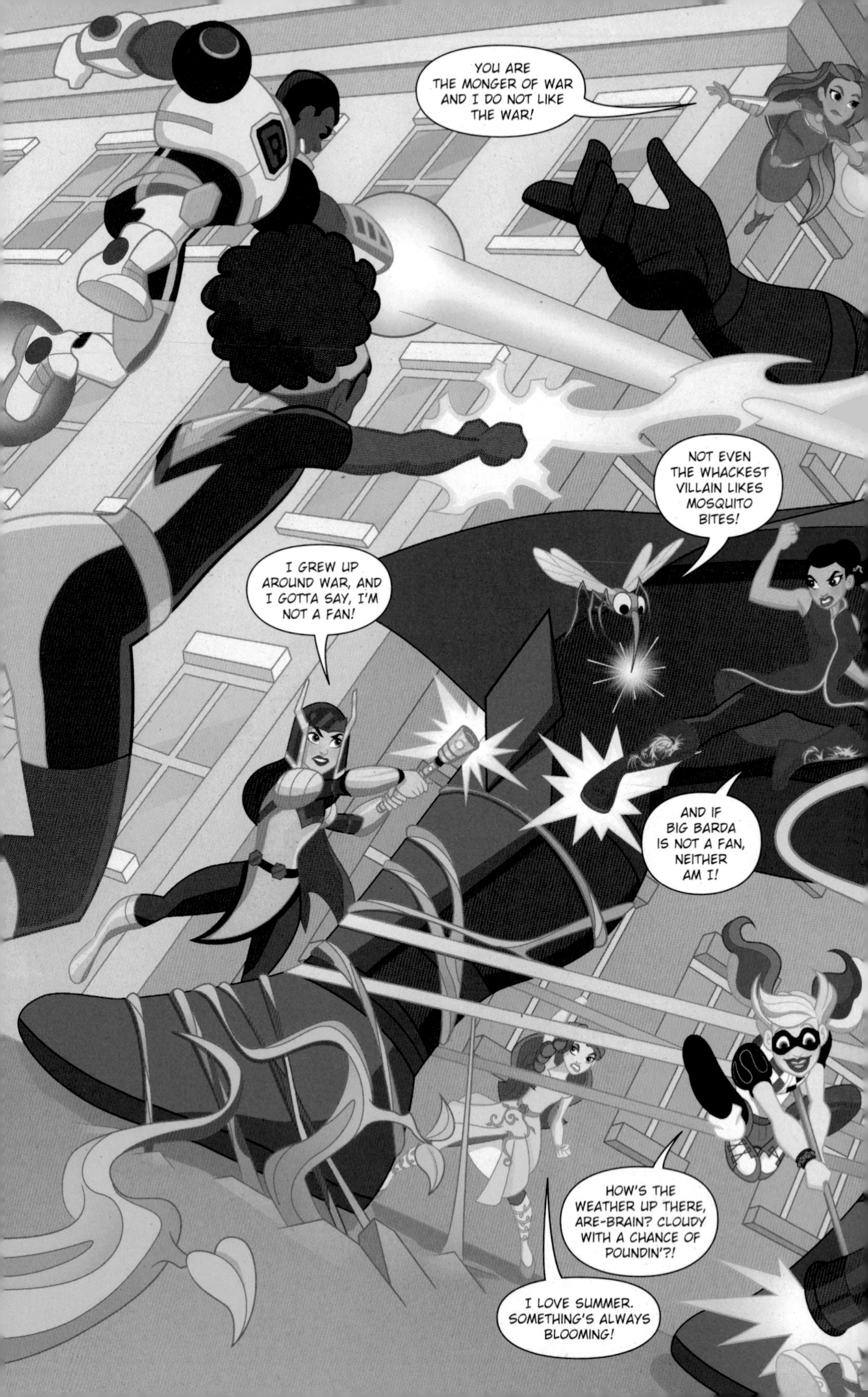
YOU ARE THE MONGER OF WAR AND I DO NOT LIKE THE WAR!
NOT EVEN THE WHACKEST VILLAIN LIKES MOSQUITO BITES!
I GREW UP AROUND WAR, AND I GOTTA SAY, I'M NOT A FAN!
AND IF BIG BARDA IS NOT A FAN, NEITHER AM I!
HOW'S THE WEATHER UP THERE, ARE-BRAIN? CLOUDY WITH A CHANCE OF POUNDIN'?!
I LOVE SUMMER. SOMETHING'S ALWAYS BLOOMING!

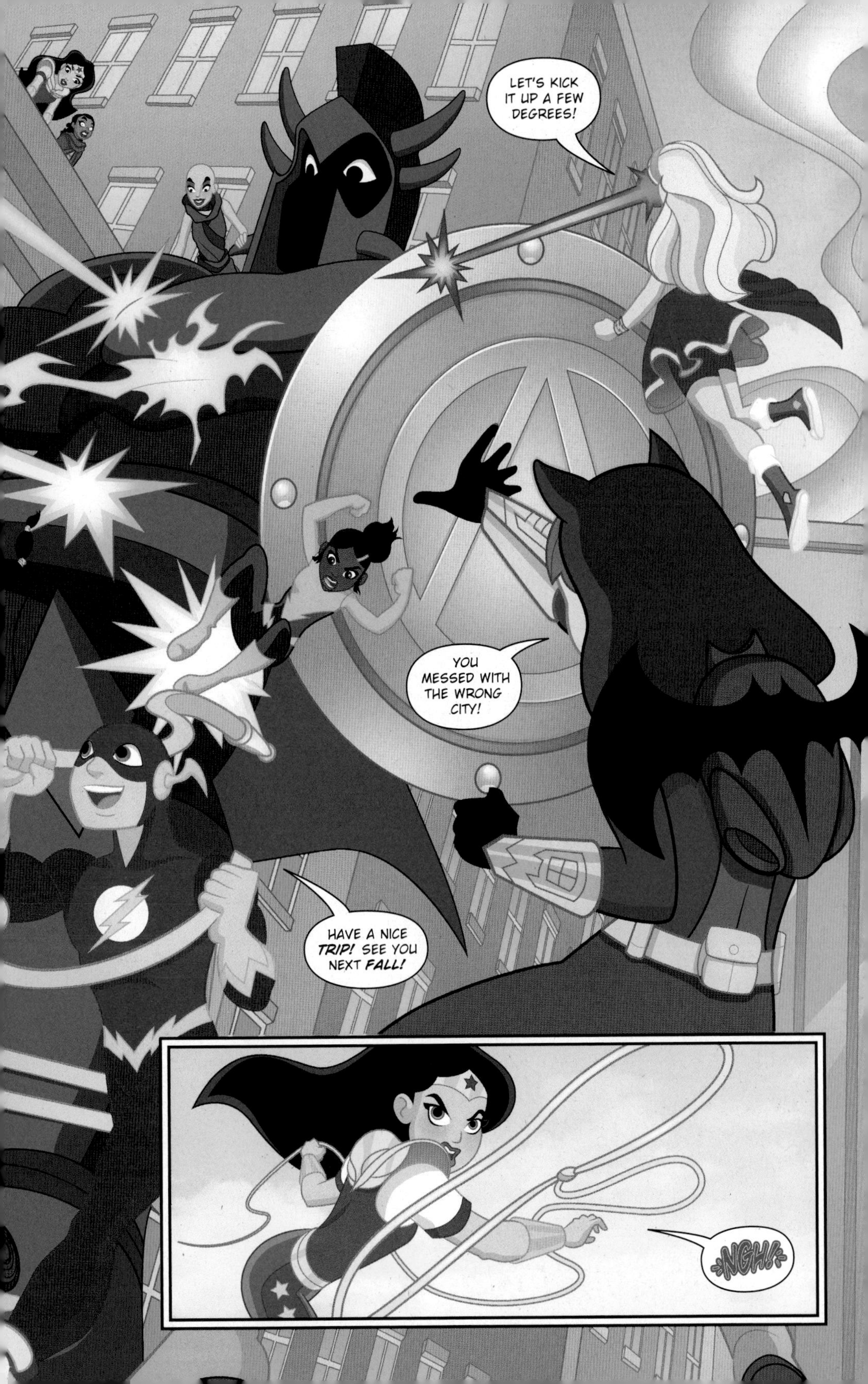
LET'S KICK IT UP A FEW DEGREES!
YOU MESSED WITH THE WRONG CITY!
HAVE A NICE TRIP! SEE YOU NEXT FALL!
NGH!

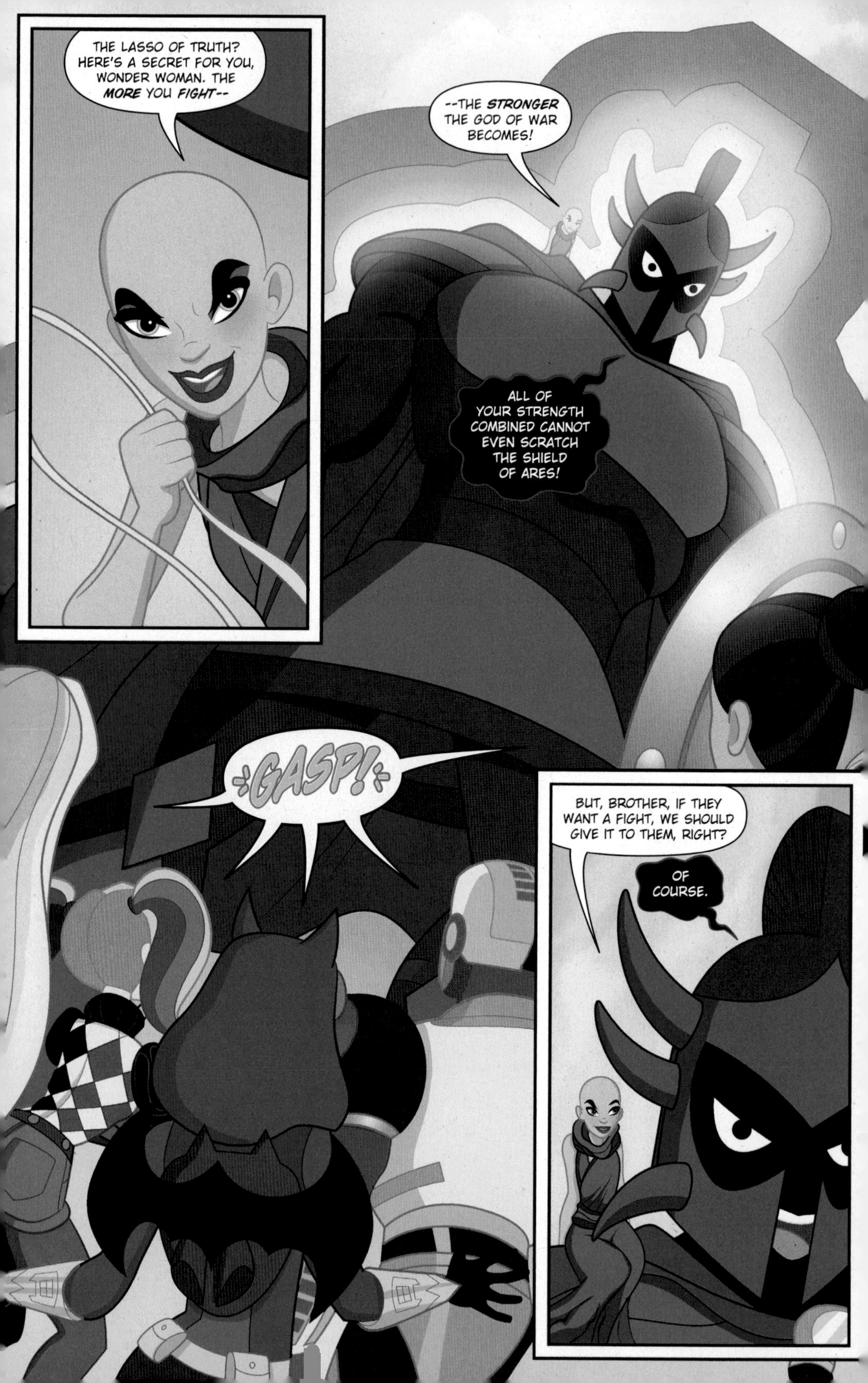
THE LASSO OF TRUTH? HERE'S A SECRET FOR YOU, WONDER WOMAN. THE MORE YOU FIGHT--
--THE STRONGER THE GOD OF WAR BECOMES!
ALL OF YOUR STRENGTH COMBINED CANNOT EVEN SCRATCH THE SHIELD OF ARES!
GASP!
BUT, BROTHER, IF THEY WANT A FIGHT, WE SHOULD GIVE IT TO THEM, RIGHT?
OF COURSE.

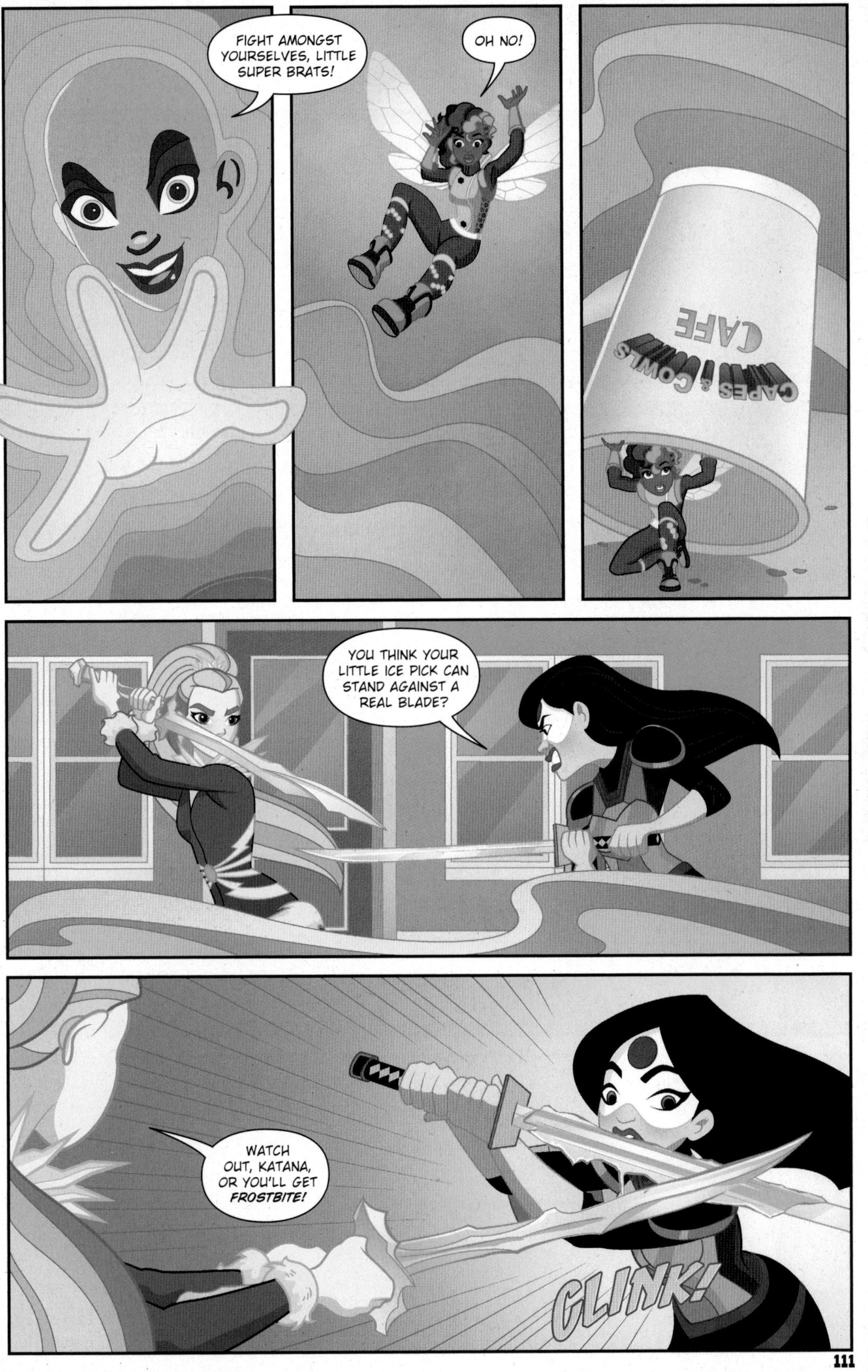
FIGHT AMONGST YOURSELVES, LITTLE SUPER BRATS!
OH NO!
CAPES & COWLS CAFE
YOU THINK YOUR LITTLE ICE PICK CAN STAND AGAINST A REAL BLADE?
WATCH OUT, KATANA, OR YOU'LL GET *FROSTBITE!*
CLINK!

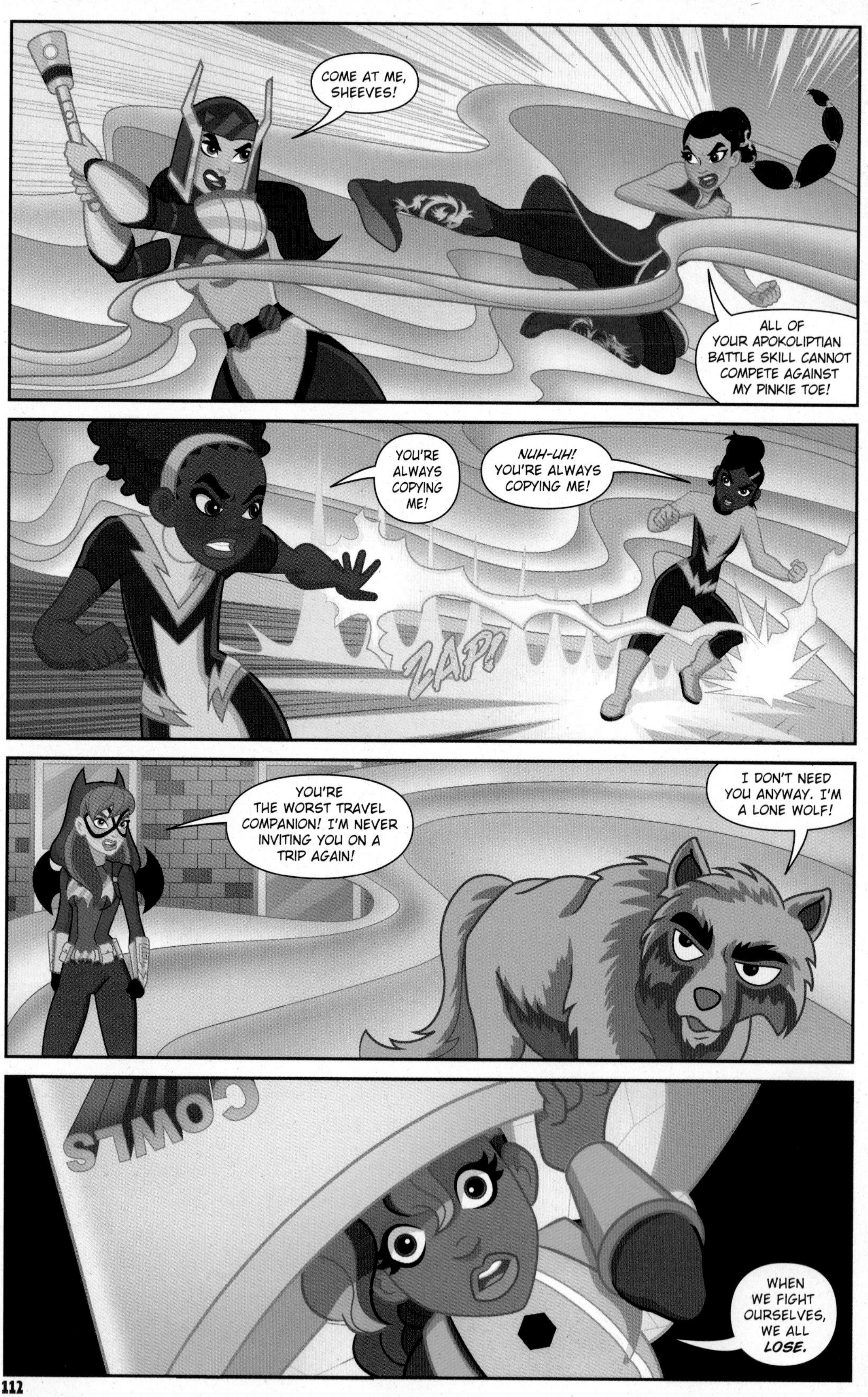
COME AT ME, SHEEVES!
ALL OF YOUR APOKOLIPTIAN BATTLE SKILL CANNOT COMPETE AGAINST MY PINKIE TOE!
YOU'RE ALWAYS COPYING ME!
NUH-UH! YOU'RE ALWAYS COPYING ME!
ZAP!
YOU'RE THE WORST TRAVEL COMPANION! I'M NEVER INVITING YOU ON A TRIP AGAIN!
I DON'T NEED YOU ANYWAY. I'M A LONE WOLF!
WHEN WE FIGHT OURSELVES, WE ALL ***LOSE.***

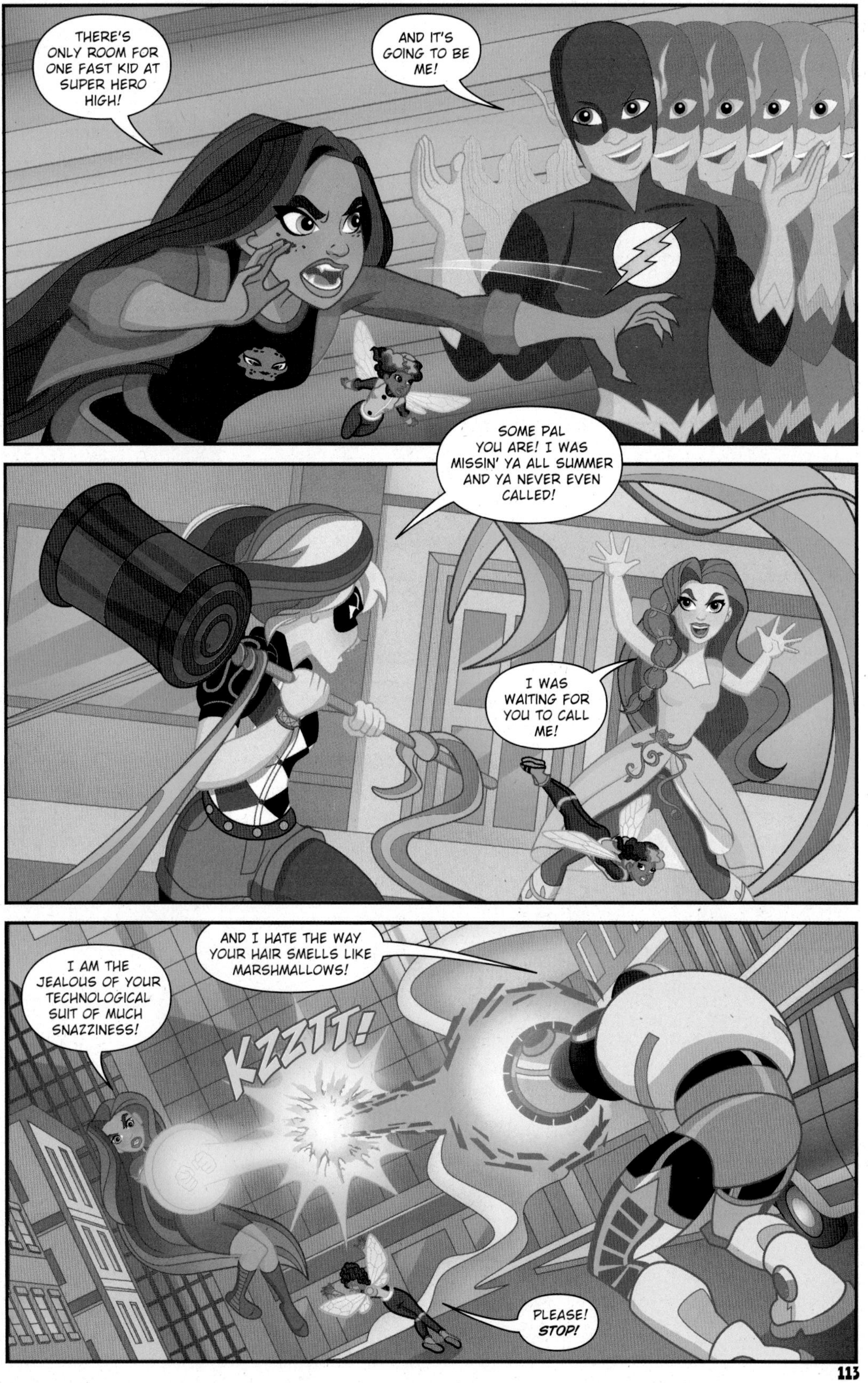

THERE'S ONLY ROOM FOR ONE FAST KID AT SUPER HERO HIGH!
AND IT'S GOING TO BE ME!
SOME PAL YOU ARE! I WAS MISSIN' YA ALL SUMMER AND YA NEVER EVEN CALLED!
I WAS WAITING FOR YOU TO CALL ME!
I AM THE JEALOUS OF YOUR TECHNOLOGICAL SUIT OF MUCH SNAZZINESS!
AND I HATE THE WAY YOUR HAIR SMELLS LIKE MARSHMALLOWS!
KZZTT!
PLEASE! *STOP!*

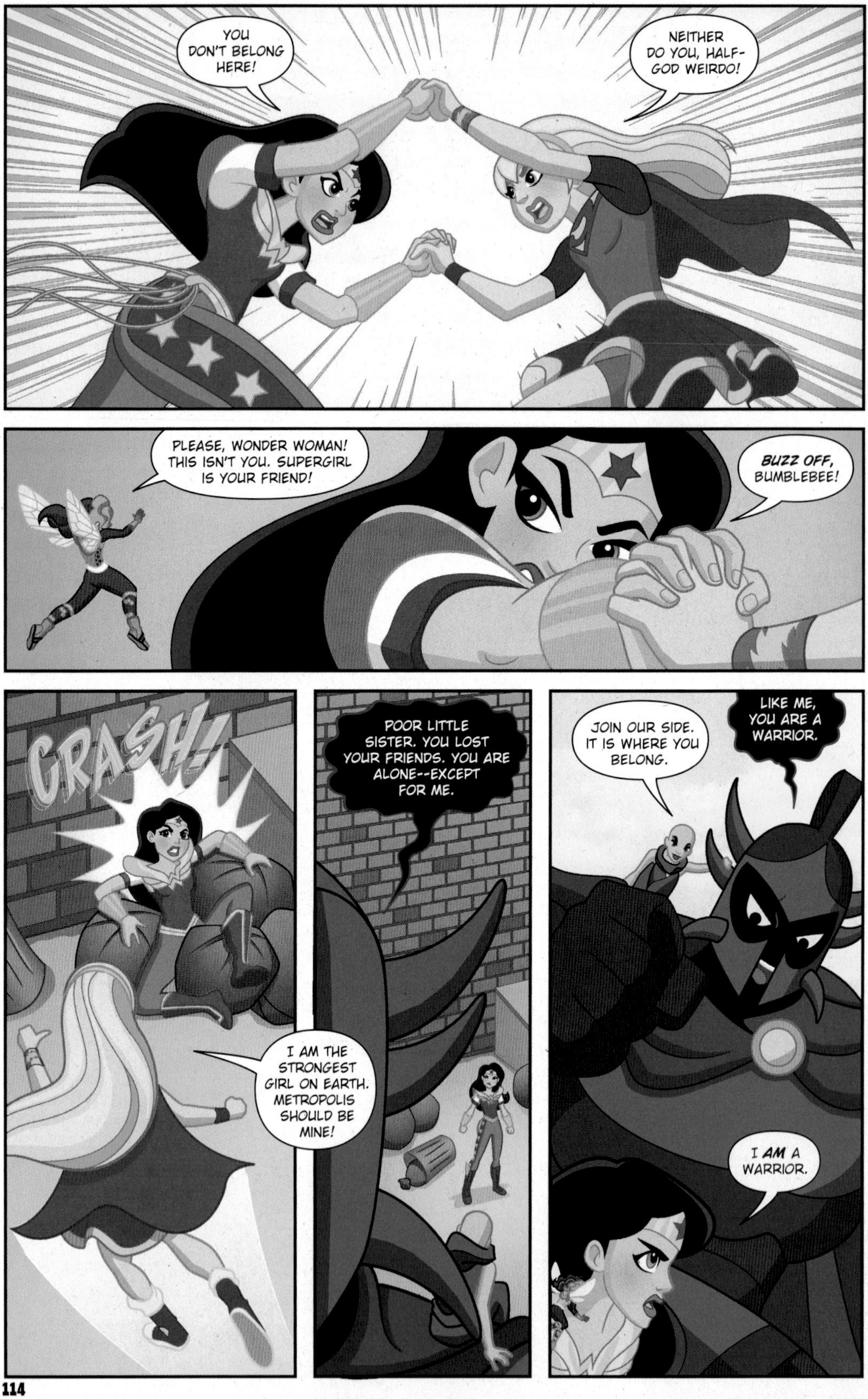
YOU DON'T BELONG HERE!
NEITHER DO YOU, HALF-GOD WEIRDO!
PLEASE, WONDER WOMAN! THIS ISN'T YOU. SUPERGIRL IS YOUR FRIEND!
BUZZ OFF, BUMBLEBEE!
CRASH!
I AM THE STRONGEST GIRL ON EARTH. METROPOLIS SHOULD BE MINE!
POOR LITTLE SISTER. YOU LOST YOUR FRIENDS. YOU ARE ALONE--EXCEPT FOR ME.
JOIN OUR SIDE. IT IS WHERE YOU BELONG.
LIKE ME, YOU ARE A WARRIOR.
I AM A WARRIOR.

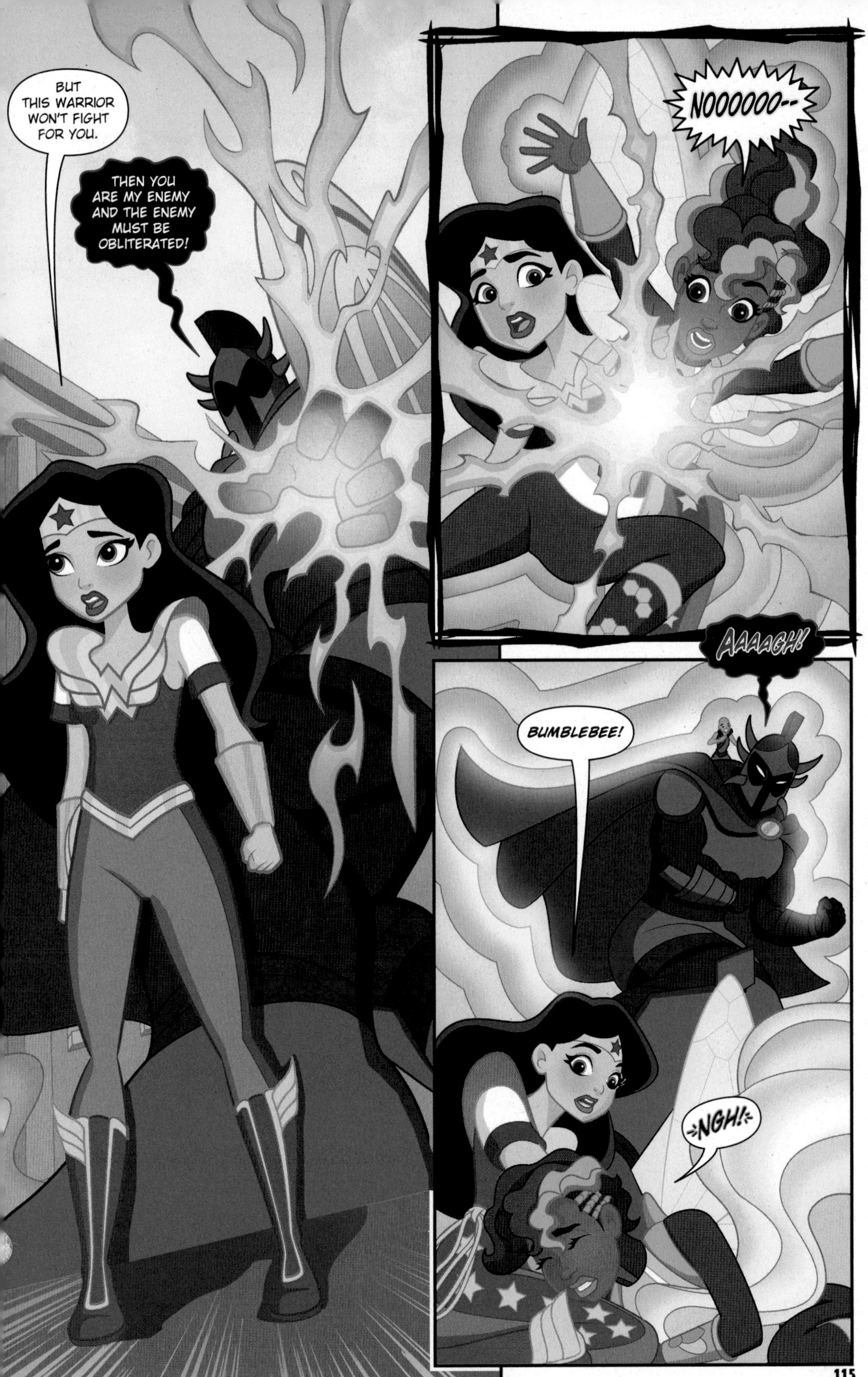

BUT THIS WARRIOR WON'T FIGHT FOR YOU.
THEN YOU ARE MY ENEMY AND THE ENEMY MUST BE OBLITERATED!
NOOOOOO--
AAAAGH!
BUMBLEBEE!
NGH!

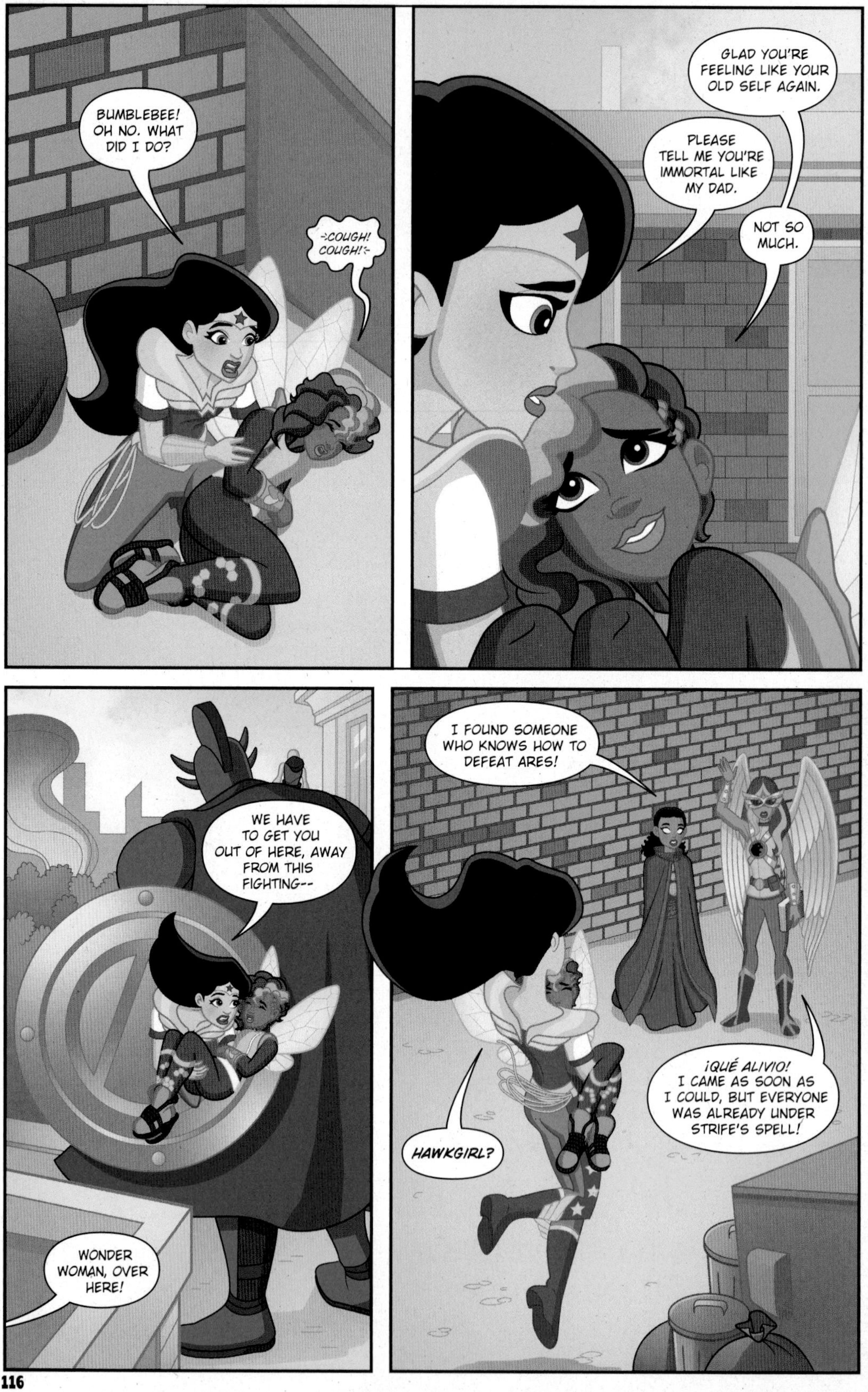
BUMBLEBEE! OH NO. WHAT DID I DO?
-COUGH! COUGH!-
GLAD YOU'RE FEELING LIKE YOUR OLD SELF AGAIN.
PLEASE TELL ME YOU'RE IMMORTAL LIKE MY DAD.
NOT SO MUCH.
WE HAVE TO GET YOU OUT OF HERE, AWAY FROM THIS FIGHTING--
WONDER WOMAN, OVER HERE!
I FOUND SOMEONE WHO KNOWS HOW TO DEFEAT ARES!
HAWKGIRL?
¡QUÉ ALIVIO! I CAME AS SOON AS I COULD, BUT EVERYONE WAS ALREADY UNDER STRIFE'S SPELL!

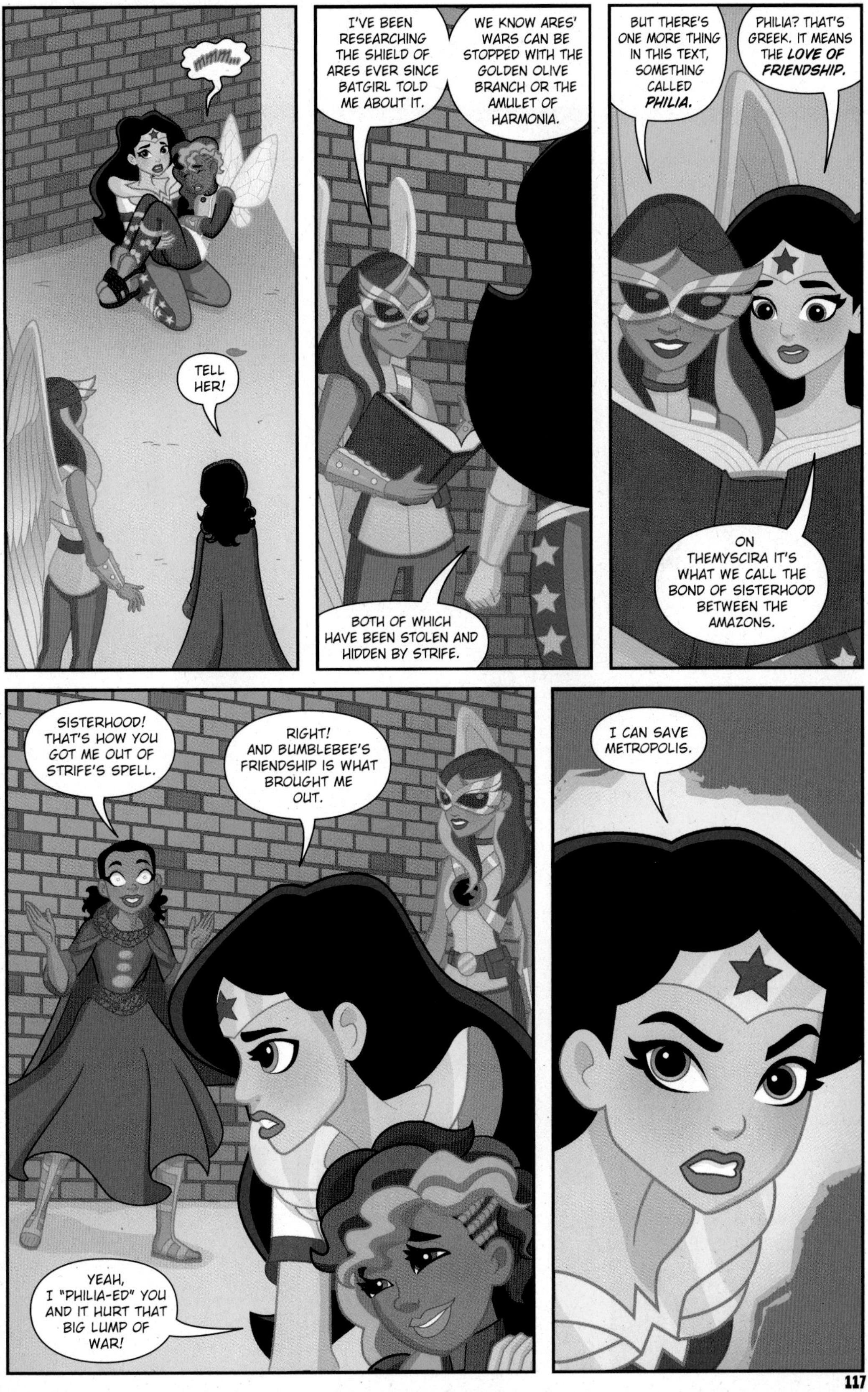
mmm...
TELL HER!
I'VE BEEN RESEARCHING THE SHIELD OF ARES EVER SINCE BATGIRL TOLD ME ABOUT IT.
WE KNOW ARES' WARS CAN BE STOPPED WITH THE GOLDEN OLIVE BRANCH OR THE AMULET OF HARMONIA.
BOTH OF WHICH HAVE BEEN STOLEN AND HIDDEN BY STRIFE.
BUT THERE'S ONE MORE THING IN THIS TEXT, SOMETHING CALLED *PHILIA.*
PHILIA? THAT'S GREEK. IT MEANS THE *LOVE OF FRIENDSHIP.*
ON THEMYSCIRA IT'S WHAT WE CALL THE BOND OF SISTERHOOD BETWEEN THE AMAZONS.
SISTERHOOD! THAT'S HOW YOU GOT ME OUT OF STRIFE'S SPELL.
RIGHT! AND BUMBLEBEE'S FRIENDSHIP IS WHAT BROUGHT ME OUT.
YEAH, I "PHILIA-ED" YOU AND IT HURT THAT BIG LUMP OF WAR!
I CAN SAVE METROPOLIS.

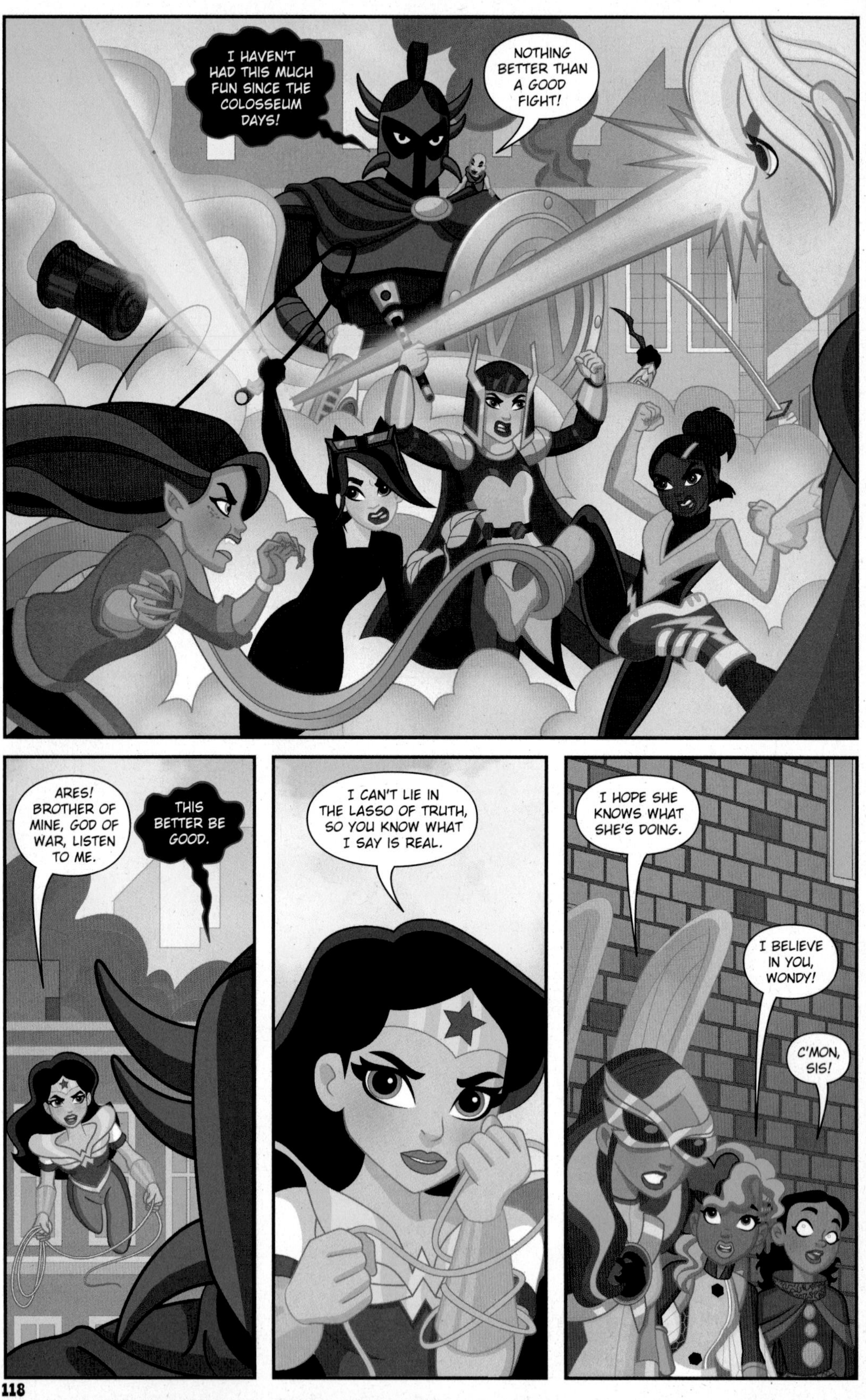
I HAVEN'T HAD THIS MUCH FUN SINCE THE COLOSSEUM DAYS!
NOTHING BETTER THAN A GOOD FIGHT!
ARES! BROTHER OF MINE, GOD OF WAR, LISTEN TO ME.
THIS BETTER BE GOOD.
I CAN'T LIE IN THE LASSO OF TRUTH, SO YOU KNOW WHAT I SAY IS REAL.
I HOPE SHE KNOWS WHAT SHE'S DOING.
I BELIEVE IN YOU, WONDY!
C'MON, SIS!

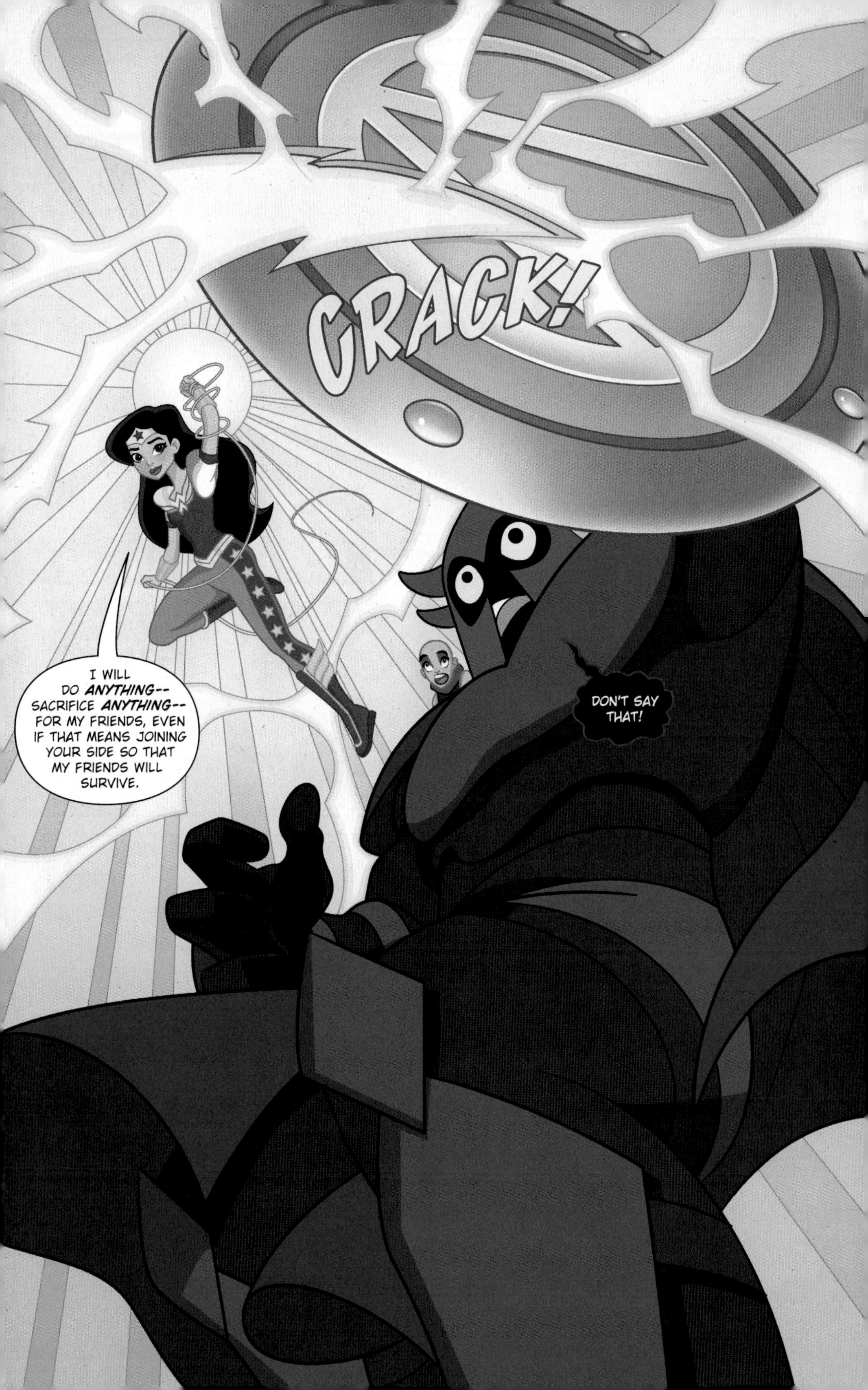
CRACK!
I WILL DO **ANYTHING**-- SACRIFICE **ANYTHING**-- FOR MY FRIENDS, EVEN IF THAT MEANS JOINING YOUR SIDE SO THAT MY FRIENDS WILL SURVIVE.
DON'T SAY THAT!

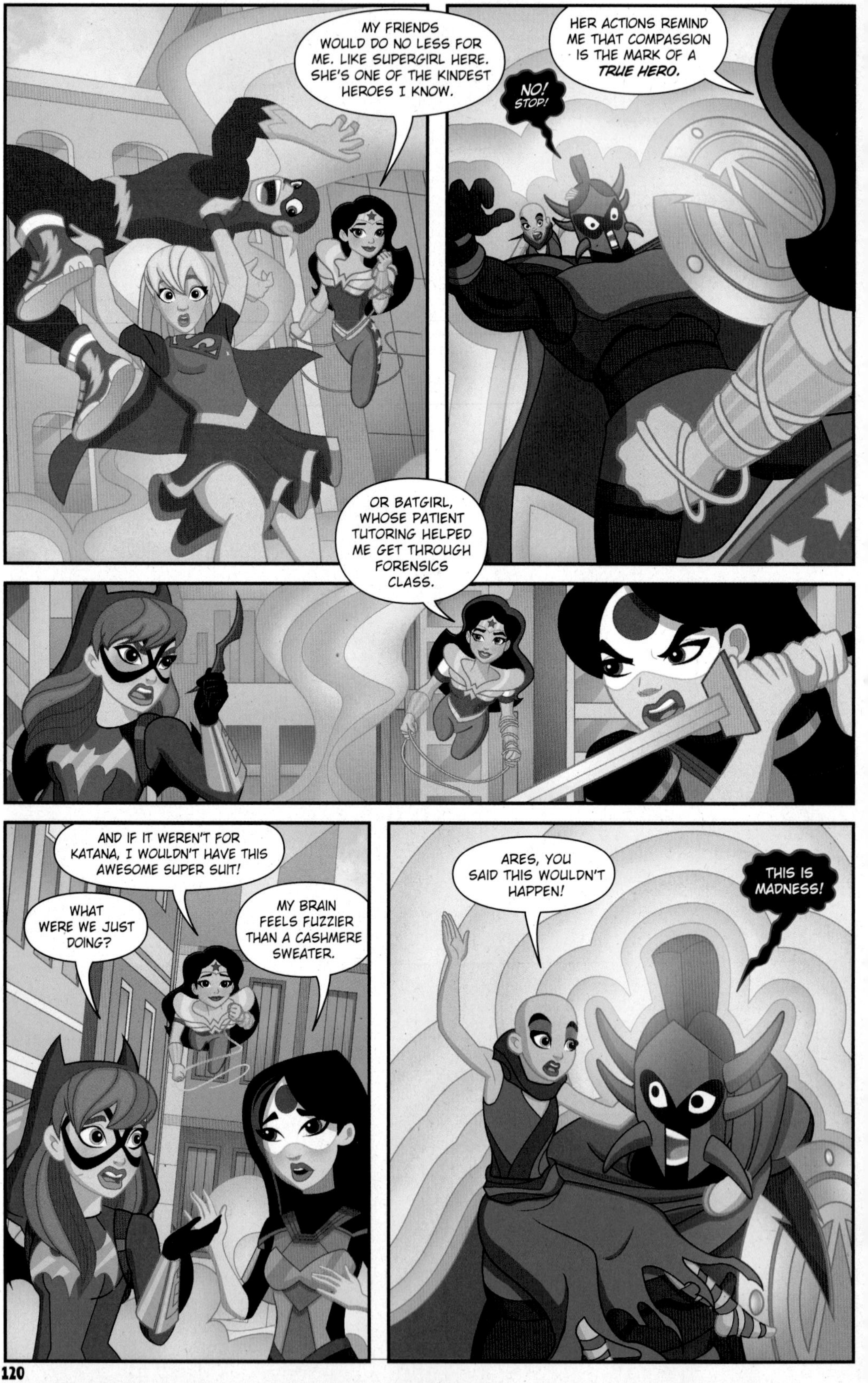
MY FRIENDS WOULD DO NO LESS FOR ME. LIKE SUPERGIRL HERE. SHE'S ONE OF THE KINDEST HEROES I KNOW.
HER ACTIONS REMIND ME THAT COMPASSION IS THE MARK OF A TRUE HERO.
NO! STOP!
OR BATGIRL, WHOSE PATIENT TUTORING HELPED ME GET THROUGH FORENSICS CLASS.
AND IF IT WEREN'T FOR KATANA, I WOULDN'T HAVE THIS AWESOME SUPER SUIT!
WHAT WERE WE JUST DOING?
MY BRAIN FEELS FUZZIER THAN A CASHMERE SWEATER.
ARES, YOU SAID THIS WOULDN'T HAPPEN!
THIS IS MADNESS!

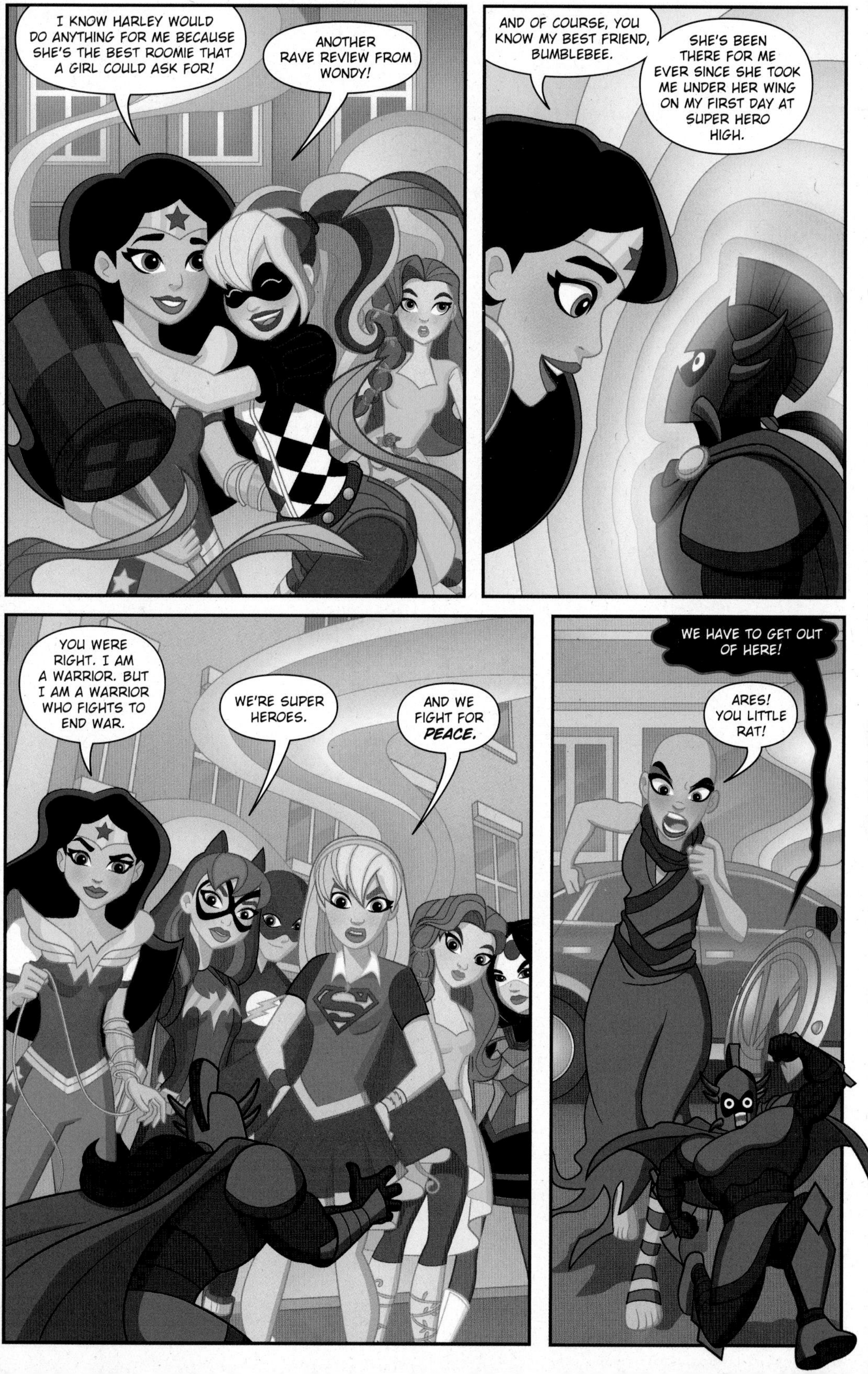

I KNOW HARLEY WOULD DO ANYTHING FOR ME BECAUSE SHE'S THE BEST ROOMIE THAT A GIRL COULD ASK FOR!
ANOTHER RAVE REVIEW FROM WONDY!
AND OF COURSE, YOU KNOW MY BEST FRIEND, BUMBLEBEE.
SHE'S BEEN THERE FOR ME EVER SINCE SHE TOOK ME UNDER HER WING ON MY FIRST DAY AT SUPER HERO HIGH.
YOU WERE RIGHT. I AM A WARRIOR. BUT I AM A WARRIOR WHO FIGHTS TO END WAR.
WE'RE SUPER HEROES.
AND WE FIGHT FOR *PEACE.*
WE HAVE TO GET OUT OF HERE!
ARES! YOU LITTLE RAT!

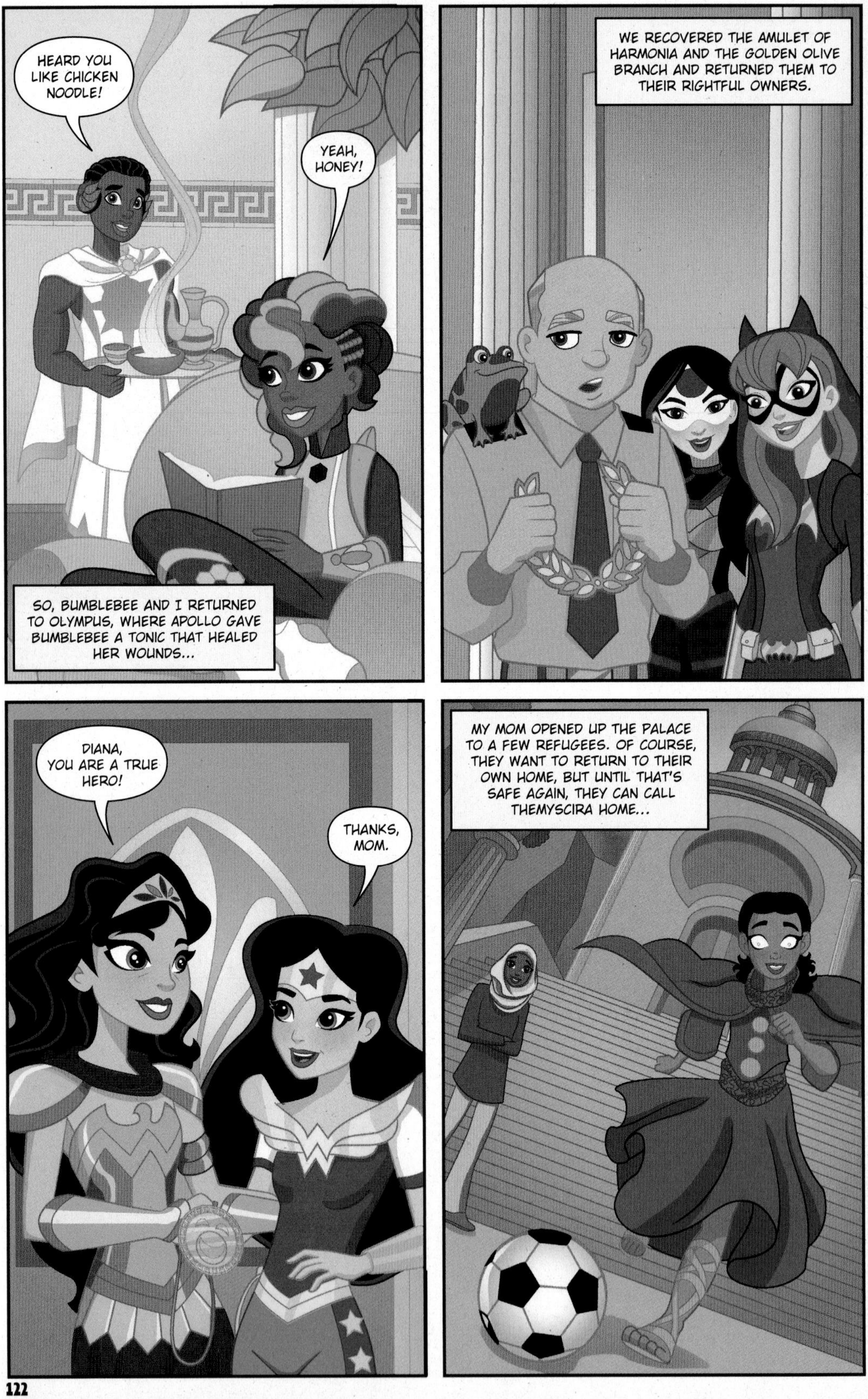
HEARD YOU LIKE CHICKEN NOODLE!
YEAH, HONEY!
SO, BUMBLEBEE AND I RETURNED TO OLYMPUS, WHERE APOLLO GAVE BUMBLEBEE A TONIC THAT HEALED HER WOUNDS...
WE RECOVERED THE AMULET OF HARMONIA AND THE GOLDEN OLIVE BRANCH AND RETURNED THEM TO THEIR RIGHTFUL OWNERS.
DIANA, YOU ARE A TRUE HERO!
THANKS, MOM.
MY MOM OPENED UP THE PALACE TO A FEW REFUGEES. OF COURSE, THEY WANT TO RETURN TO THEIR OWN HOME, BUT UNTIL THAT'S SAFE AGAIN, THEY CAN CALL THEMYSCIRA HOME...

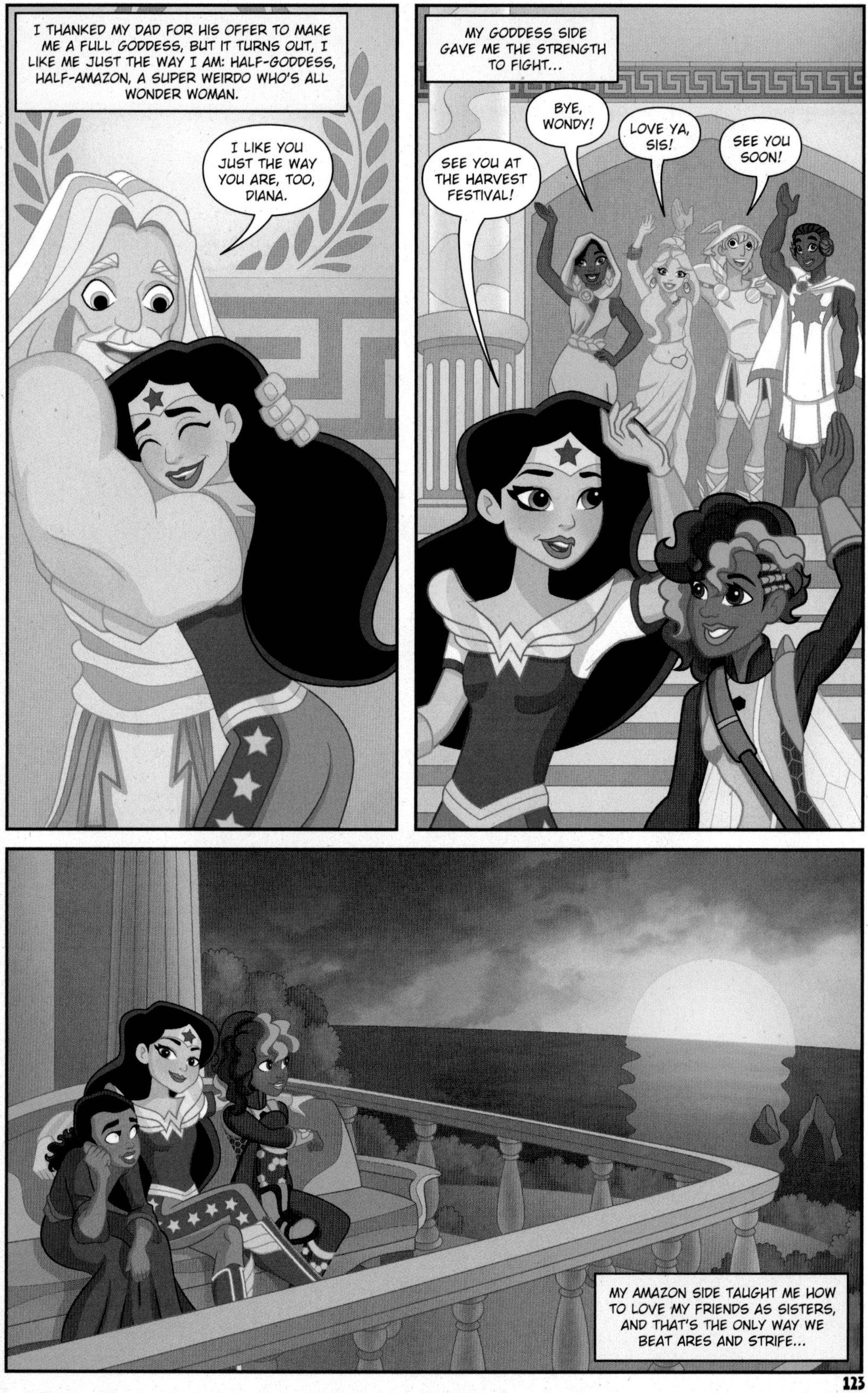
I THANKED MY DAD FOR HIS OFFER TO MAKE ME A FULL GODDESS, BUT IT TURNS OUT, I LIKE ME JUST THE WAY I AM: HALF-GODDESS, HALF-AMAZON, A SUPER WEIRDO WHO'S ALL WONDER WOMAN.
I LIKE YOU JUST THE WAY YOU ARE, TOO, DIANA.
MY GODDESS SIDE GAVE ME THE STRENGTH TO FIGHT...
SEE YOU AT THE HARVEST FESTIVAL!
BYE, WONDY!
LOVE YA, SIS!
SEE YOU SOON!
MY AMAZON SIDE TAUGHT ME HOW TO LOVE MY FRIENDS AS SISTERS, AND THAT'S THE ONLY WAY WE BEAT ARES AND STRIFE...

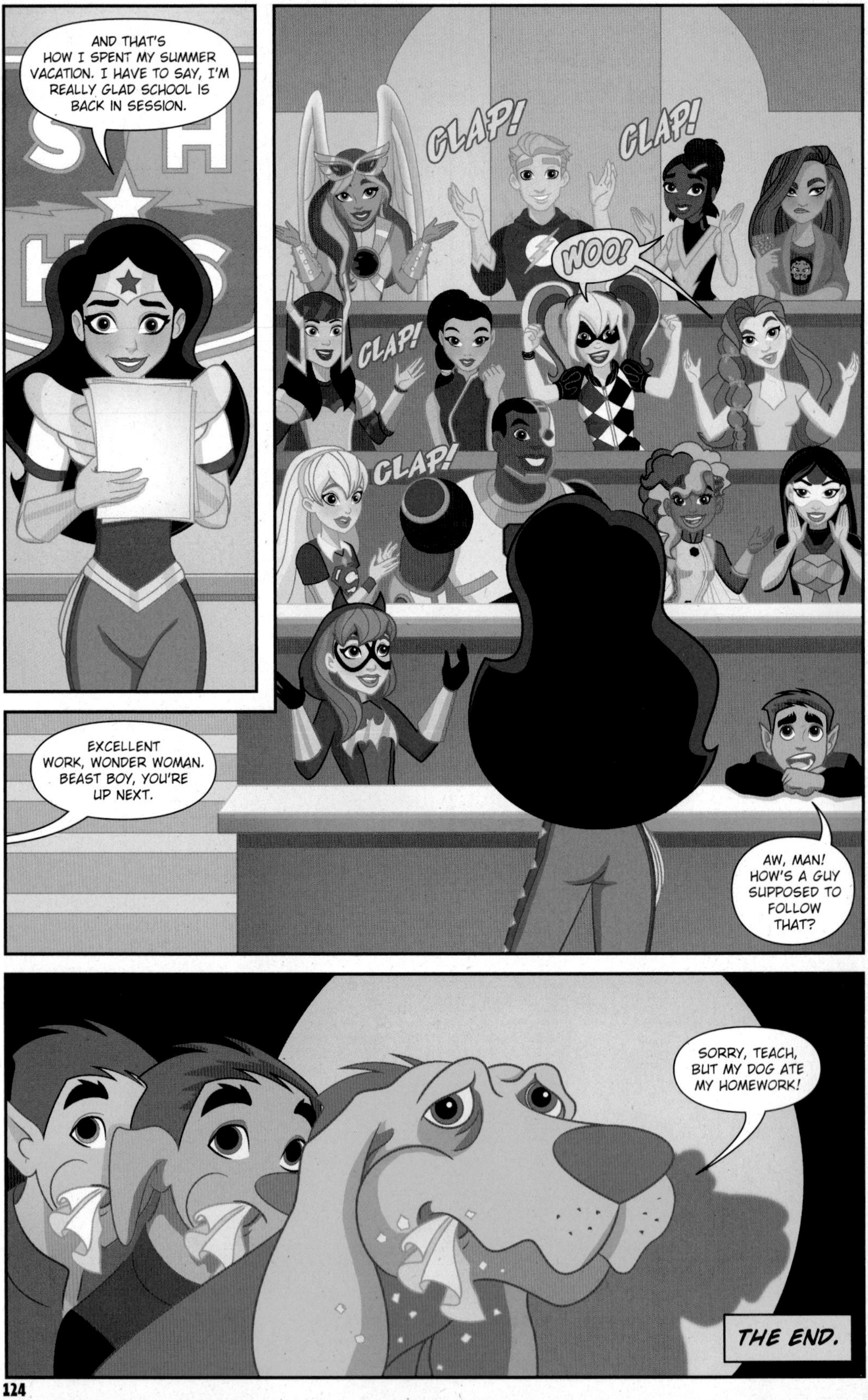
AND THAT'S HOW I SPENT MY SUMMER VACATION. I HAVE TO SAY, I'M REALLY GLAD SCHOOL IS BACK IN SESSION.
CLAP!
CLAP!
WOO!
CLAP!
CLAP!
EXCELLENT WORK, WONDER WOMAN. BEAST BOY, YOU'RE UP NEXT.
AW, MAN! HOW'S A GUY SUPPOSED TO FOLLOW THAT?
SORRY, TEACH, BUT MY DOG ATE MY HOMEWORK!
THE END.

WONDER WOMAN DAY EXCLUSIVE COVER ART

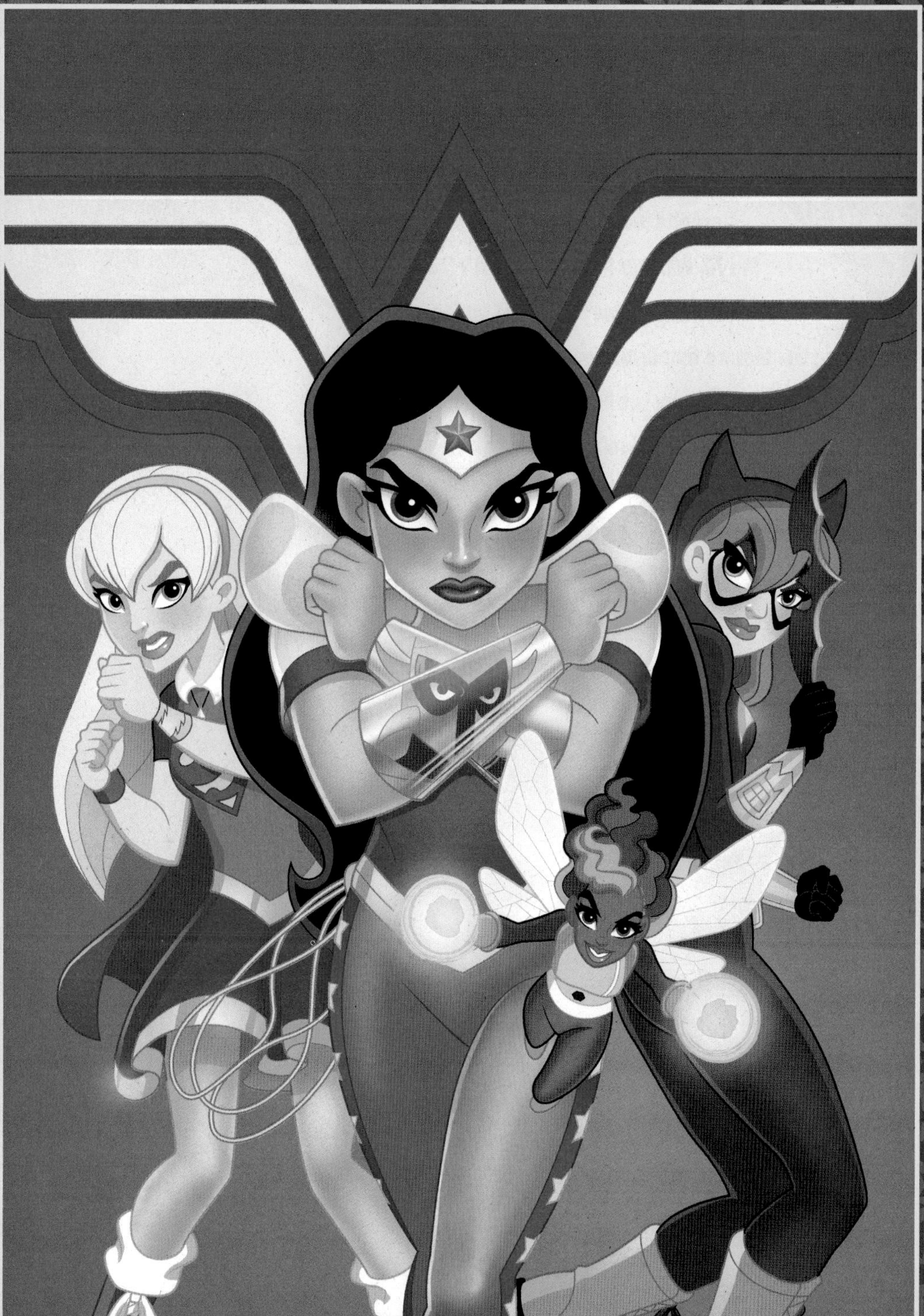

ABOUT THE AUTHOR

Shea Fontana is a writer for film, television, and graphic novels. In addition to the DC SUPER HERO GIRLS graphic novels, she also writes the *DC Super Hero Girls* animated shorts, TV specials, and movies. Her other credits include *Doc McStuffins, Disney's The 7D, Whisker Haven Tales with the Palace Pets*, live shows for *Disney on Ice*, and the feature film *Crowning Jules.* She lives in sunny Los Angeles, where she enjoys playing roller derby, hiking, hanging out with her dog, Moxie, and changing her hair color. ★

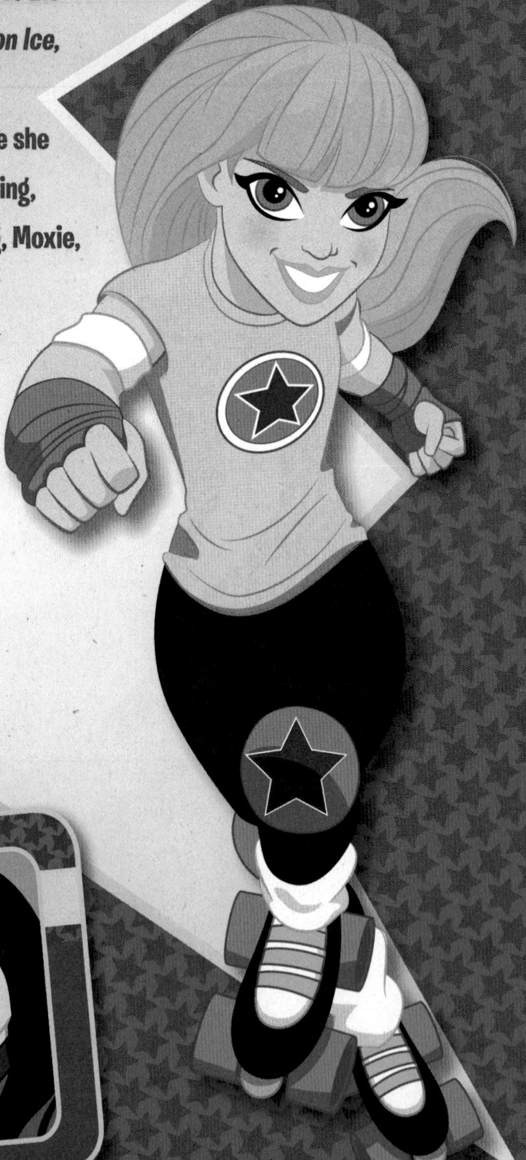

ABOUT THE COLORIST

Monica Kubina

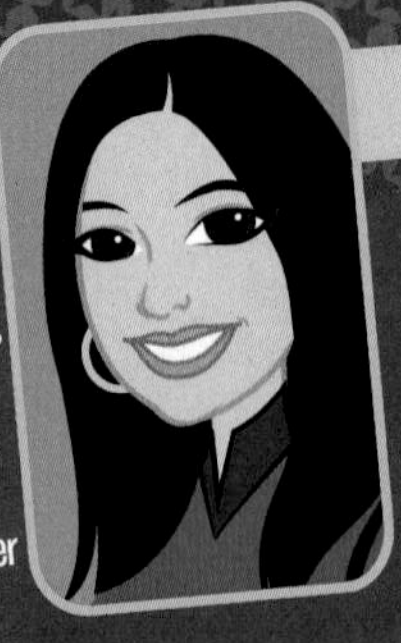

has colored countless comics, including super hero series, manga titles, kids' comics, and science fiction stories. She's colored *Phineas and Ferb, SpongeBob, THE 99*, and *Star Wars*. Monica's favorite activities are bike riding and going to museums with her husband and two young sons.

ABOUT THE ARTIST

Yancey Labat got his start at Marvel Comics before moving on to illustrate children's books, including *Hello Kitty* and *Peanuts* for Scholastic, as well as books for Chronicle Books, ABC Mouse, and others. His book *How Many Jellybeans?* with writer Andrea Menotti won the 2013 Cook Prize for best STEM (Science, Technology, Education, Math) picture book from Bank Street College of Education. He has two super hero girls of his own and lives in Cupertino, California. ★

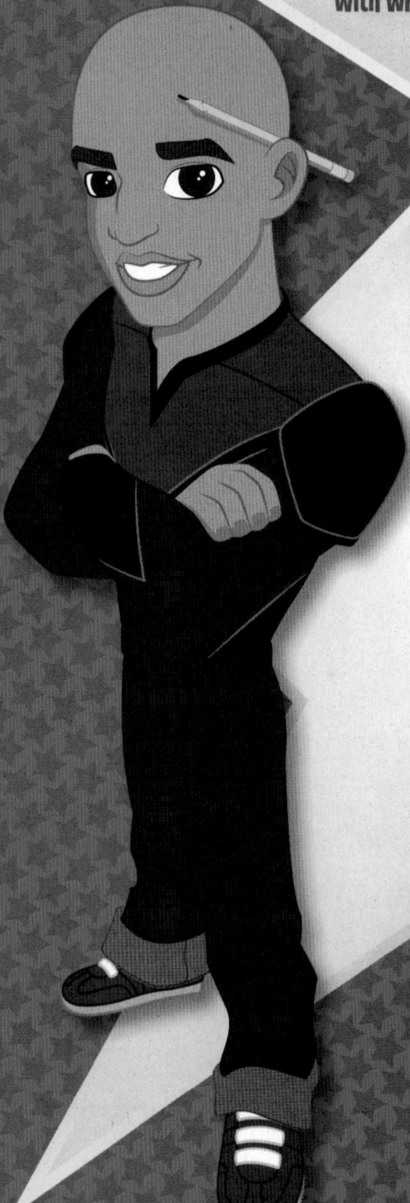

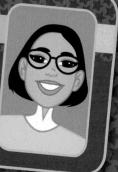

ABOUT THE LETTERER

Janice Chiang

has lettered *Archie, Barbie, Punisher* and many more. She was the first woman to win the Comic Buyer's Guide Fan Awards for Best Letterer (2011). She likes weight training, hiking, baking, gardening, and traveling.

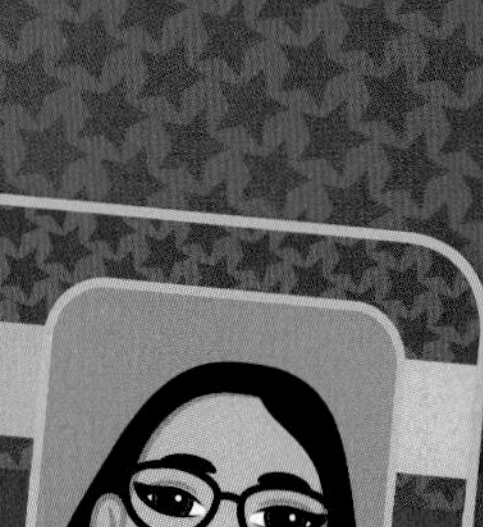